WHEN YOU REC'D MY PLANS

ROMANCE REHAB SERIES
BOOK 3

JESS CHRISTINE

Ebook ISBN:979-8-9904385-4-5

Paperback ISBN: 979-8-9904385-5-2

Cover designed by Paige Moreland (@lpmdraws)

Editing by Tina Otero

Formatting by Kalie Gerwig | Good Girl Author Services

Chapter Images by Paige Moreland (@lpmdraws)

Doodles by Matt Christine

To the brain injury warriors and the people who rally around them.

PLAYLIST

Please click the link or scan the QR Code below for the link to the Spotify Playlist created for *When You Rec'd My Plans*

DEAR READER

When You Rec'd My Plans is the third interconnected standalone in the Romance Rehab series. While it can be read on its own, I recommend the books to be read in order to avoid any potential spoilers from book one and two.

Please note that it is intended for individuals 18+ due to the mature language and open door/explicit sexual content. It also includes a side character who has suffered a brain injury and complicated family relationships. My priority is your mental health, so if these topics are upsetting to you please proceed with caution.

CONTENTS

DICKTIONARY

For those readers who want to skip the smut or go straight to it, do with this list what you will.

PROLOGUE
WREN - JULY

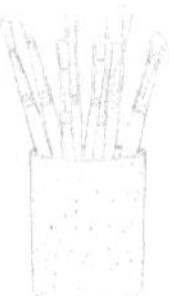

A strange sense of dread washes over me at the sight of my landlord, Mr. Fink. He's standing in front of a group of people with his wife. His face is cast downward into a frown, and his shoulders are slumped.

I search the small crowd gathered outside the front of my apartment complex and locate my neighbor, Crystal, who lives above me. She's sitting in the front row with her daughter, Sasha.

"Hey, girl," Crystal says as I approach. "We saved you a spot." She removes her bag from the chair next to her and taps the seat in between her and her daughter.

"Any idea what this is about?" I ask. "The email was so vague that I'm a little nervous about what he's going to say."

"Hey, Wren," Sasha says, pushing her glasses up her nose.

"Hey, girlie." Reaching over, I pull her into a side hug.

"My guess is that they're selling the complex, and they called us all here to tell us," Crystal says. "Someone I was talking to at Sasha's bus stop last week was saying she heard they were having some financial trouble."

My heart sinks into my stomach. Our complex is pretty small and privately owned. The Finks are as good as they come, and the fact that every single chair is full is a testament to just how much they are loved by the people who live here.

Mr. Fink is an older man, and he looks a little bit like Santa Claus—rosy cheeks, round belly, and a long, white beard. Mrs. Fink is around his age, but her hair is dyed blonde and she's much shorter than him. When she isn't making desserts to give to neighbors, you can find her in the front office answering the phones.

"I don't want to imagine losing them," I say.

"Ugh, I know," Crystal says. "It's no secret that Sasha and I wouldn't have a roof over our heads if they hadn't been so understanding when I lost my job last year. Let us live here for free until I could find something, and then when I tried to pay them for the months I missed, they refused my money. Told me to put it in an account for Sasha." She smiles warmly at her daughter, who is now staring at her mom's phone, watching a cartoon.

Crystal's words tug on my heart, and all the times that Mr. Fink came to my apartment to fix something or Mrs. Fink baked me a cake for my birthday pop into my head. When I moved in, they both took the time to get to know me, and when they found out I was saving to start my own camps for individuals with brain injuries, they offered me one hundred dollars off my rent each month and told me to put it towards my dream. "They really are the best," I say.

Mr. Fink clears his throat and quiets us down. "Thank you all for coming tonight. It's no secret that I think of all of you as family." Tears well in his eyes, and he takes a minute to collect himself. His wife takes his hand as she wipes the tears running down her cheeks.

"Cedar Hill was owned by my father, and when I took ownership, I promised him I would always do what was best for the tenants here. Lately, that has become more difficult because, if I'm honest, money is tighter than it used to be. The building is in need of a lot of repairs that I can't manage on my own, and the number of vacant apartments is the highest it's ever been."

I look around at the crowd, realizing just how small it is. Between the empty apartments, the repairs, and the Finks consistently being flexible with rent payments, I imagine money is extremely tight. Guilt pings my heart because I know if it hadn't been for the kindness they showed me, they might not be in this position.

Closing his eyes, he takes a deep breath. "So, we have made the very difficult decision to sell the complex."

Gasps echo through the group, and even Sasha's attention is pulled from the little screen in her lap.

"I know." He nods and breathes in deep again, no doubt trying to hold back tears. "This isn't what I was expecting either, but please know this decision doesn't come lightly, and the new management company has assured me that once they're done, it'll be like a whole new place. They've also assured me that they will work with each of you while the repairs are completed." He looks at his wife. "You were all in our minds when we signed the papers, and I promise they will take care of each of you."

"I want to add that we are so appreciative of all of your business, and we are going to miss this place and every single one of you very much," Mrs. Fink says. "Does anyone have any questions?"

Three arms shoot up immediately, and Mrs. Fink points to Ms. Norris sitting in the back row. "When will the new company be taking ownership?"

"We signed the papers this morning," Mr. Fink explains. "From our understanding, information regarding the acquisition will be sent out tomorrow via email, but we wanted you all to hear it from us first."

"Are we going to lose our apartments?" Crystal asks.

"No, I would not have sold it to them if I thought that was

going to happen. They assured me they would work with all of you while the renovations took place."

"Thank you," she says, looking towards her daughter.

"Will rent be increasing?" someone else asks.

"We aren't sure," Mrs. Fink says. "The new company is aware of the current rent prices, and we are hopeful that if they do raise rent, it will not be by much."

"That's not reassuring," Crystal whispers to me.

"Not at all," I agree.

They answer a few more questions before we all stand to leave. Crystal, Sasha, and I make our way over to where the Finks stand.

"Thank you for everything these last couple of years," I say, hugging Mrs. Fink tightly.

"Of course, sweetheart," she says. "I hope you all stay in touch, and Wren, I can't wait to see the magic you create one day with your camps."

My stomach twists. If the rent prices go up, then I won't be able to put aside as much money as I've been saving.

"I promise to keep you updated," I say.

"We really hate to do this, but we were out of options," Mr. Fink adds.

"We understand," Crystal says. "Y'all gotta take care of yourselves. We'll all be okay."

The three of us say our goodbyes and walk back to our apartments together.

"You think this new company is really gonna look out for all of us?" I ask when we make it to my door.

"I sure as hell hope so," she says. "I guess we'll find out tomorrow."

———

From: Austere Development Group
Bcc: Wren Dawson

Date: July 12
Subject: Cedar Hill Apartment Acquisition

We are excited to announce that Austere Development Group has acquired Cedar Hill Apartment Complex effective immediately. The current building is in need of extensive repair and renovations. After much consideration, our team has decided to demolish the current building, so that we can create a safe and livable space for the residents of Cedar Hill. We recognize that this will require the current tenants to find somewhere else to live. For this reason, we are allowing current residents to remain in their apartments until October 31st. Those who stay in their apartments should pay monthly rent to: Austere Development Group. There will be no change in rent costs prior to October 31st, and rent will be due on the first day of each month. If you decide to move out prior to October 31st, we will gladly terminate your lease early and return your security deposit, no questions asked.

Please be on the lookout for more information regarding the renovation and special pricing for current tenants once the renovation is completed. All questions regarding the acquisition should be directed to: cedarhill@austeredevelopmentgroup.com.

Best,
The Austere Development Group Team

CHAPTER 1: BEETLEJUICE!
BEETLEJUICE! BEETLEJUICE!
WREN - ONE MONTH LATER - AUGUST

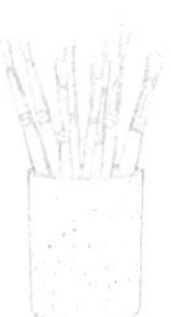

"I'm beat," Gray says, sipping from her martini glass. "Thanks for coming out with me. I've been going nonstop lately and needed a night where I wasn't cooped up in my apartment or thinking about work."

"I get it," I say, taking a drink of my water. "Thanks for forcing me to do something other than stay at home with my cat and look for a place to live."

"Cheers to us for being fun," Gray chimes, lifting her glass and clinking against my clear plastic cup. "You sure you don't want something to drink. It's ladies' night, so everything is half off."

"Maybe in a little bit." I look around The Local, and it's packed. My stomach turns. Ladies' Night has never been my favorite because it always feels like the bar is using women as bait for all the men who ultimately show up to try to get us drunk and themselves laid.

"How is the apartment search coming?" she asks.

"It's not. I'm so stressed about it. I keep thinking I'll find somewhere else to live, but it's all too expensive. My current rent is so cheap, it's no wonder my previous landlord had to sell."

"I know you don't want to hear it, but you could live with Tanner. Lacey and Jace move into their new house next weekend, so T will have a spare room."

"Jace?" I giggle. "Since when do you call Lacey's boyfriend by his actual name and not his nickname?"

"It sounded so weird, right? Maybe these martinis are already going to my head. I meant Jacks. Lacey and Jacks." She laughs.

"Much better."

"So, back to living with Tanner," she says. "Don't think I didn't see what you were trying to do there. He has a room, and he's our friend. Seems like an easy option." She shrugs her shoulders and takes another sip of her drink.

She's right, but I don't want to hear it. She and our other friends haven't left me alone about this idea for weeks, and I hate it.

I need a place to live—not a roommate. And I especially don't need *him* to be my roommate.

I like living alone. I like being able to watch what I want on TV or listen to pop music a little too loud while I clean. I like not having to talk to anyone after I've depleted my social battery for the day.

I bet he binge watches shows like *The Boys* and leaves his socks all over the floor.

I cringe at the thought of having to explain that I'm not his girlfriend, just the girl he lives with, over my morning coffee, to one of his random one night stands.

What a nightmare.

I might be desperate for a place to live, but I'm not that desperate. *Nope. Not doing it.*

"I'm not living with Tanner," I say, firmly.

"He's not that bad."

I roll my eyes. *Not that bad?*

"We are talking about the same person, right?" I laugh.

"Y'all are unbelievable if you think I'll be going anywhere near Tanner Mitchell's apartment."

"Oh, my god," Gray gasps. "Look who's at the bar! It's a sign."

My eyes jump to where she's staring. Tanner Mitchell is sitting at the bar, surrounded by no less than five women.

"A sign?"

"Yes, we're over here talking about you living with him, and there he is."

"No. I think we must have just said his name one too many times. Like Beetlejuice or something."

"Oh, but he definitely doesn't look like Beetlejuice." She laughs and twirls her olive skewer in her drink. "I know some of his choices are questionable, but you can't deny he's hot. Look at that smile."

I hate that she's right again. He's at least a foot taller than me, if not more. His chest and shoulders are broad. His sharp jawline is covered with blond stubble, and the top half of his blond hair is pulled into a bun on top of his head. He's wearing khaki shorts that hit mid-thigh and a navy button up shirt that fits snuggly on his biceps.

I wish he looked like Beetlejuice. If he did, my apartment problem wouldn't exist because I'd trust myself to live with weird-ass Beetlejuice. I don't trust myself to live with a certified Thor look-alike. No. College Wren's knees would've totally buckled and fell for his bullshit, but not twenty-four-year-old Wren. No. I know better than to get caught up with a guy like him. We might be friends with the same people, but I will *not* be living with him.

"God, would you look at him?" She laughs. "I swear he thrives on being the center of attention."

"He's such a flirt. Could you imagine the amount of women who probably go through his apartment on any given week." I laugh as I watch him flirt with a blonde. "I bet he has one of those lost and found closets full of the clothes from old hookups."

"What are you talking about?"

"You know, like the girl comes over and leaves her jacket, so instead of returning it, he puts it in a closet, and if the next girl is cold, he offers it to her."

"That's not a real thing," she argues.

"Oh, it is. My ex had one, and I would bet all my money that Tanner has one too."

She takes another sip of her cocktail and leans back into the booth, getting comfortable.

"How do you think a guy like that is friends with Logan and Jacks? It's strange right?" I ask.

"I'm a firm believer that every male friend group is made up of a Ross, a Chandler, and a Joey, and that checks out with them too," she explains.

"What do you mean?"

"Jacks is a Ross, Logan is a Chandler, and Tanner is a Joey."

"I think you're right."

"Never fails. I mean look at him over there. Total Joey behavior," she says.

We both burst out laughing, and by the time we're done, I'm sure I have mascara running down my face. I take a few deep breaths, calming my laughter. My eyes betray me, and I find him again. It's apparent he doesn't skip leg day, or arm day, or any day for that matter. *Damn.*

"For someone who acts like he annoys the shit out of you, you sure look at him like you want his tongue on you."

"Please. There is no way in hell that I'm that man's type."

"What's that supposed to mean?"

I look down at my body. "Well for starters, I'm shaped like a teenage boy. No tits and no ass. Every girl he's currently ogling over there looks like a Victoria's Secret Angel. Long legs, big boobs, and curves for days."

"You are a beautiful, kind, wonderful, smart, hilarious, bad ass woman, Wren Dawson. Don't you dare talk about yourself like that. Any man would be lucky to put his tongue on you, and don't you ever forget it."

"You're ridiculous." I offer her a small smile.

I don't know what I would do without Gray. No one prepares you for how difficult it can be to make friends as an adult, but she made that so easy.

"Wait, does that mean you do think he's hot?" she questions.

"No," I say, panicked.

"Oh, my god—you do! Is that why you don't want to live with him?" Her whole face lights up.

"No," I swat at her. "I don't want to live with him because he's insufferable, and even if I did think he was attractive, which I'm not saying I do, look at him over there. He is *loving* the attention, and I'd put money on him going home with that blonde."

"He is definitely in his element."

"Definitely." I roll my eyes.

"We should probably go say hi," she says.

"No, we should let him have his fun."

"Come on," she urges.

"No. It's girls' night, and there are no boys allowed at girls' night."

"You're right. No boys. Just us." She finishes the last sip of her cocktail.

"I'm going to run to the bathroom and then grab a drink. Do you want another martini?"

"Sure, I'll take one more. Do you want me to come with you?"

"No, stay here. That group of girls in the corner has been eyeing our table since we sat down, and if we both leave we'll lose it."

TANNER

My brother has yet to respond to the text I sent earlier. I tried calling my dad, but he sent me to voicemail, so I left the office early. My roommate, Jacks, was out with his girlfriend, and I didn't want to be alone. So, instead of sitting at my apartment stewing about my family, I changed, called for an Uber, and came to my happy place—The Local.

I'm sitting at the bar, drinking a beer, and I'm surrounded by five women all holding a drink I purchased for them. *How predictable.* My dad and brother pissed me off, and now I'm sitting here trying to find someone to bring home with me to fill the void I'm feeling after today. Despite not having done this in a while, it isn't the first time, and I'm sure it won't be the last. Maybe they're right about me.

I grab for my phone and check it again.

"Oh, come on, put your phone away, and let's go dance," the blonde says. She plucks it from my hands and moves it out of reach.

"Yeah, come dance with us," her friend whines, moving her hand down my arm.

"Can I please have my phone back?" I ask.

"Whatcha gonna give me for it," the blonde teases, dangling it in front of my face.

I snatch it and put it in my back pocket before she can react.

"Oh, you seem so grumpy. Do we need to cheer you up?" the blonde flirts, running her hands over my thighs. She leans forward, stepping between my legs, and whispers, "Let's dance...or we could find a dark corner." Her lips brush against my ear, and she catches me off guard. I stand abruptly. When I got here, I had a plan, but I can't get on board with my own idea. I frequent this bar and have taken plenty of women home with me. This one, and her friend, are obviously into me, but no matter how hard I try, I'm just not into them, and the longer I sit at the bar, the less I want to be here.

A flash of red appears in my periphery to my right, and my mind is immediately somewhere else, or rather with someone else entirely.

Wren Dawson.

The girl who's been living in my dreams since April, the first time I saw her. I don't know what it is about this woman, but everytime I see her, my brain short-circuits. You'd think at thirty I'd be able to form a coherent sentence around a pretty girl, and I usually can, but everytime she comes around, I sound like a total moron.

I turn my head, and a girl about her height is walking away from me towards the restrooms. Her long red hair is pulled up into a ponytail, and I could swear it's Wren, but why would she be here? I've never seen her here before without our group of friends. I'm sure it's just my eyes playing tricks on me. I try to push the thoughts of her away and focus back on the blonde, but I can't.

"Please dance with us," the blonde whines again.

Time to go.

"Hey, Tony," I shout. "I'm gonna close out. One more round for the ladies on me." He acknowledges me with a nod and then moves toward one of the registers.

"You can't leave," the blonde pouts.

"It's been a long day. Enjoy your drinks." Tony brings me my receipt, and I sign it. "Bye, girls."

I begin to walk away. The bar is packed, and I have to push through the crowd. I look over my shoulder one more time, hoping that maybe it was Wren, and I'll see her, but instead, I see the blonde is following me.

Great.

"Wait," she yells the minute I make it to the front door. She grabs my arm, pulling me towards her.

"You seem like a—" I try, but before I can stop it, she's up on her toes, and her lips are on mine.

Fuck me and not in a good way.

I stumble backwards, trying to pull away, but she tightens her arms around my neck and falls with me through the door.

"What the hell," I say, pushing her away as we stumble onto the sidewalk.

"I just wanted to make sure you didn't forget me," she says, giggling and taking a step toward me.

I put my hand up to stop her. "Look, you seem like a great girl, but I'm not feeling it, and I want to go home *alone*."

"You don't mean that."

Wren pops into my head again. "Actually, I've never meant anything more."

"You have got to be kidding me," she snaps, just as her friend walks out to meet us.

"What's going on?" the friend asks.

"Nothing. Let's go," she says with a frustrated breath, grabbing her friend's arm and stomping back into the bar.

I let out a small chuckle and then call for my Uber. It's definitely time to go home.

WREN

I'm in the world's longest line for the women's bathroom when I attempt to redo my ponytail. I'm almost finished twisting the elastic around my red strands when it snaps, leaving me with one of those weird creases in my hair and no way to fix it. *Shit.* I attempt to run my fingers through the crease, but it's no use.

"Do you have an extra hair tie?" I ask the girl waiting behind me. She sways back and forth, and her eyes are a little glossy.

"Nooooo, sure don't," she slurs. I offer her a small smile then get out of the line, groaning. I head back toward where

Gray sits. The moment I push my way through a small group of people, I see Tanner stumble out of the bar's doors attached to a blonde like some sort of sucker fish.

Lovely.

I roll my eyes because I was right—he's taking the blonde home. Why are men always so predictable?

I continue back to our table, wondering why my friends would ever think living with someone like him would be a good idea. No, one thing is for sure, Tanner Mitchell is the definition of a fuck boy.

Actually, if you look up that word in the dictionary, I'm ninety-nine percent certain his photo would be plastered right there in the margins.

I know his type—very pretty, very arrogant, and very much can't keep his dick in his shorts. I dated a man like him. Hell, I loved a man like him, and all it brought me was a whole lot of heartbreak.

CHAPTER 2: A SIREN LURING A SHIP
TANNER

I unlock the door to my apartment and walk inside. Jacks is sitting on the couch, watching TV.

"Where's Lacey?" I ask, shutting the door behind me.

"She's taking a bath. We just got back a little while ago," he says. "Where were you?"

"The Local. Had a shitty day at work." I walk across the apartment and into the kitchen where I begin to make a bowl of cereal.

"Surprised you came home alone," he says over the sound of the television and the Froot Loops filling my bowl.

"I just wasn't feeling it," I call back.

"That doesn't sound like you. You good?"

I add some milk to the bowl and think back on my night. The redhead walking away from me pops into my mind, and all I can think about is Wren. It's like, for months now, a switch flipped, and my brain won't let me go past flirting with anyone, and anytime I try, Wren pops up and steals my attention.

"Not sure," I say, walking back into the living room to join him. "How much longer do you think Lacey is going to be?"

"A while. She grabbed her Kindle on the way into the bathroom, so I imagine we have some time before she emerges." He chuckles.

"If I tell you something, will you promise not to tell her?"

"That's a big ask."

"I know, but if she finds out then the rest of the girls will find out, and they can't."

He eyes me. "Okay?"

"Tonight seemed like a normal night out. I was at the bar, surrounded by really pretty women, and there was this blonde who was really into me. Like I could have easily brought her home, but I didn't want to."

"Go on," he says.

"And I couldn't figure out why I didn't, but then I saw this girl walking towards the bathrooms and I thought it was Wren, but I wasn't sure, and it's like every last bit of energy I had to give the blonde disappeared."

"You don't say?"

I take a bite of my cereal. "Yeah, and that's not the first time this has happened."

"What do you mean?"

"Like me seeing a redhead and thinking it's Wren, only to find out it's not."

"Interesting," he says, leaning forward on his knees. "How long has this been going on?"

"Honestly?"

"Yes."

"Since my birthday dinner in April."

"April?" he asks, in disbelief. "Please explain."

I inhale deeply and blow out a long breath, considering how much I want to tell him, and then because he's one of my best friends, I decide to tell him everything.

"We were all at this restaurant for my birthday, and you weren't back yet. She happened to be there with the other girls. But that was even before Logan and Poppy were official, so we didn't talk to them, just kinda saw them from across the room. I don't know. I saw her and it's like my brain chemistry changed, and since then I don't even know how to act around her or other women. All I could think about after that night was learning her name. There was just something about her. She drew me in with one smile, like a siren luring a ship, and I regretted not having the courage to go introduce myself that night."

"A siren luring a ship." He looks at me like I'm some sort of alien from outer space, but I continue, because fuck it.

"I don't know how else to explain it. Then, in May, she was standing outside Logan's apartment with Lacey, and I honestly didn't think I'd ever see her again, but there she was. And since then, I've fumbled the bag every goddamn time we've been around each other."

He looks at me, shocked.

"What?" I ask, fully aware that I probably sound like a psycho, but I can't help it.

He begins to laugh and leans back on the couch, crossing his arms over his chest and one of his ankles over his knee. He's quiet for a few seconds, and uneasiness settles over me.

"It's just weird hearing you talk like this." He pauses before continuing, and then when he begins again, his words come out hesitantly. "I don't mean this in a bad way, because you know I think of you like a brother, but I'm really surprised to hear you talk about her like this. I mean, usually when we're all together, you're flirting with someone else that's not her."

"Fuck, I know." I run my hands down my face and let out a groan. "Maybe I'm just trying to get her attention." I know it sounds bad, and I internally cringe at my own words. "Because she wants nothing to do with me, and it drives me nuts."

"Very mature of you," he deadpans. "Do you think that's what it is? I mean, you aren't really used to not having a girl's attention. Could this attraction simply be you wanting what you can't have?"

"I don't know, but I don't think so."

"Who else knows?"

"No one. I mean, I think Logan might have an idea, but I haven't outright told anyone this but you."

He nods.

"Have you thought about just asking her out?"

"She'd never go for that, and then it would be awkward for everyone."

"You don't know that."

"I think I do. And if she did agree, I'd probably manage to fuck it up somehow. I mean, I'm good for a fun night, but long-term…I've never been good at that. Plus, I don't want to risk fucking up the group dynamic. You know I almost ruined our friendship with the whole Lacey fiasco. I don't need to risk anything like that again."

"You and Lacey were drunk and both regret the night. She and I weren't talking at the time, and you had no way of knowing who she was." He cringes a little as he talks. "I told you we were cool, and I meant it. But Wren isn't Lacey. You'll never know what she'll say if you don't try."

It's obvious that at best, she tolerates me, and at worst, she wants nothing to do with me. I also know that, despite what he's saying, I can't act on how I feel about her because if I screwed it up, our friends would never forgive me.

Accidentally sleeping with one girl in our friend group is forgivable. Especially when that girl was Lacey and she called me a mediocre lay. I got really lucky that Jacks is the most understanding man I know. But sleeping with a second girl in the friend group and inevitably fucking it up? Inexcusable.

"I don't know, man."

"What don't you know?" Lacey asks, walking into the living room.

"Oh, uh, nothing," I lie. "Work shit."

"Hmm," she hums, her eyes shifting back and forth between me and Jacks. "Want my opinion?"

"No," I say, a little frantic.

"Okay, asshole," she teases, rolling her eyes. "I'll have you know I'm very good at giving advice. Just ask any of the girls."

"I'm sure you are, but it's nothing. I'm tired anyway. It's been a long night."

"Suit yourself." She shrugs. "Jace, you ready for bed?"

Jacks looks at her and then to me.

"Just follow your gut," he says. "Stop overthinking it." He stands and begins to walk across the room toward Lacey.

My gut? My gut's telling me I'd fuck it up because I always do. My dick though? Fuck, it's telling me something else entirely. And if I'm honest, so is my heart.

"Night, Tanner," she chimes. "If you change your mind, I'd be happy to give you my opinion."

"Noted," I say, chuckling. "Night y'all."

I bring my bowl and spoon to the sink, turning over the events of tonight in my head. I know I'm right; it doesn't matter how I feel, she'd never go for a guy like me, and even if she did, I'd inevitably mess it up.

Despite all of this being true, I climb into bed, and when I close my eyes, it's her I see.

CHAPTER 3: SO PREDICTABLE
WREN

There is nothing worse than Monday morning. I make my way across the parking lot holding two large boxes full of supplies for Dogwood Manor's annual summer party, mentally going through my checklist of everything I need to get done this morning before it officially begins.

Robin, the receptionist, meets me at the door.

"Morning, Wren," she says, holding one of the doors open as I walk through. "It looked like you could use a hand. Can I help you with those?"

"Thank you, but I think I've got them."

She smiles and returns behind the front desk, and I continue through the front lobby and the dining room. Dogwood Manor's resident lovebirds are sitting at a table across from one another, holding hands, drinking coffee.

"Morning, Ms. Clara. Morning, Mr. Eugene," I say as I walk through the dining room.

"Good Morning, Wren," Mr. Eugene says, setting his coffee mug down on the table. He's dressed in a short-sleeved, plaid button up shirt and khakis. His gray hair is slicked back with gel, and his glasses frame his soft brown eyes. Ms. Clara is wearing one of her signature mumus—this one is teal and covered with sparkly pool floats— and matching shoes. Her white curls are styled, and she's wearing a little bit of makeup that makes her cheeks look rosy.

"You two are up and ready early," I say, stopping to talk to them.

"We're looking forward to the party today and wanted to be ready to go," Ms. Clara clarifies.

I check my watch, and it's seven forty-five. "Shouldn't you be with Lacey doing occupational therapy?" I giggle.

"No, she said I didn't have to do it today because of the party," she argues.

"Are you sure?" I ask.

"Yes, dear. I might be old, but my memory isn't completely shot."

"So, what do you have planned for us today?" Mr. Eugene asks. His southern accent rolls off his tongue like molasses.

I open my mouth to explain the schedule for today's events, but I'm interrupted when my friend, Lacey, comes around the corner breathing heavily, her blonde ponytail swinging behind her.

"There you are, Ms. Clara. I've been looking all over for you. We were supposed to start your OT session fifteen minutes ago."

I stifle a laugh.

"Do we have that today?" Ms. Clara asks, feigning igno-rance. "I thought you said we could skip it because of Wren's thing."

"No, you know we need to do therapy. Come on. Come with me to the gym, and I'll make it quick, and then you and Mr. Eugene can go to the party. I'm sure Wren needs to set up anyway."

"She's right," I say. "It won't be starting until around ten."

Ms. Clara rolls her eyes.

"I'll be waiting for you," Mr. Eugene says, offering her his hand and helping her stand. He leans down and plants a chaste kiss against her lips.

"I love you," she says, grabbing for her walker and beginning to move across the dining room.

"I love you too," he says.

"Lacey, feel free to bring any of the residents to the party for your sessions today, and tell the other girls too. I made sure to include things I thought would help you out," I call after them.

"You got it, girl!" she says over her shoulder.

I make my way to my office and set everything down on top of my desk. Opening one of the boxes, I begin to inventory my supplies. There is a knock on the door, and when I look up, I find my boss, Daryl, taking up the entire space between the door frame. He's a tall man, with rounded shoulders, and his skin always looks a little gray. His clothes never fit him quite right, and his black hair is clearly from a box and always in need of a cut. His general demeanor is like Eeyore, but he's nice enough, and I appreciate that most of the time he lets me do what I want.

"Big day today," he says flatly. "What do you have planned?"

"Pick-A-Duck," I say, holding up a reacher and a yellow rubber duck out of one of the boxes. "Kinda like the fair game, but instead of grabbing them with their hands, they'll have to use a reacher."

He nods, so I continue.

"Then I have cornhole, shirt tie-dyeing, a summer-themed BINGO game, and a POG juice tasting. Which reminds me, I need to get some thickener from the kitchen."

"Fantastic," he says without smiling. "If I haven't said it lately, we're lucky to have you."

"Thanks," I reply, offering him a smile. He turns and leaves without another word, and I get started on setting up the activities.

At ten o'clock, the residents start making their way into the rec room for the event. I'm excited when I see a couple of them are accompanied by Lacey and Gray.

We've worked together for two years now, and I don't think I would still be at Dogwood Manor if it wasn't for them, Poppy, and Chloe. It's not that I don't like working here—it's just not my dream job.

When I started here, I had just gone through the hardest thing I have ever been through. I felt so lost but was desperate for a fresh start, and while being the activities director in an assisted living facility isn't what I had in mind when I became a recreational therapist, it pays the bills and brought me the girls I consider my best friends.

The girls who have no reason to include me but still do. We don't have the same boss. My office isn't in the therapy gym, but yet they all took me under their wing, and they've supported me like no friends I've ever had before.

"Thanks for coming," I say when they walk in. I grab some Hawaiian leis and pass them out to my girls and the residents.

"This looks great," Gray says, looking at the decorations and each station that I have set up.

"Each station is labeled, and then cornhole and tie-dyeing are right outside the doors." I gesture to the double doors that take up most of the back wall.

"Let's start with cornhole," Gray says to Ms. Betty. They wander off toward where the game is set up.

"How does Pick-A-Duck sound?" Lacey says to Ms. Ethel.

"Fine dear," she says.

"Great, why don't you head over to that table, and I'll be right behind you."

Ms. Ethel walks away, and Lacey takes a step closer to me. "Gray said y'all ran into Tanner the other night. Have you thought anymore about moving in with him?" she whispers.

"How many times do I have to say it's not happening?"

"You don't have much time left to find something."

"I have plenty of time. I don't need to be out for another two and a half months."

"Regardless, Jace told me this morning that Tanner's still looking for a roommate."

"He should ask the blonde I saw him go home with on Friday night." I laugh.

"Blonde?"

"Yeah, I walked out of the bathroom and he was attached to this blonde girl like some sort of mouth leech." I shudder at the memory.

"I was at their apartment Friday, and there was no blonde."

There was no blonde?

"Maybe they went back to her place. I mean, I saw him kissing the blonde. No way he didn't hook up with her."

"You know when I got out of the bath, him and Jace were talking about something, and Tanner said it was work, but I thought I overheard him say something about a girl before I walked out. Maybe that's who he was talking about."

"Did Jacks say anything?"

Why do I care?

"We didn't really do much talking that night." She giggles. "And then by Saturday morning I forgot about it."

"Lacey, are we doing this or not?" Ethel shouts across the room.

"Coming," Lacey chimes. "We'll talk more later, and I'll see what Jace knows. Promise me you'll consider what I said about the roommate thing." She squeezes my arm and then moves away toward Ms. Ethel.

Consider living with him? *Not a chance in Hell.*

CHAPTER 4: PEPPER AND SOAP
TANNER

I decided to park my car a few blocks from work because I figured the extra five minute walk in the mid-August humidity was worth five less minutes in the office. Despite the temperature, the sun is shining, and it seemed like a crime to waste such a beautiful day in the confines of my stuffy office.

Peachtree Street is crowded with people walking to and from the surrounding office buildings and restaurants. I make my way down the street, doing my best to dodge people heading in the opposite direction. The sidewalk narrows, and I try to move around a puddle of standing liquid. It's probably water, but the air smells like hot trash, and I've lived here long enough to know that whatever it is, I don't want it on my brand new white sneakers. Just as I'm about to step around it, someone on my left runs into me, throwing me off my balance and causing me to put my right foot smack in the middle of the puddle.

"Fuck," I say under my breath, trying to shake off the brown liquid that now covers not only my shoe but the bottom of my jeans too. Frustrated, I look up to see who is responsible. A woman with long red hair and freckled skin is running a few feet ahead of me. She's dressed in a navy sports bra, matching leggings, and headphones. She looks just like Wren Dawson, and dammit, I'm doing it again.

She consumed my thoughts and my dreams all weekend, and despite my conversation with Jacks and my most valiant effort, I can't get her out of my head.

"Hey!" I yell, trying to get her attention, but she doesn't turn around. I break out into a jog, catching up to her just as the crosswalk sign turns red and she stops.

"Hey, Wren," I try again, this time touching her shoulder to get her attention.

The woman turns to face me, and it's definitely not her. *Shit.*

She removes her headphones and looks me up and down, focusing on my shoe and wet pants for a second, before looking me in the eye.

"Can I help you?" she asks, confused.

"Oh, no, sorry. I thought you were someone else. My bad. Enjoy your run," I say awkwardly.

She looks for oncoming traffic and then crosses the street. I continue my walk to the office, disappointment blooming in my chest.

Of course that wasn't her. It's Monday, and she has a job. I need to pull myself together. If I'm lucky, she'll be out with all of us on Friday, and I can maybe try to get on her good side then.

I make it to the front doors of my office building and exhale. I consider turning around and going home, but it's the second Monday of the month—and the one day my absence doesn't go unnoticed. I pull on the door handle, stand up a little taller, and begin to move across the porcelain tile floor towards the elevators, trying to ignore the whispered side conversations that stop abruptly when I get too close. I never know what it is they're saying exactly, but I know they're talking about me, and I know most of them don't think I deserve to be here. I don't think I do either, but that's nepotism for you.

Being here reminds me of the pepper and soap experiment I did as a kid. I don't really remember the point of it, but I do remember my third grade teacher showed it to us. She filled a shallow dish with water and then dumped a bunch of black pepper on top. First, she stuck a clean finger inside, and nothing happened. Then, she covered her hand with soap and repeated the experiment. The minute her soapy finger touched the water, all of the pepper retreated toward the sides of the bowl.

That's how I feel when I'm here. I'm the pepper. This place is the soap. Or maybe I'm the soap and this place is the pepper. Either way—we don't mix.

I call the elevator, tapping my foot as I wait.

I'm pleasantly surprised when it opens a moment later and is empty. I step on, and the minute the doors shut, I feel my shoulders relax.

It hasn't always been this way. When my grandfather was alive, being here felt more comfortable. He always made sure I had a place at the table, but then last December he passed away, and it became harder to be in a place that reminded me so much of the one person in my family who thought I was worth a shit.

I've considered walking away. Hell, I even asked the owner of The Local after a particularly shitty day if he'd consider selling me the bar, but I made a promise to myself to always make my grandfather proud. And while no one else seems to want me here, he did, so I'll keep trying as long as I can bear it.

I step off the elevator and move into my office. It's framed by large windows that overlook the entire Atlanta skyline. The view is absurd. I have no business calling it mine, but it is the one perk of being a nepo baby I enjoy.

Before I can sit down, my babysitter—or assistant as my

father and brother refer to him—John, knocks and enters the room with a freshly made latte.

"Good morning, Mr. Mitchell," he says, handing me the paper cup. I take a sip and breathe in the scent of brown sugar and cinnamon. It smells like fucking heaven.

I lied. There are two perks I enjoy—the view and the free lattes, but that's it.

"I've told you to call me Tanner," I say, taking a seat behind my desk and slouching down in the tall leather chair.

"Right. Um. Okay. Mr. Mitch— I mean Mr. Tan—"

I put my hand up to stop him. "Just Tanner. No mister necessary." I swallow down a long sip of my latte.

I've had babysitters since I started working here, but John is new. According to Dad, every executive vice president gets an assistant, but I've always had the suspicion that mine only exists to report back to my father. I honestly don't know where my dad finds them, but so far they've only been men.

John is the least annoying one yet, so I hope he sticks around longer than the others. He's the first who hasn't run to my dad to tattle every small transgression. He's also only been working here for a few weeks, and I'm sure he'll be fired soon for the same reason. That, or the fact that he always looks a little disheveled. His dark hair is always a little messy. His shirt is wrinkled and haphazardly tucked in, and his tie is looser than it should be. He always looks like he just fucked someone in the bathroom but didn't have time to look in the mirror before jetting off to grab me my latte. I should care, but I'm not Mitt Mitchell, so I don't.

"Oh, um, right. Tanner. Sorry."

"What time is the meeting with my father and brother?"

He fidgets nervously and pulls out his phone. I watch as his eyes scan the screen, and his face falls.

"I don't see a meeting on your calendar, sir," he says.

I check the date on my computer. "Is today not the second Monday of the month?"

"It is," he confirms.

"Then we have a meeting," I say. "My brother, Mitch, texted me yesterday, saying that he had a busy morning, and that he would have his assistant call you to set up a time for this afternoon."

"No one has called, and I've been here since eight."

"You sure?" I click on my inbox and scan the emails for something from my dad or brother. Nothing. My eyes shift to the clock. It's twelve-thirty.

"I'm sure," he says.

"Okay, well can you call and see when they want to meet. I don't need them accusing me of missing another meeting, and I specifically came in today to meet with them."

"Yes, sir," he says, turning to leave.

"Oh, and can you grab me something to clean my shoe with? I stepped in a puddle on the way here, and it's covered in street sludge."

He nods and exits my office. I send some emails while I wait and then grab my phone.

S.H.I.E.L.D.

> Did the girls say if Wren was coming out with us on Friday

LOGAN:

I think everyone is but Chloe.

> Okay cool

DONOVAN:

Why?

JACKS:

Yeah, why are you asking about Wren?

Bastard.

Just wondering

JACKS:

Is this what your gut is telling you to do?

Maybe

LOGAN:

Wait, what does Jacks know?

Nothing

ENZO:

Why don't I believe you?

DONOVAN:

Yeah, something's up.

LOGAN:

Jacks? Care to share?

JACKS:

I'll let T share.

I just want to get on Wren's good side

And I think Friday might be my chance

LOGAN:

Not this again.

She just acts like she can barely tolerate me

I didn't realize wanting to be liked by our friend was a crime

LOGAN:

I know you aren't used to girls not being interested in you, but I think it's best you let this one go.

But what if I don't want to let it go.

I'm not trying to get in her pants

I'm just trying to show her that I'm not a total douchebag

Come on please help me

Don't tell me you're all coupled up and I've lost my wingmen

LOGAN:

What did you have in mind?

Maybe she and I could play you and Poppy in ping-pong and you suggest it

LOGAN:

Haven't we tried this before?

DONOVAN:

Or you could just talk to her.

JACKS:

That's what I've been saying.

She doesn't like talking to me

ENZO:

Then maybe you should let it go.

I like the ping-pong idea better

Come on Logan

JACKS:

Why not Lacey and me?

Because the last time she and I played you and Lacey we kicked your ass and then she refused to dance with me

LOGAN:

I knew we had tried this before.

> Maybe second time's the charm

LOGAN:

> Fine, but if she wants nothing to do with you
> then you leave it alone.

My office door swings open, and I look up to find John walking in. He's noticeably a little paler than when he left. He walks over to my desk and hands me a packet of wet wipes.

"Did you get a hold of Mitch's assistant?" I ask, bending down to clean off my shoe.

"I did, um…" He swallows hard and clears his throat. "She said that the other Mr. Mitchells met this morning at nine."

What the fuck.

Without thinking, I try to stand, hitting my head on the underside of the desk with a loud thunk.

"Fuck!" I yell.

"Are you okay, sir?"

"I'm fine," I say, standing and tossing the dirty wipes into the trash. I smooth my shirt and try to ignore the spot on the back of my head that's throbbing.

We head out of my office and toward the elevator.

"Where are we going?" John asks, following behind me.

I hesitate for a minute. I'm not really sure where I'm heading. The meeting was with both my father, Mitt, and my brother, Mitch. I try to calm myself, give both of them the benefit of the doubt. I don't know that I was purposely left out of the meeting. I should talk to them. This time it could have really been a mistake, but deep down, I know this has my dad written all over it. And Mitch, being the obedient puppet that he is, probably went along with it.

"To see my father."

After a short and silent elevator ride, we step off and are greeted by my dad's assistant.

"I need to see my dad, er, I mean Mitt," I say as I walk up to her desk, rubbing the back of my head.

"He's not here," she says.

"He's not here?"

"No, he and your brother headed out thirty minutes ago."

"Why?"

"I think they had golf with a client," she says, nonchalantly. "Were you supposed to meet with him?"

"No, um, Mitt mentioned he was golfing today, but I forgot," I lie. Trying to control my breathing, I inhale and exhale slowly. It's been clear they haven't wanted me around as much since we lost Granddad. This shouldn't be a surprise, but it doesn't change the fact that it feels fucking terrible.

"Do you want me to take a message and tell him you stopped by?"

"No, I'll text him. Thank you."

Turning around, I call the elevator, and when the doors open, John and I board in silence. He follows me back into my office.

"I'm really sorry, Tanner. This is my fault. When I got here this morning, I had to use the bathroom, and they must've called while I was in there. I'm—"

I put my hand up to stop him. "This isn't your fault John. They didn't call."

"You don't know that," he tries.

"Yes, I do."

CHAPTER 5: IT'S A GOOD THING I PAY ATTENTION

TANNER

The Local is already wall to wall people when Jacks, Lacey, and I walk in. We push through the crowd, and I spot Poppy and Logan sitting at a table with our friends, Donovan and Enzo. My heart drops a little when I don't see Wren.

After the week I've had, I could use a win, and the only win I want is for her to give me a chance to show her that I'm not the guy she thinks I am.

Poppy stands and wraps Lacey up in a hug, and Jacks and I greet the guys.

"So, what's everyone drinking?" I ask.

"We hadn't ordered yet," Logan says. "We were waiting for everyone to get here."

"I think I'm gonna do a gin and tonic," Lacey says, scooting into the booth.

"I'll take a French 75," Poppy says.

"Wren and Gray will be here soon, but I'm not sure what they want," Lacey adds. "I can text them."

It's a good thing I pay attention.

"I got them. Don't worry," I say. "Donovan and Enzo, y'all good with beer?"

Both men nod, and Jacks, Logan, and I head to the bar to order.

"Yo, Frank," I yell when we find an empty space. He waves and nods his head, acknowledging us.

"You still good with our plan," I ask Logan while we wait.

"Yeah, we'll play, but I'm serious. If she doesn't want to play, then you gotta take that as a sign to leave her alone. I don't understand this obsession you have with her. Do you like her or something?"

"What can I get y'all?" Frank yells over the bar before I can answer Logan.

"Five beers, a gin and tonic, a French 75, an extra dirty martini, and a cosmo," I order.

"Y'all opening a tab?" Frank asks.

"Sure." I slide my card across the bar. He takes it and then turns to go make our drinks.

"T, I can cover me and Lacey." Jacks says.

"I was about to say the same thing about Poppy and me. You don't have to pay," Logan adds.

"It's no problem. Y'all can get it next time." I shrug them off.

"I wish you wouldn't do that," Logan argues.

"I have the money—might as well spend it."

"Regardless, we could've gotten them," Jacks grumbles.

Frank returns with our order. I grab Wren's before either of my friends has the chance. We do our best to collect the rest of the drinks between the three of us, but there are nine drinks and only six hands.

"Leave some of the beers, and I'll make a second trip," I offer. They agree, and the three of us walk back to the table.

My heart stops when I see Wren. The other girls in our group are pretty, but Wren is the type of beautiful that men would start wars over. She's stunning. Her long, auburn hair is pulled back out of her face. She's wearing pink denim shorts, a white tank top that shows off her midriff, and a matching crocheted vest with small pink flowers and green leaves down the front.

I walk up behind Logan and Jacks, clearing my throat.

"Uh, here you go," I say, offering her the cosmo.

She stares at me a little stunned and doesn't take the drink.

"You drink cosmos right?" I say, now very unsure that I remembered her favorite drink correctly.

"Yes," she says. "I'm just confused about how you know that."

"I pay attention," I say, winking.

She takes the cocktail from me and rolls her eyes. "Thanks," she mutters under her breath.

The look I'm used to her making when she sees me appears. It's official. She hates me. Why did I have to wink like a fucking dumbass?

Pull yourself together.

"I'll be right back," I blurt out, turning and heading back toward the bar to get the rest of the beers.

I gather the three remaining drinks and am about to turn around when Frank stops me.

"Hey, T. You gotta minute?" he asks.

"Yeah, what's up dude?"

"Jerry's here and wants to talk to you." He nods to the other side of the bar to where the owner of The Local, Jerry, stands. The T-shirt he's wearing is worn, and I can tell the screenprint of The Local's logo is starting to peel. He's a good dude, but despite being the owner, he doesn't come around much, unless required. Jerry lifts his chin in my direction.

My mind jumps to the conversation he and I had a month ago. The one where I asked if he'd ever consider selling The Local, and he said he'd think about it. I haven't seen him since, and if he's wanting to talk, maybe that means he's considering my offer.

"Yeah, let me just bring these beers to my friends, and I'll be right back." I grab the bottles, run back to the table, and leave again without a word.

I make my way around the bar to where Jerry is standing.

"How's it going?" I ask.

He glances around. "It's always a good night when we're busy. You got a minute to chat in my office?"

"Definitely. It's not like you to be here. Everything good?" We move out of the bar and through a door into a small room. Papers are scattered around a small desk, and a couple kegs sit in the corner.

"Oh, yeah, yeah," he begins, sitting in the folding chair behind the desk. "I guess I should just come out and say it. I've been thinking a lot about what you and I talked about, and if you're still interested, I'd be interested in selling this place."

I stare at him, surprised. "Oh, wow." I run my hand through my hair.

"Sorry for the blunt delivery, but I don't know how else to say it."

"I'll be honest. When I brought it up, I didn't realize you were so close to selling."

He nods. "This place means a lot to me, and if I'm going to sell, then I want it to go to someone who will love it as much as I do, and I have no doubt that's you." His dark brown skin creases at the corners of his eyes as he chuckles. "You are one of my best customers, and I'm not getting any younger."

My mind whirls with ideas of where I could take this place. I could finally have a project that was all mine—a project where I could really let my creativity run wild. And, the best part would be that I'd get to run it all by myself. No more answering to my dad or brother. No more getting left out of meetings or trying to prove myself to people who are impossible to impress.

Fuck it sounds nice. It sounds freeing.

A conversation I had with my grandfather interrupts my

thoughts, and I wish my life was simpler. I wish I didn't feel obligated to stay despite how they treat me. I wish I didn't want their approval so badly, and owning a bar would never make them proud.

"I don't need an answer tonight, but just promise me you'll think it over." He puts out his hand to shake mine. "When you're ready to talk about it, let me know, and we can meet and discuss the fine print."

I take a long drag from my beer. "I will."

"Good. Let's keep this between you and me for now?"

"For sure."

I follow him out of his office, still a little stunned. Turning, I walk back to my friends and find all of them staring at me. My heart skips a beat when I spot Wren, and I decide to focus on her. I can think about possibly becoming a bar owner tomorrow.

"What?" I ask, approaching the table.

"What was that about?" Jacks asks.

"Yeah, why are you sneaking off behind doors with strangers?" Lacey teases.

"Oh, that was just Jerry. He owns the bar. It was nothing."

For a split second, I consider telling them, but Jerry asked me not to, and there is no way for me to discuss this with all eight of them quietly.

"Pink Pony Club" by Chappell Roan starts to play over the speakers, and all four girls scream.

"Let's dance!" Poppy yells. "Boys, you coming?"

"Let's go, babe!" Enzo says, grabbing Donovan's hand.

"I think I'm going to sit this one out," I say.

"Yeah, me too," Logan says, making eye contact with Jacks.

"You're never any fun," Poppy teases her boyfriend.

The six of them head to the dance floor, leaving me with Logan and Jacks at the table.

"So, now that it's just the three of us, are you gonna tell us why you were talking to the owner of the bar?" Logan asks.

"Yeah, because it sure as hell didn't look like nothing," Jacks adds.

I take another long sip of my beer. Jerry asked me not to say anything, but I know I should talk about it with someone. I exhale.

"You can't say anything," I insist.

"You and the secrets lately," Jacks says.

"What does that mean?" Logan asks.

"Nothing," I say, cutting my eyes at Jacks, who shrugs his shoulders and sips from his beer.

"We won't say anything," he says, and Logan nods. "What's up?"

I turn completely to face them, lowering my voice so no one else can hear me. "He wants to sell the bar, and he wants me to buy it."

"That's fucking awesome man. You said yes, right?" Jacks asks.

"No, it's complicated. I told him last month I wanted to be considered if he ever thought of selling it, and I wasn't expecting for him to offer it to me a month later. So now I'm not sure what I want to do. As much as it's tempting, my grandfather trusted me and my brother to take over the family business one day, and I can't help but feel a little guilty about considering leaving."

"That's bullshit. You hate it there. Take it from someone who let his dad run his life for too long. You shouldn't sacrifice your happiness to make others happy. Your grandfather wouldn't have wanted that for you," Logan says.

"Speaking of your father, whatever happened to his campaign?" I ask.

Logan shrugs. "Last I heard, some of his past infidelities had come to light, and he had backed out."

"You didn't?"

"Oh, god, no. I may have cut ties with him, but I wouldn't slander his name. I think a few women came forward, but I'm not sure." He pauses. "But we're not talking about me. We're talking about you."

"I think you should buy the bar. I never thought you belonged in the office. Capable—of course you are, man, but it's not you," Jacks says.

Deep down, I know he's right. The suit and the fancy office has never been me. "I was thinking it would be cool if I expanded the bar. Maybe build some pickleball courts, and then people could come play and grab a drink after the games."

"Fuck yeah, man. I think you know what you need to do. Talk to your dad and Mitch, and then make it happen," Logan says.

CHAPTER 6: PING-PONG, ANYONE?
WREN

Poppy, Lacey, Gray, and I can't stop laughing as we walk off the dance floor toward the bar to refill our drinks.

"Y'all need another?" I ask Donovan and Enzo.

"We're good," Enzo calls back as he and his husband walk to meet the guys at the table.

"Tanner was sweet to remember what you liked to drink," Poppy says as we find an empty place along the bar.

"I don't know if sweet is the word I'd use," I say, wincing a little at the thought of him bringing me my favorite cocktail.

"I think he's trying," Gray says.

"To get in my pants?"

"I thought you weren't his type," she claps back.

"What does that mean?" Lacey asks.

"Nothing. I don't trust that his gesture doesn't have an ulterior motive."

"I think he's just being your friend," Poppy clarifies.

"Maybe, but I just don't get it. It's like a woman wrote Logan, Jacks, Donovan, and Enzo. Then there's Tanner. And, well I don't know, but he's nothing like them. The flirting is out of control. I mean he fucking winked at me. I can't."

"So, I guess this would be a bad time to remind you he still needs a roommate," Lacey says.

"Yes!" I shout, playfully shoving her shoulder. "I know y'all don't get it because you have these super sweet boyfriends who literally worship the ground you walk on, but I've dated a Tanner before, and it's not worth the trouble."

"I don't have one of those," Gray laughs.

"Well at this rate, you're probably next," I say.

"With all my issues, I doubt that," Gray says, her face falling a little.

"That's not true," I reply.

"We weren't talking about me," she says, trying to change the subject. "We were talking about how you were thinking about dating Tanner."

"I was not." A giggle bubbles out of me at the thought.

"You did bring up dating him," Lacey laughs.

"She's right," Poppy says.

"Y'all are the worst. I was just trying to say that he's nothing like your boyfriends, and that in my experience with dating a guy like him, I learned my lesson."

"But no one is suggesting you date him," Poppy reminds me.

"I know that, but I don't think he would understand that. I'm not going to force myself to live with the world's biggest flirt. I keep telling y'all I'll find something, and I will. Stop worrying."

"But we're your friends," Lacey says. "We're supposed to worry about you, and in two and a half months, your apartment will be a pile of rubble."

"It's so sad," I lament. "Did I tell y'all that I ran into my old landlords at the grocery store, and they said the new company kept them completely in the dark about demoing the building. They were devastated to find out that we're all getting kicked out because of it."

"It's so slimy," Gray says.

"So slimy," Lacey adds. "Did you ever ask about the rent special they offered the current tenants?"

"I did, and it was two and half times my current rent." I pretend to gag. "So expensive. I need somewhere cheap."

"What can I get you ladies?" the bartender asks, interrupting our conversation.

"Another gin and tonic, a French 75, a cosmo, and a martini," Lacey shoots off.

"Extra dirty," Gray yells as he walks away, and he throws a thumbs up into the air.

"Have you looked on Craigslist?" Gray asks.

"Craigslist? No. I don't want to be murdered." I laugh. "I just need to find a place that's decent and allows me to keep saving my money."

"I could talk to Jace about you living with us for a bit," Lacey offers.

"I can't do that. We're moving y'all in tomorrow, and I would totally kill the vibe."

"Then Tanner—" Poppy begins.

"Nope, we're done. Next person to bring him up is going to have to take tequila shots," I warn.

"Fine," all three of my friends say at the same time.

The bartender returns with four drinks, and we make our way back to the guys.

"Anyone up for a friendly game of ping-pong?" Logan asks, gesturing toward the table in the corner. "What do you say, Chatterbox, you and me versus Wren and Tanner?"

"I'm in," Poppy says. "Wren, want to play?"

"Oh, um, I think I'm going to sit this one out," I say.

"Come on," Poppy begs. "I'm not very good, but it'll be fun."

"Yeah, pretty please," Tanner pleads.

"Gray, why don't you play," I suggest.

"No, I'm good," she says, her mouth forming an evil grin. "You should play."

"Fine," I groan, downing the rest of my cosmo in one go.

"Hell yeah," Tanner yells, putting his hand up for a high five, but when I try to meet his hand with mine, he moves it, and it just ends up being an awkward brush of our fingers. His cheeks heat, and he heads to the bar to collect the paddles without a word.

They seriously want me to live with him, yet we can't even high five without being weird.

The rest of us head toward the ping-pong table, and I try to push my feelings aside.

"So, what are we playing for?" Tanner asks, handing each person a paddle.

"Losing team has to share a dance," Poppy says. "And the winning team gets to pick the song."

"That was the bet last time we played," I say. "Remember the night Jacks and Lacey hooked up in the bathroom?"

"Scared you're gonna lose?" Poppy teases.

"No, I was just thinking we could come up with a different bet."

"I'm good with that being the bet," Logan says, shrugging.

"Me too," Tanner agrees.

"I'm sure you are," I say under my breath, walking to my side of the table.

"What does that mean?" he asks.

"Nothing," I retort, annoyed. "Let's play."

The game begins, and with every hit, it's apparent that once again Tanner and I are the better players. In no time, we are up nine to three, and I send a silent thank you to the universe that this game is moving fast. Two more points and we win.

"I honestly thought y'all would be better competition than Jacks and Lacey," Tanner yells at our opponents.

I giggle and send the ball flying back over the net.

"We're not that bad," Poppy argues, missing the ball.

"That's our point," I shout. "10-3."

Tanner sends the ball straight at them. Logan returns it, but Tanner doesn't even try to hit it.

"10-4," Poppy calls out.

"If I didn't know any better, I'd say you were trying to throw the game with hits like that," Logan yells.

"You better not be," I yell, cutting my eyes in Tanner's direction.

Poppy serves the ball, and she and I return it back and forth a couple of times before I send it flying over the net toward Logan, who misses.

"Shall we pick a song?" I ask, turning towards Tanner.

"After you." He puts his hand out, and I move past him toward the DJ.

"We make a good team," he says.

"Hard not to when the people you're playing against suck."

"I guess so. Do you play often? You're really good."

"We need to pick a song," I say.

"Oh, um. Okay. Maybe 'Love In This Club'? Everyone thought it was funny last time."

"No, that's what they were going to pick, plus they're obsessed with one another, so they'd love it to be a hot song. It has to be something dumb," I say. "Like I don't know, maybe—"

"'The Hokey Pokey,'" we say at the same time.

"Ha! I told you we make a good team," he says, flashing me a smile that takes up his entire face.

My stomach flips, and I feel a small smile form across my lips. I try to hide it, but it's too late. He catches it, and a larger one erupts across his. "Thinking Out Loud" by Ed Sheeran pours through the speakers, and couples sway all around us, wrapped in each other's arms. He takes a step towards me, and my stomach does another swoop when his blue eyes find mine.

"I know we won, but do you want to dance before you tell the DJ to play the song for them?" he asks.

The cosmos and the music must be messing with me because there is no way I'm falling for whatever is happening right now.

"Oh, um…" I stammer. "I told Gray I'd share an Uber with her after our game."

"Yeah, you're right. It's late. No worries," he says, pushing his hand through his hair, and fuck, my stomach does it again when his bicep flexes.

"Sorry. I'm just gonna go tell the DJ," I say, more panicked than I intend.

Shit. Get it together. It's Tanner for Christ's sake.

"Yeah, for sure."

I walk toward the DJ, trying to shake off whatever the hell that was because I know better, and if my judgment is failing, it's definitely time for me to go home.

CHAPTER 7: THE ACTUAL EMBODIMENT OF ALL MY DEEPEST AND DARKEST INSECURITIES

TANNER

"You're what?" my dad's voice reverberates off the walls of my parents' dining room. He stands abruptly, causing the whole table to shift. The wine I just poured threatens to slosh over the edge of my glass, and my brother's fork clangs against the fine china plate my mother insisted we use because the whole family was together.

I look quickly between the five people in front of me. Bella, my younger sister, stares down at her phone, refusing to make eye contact with anyone. Mitch and his wife, Farah, are staring dumbfounded at my father. My mother wipes the corners of her mouth with her cloth napkin and then slowly rises to meet my dad. She moves her hand down his back, offering him a small smile. There is no mirror in the dining room, but I'm sure my face is somewhere between surprised and confused as shit because I, for one, am flabbergasted that I was not the cause of the look spread across my dad's face.

When I arrived at my parents' house tonight, I had no doubt that I would be seeing the look—this look—before the evening was over. It's the same look that tucked me into bed most nights after a long lecture about needing to listen. The look that stared back at me while I struggled with my homework from the time I was six until I was fourteen. The look that met me when I stepped off the lacrosse field after every game. The look that paints his face on the days I make it into the office.

And I was fully expecting the *"I'm fucking disappointed in who you are. Do better. Grow up. When are you ever going to make me proud?"* look when I told him that I wanted to pursue purchasing The Local and leave the family company. For three weeks, I've been waiting patiently for him to get back in town, for him to have time to meet with me, and now it's all going to shit.

Tonight was supposed to be like every other family meal we've ever had—dinner, drinks, dessert, and the actual embodiment of all my deepest, darkest insecurities.

It was supposed to start with my parents doting on my little sister over drinks and hors d'oeuvres. Then, during the main course, the conversation was supposed to switch to the part of the evening where Mitt and Mitch bore us all with talk about how fantastic the family business is doing, most of which is news to me because, despite me working with them, I'm rarely kept in the loop. And then for dessert, I would remind my dad that I once again didn't live up to his expectations. But I'm still eating my steak, and the look has already made an appearance, and I'm quickly realizing my announcement isn't going to happen.

"Dad, if you would just hear us out," Mitch tries.

My dad inhales and then lets out a long, audible breath.

"Sit down, honey," my mom encourages, rubbing his back again, but he doesn't move.

Why is he being so fucking dramatic?

"Mitt, this isn't Mitch's fault," Farah explains. My brother grabs her hand and squeezes it tenderly. "It's my job, and I can assure you I tried everything I could to stay in the country, but it's not feasible."

My dad ignores her, turning his head toward my brother. Every second of silence seems to fill the air like helium in a balloon, pulling the surface tighter and tighter until it threatens to burst completely.

"You know how much we have on the line right now," my dad barks, shaking his head.

"I know," my brother begins. "But Farah is my wife, and this promotion—"

Fleur, my parents' private chef, walks backwards through the door holding a round cake covered in white icing, interrupting my brother. "Dessert is serv—," she sings in a French accent, flipping around. She stops abruptly when she realizes she's interrupted whatever the hell is going on here. I let out a loud laugh that I quickly try to muffle when my father's eyes shoot in my direction.

"Should I come back?" she asks, hesitantly.

"No, it's fine," my mom says through clenched teeth.

She pulls my dad back into his chair, and they both sit. My father continues to glare in my brother's direction while Fleur slices the cake and serves each of us. The silence in the room is deafening, and I still can't figure out why my sister-in-law's promotion caused such a visceral reaction from my father.

"Dad, can we talk about this?" Mitch begs, once Fleur is back in the kitchen.

My father stands, throws his napkin across his plate, and then leaves the dining room.

I guess that's a hard no.

"Someone want to tell me what's going on?" I ask, looking toward my brother.

"It's complicated," Mitch huffs out. "You wouldn't understand."

"Why? Because I'm me? I know about your secret little meetings. Just tell me why you having to move is such a big deal. You're an asset to the company, of course, but why is Dad reacting like this?"

Mitch downs his glass of wine. "Should I follow him?" he asks.

My mom shakes her head. "No, let him calm down. He's stressed. We're both really happy for you, Farah. Mitt will come around. He just needs time."

My sister-in-law forces a smile, but her shoulders slouch.

"So, Tanner, what's new with you?" my mom attempts to change the subject.

Oh, let's see, I want to quit my job and buy a bar, but my big brother just completely fucked my plan with his little announcement.

"Not much. I still haven't found a roommate."

My brother picks at the slice of cake in front of him.

"You're looking for a roommate?" she asks.

"Have been since the end of July," I snap, my patience wearing thin, and my eyes shift back to Mitch. "Bro, talk to me. I think I at least deserve to know why he reacted that way."

"Honey, don't worry about it. Bella, did you tell Tanner you're the cheer captain this year?"

I blink in my mother's direction. She is actually acting like this dinner isn't completely fucked, just carrying on like nothing happened.

"Mom, can you be so for real right now? Dad just stormed out of dinner. I don't think Tanner wants to hear about me being the cheer captain," Bella says with as much drama as you can expect from a sixteen-year-old.

"No, I do want to hear about it, and we will talk about it. But, you're right. Right now, I'd like Mitch to tell me what's going on with Dad."

"I said it's complicated," he barks.

Of course he won't tell me. It doesn't matter that I work there too. It doesn't matter that I'm his brother. None of it ever matters. I'm not Mitch. I'm not Bella. I'm just Tanner, and that's not good enough. If I ever needed confirmation that buying The Local was the right move, it's this conversation.

"Right. Okay, well on that note. I'm gonna head out too." I run my hands through my hair.

"You didn't touch your cake, and I specifically asked her to make you red velvet because I know it's your favorite," my mom says.

"Red velvet's not my favorite. Lemon is, and I'm suddenly not in the mood for cake." I stand and begin to walk out of the room, only pausing to kiss Bella on the top of the head. "Bye, Bells. Congrats on the cheer thing. Farah, it was nice to see you. Congrats on the new gig."

My mom and brother begin arguing about something behind me, but I don't have it in me to listen to what it's about.

The warm, summer air and the scent of cigarettes hits me in the face the minute I swing their front door open. I quickly close the door behind me and turn left to the side of the house.

"I thought you quit?" I ask, rounding the corner.

My dad throws the butt of his cigarette onto the stone driveway and stomps it out with his foot.

"Don't tell your mother."

"Yeah," I breathe out, shaking my head.

"I'm sorry for storming out of dinner," he says.

"It's fine." I shrug. "Farah deserves the apology, not me. Have a good night." I turn to walk away, but he stops me.

"Wait, let me explain."

I freeze. Part of me thinks I should leave, but I don't. The other part of me thinks I should just tell him about the bar so that I can be done with this nonsense, but I don't do that either. Instead, we stand there in silence for a few seconds, staring at one another.

The flood light illuminates his face. It's amazing how little we look alike. He's at least three inches shorter than me. His eyes are a brownish green. Younger Mitt even had dark brown hair, but now it's gray. He looks exhausted. He looks old.

He rubs his hand down his face and exhales.

"I planned on taking a step back from the company at the end of the year."

"Mitch knew?"

"Of course your brother knew. He was set to become the next President and CEO."

"Of course your brother knew." Funny they forgot to mention this was happening. Must have been talked about in one of the many meetings I wasn't invited to.

"I'm sixty-five. I can't keep doing this forever. He was my only option," he explains. "If it's not him, then we will have to bring in someone else."

My stomach flips. Having a Mitchell lead the family business was all my granddad ever wanted. I can practically see him turning over in his grave at the thought of someone with a different last name running the company. The Local flashes in my head. I was so close to having something for me, but just like it always does, my family obligation tugs at my heart. This isn't how it was supposed to be.

FUCKKKKKKKKK.

"But it's a family business. You promised Granddad you would keep it that way."

"Your grandfather isn't here anymore. I can't keep doing this forever. I want to spend time with your mother. As hard as it is to admit, if your brother is leaving, then I have no other options."

"Aren't I supposed to be an option?" I can't even believe the words coming out of my mouth.

A loud laugh bellows out of him, filling the quiet night. "I love you, Son, but I think you and I both know that isn't in the best interest of the company."

His words are a fist to my gut, and it's clear. Mitch was the only option, not because he doesn't think I want it, but because he thinks I can't do it.

"I know I'm not Mitch, but I am a Mitchell. I closed that Cedar Hill deal this summer, and it's going well. I know you haven't had time to look at my plans, but maybe if you did—"

"The Cedar Hill acquisition is nothing compared to running an entire company. You still have a lot of growing up to do."

"Then let me prove to you that I'm ready, that I can grow up. I want to be considered for the position." I'm not sure if I'm more desperate for his approval or to prove him wrong, but once the words leave my mouth, I know I can't take them back.

"Tanner, being the president and CEO of a company is not like one of your little hobbies. It's serious, and it requires—"

"I know what it requires. I'm a Mitchell. I have my MBA. I've been an executive vice president for five years. I'm just as qualified as Mitch, and you know it."

My dad rubs his temples. "Meet me at the office tomorrow at nine, and we will discuss it. I'm making no promises. Wear a suit, and don't be late."

Dude I'm going to have to bail on pickleball tomorrow

LOGAN:

Everything okay?

Family shit

No one died just gotta deal with something

LOGAN:

I understand. Don't worry about it. Did you tell him about the bar?

Didn't get the chance

LOGAN:

Shit

I'll fill you in later

LOGAN:

I understand. Don't worry about it. tell him about the bar?

Didn't get the chance

LOGAN:

Shit

CHAPTER 8: MY FAVORITE PERSON
WREN

"I'm home," I yell, pushing open my parents' door and walking into their modest, brick ranch.

"We're outside, sweetheart," my mom shouts from the screened-in porch that is attached to the back of their house.

I make my way through the living room toward the door, taking in the home I grew up in. It's like a time capsule of my childhood, just with a little less furniture and some added ramps for my brother's wheelchair.

As I step onto the deck, my parents stand to meet me, and I notice my dad winces slightly as he gets up from his chair. I've worked hard not to feel guilty about the decisions I've made, but I can't help but wonder if I was still living here, if he wouldn't be hurt.

I set the gift I brought for my younger brother, Cody, on the table and wrap my mom up in a hug first, taking a moment to breathe in her perfume. She smells like peonies, and for the first time in a while, I feel the tension in my shoulders melt away.

"Glad you could make it, sweetheart. You're all he could

talk about," she whispers in my ear. I giggle to myself, glancing over at Cody.

I turn to find my dad. "You okay?" I ask as he wraps me in a hug.

"Always worrying about us." He shakes his head. "I'm fine, honey. Just tweaked my back helping this guy into bed the other day." He nods toward my brother.

"Aren't you going to tell me hello," a mechanical voice says through the speakers of the iPad Cody uses to speak.

"It's always all about you isn't it," I tease, flipping around and wrapping my arms around him. I place a kiss on the top of his auburn hair. "Hey, bud. I missed you."

He laughs, and it's my favorite sound. Almost six years ago, I never thought I would hear it again, and while it doesn't sound like it used to, I love his new laugh just as much as I loved the old one. It's a reminder that I still have my little brother.

He begins to type on the screen, and I wait for his response.

"Fucking liar," he says. I shake my head.

"Language," my moms scolds. "Please don't use that word under my fucking roof." Cody's whole body shakes with laughter, and he begins to type again.

"Is that for me?" he asks, using his speech device.

"It sure is. You want to open it?"

He nods his head, and I place the small bag on the tray table connected to his wheelchair. I help him hold the bag, and he pulls the tissue paper out with his left hand, and it falls all over the floor. Reaching in, he pulls out a Funko Pop! figurine of Spiderman hanging from his web. His whole face lights up.

"I didn't think you had this one yet."

My mom walks over and looks at the box. "He doesn't," she confirms. Cody begins to tap on his screen. "You don't have to bring him a present every time you come over. I mean the twenty-three gifts for his twenty-third birthday two weeks ago was plenty."

"Yes, I do," I say, smiling at my brother. "Those were birthday gifts. They don't count."

"Thank you I love it Dad can you put it on my shelf," my brother says using his iPad, the sentences coming out as one because he doesn't use punctuation when he talks.

Standing, my dad nods. He winces again and places his hand on his lower back for support. "You got it, bud." He takes the box and disappears back into the house.

"So, what's the plan for today?" I ask.

He begins to type again, and I find an empty chair.

"Marvel movie marathon," Cody says.

"Sounds perfect. What are we starting with? I guess I'll let you pick." His finger swipes on the screen, and I know he's navigating to the page of saved movies that make it easier to participate in conversations.

"Lunch will be finished around two, and then I made dessert," my mom explains.

"*Iron Man Black Panther Thor*," he says.

I check my watch. "*Iron Man* is perfect. We'll have time to watch it before lunch, then I can stay, and we can watch the others after. I cleared my whole schedule just for you."

Cody's mouth forms an asymmetrical smile, and he begins to type on the screen again. My mom stands to help him move his wheelchair into the living room. She parks it in front of the TV that hangs over the fireplace, and I curl up in my dad's worn leather recliner under a blanket then click through the recently watched movies until I find *Iron Man*.

"I feel special," he says, after typing on the screen.

"You should because you are. Now don't let it go to your head. The movie is starting."

———

My mom and I walk out of Cody's room and into the kitchen where my dad is still sitting at the table, finishing the last of his slice of pie.

"I know you were looking forward to more movies, but he seemed exhausted." Mom squeezes my hand. "Coffee?"

I nod. "It's okay. I'm not going to deprive him of a nap just because I want to watch some movies we've both seen more than a dozen times."

"I told y'all I could help," my dad says as I take a seat across from him.

"No. You can't. You hurt your back lifting him," I say matter-of-factly. My mom slides a mug in front of me and joins us. "How did that even happen?"

"Caregiver called out a couple days ago, and your mother had run up to the store. He said he was tired, and I must've lifted with my back a little too much, because the minute I got him standing, I could feel it."

"Why not use his lift?"

"That old thing?" My dad shakes his head. "I think it's broken. It's easier to just do it myself."

I exhale. The lift is broken? Caregivers are calling it out? I wonder what else they haven't told me.

"Since when?"

"A couple weeks now," my mom says. "I'm trying to get a new one or at the very least a repair, but you know how insurance can be." She shakes her head. "I'm hoping to hear from them soon."

"And how often are the caregivers canceling?"

"Depends. We have a few really good ones right now, but you know how it is. We'll find good ones, and then they move on."

For the first time today, I really take them in. Both are in their mid-fifties. My dad's hair is beginning to gray. My mom's hair used to be the same shade as mine, but now it's a deeper red that you can only get at a salon. There seems to be more creases around their eyes than the last time I saw them.

Guilt overwhelms me. I should be here helping. Maybe getting kicked out of my apartment is a sign from the universe that I need to be here, not living my life like nothing awful happened to my favorite person.

"You know, I actually have to be out of my apartment by the end of October. Maybe I should move back in. I could help. I know y'all need it."

The base of my mom's mug clatters against the wood surface of the table. "Absolutely not," she says.

"But Mom—" I begin, but this time my dad chimes in.

"As much as we would love to have you under our roof again, you can't move back here. You are going to be Cody's primary caregiver one day, but that day isn't today. Your mother and I are more than capable of caring for him."

"We do appreciate your offer, honey, but your father is right. You're twenty-four. You should be out in the world living your life. You're always welcome here, and we are so appreciative of how much you helped after his accident, but you can't put that pressure on yourself."

She grabs my hand, and tears begin to run down my cheeks. I know they're right. We spent more than a year in therapy together learning how to process everything that happened. My takeaway was that I couldn't be there for everyone the way I wanted to be if I didn't take care of myself first, but some days that fact is still hard to accept. I love my family more than anything in the world, and it feels selfish not to be here helping. It's an internal battle I fight constantly.

"Don't you start crying," she says. "Our lives were forever changed the day your brother fell, but that doesn't mean we have to live life being sad about it. We still have him, and while he may use a computer to talk to us and needs a little bit of extra help sometimes, he's still our Cody. I know for a fact he wouldn't want you to live here."

"Oh, did he tell you that?" I can't help but laugh at her frank statement.

"He did. He never liked having to share our attention."

"Very funny," I deadpan.

"Why are you moving?" my dad asks.

"They sold my apartment building, and the new company is kicking us all out to demolish it."

My mom gasps. "Why didn't you say something?"

"I didn't want to make a fuss over it. You have a lot on your plate." Her mouth droops a bit, and I know my words hit her harder than I intended. "I've been looking for a place, but everywhere is so expensive. I thought I had found something, but the rent was insane. Between that, bills, and my savings, I just couldn't swing it."

"Are you still saving to start those camps you've been dreaming about for the last six years," she asks.

"Yes, I don't make much, but every extra penny is going into my savings."

My parents look at one another and then back to me. My mom shakes her head.

"We admire you and all of your goals, honey. But have you considered saving a little less so that you can afford something better?" she asks.

I ignore her statement, sipping from my coffee mug. There is nothing wrong with planning for my future, especially when my plan would make my little brother's life so much better.

"Have y'all thought any more about hiring more help, so you don't have to do as much?" I ask, changing the subject.

"It's expensive to hire help," my dad says. "We're making do with the three caregivers we have. They're covering most of the weekdays, and then we have him at night and on the weekends. It's working."

"Is it?" I mutter. "You're hurt. It's only a matter of time before mom gets hurt too."

My mom rubs her hand down my dad's back.

"I know you don't want to talk about these things, but y'all need to consider it. The last thing I want is for either of you or him to get injured," I argue. "And if the lift is broken and the caregivers are calling out, it would be nice to have some alternates so it doesn't all fall on you."

"We'll look into it," she says. "But you need to look after yourself and stop worrying about us. Promise me you'll find a place to live that's decent."

"My current place is decent."

"Baby, you live in a shoebox that was built god knows when. You constantly complain about leaks and repairs that need to be done. No wonder they sold it." She gives me that look that moms give when they know they're right.

"It's not that bad."

My mind jumps to the bucket I placed on the kitchen counter this morning to capture the water dripping through the ceiling, and I wonder if it'll be fixed when I get home.

"Do you currently have any active leaks?" she asks like she can read my mind.

"Yes. Okay, maybe you have a point, but overall it's safe, affordable, and close to work. I like living there, and I'm really bummed that I have to move."

"I know, but maybe it's time to spend a little bit more money on the present. I know you have big dreams, and I have no doubt you'll get there one day, but you never will if you don't take care of yourself now."

"My friends have been really supportive. They all offered me spare rooms and their couches, but I don't want to intrude."

"It might be a temporary solution until you find something more permanent," my dad says.

An unwelcome Tanner thought pops into my head, but I push it away.

"Yeah, but Poppy and Lacey moved in with their

boyfriends. Chloe is a single mom, and Gray's in a studio. They don't need me barging in and taking up space."

"I'm not surprised," my mom says.

"What do you mean?"

"It's just you always think about others before you think about yourself. It's admirable until it starts to affect your quality of life."

Okay, ouch.

"I agree with your mother." Dad sips from his mug.

The chances of me finding something as affordable as Cedar Hill is slim. I refuse to stop saving money, so maybe I should just give in. I stand from the table and load my mug into the dishwasher.

"I'll find something. Worst case scenario, I'll take one of my friends up on their offer until I can find something."

Mom smiles. "Now that's a plan I can get behind. I'm glad you've found a good group of friends."

"Me too." Poppy, Logan, Lacey, Jacks, Donovan, Enzo, Gray, Chloe, and Tanner pop into my head. For the first time in I don't know how long, the world around me seems a little more settled, and I don't feel so lost. After Cody's accident and all of my friendships ended, I dreamed of being a part of a friend group like this, and while we've had some ups and downs, I'm so glad to call each of them my friend—even Tanner.

I lean against their counter, and my eyes land on the calendar hanging on the fridge. My mom, always one to be thinking ahead, has already changed the month to September. A big heart is drawn on the thirtieth around the words *twenty-five years*.

"Are y'all going to do anything for your anniversary? Twenty-five years is a big deal."

"We talked about going out to eat, but we'll probably just grill some steaks here and open a nice bottle of wine," my dad explains. "Mondays the caregiver gets off at three, so we'll need to be here with your brother."

"Y'all are trying to convince me to look after myself, and you're not looking after you. I know it's hard to take a break, but y'all deserve a night out. Do you want me to come over and hang with Cody while y'all go to dinner?"

"You don't have to do that," my mom says.

"Please, hanging out with him is my favorite thing. If I had it my way, I'd send y'all away for a week so you could actually take a vacation, and one day I will. But, in the meantime, I can come hang out with my brother, and y'all can go to dinner."

"Goodness, who raised you to be so caring and wonderful?" my mom teases.

"You did." I roll my eyes, and both of my parents stand, laughing. My dad winces again.

"I think I'm going to head out," I say. "Please consider hiring more help. Dad, please go see a doctor about your back. And Mom, if you need help with the insurance stuff, call me, and I can see what I can do."

"We will," he says, wrapping me up tightly. "But you need to consider what we said too."

"I will. Love you both, and I'll put your anniversary on my calendar. Dad, you better take Mom somewhere nice."

"Consider it done. I love you." Dad kisses the side of my head and releases me. I turn to find my mom. She sets down her mug and pulls me into her. I'm wrapped up in her scent once more, and I breathe her in, instantly calming my nervous system again.

"I'll call your dad's doctor tomorrow," she whispers in my ear.

"Thank you." I squeeze my arms around her.

On my way out the door, I stop by Cody's room and peek in. I smile when I spy the Spiderman I gave him on the shelf among the hundred or so figurines that line the top of his room. He's sound asleep. "Love you, bud," I whisper before closing his door softly.

CHAPTER 9: BOO!

WREN

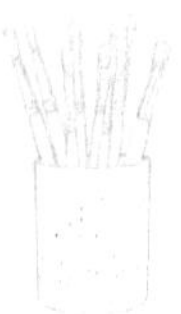

I'm still reeling from the conversation with my parents when I pull into The Local. It's not lost on me that I need to find a place to live, but not being able to find something affordable is stressful and overwhelming.

I'm not even sure why I turned in on my way home. It's not like me to go for a drink, but I saw the sign and it felt like the right call. I blow out a long breath, trying to calm my racing thoughts, and grab my phone.

The Tortured Therapists Department

I know it's last minute, but anyone want to meet at The Local for a drink?

CHLOE:

Wish I could, but Ava was with a sitter all day. Next time!

LACEY:

Poppy, Logan, Jace, and I are out on a double date. We can come meet you after?

Don't worry about it. Y'all have fun!

Gray?

GRAY:

I fear I already took off my bra. Don't hate me!

I understand! I guess I'm drinking alone.

GRAY:

Unless you meet someone cute!

Very funny.

POPPY:

Be safe. If you need a ride, call one of us.

I will. See you all in the morning.

I HESITATE FOR A COUPLE MINUTES AND THEN GET OUT OF MY CAR to walk across the parking lot. The bar is surprisingly empty for a Saturday night, and when I check the time on my phone, I realize it's only six thirty, so the main crowd isn't here yet.

I find an empty barstool and wave the bartender over.

"Whatcha drinking?" he asks.

"Any specials?"

"No. Just the usual."

"I think I want an amaretto on the rocks tonight." He nods and walks away. I pull out my phone and type *apartment for rent near me* into the search bar. I scan the available listings.

Fourteen hundred dollars a month.

Twelve hundred dollars a month.

Twenty-four hundred dollars a month.

Every single one of them is so expensive.

Eight hundred dollars a month. I click on the listing, and my stomach turns when the pictures pop up on the screen. It's an apartment in the basement of someone's house. It's totally giving *live with me so I can use your skin to make a suit* vibes. Hard pass.

I click back and keep scrolling. Realistically, I have time. I don't technically have to be out until the end of October, but everyday it seems like more of my neighbors move, and it's starting to creep me out. I stretch my neck from side to side.

A thousand dollars a month.

Money would be tight, but I could make it work. Maybe.

I click on the listing. Immediate no. Ugh. Why is this so hard? Feeling frustrated, I put my phone back in my purse.

"Thank you," I say, offering a small smile when the bartender returns with my drink.

Taking a sip, the aroma fills my nostrils. The flavor of almond liquor dances on my tongue before warming my throat as I swallow down one sip and then another. I'm staring off into space when I feel a firm grasp on my shoulders.

"What the hell?" I yell, whipping around.

"Boo!" Tanner says, letting go of me.

He looks like he came straight from a business meeting. He's wearing dark dress pants, expensive shoes, and a white button up shirt. His sleeves are rolled up, and the top couple buttons of his shirt are undone.

I didn't know he owned clothes like this. My brain starts moving in a weird direction, thoughts about how good he looks beginning to trickle in, and I internally panic. I try to hide my emotions, but that's not a skill I've ever acquired, and he catches me.

"Like what you see?" he asks, a little too cocky for my liking.

"Nope," I grumble out as I take another sip of my drink.

"Is this seat taken?"

"Nope."

He slides onto the stool next to me. "Frank," he yells, waving to the bartender.

"Hey, T," Frank says, putting out his hand and pulling Tanner into a hug over the bar. "What can I get you?"

I continue to stare straight ahead.

"It's good to see you, man. Is Jerry here?"

"No," Frank says. "He's out of town until next week."

"Okay, then I guess I'll have what she's having," Tanner says. Frank moves away from us, and in my peripheral vision I can see Tanner has turned his body so he's facing me.

"Are you waiting on a date to meet you?"

"Nope."

"Are the girls coming?"

"Nope."

"Are you going to say more to me than nope?"

"Nope." I glance over at him, and a wide smile erupts across his face. His chest rumbles with a loud laugh that makes the blond knot on the top of his head wiggle a little.

"Okay. I take it that means you're drinking alone?"

Frank slides his drink across the bar and then walks away to help another customer. Tanner lifts the glass to his lips.

"Not bad," he says. "Amaretto isn't your usual. Rough day?"

"What are you doing? Isn't there some other girl here you want to try to convince to sleep with you?" I ask, looking around the bar.

"You think I'm trying to convince you to sleep with me?" He smirks. "Bold of you."

"No. That's not what I meant." I take a sip of my drink before placing it back on the counter. "I think I'm going to go." I stand quickly, waving at the bartender.

"Wait, don't go. I was kidding."

"Whatcha need," the bartender says, walking back over to us.

"I'm going to close out."

"Hold on. You haven't finished your drink. We've never gotten to hang out just us. It could be fun," Tanner offers.

The bartender looks back and forth between the two of us.

"I think you and I have two very different ideas of fun," I say, turning to face Tanner.

He pats the barstool, looking up at me with the stare of a puppy dog. It's the look of a man who always gets what he wants. *God dammit, it's working.*

"For Christ's sake," I huff out. "I'll finish my drink, just stop looking at me like that."

"So, you gonna leave it open?" the bartender asks, hesitantly.

"I guess."

"Works every time." Tanner chuckles, sipping from his glass. "So, why are you here drinking alone?"

"I could ask you the same question."

Silence hangs between us. We're friends. We've hung out numerous times with other people, but never alone—never just the two of us. Come to think of it, I don't think I've ever had a real conversation with Tanner Mitchell that didn't involve at least one other person. Not that I've wanted to or had the chance. When we're together he's usually too busy flirting or goofing off to be serious, but maybe tonight will be different.

TANNER

Wren's eyes are the most beautiful shade of green and blue. They look like the ocean. Her auburn hair hits right above her ass. She's wearing a green tank top that brings out her eyes and denim overalls covered in a floral pattern. The smallest bit of stomach is visible on each of her sides. Small freckles contrast against every inch of her milky skin, and I'm completely enchanted.

She clears her throat, and I realize I haven't answered her question. Or did she not answer mine? I don't remember.

"You good?" she asks.

"Yeah, sorry. Really long day. What did you ask?"

"Why are you drinking alone tonight?"

"Technically, I'm not alone. You're here," I say.

She rolls her eyes. "Shit, did they text you and tell you to come meet me?"

"Who?"

"The girls."

"Nope. I haven't talked to anyone all day. I was stuck at the office. I'm here because my day totally blew, and I needed a drink before I went home. You?"

She tips her head ever so slightly to the right and squints her eyes. "The office?"

"Yeah, the place I work. My own personal version of hell."

She lets out a little giggle over the rim of her glass. "I didn't have you pegged as the office type."

"No? What did you think I did?"

"Honestly, I had no idea." She shrugs her shoulders. "But the whole white-collar businessman who works weekends was not in my top five guesses."

"Well, if it makes you feel any better, I don't love it, so I guess you're right that I'm not the office type."

"Hmmm," she responds. "Why was today bad?"

I don't usually talk about this part of my life, but something in the way she's looking at me makes me think I might want to tell her all of my secrets. I throw back the last of my drink. "Play me in a game of ping-pong. If you win, I'll tell you, and if I win, you have to tell me why you're here."

She studies me for a quick second. "I really should go home."

"Scared I'll beat you? I get it." I pick a piece of lint off of my shoulder. "I am one half of the Dink and Balls pickleball team and arguably our best player. I would be afraid I'd beat me too."

"How do you do that?"

"Do what?"

"Be so insanely insufferable." Her brow furrows, and she waves towards Frank. "I'll see you later. Goodbye."

Frank walks over. "Another round?"

"No," she says at the same time I say, "Yes."

"We're not doing this. I'm leaving."

"It's one game. Indulge me. I know you know how to play."

"I drove here. I don't need to have more than one drink."

"I'll make sure you get home safely."

Her breath hitches. "Do I even want to know what you mean by that?" She shakes her head.

"One game. Pretty please." I do the puppy dog eyes again.

"Goodbye, Tanner."

I'm desperate for her to stay. Partly because I don't want to be alone, and partly because I don't know when I'll get the chance to hang out with just her again, and by some miracle this conversation is actually going kinda well.

"Pretty pretty pretty please," I beg, clasping my hands in front of my face. I make my eyes even bigger and protrude my lip a little more.

"Fine. One game, but then I'm leaving."

Jackpot!

"Told you that look never fails me," I boast.

"And I wasn't lying when I said you're insufferable."

Fuck, I like when she gives me shit.

I shift my gaze to Frank. "Another round of drinks and two ping-pong paddles, please."

We collect the items and walk over to the ping-pong table in the corner of the bar. "Okay, so to recap, if I win, you have to tell me why you're drinking alone, and if you win, I'll tell you about my day."

"This seems unnecessary, but if you insist. I'll serve first," she says, rolling her eyes and taking a sip from her glass.

She throws the little orange ball and sends it flying over the net. I hit it back. We continue that way for a few exchanges before she hits the ball with as much force as I think she can, causing me to miss it completely.

"Ha!" she shouts as I sip my drink. "Thought you were good."

Her statement makes me choke, and I realize I don't just like when she gives me shit, I might be addicted.

She serves the ball again, and I hit it so hard it spins. She misses it completely. "Still think I'm bad at this game?" I tease.

"Do you want my honest answer?" she asks.

We go back and forth, matching each other point for point.

"8-7," she shouts. She finished her drink two serves ago, and I can tell the alcohol has loosened her up a bit. "Your serve, playboy."

Fuck me. I like when she calls me that.

"Playboy?" I shake my head and smack the ball in her direction. She stumbles and misses it. "8-8. I think those drinks are catching up with you."

She sticks out her tongue.

The ball bounces between us. Each of us scores point after point. "10-10. You gonna let me win, uh…" I pause. I want to nickname her too, but I'm not sure what to call her. The first words that pop into my mind are dream girl, but I say my second choice instead."Wrenny."

"Nope. Don't call me that."

Wrenny? What the fuck, man?

She hits the ball straight at my head and scores again.

"Hey, no cheap shots," I warn, pointing my paddle in her direction.

"11-10," she chimes. "Looks like I might just beat the best player on the Dink and Balls pickleball team."

I smack the ball in her direction, and she sends it back over the net. The edge of my paddle barely grazes her return, and I miss.

"I win," she squeals, throwing her hands above her head and doing a little twirl. I know I shouldn't be staring, but I can't help it. She looks so fucking happy, and I like that I played a part in it.

Walking over to where I stand, she pats my chest. "Alright, pay up! Why did your day suck?" She pushes herself onto the top of the ping-pong table, leaning back ever so slightly on her hands and crossing her legs.

I take a deep breath and stuff my hands in the pockets of my pants, rocking back on my heels. "I work for my family's company. Last night my brother announced that he and his wife are moving to Germany for her job. He was supposed to take over as president and CEO at the end of the year. I'm not sure why I did it, but I told my dad I wanted to be considered for the position, and he spent today trying to prove to me that I wasn't suited for the job."

"Damn, I'm sorry." She shifts her weight to sit up a little straighter.

I shrug. "It's honestly nothing new."

"Did he say why he thinks that? I'm sure you'd make a great CEO." There's a hesitation in her voice, and I can't help but wonder if she doesn't think I can do it either.

"No, he didn't. I'm currently working on this multi-use development project, and I'm really proud of it." I start to pace. "We acquired the Cedar Hill complex back in June, and I have plans to turn it into this really cool residential and commercial space."

Wren's mouth falls open, and her eyes go wide. "Did you say Cedar Hill?"

"Yeah, the shithole complex over on Maple Street. He seems to think that the future CEO should tow the line. Apparently, not only did I fuck up the timeline because I decided to be a decent human and give the current tenants three months to find a place to live, but according to him I also took too many creative liberties with the project."

She lets out a hum, and the corners of her mouth fall a little.

"Don't tell me you agree with him?" I laugh.

"Uh, no, it's not that," she says. "I'm just trying to process what you just said, and I'm feeling a little woozy. I need a minute."

She pops off the table and walks back toward the bar silently, so I follow her.

Frank sees us and walks over. "Can I get you something?"

"Water," she says.

"Are you okay?" I ask, confused as hell, but genuinely concerned that something might be wrong with her.

"You're talking about Cedar Hill Apartments?" she asks.

"Yeah, why?"

She starts to laugh and doesn't stop. It's not a normal laugh. It's unhinged, bordering on deranged, and if I'm honest, a little scary.

"What's so funny?"

"You're the asshole kicking me out of my apartment," she says in between the deep breaths she's attempting to take to calm herself.

My heart sinks into my gut. "Your apartment?"

"Yeah, I live in the—what did you call it—shithole complex over on Maple Street that you're tearing down." She throws air quotes up as she speaks.

"Did I call it that?" I wince. "I meant the super nice complex that I wish I lived in."

She laughs. "Part of the reason I was drinking alone tonight was because I can't find a place to live. This is unbe-lievable."

"I'm so sorr—"

"Please, I don't want your pity or your apology." She shakes her head, looking toward the bartender. "Can I close my tab?" He nods, tapping on the screen of the register. She takes the receipt, fills in the tip, signs her name, and then looks back at me.

"It sounds like it's been a long day for the both of us," she says.

"If I had known you lived there…"

"You would have what? Not done your job?" She shakes her head. "It's business, not personal. I mean, it's very inconvenient, and I think it's really shitty that you or your company promised to preserve the building and then went back on that promise, but I'm not mad at you."

"I never meant for you to get caught up in this."

"I'm sure you didn't. Tonight was…" She hesitates for a second. "Fun. Tonight was fun. Bye, Tanner." She turns to walk away, and I go to grab her hand, but I miss and make contact with her purse instead.

"Please don't leave. I'm worried I upset you."

She takes a deep breath. "You didn't. I'm tired and a little drunk. I need to go home. I have a long day of apartment hunting tomorrow because as you know, soon, I won't have a place to live. I'll see you later."

All the joy that radiated off of her during ping-pong is gone, and I want so desperately to get it back. I might be a huge disappointment to my dad, but I don't want to be a disappointment to her.

"Live with me," I blurt out.

Her mouth falls open.

"You know Jacks moved out. I have space."

"Nope. Not happening."

"It's the least I can do."

"I'm not living with you."

"Give me three reasons why you shouldn't?"

"I'll give you four." She holds up a finger and takes a step towards me. "One. Living with your friend, who's a girl, is a real cock block. I'm not going to be responsible for you getting blue balls."

She already is.

She holds up another finger. "Two. Men and women cannot live together and just be friends. You flirt with every-thing that moves, and I move. I'm not going to force myself to live under the same roof as your bullshit."

But flirting with her sounds fun.

She holds up a third finger. "Three. I'm tipsy, and I'm not about to agree to something while under the influence. I'm more responsible than that."

Man, she's cute when she thinks she's getting her way.

"And four." She puts up the last finger. " I've been to your place. I could never afford it."

I'm about to blow your mind, Wren Dawson.

"True, I guess," I reply, shrugging my shoulders. I close the remaining space between us. Looking up at me, she swal-lows hard. She freezes and her hand remains upright, like she's afraid to move, for fear it'll put us even closer together. "But, have you considered there might be actual legit reasons why we *should* live together?"

"No, because there are not."

Smirking, I move one of her fingers down, leaving only three still upright. "One. You currently have no place to live, and I have a spare room."

I push the second finger down, and she remains frozen in place.

"Two. I don't know if you noticed, but I'm really strong, which means living with me is safer than living alone."

She lets out a laugh, and I push the third finger down.

"Three. I'm a lot of fun, and you look like you could use some fun."

She rolls her eyes. I move the last finger down, and her hand falls to her side. Her lips part ever so slightly.

"And four, I'm also a little drunk, and I feel really bad about the whole ordeal, so I won't charge you rent. What do you say, roomie?"

She bites her lip, and I watch as her throat bobs up and down. I can see the wheels turning in her head. Is she actually considering living with me?

"I don't know," she says, hesitantly.

"Come on. Give me a chance." I give her the look that's gotten me my way with her all night, but this time I push my bottom lip out a little bit more than before. "Please."

"Fuck," she grits out. "Fine." She takes a step back, and crosses her arms.

"Fine?"

"Yes, fine. But it's only until I find somewhere else to live, and I'm paying you something. I don't want your pity money."

"We can work out the details later. It's a deal then." I smirk and put out my hand to shake hers. The minute her skin touches mine, electricity pulses through my veins.

"Hey, Frank," I yell. "How about another round on me. We need to celebrate."

I can't believe I get to live with my dream girl.

CHAPTER 10: THE RED SUITS YOU

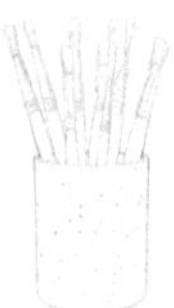

Dolly, my cat, kneads her paws into my back, causing me to stir. I open my right eye and wince as the sun streaming through the window hits me smack in the face.

"Dolly," I whine, stretching and flipping over. "Some of us drank too much last night and want to sleep."

Rubbing my hands over my eyes, I attempt to shake off my hangover and think through my evening. Bits and pieces of my night are blurry, but I'm slowly piecing it all together when it hits me.

Oh. My. Fucking. God. I agreed to live with Tanner last night.

I jolt up in bed at the thought, making my head spin a little and startling Dolly.

What was I thinking?

I wasn't. I was drunk, and he said something about it being free, and dammit free sounded good, and then…did he order shots? Given the way my head feels, I'd say there were definitely shots.

Moving slowly, I crawl out of bed to get ready for breakfast with the girls.

Shit, did I drive home?

I peek out my blinds and don't see my car parked in my usual spot. Did Poppy pick me up? I grab my phone and scroll through my texts. The last text I have from any of my friends was Poppy's offer to pick me up if I needed, so I guess that's a no. I click on Gray's name.

> Any chance you could come pick me up and then take me to get my car at The Local after we eat?

GRAY:

Oh no! Did you get sad drunk last night by yourself? I feel bad I didn't come.

> I wasn't alone. Can you help me?

GRAY:

YOU WEREN'T ALONE?!?!?!

GRAY:

OMG! Did you meet someone?

> Focus. Can you take me to get my car or do you have to work?

GRAY:

Of course. I don't have to be at the hospital until 1:00 but you need to explain. Did you meet a guy?

> It's a really long story, and I need a shower and caffeine.

GRAY:

No, you need to tell me what happened!

> I'll see you soon.

I put the phone down and turn on the water, ignoring the assault of text messages that are now threatening to make my phone vibrate off the counter. I need to shower. I need to clear my head, and then I need to come up with a plan. I can't really live with him. Can I?

I'm feeling a solid thirty percent better after my shower, and I know coffee will help get me to at least fifty percent before Gray arrives. I wrap my hair in my towel, throw on my bra and thong, and head toward the kitchen.

"Morning, roomie," a deep voice says behind me, causing me to scream and sending me into the air. The towel topples off my head and onto the floor. Spinning around, I find Tanner laying on my couch, shirtless, playing on his phone.

I have no words. Why is he here? I don't have any memory—shit, we shared an Uber and he walked me to my door, but he didn't come in. Did he? Well, I guess he must have because I'm staring at his bare chest on my sofa right now.

A wide, goofy grin spreads across his face. Calm down, Wren. This is totally—

"Special occasion?" he says, the corners of his mouth tipping even more upward.

"What?"

His gaze drops to my tits, and he gestures toward me with his hand. "The red suits you."

I look down and realize what I'm wearing. Or, rather, what I'm not wearing. My face heats.

"Oh, for fuck's sake," I say, bending down to grab the towel. I do my best to cover myself and stomp back to my bedroom as quickly as I can. I hear him laugh behind me.

When I emerge again, I'm fully clothed and ready for breakfast. And in the least surprising turn of events this morning, he's still here—and still not fully clothed. He's sitting on the couch, one ankle crossed over his knee, with his abs on full display. A cocky grin is painted across his face.

"I like your cat," he says.

"My what?"

"Your cat." He scratches Dolly between the ears. "I didn't know you had one. What kind is she?"

"A cream point ragdoll. I should've mentioned her. You're not allergic are you?"

"No, I'm definitely not allergic to cats." He winks at me, and the corners of his mouth tip up. I let out a frustrated breath.

"Can you put on a shirt?"

He flexes his chest and ab muscles. "Why? Are you distracted?"

"Can you be serious for one fucking minute?"

He laughs again, grabbing his white button-up off the other side of the couch. He pulls it on each arm and then stands to button it, slowly.

"Why are you here?" I ask, walking into the kitchen to make my cup of coffee.

"You don't remember?"

"Remember what?"

"Our night together, Wren. Honestly, I thought I meant more to you than that."

I stop pouring my cold brew and turn to face him. I was drunk last night, but not so drunk that I would have slept with him and forgotten about it. Is he actually insinuating that we slept together?

"Oh, relax," he teases. "I'm just fucking with you."

"That's not funny."

"I think it's kind of funny. You should've seen your face."

"Why are you here?" I ask again, flipping back around to finish making my drink.

"We were both pretty drunk last night and shared an Uber. You offered me the couch, and I passed out. It wasn't that big of a deal."

I place the cold brew and creamer in the fridge.

"Okay, but why did we share an Uber?" I ask, moving into my small living room to join him.

He shrugs. "I told you last night I'd get you home safely, so I did."

I don't know why his statement makes my heart flutter. We're friends. Friends want their friends to get home safely. Right? Like if it was Gray, I would've seen that she made it home. "Do you have any hot coffee?" he asks, standing from the couch and stretching dramatically, breaking me from my thoughts.

"Oh, um, no. I drink iced year round."

"Really? Cold coffee even when it's cold?"

"Yes, cold coffee. It's currently September in Georgia. It's not that cold."

"I'm more of a hot coffee year round kind of guy." He plops back down on the couch and yawns. "So, should I call us an Uber?"

"Oh, actually—" A knock on the door interrupts me. "That's Gray. We have breakfast with the rest of the girls this morning," I explain, swinging the door open.

"Are you really not going to text me back? Who did you meet?" She pushes past me, stopping abruptly when she sees Tanner.

"Morning, Gray," he says, a little too chipper.

"Tanner?" Her eyes find mine in a slow but very dramatic movement. The look on her face is borderline psychotic.

"Tanner was just leaving," I say. "Right?" I shove my hand in the direction of the door.

"Oh, yeah. Uber should be here any minute," he says, walking toward us.

He stops before walking out, wrapping his arms around me. My whole body stiffens under him, and he lets out a loud chuckle. "Talk to you later," he says, releasing me and winking. "Bye, Gray."

"Bye?" she says in disbelief.

"You want to tell me why he was at your apartment this morning?" she asks as soon as the door is closed.

"It's not what you think." A rush of heat covers my face. "I'll explain in the car. We're going to be late."

We walk out of my apartment in silence, and I spot Tanner a few feet from Gray's car, standing on the curb, grinning from ear to ear. Of course he's still here. It was obvious he hadn't ordered a car yet, and a tinge of guilt pulls at my heart for kicking him out, but it quickly disappears when I remind myself that him being on my couch this morning was insane. I offer him a wave and then climb into Gray's car.

"Should I offer him a ride?" Gray asks, following right behind me.

"We're gonna be late if we stop by The Local first," I say, guilt still hitting me square in the chest. "He's a big boy; I'm sure he'll find his way."

"Is he a *big* boy? I wouldn't know," she says, trying to hold back a laugh.

"Stop it and just drive." My head falls against the back of the seat, and she honks her horn as we pass by him.

We immediately get stopped at the first red light when she turns out of my complex's parking lot. "Tanner was at your apartment this morning," she says.

I let out a grumble, and my friend begins to laugh again. "Please explain. Because my imagination is running wild, and I have to say I don't hate the idea of you and him."

"There is no me and him. The short version is that you all abandoned me last night. He showed up at The Local. We drank too much, and then he made sure I got home safely."

Her head whips in my direction. "He made sure you got home safely. That's sweet."

It is sweet, and I don't know how I feel about it.

"The light's green," I say, and she begins to drive again. "Yes, because he's our friend. He slept on the couch, and he was still there because he thought we were going to go get our cars together. He didn't know about breakfast."

"Oh."

"Don't sound so disappointed. There's more."

"Oh?" The corners of her mouth lift into a devious grin.

"I might've agreed to live with him." I cover my face with my hands and peek through my fingers.

Laughter begins to bubble out of her, tears streaming down her face.

"It's not funny. I honestly don't know what I was thinking," I say.

"Have you told anyone else?"

"No. Because I think I'm going to tell him it's a horrible idea. He caught me in a bad moment. Yesterday was stressful, and I was drunk. I can't live with him."

"Wait, why was yesterday stressful? Everything okay with your brother?"

"Oh, yeah, Cody's fine. My parents need more help. My dad hurt his back helping my brother into bed the other day. I offered to move home, but they said no. I can't find anywhere affordable to live. My mom actually suggested that I stop saving money for my camp idea, and you know I can't do that."

"Is Tanner's place affordable?"

"I don't know. He told me he wouldn't charge me rent."

She pulls into a parking spot in front of the restaurant and turns off the car. She unbuckles and flips toward me. "He offered you the room for free?"

"Yes, and don't look at me like that! It's not that big of a deal."

"I would argue it's a very big deal. Like I know you're friends, but I'm your best friend, and I'd probably charge you something."

"Wow, I'm so lucky to have you in my life," I say sarcastically. "I don't know what I'm going to do."

"I don't think you have a choice."

"I don't want to be anyone's charity case. I'll figure—"

Banging on my window interrupts me, and I turn to see Poppy and Lacey.

"Let's go, you two! I'm starving," Lacey yells through the window.

I glance back over at Gray. "I'll figure it out, but until then, let's keep this between us."

She nods, and we both make our way out of her car and into the restaurant. The last fourteen hours might have been weird as hell, but I'm with my girls, and I'm going to focus on them. I'll deal with my living situation once my head isn't pounding and my stomach isn't grumbling.

———

Ava nestles into my chest, letting out a little hum as I stroke the back of her blonde curls.

"I'm so glad you brought her," I say to Chloe, who is sitting across from me.

"I appreciate you holding her so I can eat."

"Say we don't mind, do we sweet girl?" I make a silly face, and Ava giggles.

"What's it like living with the guys?" Gray asks Poppy and Lacey.

"Honestly, I love it," Lacey says. "I mean, I miss Poppy, but it's so easy with Jace and the hot as sin sex isn't half bad either."

Poppy takes a sip from her mimosa. "Honestly, same. Logan woke me up with his head between my legs this morning, so I'm not complaining."

"Little ears, you two," Chloe scolds.

"Oh, shit, I mean shoot. Sorry Ava," Poppy says.

Chloe shakes her head. "Any luck with the apartment hunt, Wren?"

I glance over at Gray. "Oh, um, maybe, but I don't think it's going to work out. I might have to take one of you up on your offer." Ava slaps at my face and babbles out a stream of consonants. "Does that mean I should move in with you?" I ask her.

"Wait, why did you look at Gray?" Lacey asks.

"I didn't," I say a little too quickly.

"Oh, my god. You're lying. What's going on?" Poppy questions.

My eyes bounce between my friends.

"Might as well tell them," Gray says, shrugging her shoulders and sipping her water.

"Tell us what?" Chloe asks.

"I might have agreed to live with Tanner last night." I wince as I say it.

Everyone stares back at me with wide eyes and open mouths. Our waiter returns to clear the plates covering the table.

"What in the actual fuck? I mean, frick. Sorry, Ava. So much for *I'll never live with him*," Lacey says, shaking her head as soon as the waiter disappears. "Come on." She gestures her hand in my direction. "Tell us we were right."

"It was a weird night," I start.

"Like how weird?" She wiggles her eyebrows and smirks.

"Not weird like that. Weird that I hung out with him without any of you. We drank, played ping-pong, and then he slept on my couch."

"We're going to circle back to the couch. But ping-pong at The Local?" Poppys asks.

"Yeah, why?"

"Holy shit! That table is magic," Lacey says.

"Truly," Gray laughs. "I didn't realize the table was involved."

"Why does that matter?"

"Logan and I literally ran into each other while he and T were playing ping-pong. They had a bet that if Logan won, he could go home. If Tanner won, Logan had to stay. Logan won, but then we met and he stayed. Magic." Poppy takes a sip from her mimosa.

"Exactly. You were there for my ping-pong story with Jace. Loser had to dance together. You and T kicked our asses, and Jace almost got me pregnant during that dance."

"Y'all are ridiculous. That was the third game I've played with him at that table. I agreed to live with him, not fall in love with him. If anything, y'all are just proving that this is a terrible idea. We're only friends, and I can assure you that's all we'll ever be."

"Ping-pong table says otherwise." Lacey giggles.

"What was the bet?" Gray asks.

"What do you mean?"

"Tanner never plays a game on that table without some dumb bet being involved," Poppy explains.

"Loser had to share why they were drinking alone."

"And that somehow led to you moving in with him?" Chloe asks, confused. "I'm not following."

The events of the night play in the back of my mind. The game. His admission. Those puppy dog eyes he kept flashing at me all night. The way his abs flexed this morning while he buttoned up his shirt. I take a deep breath.

"He works for the company that bought my building. And I don't know." I shrug my shoulders. "I was desperate. He felt guilty."

"Well, this just keeps getting more interesting," Gray says, resting her elbows on the table and placing her chin on top of her fists. "You left out that little detail on the car ride here."

"It doesn't matter. I shouldn't have agreed, so I'm going to tell him today it's not happening."

"Might I remind you that he offered to cover your rent. You're saving to start a non-profit that would help your brother and so many people like him. You need a place to live. It doesn't seem like you have a lot of options," Gray says.

"He's paying your rent?" Poppy exclaims as mimosa sprays from her mouth.

"Nice," I say, scowling. "It's not that big of a deal. Friends help friends out."

All four of them look at each other, and then back at me.

"Gray's right. This does keep getting more interesting," Lacey says.

"Technically, I have four other options sitting at this table with me," I say, looking back at each of them.

"I rescind my offer," Chloe says.

"I do too," Poppy says, wincing. "Sorry."

I look at Lacey and Gray.

"I'm going to have to agree," Lacey says. "Looks like your only option is Gray's couch or the big bedroom at Tanner's apartment." Ava giggles in my lap.

"Oh, you think they're funny too?" I laugh. "I can't live with him. I mean he slept on my couch last night, and I forgot and walked out of my room wearing only a bra and my underwear. That cannot happen again."

"Wait, what?" Poppy asks. "How does this story keep getting better?"

I take a deep breath. "Y'all, I was so embarrassed."

"Why? Were you wearing your period underwear?" Chloe asks.

"God, I wish. My ass would have at least been covered. I was wearing a matching red lace bra and thong set. He probably thinks I put them on for him." I take a sip of my bellini and groan.

"Oh, he definitely thinks you put them on for him," Lacey says with a laugh.

"What am I going to do?"

"You're going to live with him until you have another viable option," Gray says.

Cody and my dreams flash in my head. A pang of guilt washes over me.

"I'm going to live with him," I repeat. Ava claps her hands. My four friends tap their glasses together in dramatic cheers, and I grumble.

CHAPTER 11: I CAN KEEP MY DICK IN MY PANTS
TANNER

The image of Wren in red lace lingerie has not left my head since I saw her this morning. Every inch of her creamy skin was painted with freckles, her ass on full display, and thin lace covered both of her perfect breasts.

I'm in deep shit, and I know I should stop because I can't be anything more than her friend, but it's like I'm a boulder on the side of a mountain, and I'm free falling.

Not to mention, I'm the reason she is being kicked out of her apartment. She might be my dream girl, but there's no way in hell I'm her dream guy.

S.H.I.E.L.D.

Found a roommate

DONOVAN:

Do we know him?

Her

DONOVAN:

Her? Do we know HER?

Wren

LOGAN:

No way she agreed to live with you. She barely wanted to play ping-pong with you the other night.

ENZO:

Yeah, I call bullshit too.

Well she did

JACKS:

This is an interesting development.

DONOVAN:

How did that happen?

We ran into each other last night at The Local and I'm the asshole kicking her out of her apartment

ENZO:

No!

I feel awful so I offered her the spare room and she agreed

JACKS:

Another interesting development.

LOGAN:

You can't sleep with her. The girls would kill you.

Well aware

I can keep my dick in my pants

LOGAN:

Since when?

April

LOGAN:

WTF?

DONOVAN:

Seriously?

> Hand on the Bible

> Haven't slept with anyone since the night before my birthday

LOGAN:

I'm speechless.

My phone vibrates, and I see a separate message from Jacks come through. I click out and over to his message thread.

JACKS:

Are you sure this is a good idea?

> Why wouldn't it be

JACKS:

I can just tell you like her, and the guys are right. I know it sucks, but she friend-zoned you. I don't want you to get the wrong idea about this roommate situation.

> I can just be roommates

> It'll be fine

I click out of the messages and back to the group chat.

S.H.I.E.L.D.

ENZO:

Are you sick?

DONOVAN:

Are you fucking with us?

I'm changing the subject

Can I count on all of you to help her move

JACKS:

Of course.

Glad to see he's coming around.

LOGAN:

Sure. When?

She has to be out of her apartment by the end of October but I'm going to tell her she is welcome whenever she wants

I'll keep you posted

I run my hand through my hair and look around my apartment. Since Jacks officially moved out, I've allowed the mess to get a bit out of hand. Socks are scattered all over the floor and used bowls litter the coffee table. It's not like me to let things get this bad, but I've been pulling long days at the office, and haven't had time for much else. I stand, grabbing the four bowls that sit in front of me. If she is going to live here, I can at least make her comfortable.

———

AT TEN THIRTY, I COLLAPSE ON MY COUCH. THE APARTMENT IS clean, so Wren can officially come whenever she wants. *No, not come. Move in. Wren can move in whenever she wants.* I grab my phone then click on her name.

Hey roomie

WREN:

It's late.

Sorry I was just thinking about you

Three dots appear and then disappear.

I mean you moving in

Not you

I was thinking about you moving in

Three dots appear again and then disappear.

Anyway when are you moving in

Do you want to come by this week and see the apartment

WREN:

Why don't you use any punctuation when you text?

Periods make everyone sound so angry

WREN:

If you used them, all of whatever that was could've been one text.

You're right. I will try to use punctuation from now on.

WREN:

Thank you!

Actually no

It feels really weird

I prefer no punctuation

> Less formal

> More fun

WREN:

You're unbearable.

> See you sound so mad

WREN:

This week is really busy, but I can come over next Wednesday after work.

I look around my clean apartment. I guess I'm going to have to try my best to keep it looking like this for the next week and a half. Fuck, I need to chill.

WREN:

I'd like to be out of my current place sooner rather than later. Most of my neighbors are already gone, and it feels like a ghost town.

> You're welcome whenever you're ready

> I talked to the guys earlier and they all agreed to help you move

WREN:

I really appreciate that and you offering me the room, but this is a very temporary plan. My parents said I can store some of my stuff at their place until I can find something more permanent, so I won't have much to bring.

Temporary. This is temporary. I'm the guy who put her in this predicament. It's obvious she hates this idea, and I need to follow her lead.

> Sounds good

> The room is yours as long as you need it

WREN:

Thank you! I'll see next week!

CHAPTER 12: THE CHEETAH AND THE DOG
WREN

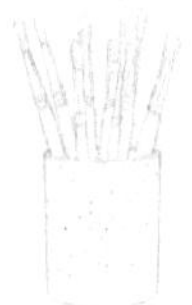

The Tortured Therapists Department

Would it be crazy to ask Tanner if I could move in this weekend instead of waiting?

LACEY:

I mean the room is available, so no. Why?

My upstairs neighbor moved a month ago, and I swear I heard footsteps coming from that apartment last night. I'm so ready to be out.

GRAY:

Like a ghost?!? 👻

POPPY:

OMG! So scary.

I hope it wasn't a ghost, but whatever it was confirmed I'm ready to get the hell out of here. It's too quiet.

LACEY:

Yeah, we need to get you out. Jace and I are free to help if you need. We've got nothing going on this weekend.

POPPY:

Logan and I can come too. Are you packed?

Thanks! I've started to, but I'm slow.

POPPY:

I'm an excellent packer. Why don't we finish up Saturday morning?

CHLOE:

I can see if my mom can take Ava for a few hours.

GRAY:

I'm working on Sunday, but I can help Saturday.

Thanks y'all! I'm going over to Tanner's tonight to measure, and I'll let you know what he says. 🤍

GRAY:

Measure what? 😏

Bye.

I walk into my office and set my things down on top of my desk. I check my schedule, breathing out a sigh of relief when I realize it's Wednesday.

There is a Bible study group coming from a local church at nine. Art group—my favorite thing in the world—starts at ten thirty and goes until lunch. Then, I'll run a chair yoga group before taking a small group of residents to rec center at two for their bi-weekly pickleball lesson.

A knock on my door grabs my attention, and I find Gray standing there.

"Hey, girl," she says, walking in and sitting down in front of my desk.

"Hey." I check my watch. "It's seven thirty. Shouldn't you be doing therapy by now."

"My first patient cancelled, so I don't have to clock in for another fifteen minutes. Plus Margaret's off until Monday for a family wedding or something. I wanted to check on you after your close encounter with that ghost last night." She laughs.

"Laugh all you want, but my building is old as fuck and now very empty. Even Dolly acted like she heard it too."

"Okay, I'll believe you." She giggles. "I'm a little offended you didn't think my measure joke was funny?"

"It wasn't."

"Come on, you aren't even a little curious how big his—"

"Please do not finish that sentence."

She begins to laugh. "Did you tell your parents about moving in with him?"

"Wow, what a transition."

"Well, you didn't seem interested in discussing Tanner's dick size."

"And that led you to asking about my parents?" I eye her, sipping my ice coffee.

"My brain's a weird place. Did you tell them?"

"Yeah. I broke the news last Sunday after breakfast. I don't know if my dad is thrilled I'm living with a guy, but like you said, I don't have a choice in the matter. He did seem more up for the idea once I asked if I could store some of my things in their basement."

"Wait, why?"

"Because my dad is traditional and thinks men and women shouldn't live together before they're married. One of the most liberal people I know, but he can't get behind me shacking up with a guy he's never even met. Especially one who is six years older than me, but once I explained I didn't want to have to move in a bunch of boxes that I'll never unpack, he calmed down a bit."

"No, why aren't you bringing all your stuff?"

"Because it's a very temporary solution, and I don't think I'll need all of my furniture because Tanner's place is mostly furnished."

"So you aren't bringing anything? Not even your art?"

"No, he already has stuff on the walls; he doesn't need my artwork crowding up the place. I think I have to bring my bed, but I'm not sure. It's part of the reason I'm going over there after work today. I'll figure out what I need, and then I'll bring just the essentials to get me through six months or so."

Her mouth drops into a frown, and she studies me.

"Anyway, I talked to my therapist about it last week and I'm feeling better. She helped me come up with the plan."

She nods her head and sips from the thermos she's holding. "The plan?"

"Yep, my goal is no more than six months. I'm honestly hoping to be out in three, but I know that puts us around the first of the year, and it might be hard to find an apartment. I'm hoping that come the end of January, Dolly and I will be settled in our new place."

"And then what?"

"I'm not sure yet. It definitely takes some of the pressure off of finding a place sooner, and it gives me time to look for something more permanent, maybe even a second job. "

"A second job?"

"Yeah. I don't plan on stopping my savings account, and I plan on giving Tanner something, so a second job will be good. Plus, it'll also keep me busy, so I won't be forced to be around him more than I have to."

"I know the camp thing is important to you, but he said you didn't owe him anything. Let him help you."

"A second job isn't that big of a deal."

"I just don't want you working yourself into the ground."

"Says the person who works three jobs and barely has time for a social life."

"Fair," she puts her hands up. "It's just I have to pay back my loans. You don't have to stress out about Cody or the future. It's okay to relax and take things easy."

"You sound like my therapist."

"Maybe we both have a point."

I offer her a small smile. I wish life was that simple. I wish it was that black and white, but the truth is, every decision I make includes me thinking about my brother.

"It's complicated. Opening up camps like this would be huge for my family and so many other people. You should have seen my parents...they're exhausted. If there was a camp they could send Cody to for a week, and they could get some respite, do you know how huge that would be for them and him?"

"I just wish you'd put yourself first and stop worrying about everyone else. Tanner isn't going to force you out. You could literally ride that wave as long as you wanted."

"I will not be riding anything," I deadpan. "They did finally agree to start looking for backup caregivers next week, which is a relief. I told them I'd help with the interviews if they need me to, so maybe I don't have to worry about them getting hurt."

"You're a good sister."

I take a deep breath and force a smile. "It's nothing you wouldn't do for your brothers."

She smiles. "When was the last time they had a physical therapist train them on how to properly lift and transfer your brother?"

"Maybe a year and a half ago. They had been using a lift until recently. My parents said it's broken and the insurance company is giving them the runaround."

"What if I give them a refresher. See if there is anything I could suggest to make things easier on them and Cody."

"When are you going to have time to do that?"

"It won't take long, and they don't live that far from me. I'll just pop in, or I could even do it this Saturday since we are moving all your stuff into their basement." She rolls her eyes.

"Very funny, but you don't have to."

"Stop. You're one of my best friends. I should have offered it a long time ago. I can't treat him, but I can go make sure your parents are doing a proper transfer."

Tears prick the back of my eyes. "Thank you. Dad did say he was lifting with his back."

"No!" She rubs her hands down her face. "No wonder he hurt it."

"I know. I tried to tell him, but they don't always listen to me."

She stands from the chair and walks around the desk, pulling me into a hug. "Stop trying to do it all on your own. No one expects you to."

My eyes find the clock on the wall behind her. "You better go clock in. I need to prepare for Bible study."

"Sounds thrilling," she deadpans. "Oh, I know Clara has signed up for pickleball, but she really shouldn't be playing. I told her she could cheer Eugene on from the sidelines."

"I bet she hated that."

"Oh, yeah. Told me that it was none of my business what she and Eugene did." She laughs.

"Don't worry, I know her balance isn't great. She watches with Ethel from a bench."

"Perfect." Gray disappears out of the door, and I gather what I need to get my day started.

————

At six o'clock, I knock on Tanner's door, and it swings open immediately. He's wearing a black T-shirt with the words "nepo baby" in white letters across the chest, dark gray joggers, and his hair is tied up on top of his head.

"Hey, roomie."

"Nice shirt."

He looks down at what he's wearing and laughs. "My dad hates it."

"I'm sure he does." I fidget, rubbing my hand up and down my arm. There's an awkward pause, and I wish I had a drink. The night at The Local felt easier. I'm overcome with nerves, and I'm not sure why. "Um, can I come in?"

"Oh, shit, yeah." He moves out of the way.

I walk into the apartment and am immediately hit with the smell of maple syrup and bacon.

"Are you about to eat breakfast? It smells like a pancake house in here. I could've come over at a different time."

The faintest tinge of red paints his cheeks.

"I made us food."

"Food?"

"Yeah. I got the idea from Jacks. He made Lacey fries before their big talk, and it seemed to make it less awkward. I don't know. I thought you might be hungry, and if we're going to live together, then we should get to know each other better."

"You made breakfast for dinner?"

He rocks back on his heels, stuffs his hands in his pockets, and shrugs his shoulders. "Lacey said that's what you liked."

"Did she?"

"Is she wrong? Jacks told me she said you liked waffles."

"They're my favorite."

"So, what do you say roomie? Want some waffles and to get to know each other a little better?"

I manage a small nod, and he begins to walk toward the kitchen. "So, do you want the grand tour before or after we eat?"

"After? I've been here before, so I really just need to

measure the room to figure out what furniture I need to bring. Remind me where the bathroom is."

He points down a small hallway, and I make a beeline for the door.

God, why does this feel so awkward?

The Tortured Therapists Department

> He made me dinner.

GRAY:

Tanner?

> Lacey, did you tell Jacks I like waffles?

LACEY:

Tanner made you waffles?

> Yes. What else did Jacks ask you?

POPPY:

Aw! That's so sweet.

> Lacey?

LACEY:

He said Tanner was making dinner and wanted to know what you liked. I didn't think much of it.

> It doesn't mean anything, right? Like this is just our friend being nice. Not trying to get in my pants?

POPPY:

I'm telling you he's not the guy you think he is. I think he wants to make you feel comfortable and feels really bad about your apartment. You can trust him.

> Okay.

LACEY:

Poppy's right. He's a flirt and goofball, but I
don't think they're fuck me waffles.

GRAY:

Get back out there, get out of your head, and
stop making it weird.

They're right. They aren't fuck me waffles. They're platonic roommate waffles. Now, get back out there, and be an adult.

I wash my hands and then walk out of the bathroom and down the hall toward the kitchen.

"Sorry about that," I say.

"You don't have to apologize. Hungry?" He gestures to the table, and I see two plates sitting across from each other. Both are stacked high with freshly made waffles, bacon, and eggs prepared my favorite way—scrambled with cheese.

"Starving." I take a seat in front of one of the plates, but he remains in the kitchen.

"What do you want to drink? Mimosa?"

"Oh, I don't like orange juice."

"Then it's a good thing I wasn't planning on making them with orange juice." The corner of his mouth tips upward.

I watch as he walks over to the fridge, and pulls out strawberries, elderflower liqueur, champagne, basil, and something I can't identify.

"What's that?" I point at the little jar filled with pink liquid.

"Strawberry juice that I made earlier," he says nonchalantly, pouring a little into each glass. He tops each one with some champagne and a shot of St. Germain.

I don't know how to describe it, but he seems so natural at making it. Practiced even. He tops each one with a basil leaf and a sliced strawberry.

"Are you some type of secret mixologist?" I ask as he hands me one of the glasses.

"Just a hobby," he says, taking the seat across from me.

"So, you wear suits to work and make cocktails in your spare time? Who knew you had a secret double life?"

He laughs. "No, I've just taken a couple cocktail making classes for fun. It's nothing. I also don't usually wear suits to work." He takes a long drink of the cocktail. "So, tell me about you. Any secret double life I should know about?"

"No secret job, but I do paint in my spare time." I take a bite of my waffles. An accidental moan escapes when the mix of butter and syrup hits my tongue.

"You like them?" he chuckles.

"Sorry. Yeah they're really, really good."

"You don't have to apologize. It was hot…I mean cute… no, funny. It was funny. I'm glad you like them."

I offer him an awkward smile. "Shall we talk about the move in plan?" I suggest.

"Yeah. Let's do that."

"Okay, well I was thinking there's really no need for me to wait until the end of next month. Your company was so kind to offer to let us cut our leases whenever we want, so would it be weird if I moved this weekend?"

"This weekend?"

"Is that too soon? It's just that most of my neighbors have already left, and I'm certain a ghost has taken up residence in the apartment above mine."

"A ghost?"

"Yes, a ghost. My upstairs neighbors moved, and Dolly and I heard footsteps last night. How else would you explain it?"

"Do ghosts walk? I thought they floated."

"I don't know what they do, but I know what I heard."

"Okay," he chuckles. "That's fine."

"Are you sure?"

"It's perfect."

"Thank you. I'll just need to crash for six months max, but

hopefully I'll be out in three. I'd like to pay you rent. I don't want to be your charity case."

"I'm not accepting your money. I fucked you."

I choke on my drink.

"No. Shit. I meant I fucked you over with the apartment."

He takes another large sip from his glass, and I try to stifle a laugh. The slightest hint of pink colors his cheeks and the tips of his ears.

Is he really this awkward or am I making him nervous?

"Let me try again. We're friends," he says. "I feel bad about you getting kicked out of your apartment. Letting you stay here for free is the least I could do."

"I appreciate that, but I want to at least pay my half of utilities and bills. Just tell me how much I owe you a month, and I'll send you the money."

"You know I'm, like, really rich, right?"

"No, you aren't."

"I've got a trust fund and a paycheck that says I am." His eye shifts down to his shirt. "And I'm not telling you that to be a tool. It's just I don't need your money."

He's rich? I glance around his apartment. I mean it's a nice place, but it doesn't scream I have all of my daddy's money at my fingertips.

"Well regardless, I can still pay you something."

"That won't be necessary." He shakes his head.

"Tanner." I put down my fork, looking him dead in the eye. "I know you feel bad, but I can't let you pay for everything. It's not right. I have a job. I'm a semi-functioning adult. I'm very appreciative of your offer, but I have to give you something."

He takes a huge bite of food, and I can see the gears turning in his head.

"Hang out with me one night a week, and we'll call it even."

What the hell?

"I'm not dating you," I say a little too quickly—and harshly.

His jaw ticks.

"No, they wouldn't be dates. Hang out with me as my friend. Let me get to know you, and let me show you I'm not the douchebag you think I am."

"I've never called you a douche—"

"You didn't have to." His shoulders sag, and he tries to hide the downhearted look on his face behind another bite of his food. My whole face heats with embarrassment as guilt radiates off of me.

"I don't think you're a douchebag. You just remind me of someone from my past." The minute the words come out of my mouth, I wish I could take them back.

"I'm guessing he wasn't the best guy?" he asks, totally defeated.

"No," I say quietly. "He wasn't."

"Then let me prove to you that I'm nothing like him. One weekly roomie night, and we'll call it even," he repeats.

I turn over his offer in my head. It would be much more affordable than paying him, but it still doesn't feel like enough. Plus, now I feel like a total asshole, so I'm going to have to do so much more than one measly roomie night a week.

"What will we do on these roomie nights?"

"Whatever we want. No rules. Just two friends hanging out."

I study him for a few more seconds.

"I have no ulterior motives. You said you want to pay me back, so give me your time. You can trust me," he says. "I promise."

"Alright," I agree. "You have a deal." I put out my hand, and his large hand envelopes mine completely. My eyes lock on where we connect. My skin buzzes under his touch, and I quickly tug away.

"Deal," he says as a goofy grin spreads across his face. "Now that that's settled, I bought us a game to play."

"A game?"

"Yeah, we don't have to play if you don't want to, but I thought it was important that we get to know each other better since you'll be living here." He gestures to a box of cards in the middle of the table. I pick it up and read the back.

"So they're just like icebreakers?" I ask, setting it back in between us.

"I think so," he says. "If you think it's dumb we can skip it."

"It's not dumb." I pop the lid off the box, grabbing the top card. "What's your favorite conspiracy theory?" I read.

"Aliens are real, and the government is hiding them from us," he says with no hesitation.

"Aliens?"

"Yeah. You don't believe in them?"

"I've never really given them much thought," I say, taking a bite of waffles. "But maybe."

"What conspiracy theory do you think is real?"

"That's tough. I don't think I believe any of them. Maybe that Princess Diana was really murdered."

"Oh that's a good one."

I shrug. "I guess we'll never know. Your turn to pick a card."

He digs down in the box, grabbing one halfway down the stack. "What's your favorite color?"

"Easy. Orange."

"No, it's not," he says.

"What? You don't think orange is a good color?"

"No, I think it's the best color."

"You don't."

"I do."

I study him, not sure I'm buying the whole we have the

same favorite color move, but I let it slide. I grab a card off the top. "What's your favorite animal?"

"Dogs."

"That tracks." I laugh. "So basic."

He sips his drink. "I bet my reason isn't what you think."

"I imagine you like them because they're man's best friend or something. Doesn't every guy like dogs?"

"I mean, Jacks is obsessed with birds, so no."

"Okay, then why do you like them?"

"I went to the San Diego Zoo as a kid, and they have this program where they pair cheetahs with dogs. It's so funny because the friendship makes no sense, but they become best friends despite their reputations."

I put my fork down and stare at him.

"The cheetahs aren't used to living in the new environment, and despite their power are really anxious animals. It's their instinct to run because they're so damn fast, but the dogs help make them comfortable. I just think it's really cool that a dog can befriend anything, even something as beautiful and wild as a cheetah," he explains.

"Are you bullshiting me right now?"

"What? Why would you think that?"

"Is this some sort of metaphor? Am I the cheetah?"

"That depends. Are you saying you're wild and beautiful?" He smirks.

My face heats.

"Forget it." I take a bite of waffles.

He begins to laugh. "Oh, I get it," he says. "You're the cheetah and I'm the dog. Our friendship doesn't make sense, but we're going to be best friends. Is that right?"

"Forget I said it." I roll my eyes.

"No, I like it. I know you're nervous about moving in with me, but I'll help make you feel comfortable. I promise." Another goofy grin spreads across his face, and my stomach flips. I stuff another bite of waffle in my mouth, pushing whatever the hell that feeling is as far away as humanly possible.

"So what's your favorite animal?"

"A cat," I say around the bite of food.

"Ha!" he laughs. "And you called me basic. Why do you like cats?"

"I don't know; I've just always liked them."

He chuckles and grabs a card. "What's your favorite food?"

"You already know it's waffles, but what you don't know is that I usually like to eat them with mini marshmallows on top."

"Mini marshmallows?"

"Yeah," I smile at the memory that pops into my head. "When my brother and I were younger, my dad used to cover them with butter, mini marshmallows, and syrup. It's delicious."

"Noted," he says. "Next time I'll have mini marshmallows."

A small smile breaks across my face.

"What's your favorite food?" I ask.

"Tacos."

"So basic," I say, giggling.

"Tacos are a superior food," he argues. "Don't tell me you're anti-tacos. I will have to rescind the roommate offer."

"No, I'm definitely not anti-tacos."

"Thank god!"

We finish eating, asking a few more rounds of questions. I'm surprised to find out that there might be more to him that meets the eye.

After helping him clean up the kitchen, he gives me a quick tour, and despite my prior thoughts, there is no lost and found closet full of clothes from hookups past to be found, and the apartment is really clean.

We measure the room that will be mine, and I jot down notes in my phone. When we're done, he walks me to my car.

"I'll see you this weekend for the move," he says.

"Sounds good," I say. There's an awkward pause, and he gives me a weird side hug. "Thanks for dinner."

"Anytime, roomie," he smiles, and I climb into my car, unsure of what to make of our evening.

The Tortured Therapists Department

Update: They definitely weren't fuck me waffles. But we are on for the move this weekend! Y'all want to start Saturday morning? Is 8 too early?

LACEY:

Not for you.

POPPY:

Yay! We'll be there.

GRAY:

Count me in!

CHLOE:

Me too! I'll head over once I get Ava settled with my mom.

Y'all are the best!

CHAPTER 13: BAD EXAMPLES
TANNER

I walk into work still buzzing from the high Wren left me on last night. The moan she let out when she took a bite of the waffles I made for her went straight to my cock, and I haven't been able to get it out of my head.

I know I can't cross any lines. I would no doubt do something to screw it up, and I value her friendship too much, but damn I liked hearing her make that sound. Being in her orbit scrambled my brain, and I'm kicking myself for sounding like a tongue-tied teenager.

I don't want to make her uncomfortable, so I need to get a fucking grip. I completely pulled roomie nights out of my ass, but sometimes I surprise myself with a good idea, and I'm glad she liked it too. She doesn't owe me anything, but if she's going to insist on paying me something, I'd rather it be her time. I grab my phone and open the group chat I have with my friends.

S.H.I.E.L.D.

Can y'all come help Wren move this weekend

DONOVAN:

That's fine, we'll be in town.

LOGAN:

We'll be there. Poppy already talked to Wren.

JACKS:

Same here. Lacey said the girls were going over early.

Cool

Thanks guys

I'm also gonna need y'all to help me with some recon

JACKS:

This isn't one of your missions. LMAO!

LOGAN:

Gotta agree with Jacks on this one.

Just trying to make our friend comfortable

JACKS:

Subtle.

ENZO:

I don't think he could be subtle if he tried.

LOGAN:

What do you want help with?

Hell yeah

I need you to find out what she likes to eat and drink

Gonna make sure the fridge and pantry are stocked with all the stuff she likes

JACKS:

Just ask her.

I don't want to keep bothering her

Please 😊

JACKS:

I asked Lacey her favorite meal. Logan, you
want to take this one?

LOGAN:

Sure.

———

Guys said they are on for the move

WREN 🐺:

Cool! Thanks for checking with them.

JOHN KNOCKS AND ENTERS MY OFFICE WITH MY FRESHLY MADE
latte.

"Good morning," he says, handing me the paper cup.

"Morning."

"Mr. Mitchell called a meeting with you at eleven thirty,"
he says, causing my Wren buzz to disappear entirely.

I check my watch. It's ten fifty five. *Fuck.* I knew I
should've gotten here earlier.

"Do you know what he wants to meet about?"

"Sarah didn't say."

"Sarah?"

"Mr. Mitchell's assistant."

"Oh, right. Okay. Did you tell her I wasn't here yet?" I
move my head from side to side, stretching my neck, trying to
relieve the tension I can already feel building.

"No, sir. I told her you were on an important call and that
you were available at eleven thirty."

I nod.

"Is there anything else I can get for you?" John asks, adjusting his glasses on the bridge of his nose.

"No. Thank you."

The last big meeting I had with my dad ended with me at The Local, and that was the night I ran into Wren. I can only imagine this one will go similarly.

At eleven twenty, we make our way to my father's office. Sarah greets us with a wide smile.

"Is he ready for me?" I ask.

She places one manicured finger up and picks up the phone.

My palms are a little sweaty, and my heart thumps against my ribcage. I take a couple of deep breaths, wiping my hands down the denim covering my thighs. It doesn't matter if I'm thirteen or thirty; my body still reacts the same way around him every time.

Sarah murmurs something into the phone and then hangs up the receiver. "You can go on in," she directs.

She leads me to his office door, tapping her fist against the wooden surface before swinging it open and revealing the large, cold room. Compared to this space, mine looks like I work in a closet. I let out a long breath, trying to calm the nerves pulsing through my body.

"Morning, Mitt," I say with as much forced confidence as I can muster.

"Tanner," he says, not looking up from his computer.

"Can I get you anything?" his assistant asks me.

"No. I'm good."

"Mr. Mitchell?" She looks toward my father.

"No. This shouldn't take long," he responds.

She nods and moves out of the room, closing the door behind her. I take a seat in one of the leather chairs in front of his desk. Tapping my thumb against my thigh, I wait for him to start, but he doesn't, so I clear my throat.

His gaze finds mine and he scoffs. "I thought I told you

that moving forward you would need to be wearing a suit while in the office. You have a precedent to set. If people see you not taking your job seriously, that trickles down. Have you seen the way your assistant dresses? You're already setting a bad example." He rubs his temples.

I look down at my dark jeans and T-shirt and shrug. My wardrobe decisions have been a point of contention for years, but I can see they will be even more of an issue now. Wearing a suit makes me crawl out of my skin. When I'm sitting behind his desk, that'll be the first thing to go.

"Granddad never wore a suit."

"He also got his receptionist pregnant. He may have led this company for years, but I've told you before, and I will remind you again today, my father was far from a good example."

I suppress a laugh at how incredibly cliché our family must seem.

"You say that like you're not talking about your mother."

He looks up from his computer with a stern expression but doesn't respond.

"You told me you wanted to prove that you could take this over. You said that it was important to you to keep your great grandfather's business in the family, but I've yet to see you try."

When I don't take the bait, he continues, "Your brother is leaving for Europe whether I like it or not, and then it'll just be you and me. It's time you grow up and start taking this seriously. I would like to move forward with my plans by the end of the year, and currently I don't have much confidence that is going to happen."

That look I know too well covers his face, and my heart sinks into my stomach. He's right. I'm fucking it up, and it's been less than two weeks. I don't know why I thought I could do this. It's clear I'm in way over my head.

"Are you listening to me?" he asks.

"Yes."

He checks his watch and continues, "I need you to grow up. Stop the partying, or whatever it is you do with your free time. Try showing up to work before eleven."

"I show up before eleven."

He shakes his head. "That attitude is precisely why I doubted you would ever be ready for this amount of responsibility, but you assured me. Your mother assured me. Hell, when your grandfather was alive, he constantly championed you for this role, but it's been twelve days and you're still dressing like that and waltzing into the office at eleven. If I didn't know any better, I'd think you were self-sabotaging."

My jaw ticks at the dig, but I internally stop myself from saying anything else that might prove he's right about me.

"I'm sorry. I'll do better. I promise."

"Good. Now onto business. We are scrapping your plan for the Cedar Hill project."

"You're what? But we're set to break ground at the beginning of November," I reply incredulously.

"Then it looks like I caught your fuck up just in the knick of time. I reviewed the proposal again, and the cost is unnecessary. We will move forward with demoing the building, but it will be solely a multi-family complex."

"But I worked so hard on that plan. My team worked so hard on that plan."

"First lesson in being the CEO. Sometimes it isn't about what you want; it's about the bottomline. The money it would take to bring your little project to light would be a financial nightmare. Think of this as your opportunity to show me what you can do here. If you want me seriously to consider you for my position, I need to see that you can put your wants aside for the sake of the company."

I've already volunteered myself like some sort of Mitchell family martyr. Shouldn't that be enough?

"At the end of the project, if I'm impressed and it's profitable, then I'll know you're serious about your future, and I will begin to move forward with the plan. You will take over my role, and I will fall into the background as chairman of the board, just like your grandfather did."

My stomach turns.

"I expect the revised plan on my desk by the end of the day Monday. Is that understood?"

"But my new roommate is moving in this weekend."

"And?"

"I wasn't planning on working. I need to be there to help."

His head falls back, and he audibly exhales. "I need the plan by the end of the day Monday. This is not negotiable. If that doesn't work for you, then I will start looking for a new CEO *outside of the family.*"

He emphasizes the last four words.

"No, I'll get it done," I assure him.

I don't know how, but I'll have to. I check my watch. It's only eleven thirty-six. I still have the rest of the day and all of tomorrow. There is a small chance that if I work late, I could get him the plan before Saturday morning.

"Good. If there is nothing else, you're free to go."

I stand from the chair and walk toward the door.

"Oh, and Tanner?"

"Yeah?" I freeze, looking over my shoulder.

"Don't make me regret this."

His words knock the air out of my lungs, and my blood runs cold. I clench my teeth together, breathe in deep through my nose, and try to calm the emotions flooding my head. No doubt about it. He thinks I'm going to fuck it up.

CHAPTER 14: MOVE IN DAY
WREN

At the sounds of my alarm, I roll out of bed and shuffle to my bathroom. I brush my teeth and check the time on my phone. It's seven thirty, which means my friends should be here in thirty minutes or so to help me pack.

My nerves have me feeling a little nauseous. Originally, I was worried that living with Tanner would be like living in a frat house, but after dinner the other night, I'm just worried it's always going to be awkward between us.

I'm about halfway done with packing, and I'm sure the girls and I can knock the rest out pretty quickly. The guys will be here at eleven to start moving my furniture to my parents' house and to Tanner's, so we have a lot of work to do in a few hours, but it's not impossible.

Dolly walks into the bathroom and sticks her butt into the air, stretching her back. "You ready to move, baby girl." She mazes through my legs, only pausing to rub the side of her head against my shin. My phone vibrates, and I swipe up on the screen.

The Tortured Therapists Department

GRAY:

Stopping to grab a pumpkin spice latte, and then I'll be over!

POPPY:

That sounds so good! I think I'm going to stop on my way to Wren's to get one too. Anybody else want one?

CHLOE:

Me! Ava was up all night. Can you add an extra shot of espresso? I have cash.

I'll take one, but can you make it iced? A PSL sounds like the perfect thing.

POPPY:

Y'all got it! Lacey, do I dare ask if you want one?

LACEY:

Jace already made me my London fog, so I'll pass.

POPPY:

Okay, I'll be there soon with the caffeine.

I finish my morning skincare routine, put my hair in a ponytail, and walk back into my room to get dressed in leggings and a T-shirt with a large bouquet of wildflowers on the front. Surveying the space, I make a mental list of everything that needs to be done and then walk into my kitchen to try to find something to eat. There isn't much, but I manage to find a granola bar. I'm savoring the last bite, starting to feel a little better, when someone knocks.

"Morning, lady!" Gray chimes as she walks through the door. "Are you alone?"

"Yeah, the rest of the girls aren't here yet."

"Oh, I know that. I was wondering if Tanner was going to be on your couch again."

"Not funny," I deadpan.

"Yes it is," she chuckles. There's another knock, and Lacey and Chloe walk in.

Lacey's eyes dart around the space. "Wait, Tanner didn't sleep on the couch?" she asks, gesturing towards the sofa. "I was fully prepared for him to be here."

"I had the same thought," Gray says. "It's a shame."

"I hate all of you but Chloe."

"How are you feeling about the move?" Chloe asks.

"I don't know. He cooked me dinner the other night, and it was honestly a little awkward. Nice, but he seemed so nervous, and then when I offered to pay, he told me he was rich and said he didn't want my money, just the opportunity to prove he's not a douchebag, and I felt like the biggest bitch."

"It's not your fault he's a flirt," Chloe says.

"I know. I just hope this doesn't go up in complete flames."

"It won't," Lacey smiles. "It'll be fine. I keep telling you he's a good guy, and it's because he is. You just need to get to know him."

"Well I've agreed to roomie nights once a week, so that shouldn't be a problem."

"What the hell is a roomie night?" Gray asks. There is another knock. I walk over and swing it open.

"Here, take these. I need to go get the supplies I brought," Poppy says, handing me a tray full of coffee. She turns on her heels and heads back to the car.

I walk back into my living room and hand Chloe her drink before taking mine. "I don't know. I guess we're just gonna hang out platonically and get to know each other."

"Platonically," Lacey says, using her fingers to make air quotes.

"Yes, platonically. He said something about not wanting my money, he'd rather my time." All three of my friends make eyes at each other and then me. "Don't look at me like that."

"Like what?" Poppy asks, walking in, holding a bin full of colorful tape and markers.

"Wren was just explaining that T asked her to pay him with her time, not money."

Poppy's eyes go wide.

"It's nothing, and it's not all I'm going to do. I think I might try to make an effort to cook him dinner as part of my payment."

"You cook?" Gray asks.

"Well, no, not really, but I gotta do something."

"Seems like you could pick something you're better at?"

"Not funny," I say, blankly.

"So, whatcha got there, Pop?" Lacey asks.

"Moving supplies." She sets the bin down and starts pulling out colorful tape and markers. "Kitchen can be pink, bathroom can be blue, art supplies can be yellow, living room can be purple." She holds up each roll of tape as she talks. "Bedroom can be orange, and so on."

"Genius," I say.

She turns and looks right at Lacey. "When you pack a box, put the coordinating tape on the box, and then use the markers to write what's in the box. This way Wren will know where all her stuff is."

"Why are you looking at me?" Lacey asks.

"No reason," Poppy takes a large drink from her latte, and we all laugh.

"What's going to your parents' and what's going to Tanner's?" Gray asks.

"Clothes, everything in my bathroom, a few towels, my bedding, my bed, one nightstand, my dresser, and all of Dolly's things go to Tanner's. The rest is off to my parents' house."

"You don't want to bring any decorations, or paintings, or anything?" Chloe asks.

"I'm not going to be there very long, so there's no need." My friends look at each other again.

"What?"

"Oh, nothing," Lacey singsongs. "Should we get started?"

My phone vibrates, and I swipe up on the screen.

TANNER:

Hey I'm swamped with work so I can't be there today

I feel my face fall as I read. He's really not going to help?

Oh, okay, that's fine!

TANNER:

The other guys will be there and Jacks still has his key so he can let you in and then just take it from him because that's the only spare

"You okay?" Chloe asks.

"Oh, yeah. Tanner had to go to work or something, so he can't come help."

TANNER:

I'm really sorry and I'll explain later

"So weird he bailed again," Poppy says.

"Bailed again?" I ask.

"Yeah, he was supposed to play pickleball a couple weeks ago, but he bailed the night before. Logan's worried about him. Said he hasn't been acting like himself lately."

"Jace said the same thing," Lacey says. "What does he do for work again?"

"He works for his dad," I say, remembering the conversation he and I had at The Local, wondering if whatever is going on is related.

> Don't worry about it! You okay?

TANNER:

Yeah

TANNER:

See you later roomie

"We should start packing so we can be finished before the guys get here," I say.

The girls each grab a different colored tape roll, and we disperse across my apartment to the coordinating area. I put on my favorite playlist, and "Wannabe" by The Spice Girls begins to play. For the next hour and a half, we pack up my apartment and sing pop music at the top of our lungs, and I'm reminded once again that I'm the luckiest girl in the world to have these four as my friends.

CHAPTER 15: OH SHITSHITFUCKINGSHIT!

TANNER

It's eight o'clock in the evening when I pull into my designated parking spot outside my apartment, next to Wren's car. I guess that means my new roommate has officially moved in, and I missed it.

The new proposal is nowhere near done, so I'll most likely be in the office tomorrow and Monday working on it. I massage my temples and run my hands through my hair, trying to shake off my day. Grabbing my tie and jacket off the passenger side seat, I open my door and slide out of the car.

I'm exhausted and starving. I should've stopped for food, but it didn't cross my mind until I was almost home, and I was too tired to turn around to grab something.

The scent of tacos hits me the minute I open my door. Every light in the apartment is on, and pop music is blasting over a speaker. Wren's cat meets me at the door, and I bend down to scratch it between the ears. "Welcome home, kitty." I stand, walk around the corner, and my whole day melts away.

Wren's dancing and stirring something on the stovetop. The kitchen is a mess. The counter is covered with pots and pans and most of the food from my fridge.

My heart swells. I was fully expecting her to be hidden away in her room, and instead she's made herself right at home. She seems comfortable. She seems happy.

I prop myself against the wall as she brings the wooden spoon to her mouth and begins to belt the chorus of Whitney Houston's "I Wanna Dance With Somebody." She's wearing a green silk tank top, shorts that are rimmed in lace, and cat slippers. Her ponytail and hips rock in sync with the music, and her other hand moves to match the words of the lyrics. I have to stop a laugh from bubbling out of me when she tries to hit the high note. She looks so damn cute. It's clear she didn't hear me come in, but I stay quiet, not wanting her little show to end.

Her happiness is contagious, and I fear the minute she sees me, it'll disappear. I wish I could bask in it forever.

The bridge begins and she starts to spin in a circle, but her eyes are closed. I wait until she's facing me and then clear my throat. Her eyes pop open, and the spoon flies into the air and then clatters to the ground.

"Boo," I say with a wide grin.

"What the fuck, Tanner!" she yells. "How long have you been standing there?"

"Long enough." I smirk. "Very valiant effort with the high note on the word heat. I didn't know you sang."

"I don't," she grumbles, bending down and picking up the spoon then tossing it into the sink. She moves around the kitchen, opening drawers. "Do you have another spoon?"

"Top drawer on the right." She opens it and grabs one out.

The scent of charred something wafts by me. "Is something burning?" I ask, raising an eyebrow.

She flips around. "Oh shitshitfuckingshit!" She grabs a pot holder and smoke pours out when she opens the oven. She reaches in and pulls out a tray of what I think may have once been taco shells. Placing them on the stove top, she kicks the oven door closed. The smoke alarm begins to sound, so I quickly grab a towel and begin to fan the air around it.

"You trying to burn down my place on day one?" I say with a chuckle once the beeping stops. "Turn on the exhaust fan, would you?"

"The what?"

"The exhaust fan." I move into the kitchen and flip the switch above the stove. The sound of the fan begins to compete with the music that is still playing.

"What are you doing?" I ask, muting the speaker.

"Cooking us dinner." Her cheeks turn pink. "You made me dinner the other day, so I was trying to return the favor."

"You were making me dinner?"

"Well I was, but the shells are burnt, and I'm honestly not sure if the meat is done. I used the ground turkey you had in the fridge."

"How long did you cook this for?" I ask, pointing to the pan on the stove. The meat looks…dry. Really fucking dry.

"I don't know, but I kept cooking it because I didn't want to give us salmonella."

"Based on the looks of it, I can assure you there is not a chance any salmonella is left on that meat." I chuckle.

"I'm sorry," she says, fidgeting. "I was trying to do something nice, and I ruined it."

"You didn't ruin anything. This was the best part of my day. I promise."

"Well then your day must have really sucked."

Understatement of the year.

"Here, let me help you get all this cleaned up, and I'll order us a pizza."

She scrunches her nose. "You don't have to help. I made the mess."

"I don't mind. Let me just get out of these clothes, and I'll be right back." I click through the pizza delivery app on my phone as I walk to my room. "What kind of pizza do you like?"

"Barbecue chicken? But this dinner was for you, so pick what you like."

"That sounds delicious." I finish placing the order before stepping into my room and closing the door. I discard the suit, pull on sweats, and grab a T-shirt.

"Pizza should be here in thirty minutes," I say, walking out of my room still holding the shirt. Wren's eyes dip to my abs.

"Can you please clothe yourself," she says from the sink where she's trying to scrape burnt taco shell pieces off the pan.

"My bad. I'm not used to having a roommate." I pull the shirt over my head, and she starts to giggle.

"What the hell is that?"

I look down and study my shirt. "Oh, that's the mascot for the pickleball team Logan and I are on."

She cocks her head to the side. "Is that a pickle with balls?"

"Yep, that's Willie."

"You did not name it Willie."

"Well, Logan refuses to acknowledge him by his name, but I like to call him Willie."

She shakes her head. "Living here is going to be interesting isn't it?"

"I like to think it'll be fun." For the first time since I got home, I scan the living room and kitchen for any sign of her belongings. There's nothing.

"Where's all your stuff?"

"Oh, everything is in my room, except for my mattress. Logan's mom called while he was helping, and he and Poppy had to leave right after they dropped off the bed frame."

"Was everything okay?"

"Oh, yeah. A squirrel got into her house, and she was

freaking out. It actually sounded kind of funny. Could you imagine? A squirrel! Anyway, Logan went to help catch it. He's going to help me move my mattress tomorrow."

"So where are you going to sleep tonight?"

"I'll just crash on the couch. If that's okay? I thought about staying at my place for one more night, but I had already moved all of Dolly's stuff over here."

"You can take my room, and I'll sleep on the couch."

The thought of her in my bed pops into my head, and my cock twitches under my sweatpants.

Bad fucking idea, Tanner. She's your friend. You're really pretty, incredibly sexy, absolutely under no circumstances can you try anything with, friend. This is only night one of her living here.

"No way. I'm smaller than you, and I really don't mind. Plus, you look exhausted. I'm not letting you sleep on the couch after you had such a bad day." She smiles.

"Okay, if you're sure."

"It's fine, I promise."

I begin to help clear the counters, and as she taps the speaker, music fills the space again. We work mostly in silence, other than me telling her where things usually go. When we're done, I grab a beer for me and one of the canned cocktails Logan told me she liked for her, and we head into the living room.

"Pizza should have been here ten minutes ago," I say, checking the app.

"I'm sure it's coming." I hand her the can. "Thank you," she says.

"It's no problem. Figured you were probably parched after all the singing."

"No, I meant thank you for stocking the pantry and fridge with things I like." She opens the can and takes a long sip.

"Oh, good, so you saw the snacks?"

"I did, and you don't have to keep doing nice things for me. At this rate, I'm never going to be able to repay you."

A knock on the door echoes through the room, and I jump up and grab it. The man hands me the box of pizza, and I slide him a twenty dollar bill. "Thanks man; have a good night."

I turn back to Wren, carrying our dinner inside. "You don't have to repay me. I like helping out my friends," I assure her, setting down the pizza box and flipping open the lid.

"Can I at least send you money for the pizza? I was the one trying to make you dinner."

"Not a chance." I grab a slice and take a bite. "Fuck, fuck, fuck, it's hot!" I say around a swig of beer.

She giggles and blows on her slice but waits to eat it. "So, how's the whole CEO thing going?"

"Awful."

"Really?"

"Yeah, I don't know what I was thinking."

She blows on her slice again and then attempts a bite.

"Lacey and Poppy mentioned the guys were worried about you," she says a little hesitantly. "Do they know what's going on?"

"Nah. They don't want to be bored with my family and work shit. They both have enough going on in their own lives."

"I don't think that's true."

I shrug. "Maybe not, but usually by the time I get home from work I don't want to rehash it all. I'd rather pretend like it doesn't exist."

"Oh, sorry if I overstepped. If you don't want to talk about it, we don't have to." She bites her lip, looking down at her plate.

"No, that's not what I meant. I like talking about it with you."

Her breath catches, and her eyes find mine. I do like talking to her. Something about being near her calms me. I want to open up to her completely and let her get to know every part of me.

"I don't know what your parents are like, but my dad has always been really hard to please. I've spent my whole life chasing the feeling of him being proud of me, and it's never happened. The closest I ever got to that was when my grandfather was alive. He always made sure to tell me he was proud of me. He and I were a lot alike," I explain.

"It sounds like you were really close with him. When did he pass away?"

"Last December."

"I'm sorry," she says.

"It's okay. He was old and not in the best health."

"Is he why you volunteered to take over as CEO?"

"Yeah, it might sound dumb, but I felt obligated to keep the position within the family." For a split second, I consider telling her about the bar, but don't. I still haven't gotten back to Jerry. I know he needs an answer, and I know I can't do both even though I wish I could.

"I get it," she says, tipping the can up and taking a sip. "I feel obligated with my family too."

"What do you mean?"

CHAPTER 16: I'M NOT A NERD
WREN

I hesitate before answering his question. Tonight has been a little strange—but nice. I could have done without him catching me dancing, or burning dinner, but I don't hate hanging out with him, and the pizza is good.

"My younger brother had an accident six years ago and requires a lot of help. After it happened, I felt obligated to be there everyday and to help my parents. I really threw myself into caring for him and helping them. I still struggle with it sometimes, but moving out and living somewhere else was a big step for me."

His face falls. "I didn't know that," he says. "Here you are dealing with real shit, and I'm complaining about being a nepo baby."

"I didn't take it that way. Just because my family stuff sounds more tragic, that doesn't make the way you're feeling about your stuff less valid."

"Is he okay? Your brother?"

"He's doing okay now considering everything he's been through. The accident left him with a brain and a spinal cord injury, so he's in a wheelchair, and he uses a computer to talk."

"What happened?" He looks a little nervous. "Is that okay to ask?"

"Yeah. Um, he was in high school, and was decorating for the homecoming dance. They had propped one of those really tall ladders against the retracted bleachers, and it wasn't stable." My voice shakes a little as I tell the story. "When he climbed to the top to hang a backdrop, he fell."

His eyes go wide. "Oh, my god, Wren. That's terrible."

"Yeah, it was really bad. We almost lost him, but we didn't." I play with the hair tie around my wrist. This isn't the first time I've explained what happened to him to someone, but it always brings up the emotions associated with it.

"I'm sorry. We don't have to talk about this," he says. "I didn't mean to upset you."

"You didn't. It's just hard to remember."

"Will you tell me more about him?"

The question takes me by surprise. I'm used to people feeling bad for my family. I'm used to hearing their apologies and being told we're in their prayers, but I'm not used to people wanting to get to know about my brother.

"He's really funny, and he loves to curse. He was seventeen when it happened, so he still acts a lot like a teenager, and he likes the same things. We watch a lot of Marvel movies."

"I fucking love Marvel. What's his favorite?"

"We watch them all, but lately he's been on an OG *Iron Man* kick."

"Wait, is that why you knew the answer to the trivia question this summer?" he asks.

My mind drifts back to trivia night and how Tanner and I were the only two who knew which song played in *Guardians Of The Galaxy* and *Reservoir Dogs*. An unwanted thought of him flirting shamelessly with the waitress assaults my memory, and I try to push it away. He's being nice, and I'm living with him now. I should try to give him the benefit of the doubt.

"Oh, yeah. *Guardians* is one of Cody's favorites. I think I have that movie memorized. I've seen it so many times. The soundtrack is great too."

"Your brother has good taste. If I had to rate my top five it would be *Thor: Ragnarok* as number five, then *Guardians of the Galaxy: Volume 1*, then *Avengers: Infinity War*, then *Black Panther*, and then *Iron Man*."

I grab another slice of pizza, staring at him in disbelief while I chew.

"Did you see they're bringing back RDJ as Doctor Doom? I'm not convinced it's a good idea, but I guess we'll see," he says.

"RDJ?"

"Robert Downey Junior," he says.

"Yes, I know who the actor is, but I'm confused as to why him being cast in a role is bad."

"I just don't understand how you use the same actor for two roles in the same universe." He takes a long sip of his beer. "Like, are they going to try to say Tony Stark didn't die and he's now the villain?"

"Are you actually discussing Marvel movies with me?"

"Yeah. What? Is it that hard to believe I like superheroes?"

I laugh out loud. "I mean you look like one, so I guess not." My whole face heats the minute the words fall out of my mouth.

"You think I look like a superhero?" He smirks, and I wish more than anything I could go back in time and not say it.

"No, I just meant…your hair. It's like Thor's. It was meant to be a joke; don't let it go to your head."

"Sure," he says, taking a long pull from his beer. "I'm actually a very big Marvel fan. I've seen every movie."

"Don't tell me you have a gigantic comic book collection too?" I tease.

"No, it's not gigantic" he argues. His cheeks turn beat red, and he grabs another slice of pizza.

"Oh, my god! You totally have a gigantic comic book collection, don't you? Are you a secret nerd?" I gasp.

"I'm not a nerd."

"Says the guy who just listed off his top five Marvel movies without being asked, has an opinion about the actor playing a fictional villain, and has comic books hiding under his bed."

He blushes again. "I would never store them under my bed."

"Oh, you *are* a nerd." I cover my mouth with my hand. "I don't mean it in a bad way. I think it's endearing."

"Endearing?" he questions.

"Yeah, endearing."

"Would you want to see my collection?"

"Sure." I giggle in disbelief. He stands, goes into the kitchen to wash his hands, and then jogs into his room. After a minute, he returns with a stack of comic books. Each one is placed inside a clear protective wrapping, and the one on the bottom of the stack is framed.

He takes his time, showing me each one, telling me what makes it special. He seems like a completely different person when he's talking about them, and I hardly recognize the man in front of me.

Maybe I had him all wrong?

There must be a least fifteen spread out across the floor when he's done, and I have a sneaky suspicion there's more in his room, but this is him attempting to play it cool. I wonder if anyone else knows he likes them this much, or if this is something just for him, and if it is, then why is he sharing it with me? The final framed book has a large signature on the front.

"Who's Tanlee?" I ask through a yawn, trying to read the signature.

"Tanlee?" He gasps, and his eyes go wide. "Did you just ask me who's Tanlee?"

"Yeah, am I supposed to know?" I study the name a little closer, but it's hard to read.

"It says Stan Lee!" He laughs and looks at me like I should know who he's talking about. "The creator of Marvel. You don't know who Stan Lee is? He's literally in every movie." His face twists.

"Oh, no. I mean, maybe it sounds familiar." I shrug. "So, I guess that one is a really cool one to have?"

"Yeah, you could say that." He chuckles, shaking his head. "My grandfather gave it to me for my thirteenth birthday."

"I bet Cody would know what you're talking about." I finish the last of my drink and set the can on the coffee table.

"If your brother ever wanted to see it, I'd be happy to show him. I'm sure he'd get a kick out of you calling Stan Lee, Tanlee."

My stomach does a flip with his offer. *Weird.* It feels like butterflies, but that would mean... No. That's impossible. It has to be the pizza. The chicken was a little weird, tasted a little too much like chicken. I try to shake the feeling, but it doesn't go away. I should go to bed.

"What's that look on your face?" he asks.

"Oh, um, I'm tired. That's all." I yawn again. "It's getting late. I think I'm going to go get ready for bed and then pass out on the couch."

"Yeah, that's a good idea." He checks the time on his phone. "I've got an early morning, so I'll do my best not to wake you when I leave. Do you need a blanket or anything?"

"No, I'll just use the one I brought. Thanks."

He grabs the pizza box and our empty cans then walks back into the kitchen. I stand to go to the bathroom.

"Night, roomie," he says, returning to grab the comic books, then turning to walk back towards his room.

"Night, nerd," I say.

He shakes his head and his whole chest moves when he laughs. Then he disappears behind his door.

CHAPTER 17: IS THAT RAIN?
WREN

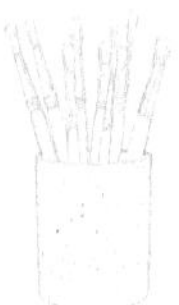

The door shuts, and I open my eyes. That must have been Tanner leaving to go to work.

The apartment is still dark, but the morning light is creeping in between the blinds. What time is it? I flip around and grab my phone. Eight fifteen. I sit up and stretch my neck from side to side. Thank god I'm getting my mattress today because for as nice as this couch is, it's not meant to be slept on.

Slipping my feet into my cat slippers, I begin to move toward the kitchen. I freeze when I reach the fridge. Stuck to the front are two yellow Post-it notes. One has a doodle of a cat with spots alongside a dog. There is a hammer, I think, sitting next to the dog, and I'm not sure what it means. I pull off the other, and study the handwritten note.

Hey Roomie! Coffee and creamer are in the fridge.
Try mixing the amaretto with the white chocolate
raspberry!
–T

I set it on the counter and open the fridge. I take out a container of pre-brewed iced coffee before perusing the creamer selection. There are five different flavors: amaretto, white chocolate raspberry, coconut cream, mocha, and caramel. I reach for the coconut cream but then pause. I grab the amaretto and white chocolate raspberry instead. After adding a small amount of ice and chilled coffee to a glass, I pour in even amounts of both flavors. I take a sip, fully expecting to hate it, but I don't—it's delicious.

> Thanks for the coffee! You were right, amaretto and white chocolate raspberry is delicious!

TANNER:

> Shit you're already up

TANNER:

> Did I wake you when I left

> It's fine. I need to get a move on it so I can help Logan get my mattress.

TANNER:

Glad you liked the coffee

TANNER:

Did you like the drawing

Yes? I'm sorry I don't get it.

TANNER:

It's a cheetah and dog

Fuck, I should've remembered that. I stare back at the little drawing and smile at the thought that maybe we are like the cheetah and the dog.

I love it. Thank you!

TANNER:

I drew Thor's hammer next to me since you think I look like him

I said your hair reminded me of him.

TANNER:

I don't know we're a similar build and I'm super strong

A vision of Tanner shirtless pops into my head, and I shake it away.

LOL!

TANNER:

Pulling into hell

TANNER:

See you later roomie

I grab the notes off the counter and walk toward my bedroom to get ready. Pulling open the top drawer of my nightstand, I set them inside. Swiping up on my phone, I find

Tanner's contact. I'm not sure why, but I add the golden retriever emoji next to his name and then check in with Poppy.

> I'm getting ready, and then I can meet you at my old place to grab my mattress. Want to meet at 9 or 9:15?

POPPY:

> Sounds good. We're up and ready when you are!

Thirty minutes later, I'm out the door and in my car. The pizza, the conversation, and the comic books from last night rattle around in my head. Guilt strikes, and I wonder if maybe I judged him too harshly. Since we decided to live together, he has done nothing but surprise me, and for the first time since I've met him, I don't want to just tolerate him; I want to try to get to know the guy he pretends not to be.

I pull into the parking lot of Cedar Hill and park my car. Yesterday, I didn't really get to process not living here anymore, so I make my way over to my old apartment, alone, for one final walk through and goodbye.

It looks so empty without my stuff, and I send a silent thank you to the universe that I didn't have to fill all the holes that cover the walls from the art and pictures that used to hang there. I guess there are some perks to getting kicked out so that the company can demolish the building.

There's a small knock, and then I hear the door swing open. "Wren, we're here!" Poppy yells. I walk out to meet them.

"Thanks for doing this. I fear if I have to sleep on Tanner's couch another night, my back will never be the same."

"It's not a problem," Logan says. "You girls ready to get this thing out of here?"

The three of us walk in the bedroom, assessing the best

way for us to carry my queen-size mattress out of the apartment.

"I think we turn it on its side, drag it to the front door, and then we can pick it up and walk it to the bed of the truck. It doesn't look very heavy, so if y'all take one side, I'll take the other," Logan explains.

We work together to lift it onto its side. Poppy and I pull from the front, while Logan pushes from the back.

"Turn," Logan says when we get to the bedroom door. "The hallway is really narrow, so we're going to have to angle it so it fits." Poppy and I try, but it starts to bend in the middle.

"We might need your help up here, babe," Poppy says. "Wren, how old is this mattress?"

"I've had it since I was probably ten," I explain with a laugh. "She's floppy, but she's broken in and comfortable."

The whole thing begins to tip and, despite our best effort, somehow wedges in the door frame. "Logan, a little help!" I yell.

"How am I supposed to get over to that side? It's stuck," he argues.

"Just walk through the bathroom. It connects." He lets go of his side, and Poppy and I take on the weight of it.

"Hurry," Poppy yells. "For as floppy as this thing is, it's heavy as shit."

"Sorry," he says, walking out of my bathroom to join us in the hall. "Y'all move and I'll hold it up." He grabs our side, and we move out of the way.

"How did this even happen?" Poppy giggles, tilting her head to the side and studying my mattress.

"It started to fall, and I think when we tried to save it, we made it worse." I shrug.

"Y'all go to the back, and I'm going to try to pull and tip it back up onto its side." We walk through the bathroom and back into the bedroom.

"Okay, y'all each grab a handle, and then on the count of three, I'll pull and you push. One, two, three." The three of us follow his instructions, and the mattress flips back up right and out into the hall.

"Yes," Poppy chimes. She lifts her hand, meeting mine in a high five. We manage to get the mattress to the front door, and then we pick it up and slowly move it to his truck. Logan jumps up, and in one swift motion pulls the mattress into the bed before beginning to tie it down.

"How was your first night at Tanner's?" Poppy asks.

"A bit of a disaster, but then it ended good."

"What happened?"

"I tried cooking him dinner as a thank you and then burnt it, so we ordered pizza and stayed up late talking. He surprised me actually."

"We've been trying to tell you he's a good guy," she says.

"I know, I just hadn't really seen it, but last night I think I got a glimpse. Now I just have to figure out how else I'm going to repay him because I think cooking him meals is definitely out."

"How bad could it have been?"

"I almost caught the taco shells on fire." I cringe.

"Yes, I'd say that's definitely out." She giggles. "Any other ideas?"

"Not yet, but I'll think of something." The sunlight dims, and I look up at the sky to see that a few clouds have moved in. "It's not supposed to rain is it?"

Poppy checks her phone, shaking her head. "No, my weather app says it's supposed to be sunny all day."

"We're all set," Logan says, jumping down from his truck. "Wren, you want to follow behind me?"

"Sure. I've just got to drop off the keys." We move to our respective cars. I pull out first, heading to the front office. It's closed, but I put them in a labeled envelope and drop them into the designated drop box. I'm almost back to the car when a raindrop falls and hits the top of my head. My head swivels to where Poppy and Logan are parked, and I feel three more fall.

Shit!

"Is that rain?" Poppy asks from the passenger seat of the truck.

"Yeah. It might hold if we hurry."

"Then let's go girl!"

I slide into the driver's seat of my car and pull out of Cedar Hill for the last time. If it rains, that mattress is fucked. My whole body is drumming with nerves as we drive back to Tanner's. My eyes keep darting between the road ahead and the very dark clouds that are rolling in and starting to spit rain across the windshield.

At the next light, we turn left, and I'm met with my worst nightmare—brake lights. We're at a complete stop. My eyes shift upward, only to find more gray clouds. *Fuck.* My phone rings.

"Hey, it looks like the church up ahead is letting out, so it might be awhile," Poppy explains.

"Dammit, there is no way we're going to make it."

"You don't know that. We…" The whole sky opens up, and sheets of rain hit the outside of my car and my mattress. "I'm sorry, babe," she says.

"Should we try to turn around and find cover?" Logan asks. "I think there's a gas station about a half a mile in the other direction."

"No, that seems pointless. It's already getting soaked. It hasn't rained like this in weeks." I rub my hands down my face.

"I'm sorry," Logan says. "I'll help pay for a new mattress. If my mom hadn't needed me to handle that fucking squirrel yesterday, this wouldn't have happened."

"It's not your fault. What are the chances?" I laugh. "I guess once we're moving again, let's head to the dump. I'll order a new one when I get back to Tanner's. The couch will be fine for a couple more nights."

How fucking perfect.

> My mattress got caught up in the rain, so if you find me on the couch again tonight that's why.

TANNER 🦌:

Noooo that sucks

> Yeah, I ordered a new one, but it won't be here for a few days.

TANNER 🦌:

I'll be working late trying to get this proposal done

TANNER 🦌:

You should take my bed

> No, thanks. I'm fine on the couch.

TANNER 🦌:

I wish you would just take the bed

TANNER 🦌:

I don't mind

TANNER 🦌:

I swear

> I wasn't telling you so that you'd offer. Just didn't want you to get a jump scare when you got back later. Really, it's okay.

TANNER 🦌:

So stubborn

CHAPTER 18: 100% AUTHENTIC FOAM
TANNER

When I've gotten home the past few nights, Wren has already been asleep on the couch with Dolly curled up at her feet. The blanket she brought with her somehow always found its way on the floor next to the couch, so each night I picked it up and covered her with it before heading to my own bed and passing out.

Work has been a lot. I hate that I haven't really gotten to spend time with my new roommate, worried that it's not helping her impression of me.

I was supposed to meet with my dad this morning about the new proposal I worked on all weekend, but he didn't show. Once again my calls went unanswered, and my texts went unread.

Since announcing his move, Mitch has made himself sparse, and so when I tried to find him after my dad stood me up, he wasn't there either. I thought about leaving early, but I knew that would just further prove my father's thoughts about me, so I stayed. I should've been diving into my next project, but I couldn't focus. Instead, I sat at my desk and drew up imaginary plans for The Local, daydreaming about all the what ifs.

I pull into my apartment complex and try to loosen up the tension between my shoulder blades. I told Wren I'd make us dinner for our first official roomie night, and I really wanted tonight to be special, but I'm exhausted.

Climbing out of my car, I grab the bag of groceries and my necktie off the back seat. Maybe I'll feel better after a shower and some food.

As I approach our door, I notice a long cylindrical box leaned up against the siding. It looks like Wren's mattress made it.

I push the front door and set the bag on the coffee table. "Wren, you here?" There's no answer, but I can hear water running from her bathroom.

Returning outside, I study the box a little closer. It's long and thin. It's addressed to her, so I pick it up, and I'm surprised by how light it is. I back through the door and place it up against the wall inside.

I move to the pantry and begin putting the groceries away. My mind is still reeling about work, and I'm distracted. Grabbing the jar of pesto from the bag, I attempt to place it on the shelf at the same time my phone chimes. Without thinking, I grab for my phone, causing the jar to fall and shatter all over the floor. Welp, there goes dinner.

The text isn't even from my dad or brother, just some spam.

Fuck me, dude.

I carefully clean up the mess of sauce and sweep up the glass. When I'm sure it's completely taken care of, I head to the shower to wash off my day. The last thing I want is to be in shit mood when I'm hanging out with Wren, and I currently feel like shit.

The warm water pelts against my muscles and runs through my hair, my mind drifting back to work. They must think I'm the biggest fucking joke, and as much as I should want to quit, it's just pushing me harder to prove them all wrong.

I turn the faucet off and climb out to dry myself. Pulling on gym shorts, I make my way back into the living room, shirt in hand.

"My new mattress came," Wren says, standing next to the box with scissors. She's wearing blue plaid pajama pants, a tiny tank top, and her wet hair is pulled to the side in a long braid. Her eyes run down my body and stop at the V-shaped cut that disappears below my waistband. Her eyes linger there for a second too long, so I clear my throat, causing her to jump. Her gaze finds mine, and her whole face turns pink.

"You okay?" I ask, smirking.

"Oh, yeah, I'm fine. Why wouldn't I be fine? Just trying to figure out the best way to get it out."

"Get it out?"

"The mattress. How to get the mattress out of the box," she says, embarrassed.

"I know. What else would you have been referring to?" Her eyes shift to my crotch, and I let out a laugh. Her face turns a shade brighter. "You sure you ordered a mattress? I mean I know I'm strong, but it seemed awfully light when I carried it in."

"It's one of those foam ones that they shrink wrap really small, and then when you open it, it expands into a whole-ass mattress. Here, help me get it into my room and onto my bed frame."

"If you say so," I say, pulling my shirt over my head. I walk over and grab the box before she has a chance, carrying it into her room one handed.

There is no way this is a mattress.

We work together pulling it from the cardboard, and she carefully cuts the plastic shrink wrap. It flops open.

"What the fuck?" she shrieks. "*This* is supposed to be a mattress?"

"Kinda looks like one of those mattress toppers." I shrug.

She cuts her eyes at me. "I know what it looks like, but I didn't order a mattress topper. I ordered a mattress." She storms out of her room, so I follow. Grabbing her laptop, she plops down on the sofa and wildly begins to type on the keyboard.

"See," she says, flipping the screen towards me when I sit down next to her. "Deluxe ultra soft 100% authentic foam with cooling feature queen size mattress..." She reads the insane description on the product, pointing at each word. Her other hand bumps the mouse pad, and the cursor reveals the rest of the description.

"Topper," I finish reading for her.

"No, it didn't say that when I ordered it," she says, frantically.

"I bet you just missed it because it cuts off after the word mattress."

"God, I'm such an idiot. I saw mattress and one hundred dollars, and I was sold."

"You really think a 100% authentic foam mattress with cooling feature would only cost a hundred dollars," I say, laughing.

"Stop it," she says, swatting at me. "It's not funny."

"It's a little funny. What does 100% authentic foam even mean?"

"I don't know," she grumbles, rolling her eyes. "I guess I'll just return it and buy an actual mattress. Goodness, what a mess."

"You can take my bed until the new one comes. I don't care."

"No," she says firmly. "This is my fault. If I wasn't so cheap, I wouldn't be in this predicament. I'll just swing by the store tomorrow and grab an inflatable one to sleep on until it gets here."

"Okay, but I really don't mind."

"I appreciate it, but it's fine." She begins typing in the search bar and hits enter. A dozen or so links to top-rated mattresses pop up. I watch as she scans them, biting her lip.

"Buy yourself a nice one. You deserve a good night's sleep." She shifts her eyes toward me. "Or, I can buy you one if you're worried about the money."

"Absolutely not. This one looks nice and it's not very expensive."

"Wren, the models don't even look comfortable on that thing. Look at that guy; he's grimacing."

She giggles.

"If you don't want me to buy it, I understand, but buy yourself something nice," I encourage her. "Like this one." I move my hand to the mouse pad, and our fingers brush. I freeze, and so does she.

"Sorry," I say, as she pulls her hand away.

"It's fine." She smiles. "Which one were you going to say?"

"This one." I click on a nice mattress that is moderately priced. "It's not the most expensive option, but it has good reviews and doesn't look like it'll cause you to need a chiro-practor."

She hesitates.

"Buy it," I urge, and, to my surprise, she adds it to the cart and begins to check out.

"Just to clarify, this is not a mattress topper," she says, when she gets to the *confirm your order* page.

"It's a mattress," I verify, and she presses the purchase button.

"So, now that that's taken care of, what's for dinner?" she asks. "I'm starving."

My heart sinks.

"I was going to make pesto chicken pasta, but I dropped the pesto jar when I got home. I'm sorry."

"It's no big deal. Accidents happen," she says. "Did you get anything else?"

"I didn't," I say, desperately trying to come up with an alternative idea, and then it hits me. "Would you want to go to Waffle House?"

"Yes," she says, grinning from ear to ear. "Let me throw on a sweatshirt and some shoes. Waffle House sounds perfect." She jumps up, and when she returns, she's still wearing her pajama pants, but she's thrown on a black sweatshirt and tennis shoes.

"What's Va–lar–is," I ask slowly, trying to pronounce the word across her chest.

"It's a fictional city in a book I like."

"Hmm, I've never heard of it," I say. "Would I like the book?"

"Do you like books?" she asks.

"I like comic books." I laugh. "Do you read a lot?"

"Yeah, mostly fantasy or romantasy books, but I do like to read."

"Romantasy?" I question, as we walk out to my car.

"They're fantasy books with a love story and some spice."

"Spice?"

"Yeah, like sex."

Wren Dawson just said the word sex, and I'm officially the least mature man on the planet.

"Got it, but it's fantasy. So, is it like aliens having sex with aliens?"

"That would be more like sci-fi." She gestures to her shirt. "Like this book is humans having sex with men that have bat wings and magical powers."

"That sounds cool."

"I think it is," she says.

"It's not that cold out; why the sweatshirt?" I ask when we're almost to the car.

"Have you ever eaten in a Waffle House?" She giggles. "If I were you, I'd go grab a jacket. They keep them freezing."

I don't think I'll need a jacket, but an idea suddenly pops into my head, and I turn around heading back to our door.

"I'll be right back," I say. "Good call on grabbing a coat." I toss her my keys and head back to the apartment to grab a surprise along with my jacket to hide it in.

When I get back to my car, she's already started it and taken over the music. One Direction blares through my speakers, and it's not my usual taste in music, but it's not bad. We don't talk much on the quick five minute drive, but in my periphery I can see her dancing as she sings along.

I park in the empty parking lot, and we make our way inside the brick building, where we are greeted by the only waitress working and a very grumpy looking line cook.

"Sit anywhere, y'all," the waitress says. I follow Wren over to a booth and sit across from her.

"I'm so hungry," she says.

"You need a menu?" I ask, offering her the one that's sitting behind the napkin holder.

"Do I need a menu?" she scoffs, a little offended. "I've lived in Georgia my entire life. Do not insult me by giving me a menu at Waffle House."

I put my hands up in defense. "Sorry, I wasn't trying to offend you."

"Do *you* need a menu?" she asks.

"No," I say. "I know what I'm ordering."

"Y'all know what you want, or do you need a minute?" the waitress asks.

"I'll have water, two eggs scrambled with cheese, bacon, hash browns, raisin toast, and a plain waffle," she says.

"And for you, hun?" the waitress looks at me.

I hesitate for a split second. "What she's having, except plain toast instead of raisin."

The waitress walks away without another word.

"Oh, my god, you didn't know what you wanted, and you totally panicked and just copied me."

"Or we have more in common than you think, and that's what I usually get too," I counter.

She blushes a little, and I don't tell her that I had no fucking clue what I wanted for dinner.

"How was your day?" I ask.

"Same as every Wednesday—Bible study, art group, chair yoga, and pickleball lessons."

"You run a Bible study?"

"Oh, no, I just coordinate it with a local church. I do run the other groups though, and I supervise pickleball lessons."

"I didn't realize rec therapists do all of that stuff."

The waitress returns with our waters, and we both thank her.

"Technically, I'm the activities director, so that's why I do all of that."

"I thought you were a rec therapist?" I ask, a little confused.

"Oh, I am. It's just rec therapy jobs are hard to find in traditional rehab settings because insurance doesn't like to cover our services, so when I graduated, I found the activities director role."

"Well that seems like bullshit."

"What does?"

"Insurance not covering what you do. I don't know much about it, but I know you help people get better, and isn't that why we have insurance? It's supposed to cover the costs of things that can help us get better."

"In theory." She lets out a long breath. "I guess. But the insurance companies don't really see what I do that way."

"Then that's bullshit." A smile ghosts across her face, and my heart swells with the thought that I had something to do with making her feel a little bit of happy.

"How was your day?" she asks, and I know she doesn't

mean to, but all the feelings I was having earlier return. The tension that had mostly disappeared pulls at the base of my skull, causing me to wince. "That bad?" she asks.

"I was supposed to meet with my dad, but it didn't happen. He went golfing with a client instead," I say.

"You're kidding?" she says.

"I wish."

"Did he cancel it?"

"No, just stood me up. It's not the first time. It's okay."

"It's not okay," she says.

Maybe she's right, but I'm used to it at this point, so I just shrug. She studies me, her face falling a little, and then out of nowhere it shifts and I can practically see a light bulb go off above her head.

"Stand up," she says.

"What?"

"Stand up. You had a shitty day, and you were in a good mood until I brought it up again."

"Why should I stand up?" I chuckle.

"Because we're gonna dance?"

"I'm sorry?"

She stands, walks over to the music player, and slides her card. She starts tapping through the selections and then picks a song. A few seconds later, "Shut up and Dance" by Walk the Moon begins playing through the speaker. She walks back over, putting out her hand.

"Come on," she says.

"We can't dance in Waffle House," I argue.

"No one is here," she says, looking around. "Now come on; get up." She grabs my hand and pulls me from the booth.

She begins to dance, and I just shake my head.

"Dance with me, Tanner," she says, her mouth forming a heart-stopping grin.

I begin to move my feet, and when her smile grows bigger, I let all of my insecurities disappear.

For the rest of the song, we dance around like we're two little kids. It's pure silliness, and with every move, all the negativity about my dad and my day melts away. It's just her and me, and nothing else matters. The music fades, and we both have to wipe the tears streaming down our faces from laughing so hard. We turn to sit back down, and the waitress is standing with our food, completely unamused and scowling.

"Sorry," Wren says, giggling and sliding into the booth.

"I've seen some weird shit here, but that might've been the weirdest," the waitress deadpans, setting our plates on the table before turning to walk away.

Another giggle bubbles out of Wren, and she slaps her hand across her mouth.

"You're gonna get us kicked out of here," I say, shaking my head.

She begins to butter her waffle and then pours syrup all over the top. I watch her with amazement.

"What?" she says, catching my eye.

I shrug.

"Come on. I know me pouring syrup on my waffle is not that interesting. Why are you looking at me like that?"

"Oh, it's just I'm not used to someone listening to my family stuff and trying to cheer me up. Thank you for the dance."

"Of course. Dancing always makes things better." She smiles from across the table and then takes a bite of her food.

She's right. Dancing with Wren Dawson could make anything better, and I hope I'll get the chance to do it again.

"Hey, I almost forgot," I say, after buttering and adding syrup to my waffle. Reaching into my jacket pocket, I pull out a bag of mini marshmallows. "Look what I snuck in."

She shakes her head, and her whole face lights up. "And you said I was going to get us kicked out. I can't believe you remembered."

"I think I've told you I pay attention."

The slightest shade of pink warms her cheeks, and I hand her the bag. She adds a handful to the top of her waffle, and then without asking does the same to mine.

"Thank you," she says. "Now try it—you're going to love it."

She watches me with anticipation as I take a large bite.

"Wow," I say around all the sugar. "That's good."

"Told you," she says, clapping her hands. And in that moment, I fall a little bit harder.

CHAPTER 19: YOU'RE INCREDIBLE
TANNER

I fucking hate Mondays. I ignored my gym alarm, and I've been laying in bed for the last thirty minutes, trying to will myself to get up and ready for work, but it's no use. All I've accomplished in a half hour is creating a list of thirty things I'd rather do than go to work and most of them include Wren, which is probably unhealthy.

There's a clatter from the kitchen, and I guess that means she's awake. The gym or work might not get me moving, but she sure can. I climb out of bed and jump into the shower. The hot water washes over my body, and I take my time massaging my scalp, trying to get rid of the headache that seems to have taken up residency behind my eyes these days, but it's no use.

Grabbing my towel, I shut off the shower, climb out, and dry off.

"Morning, roomie," I say, walking out of my bedroom, drying my hair.

"Morning," she says, looking over her shoulder. Her eyes dart down my abs to the towel hung around my waist then move quickly back up my body. "Geez, do you ever wear clothes?"

"To be fair, my clothes are in the laundry room, and I was just coming to get them. I also didn't know you'd be out here." I put my hands up in defense.

She flips around, leans against the counter top, and sips her iced coffee, studying me. She's wearing the same green silk pajamas from the first night she moved in, and her hair is pulled up on top of her head in a messy bun. She looks fucking stunning, and my dick begins to harden.

Now is not the time. Pretend you're in an ice bath. A really cold ice bath.

Dolly weaves in and out between my legs, almost tripping me.

"Woah there, girl. We don't need to be giving your mama a show."

She purrs against me.

"I think she likes you," Wren says, giggling.

"Well, I'm very likable." I smirk.

"Verdict is still out on that one," she teases, taking another sip of her coffee.

"What flavor did you go with this morning?"

"The mix you suggested yesterday. It's delicious." She smiles and my dick strains again. "Are you working today?"

Ice baths. Being naked in the snow. Jumping into a frozen lake.

"Yeah, I'm gonna try to finish early though. You?"

"Yeah, but I'm getting off around three." Her eyes dart down my body again, and she bites her lip. With one fucking look, I'm hard as a rock under my towel. *Shit.*

"I should get dressed," I spit out a little panicked. Moving past her, I quickly try to cover my crotch with the other towel and walk into the laundry room to grab my clothes. Luckily, they're easy to find, and I briskly make it back to my room, clothes in hand, before she realizes I'm hard.

I get dressed, all the while trying to will my cock to calm the fuck down, but thinking of cold things isn't working, so I switch my train of thought.

Wren is my friend. She is my friend. She is my fucking friend.

"You okay?" she asks from right outside my door. "You kinda just acted like you were on fire."

"Oh, yeah, just getting dressed. We haven't really gotten to hang out. You want to do something tonight?"

"I'm going to see my brother," she says. "It's my parents' anniversary, so I promised I'd go hang out with him. Plus, aren't roomie nights on Wednesdays?"

I open the door and lean against the frame.

"Roomie nights can be any night we want them to be." I walk past her and into the kitchen. "I was planning on leaving the office early. Mind if I tag along? I'd love to meet him."

"You want to meet my brother?"

"Yeah, I'll even bring my Tanlee comic."

She rocks back and forth on her heels, sipping her coffee.

"We're just going to be watching movies. I don't want to bore you."

"Do you even know me at all?" I ask. "A movie night sounds like just what the doctor ordered after the last couple days I've had."

She smiles, and it's official, I'm addicted. "Okay, I guess I'll see you after work then?"

"I can't wait."

———

I rushed through everything I needed to do at the office today to make sure I was home in time to go with Wren. I was a little surprised this morning that she agreed to let me tag along, but I'm excited I get to meet her family, especially her brother.

"How was work today?" I ask, climbing into her car after work to head to her parents' house. She insisted on driving, and when I argued, she shut me down so fast that I didn't try again.

"Same old, same old," she says, buckling her seatbelt. "You?"

"Busy, but not terrible."

"That's good." She stops at the stop sign and clicks through her phone. "Hooked On A Feeling" by Blue Swede begins to play in the car. When the street is clear, she turns out and sings along with the song, and I spend my time taking her in.

Her hair has a slight wave to it. Today she's wearing jeans with strawberries embroidered all over them, a vintage MTV T-shirt, a light pink blazer, white sneakers, and aviators. She really is the most beautiful girl I've ever seen, and despite my trying, I can't help but fall a little harder for her when she tries to hit a high note and completely misses.

"How'd you come up with this playlist?" I ask, after the song fades into "Paper Rings" by Taylor Swift.

"I just picked all the songs that make me happy," she says, turning the music down a little. We pass The Local, and my heart skips. I still haven't accepted or turned down Jerry's offer. I know I shouldn't string him along, but I keep thinking there might be a way for me to be happy and make my family proud. Maybe there is a way I could have both.

"Do you ever wish you could do something else?" I ask.

"Like my job? Yeah, all the time. Why?"

"I was just wondering. What would you do if you could do anything?"

She lets out a long breath. "Well, before Cody's accident, I thought I'd be an artist."

"That's right, you mentioned that you paint and wanted to own your own studio at Donovan and Enzo's wedding."

"You remember that?"

I shrug. "I pay attention. Is that what you'd want to do if you could do anything?"

"Maybe in a past life," she says wistfully. "But then he had his accident, and my dreams changed."

"In what way?" I ask, and she hesitates, quickly looking between me and the road.

"You can trust me," I assure her.

"I'd want to start a non-profit and run camps for people with traumatic brain injuries."

"That sounds cool."

"It would be so cool," she says, her mouth forming into a wide smile. "There is something similar on the west coast, but it's just your typical sleep away camp, which I'd love to do, but I was thinking I could also host art camps or sports camps or anything really." She is practically glowing as she talks. "With my degree in rec therapy, I know how to modify and adapt all the activities, so everyone could participate, and I think I could get physical therapists, speech therapists, occupational therapists, and maybe even therapy students to volunteer to help me run them. My brother was so active before his injury, and now he just sits at home. I know being able to attend camp would be life-changing for him, and I think that would be really cool."

"You're incredible."

Heat creeps up her neck and covers her face.

"It's not that big of a deal," she says.

"Yes, it is. I've never even thought about that. I think it's incredible that you want to help improve the lives of so many people. I think you should do it."

"I wish it was that simple." She relaxes in her seat, leaning back on the head rest. "The amount of money required to start up that kind of thing is enormous, and while I've tried really hard to save, I'm nowhere near where I need to be."

My gears start turning. I have money. All she'd have to do is ask, and I'd do anything to help her make her dream come true, but I know she never will, and I can respect that. She's so fucking strong, and I never want to make her feel like I don't believe she can't do it on her own.

"You'll make it happen. I know it."

"Maybe." She smiles softly. "So, what would you do if you could do something else?" she asks.

I hesitate before answering her question. Logan and Jacks are still the only friends who know I was offered the bar, and after her confession, mine seems silly and unimportant.

"I don't really have a choice. I'm a Mitchell, and Mitchells work at Austere."

"You always have a choice," she says. "Come on. I told you my dream, and I know something spurred this conversation, so what is it? What would you do?"

I breathe in deep and then say it fast. "I'd buy The Local."

"Like, the bar?"

"Yeah. A month and a half ago, the owner offered to sell it to me, but then my brother quit, and you know the rest. I think it would be cool to own The Local and make it my own."

"I mean, that seems like a no brainer," she says without hesitation. "I think you should do it."

"Ha!"

"I'm serious. I think your family would want you to be happy, and it's not that hard to see that you hate your job."

"I don't know about the first part, but is it that obvious that I hate being at Austere?"

She pulls into the driveway of a small, brick ranch and puts her car in park.

"It's very obvious." She unbuckles and turns to face me, pushing her sunglasses onto the top of her head. Her ocean eyes find mine, and the golden hour sun pouring into the car makes her look like some sort of goddess. "As your friend, I think you should do what makes you happy."

Friend.

CHAPTER 20: WE MAKE A GOOD TEAM
WREN

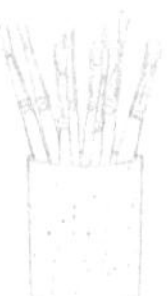

When Tanner said he wanted to come with me to hang with Cody, I wasn't sure. The last guy I brought home was my ex, Chad, and after months of pretending like he cared about my brother and what my family and I was going through, he broke up with me so that he could experience college life to the fullest.

Fucking jackass.

I almost told Tanner not to worry about it when I got to the apartment after work, but when I walked in, he was on the couch petting Dolly, wearing a Captain America T-shirt, and the framed comic was already sitting on the coffee table ready to go. He looked so excited that I didn't have it in me to cancel our plans, and so here we are, about to walk into my childhood home, together.

He's my friend, so this isn't the same thing as bringing Chad around, but I also know that not everyone has experience with brain injury like I do, and I never know whether to over prepare people or just let it happen naturally.

The car ride has been interesting. I'm quickly learning that there is more to Tanner than meets the eye, and that terrifies the shit out of me. We also didn't have time for my normal brain injury spiel because he distracted me with talks about our dreams.

"It's very obvious." I say, unbuckling and turning to face him. I push my glasses onto the top of my head. "As your friend, I think you should do what makes you happy."

I don't miss his jaw ticking when I say friend. His baby blues lock on mine, and I have to physically shake myself to break our eye contact.

"I'll think about it," Tanner says, offering me a small smile.

"Good. You ready to go inside?"

"Hell yeah, let's go," he says, climbing out of the car with his comic. We follow the sidewalk up to the front door, and I pause before opening it.

"I should've mentioned it before, but my dad was a little weird about us living together. He knows you're coming, but please just ignore anything he says. Also, Cody likes to give me a hard time, so if you could just ignore everything he says too, that'd be great."

Tanner laughs. "And your mom? Am I allowed to listen to what she says?"

"Best if you just ignore all three of them."

"Ignore your whole family. Got it."

"Good."

I push the door open, and he follows me inside. "Anybody home?" I shout.

"In the kitchen," my mom yells. We make our way down the hall, following the sound of her voice. My mom is at the stove stirring something, and my dad and brother are sitting at the table.

"You both look nice," I say, walking in and over to my mom, who's wearing a green dress that brings out her eyes. She wraps me in a hug, and I inhale her perfume, relaxing immediately.

"You must be Tanner," my dad says, standing and shaking his hand. "I'm Paul, and this is my wife, Charlotte."

"It's nice to meet you both."

Tanner turns to my brother. "How's it going man? I'm Tanner." He puts his hand out and shakes Cody's.

My brother lets go and immediately begins to type. To my surprise, Tanner takes a seat at the table and waits for him to finish. He doesn't look over Cody's shoulder and try to read what he's typing either. He just sits there, still holding his framed comic, his ankle crossed over his knee, like this is the hundredth conversation he's had with my brother and not the first.

"I'm Cody are you dating my sister," my brother says in one long stream of text.

"Dude!" I shriek. "See, I told you to ignore everything he says." I walk over and ruffle my brother's hair. "Tanner is my roommate, and he happens to be a huge nerd like you. He found out we were watching Marvel movies tonight and practically begged me to come."

Cody's whole body shakes with laughter, and he begins to type again.

"I'm not a nerd," Tanner argues.

"Says the man wearing a Captain America T-shirt," I tease.

"Can we watch *Iron Man*?" Cody asks.

"Of course we can," Tanner says before I have the chance. "I was telling your sister that it's my favorite movie of all time."

Cody nods and begins to type again. "What are you holding?" he asks after a few seconds.

"Oh, this?" Tanner flips the frame around. "It's a framed copy of *The Avengers #1* signed by... what did you call him Wren? Tanlee?"

Everyone laughs but me. Returning next to my mom, I steal a green bean from the pan, grumbling while I chew it.

"It's not my fault the signature is hard to read," I say, crossing my arms.

"You have a comic signed by Stan Lee?" my dad asks, walking over and looking at the frame. "Well that must be worth ten grand."

"Dad!"

"What?" he asks. "Am I wrong?"

Tanner chuckles. "I'm actually not sure how much it's worth. It was a gift from my grandad, and to me it's priceless."

"He seems nice," my mom whispers, nudging me with her elbow.

"He's a really nice roommate," I whisper back.

"Mmhmm," she muses.

I'm in absolute awe of the man sitting next to my brother. I don't know why I was worried for him to come. That feeling I've been pushing down returns to my stomach, and this time there is no weird chicken to blame. No alcohol either. Tanner Mitchell is giving me butterflies, and I don't hate them.

Cody begins to type once more, and we all wait for him to speak. Tanner's eyes find mine, and I offer him a thankful smile.

"That's fucking awesome," Cody says.

"Language," my mom scolds. "We have a guest."

"Oh, I'm not offended," Tanner assures her. He turns back to Cody. "And that's what I tried to tell your sister, but she wasn't impressed."

My brother laughs again, and I honestly don't know the last time I saw him this happy.

"Dinner is ready," my mom says. "And we need to get going, honey." She checks her watch.

"We're just going down the street, so if y'all need anything, call us," my dad says, grabbing his sports coat off the back of the chair.

"Y'all have fun and enjoy yourselves," I urge. "Cody,

Tanner, and I have everything under control. Isn't that right boys?"

Both men nod, and my mom wraps me in another hug. "Thank you for this, sweetheart," she says, squeezing me. "It means a lot."

"Don't mention it." They leave, and Tanner immediately jumps up to help me plate the food. I remove Cody's tray table, moving him as close to the table as I can, and then I set his iPad within his reach.

"Looks like your mom made chicken, mashed potatoes, and green beans," Tanner says. "You want a little bit of every-thing, man?"

Cody taps the screen and says, "Yes."

"Here," I say, handing Tanner a divided plate with built up edges for my brother. He spoons out the portions and then turns to walk the plate over to Cody.

"Oh, actually, can you hand it to me? I need to cut up the chicken."

"Shit," he says rather discouraged, turning back around. "I'm sorry."

"Why?" I ask.

"Because I talked to Poppy, and she said that sometimes people with brain injuries might need help cutting up their food, but I should ask, and I forgot to ask, and then I tried to give him a whole piece of chicken, and I should've asked," he rambles quietly and a little panicked.

I stare at him, speechless. "You talked to Poppy?" I whis-per. Those butterflies swoop low in my belly, and my heart skips a beat.

"Well, yeah, I figured I'd eventually meet Cody, and I just, I don't know. I messed up, and I'm sorry. I just wanted to make sure I didn't fuck up his first impression of me I guess."

"You didn't fuck up," I say, giggling at how flustered he is. "He does need help cutting the chicken, but I forget some-times too."

Cody begins typing on the screen on his iPad. Tanner sets the plate back on the counter, and I hand him a fork and a knife.

"She does forget," Cody says.

"Well, I'm glad I'm not the only one," Tanner says, nudging me with his elbow. He begins cutting, and then when he's done, he looks at me.

"Is this okay?" he asks, nervously.

"It's perfect."

He walks the plate over to Cody, and places it on the table in front of him.

"Utensils?" he asks, flipping back and looking at me.

"Top drawer on the left. He uses the spork with the fat gray handle."

"Got it," Tanner says.

"Thanks," Cody says, before taking the spork and digging into dinner. I fill his special cup with water, and then once he's settled, I serve myself. Tanner is leaned up against the counter holding a plate, watching me.

"You gonna get some food?" I ask. "I promise my mom is a better cook than I am."

He laughs and shakes his head. "I have no doubt. I was letting you go first."

"It's okay. Dig in."

He walks over, invading my space, and we both reach for the mashed potato spoon at the same time. Our hands connect, and I do my best to ignore the surge of electricity that shoots up my arm.

"Oh, sorry," he says.

"No, go ahead." I release the spoon and move towards the table. It doesn't dawn on me that I walked away without getting any potatoes until I'm already sitting down.

Dammit.

Tanner joins us and eyes my food. "You didn't get mashed potatoes?" he asks.

"Changed my mind," I lie, still trying to ignore the feeling his touch left me with. A smirk spreads across his face, like he can read my mind, and I quickly shove a bite of green beans into my mouth to hide my reaction.

Throughout the rest of dinner, I watch as the man across from me continues to make my brother laugh, and I'm a little jealous at how good he is at it.

Once we're done, I help Cody navigate his chair into the living room to get ready for the movie, and Tanner tackles the dishes.

"We're all set for the movie," I say from the entry to the kitchen. "You didn't have to clean all that up. I could've done it."

"It was no problem," he says, drying his hands on a dish towel and then walking towards me. "We make a good team."

My breath catches as he passes me, and I swallow hard when the mix of woods, amber, and the slightest hint of something floral overwhelms my senses, causing my knees to buckle.

Does he always smell this good?

"I'll be right back. Gotta pee. Y'all good?" I stammer.

"Yeah," Tanner says, his face twisting with a little confusion as he looks back over his shoulder. "Are you good?"

"Yeah, great," I say, trying to slow down so it doesn't look like I'm running away uncomfortably as I make a beeline for the hall bathroom.

Closing the door behind me, I begin to pace the small space. I need to get it together. I'm living with this man. Just because he's absolutely incredible with my brother doesn't mean I need to melt for him. Plenty of people are great with Cody, and I'm not swooning over them.

A couple months ago, I could barely tolerate him. Nothing has changed. Just because he's a little nerdy and sweet doesn't mean he's not a fuck boy. I'm being blinded by my love for my brother…that's what this is. I take a few deep breaths, calm myself, and then pull my hair up into a ponytail.

Feeling a little less crazy, I walk out of the bathroom, and my eyes immediately land on Tanner. He's leaning over my brother, and they're looking at something on his iPad.

I clear my throat, "Y'all ready to start the movie?" I ask, sitting down on the sofa.

"Let's do it," Tanner says. His eyes shift between the leather recliner and the cushion next to me.

Please pick the recliner. For the love of god, please do not sit next to me.

He struts over and plops down to my left.

Shit.

I start the movie and try to relax, but I can't. He's sitting so close that I can smell his cologne. He laughs at something in the movie, and my stomach bottoms out again. It's official. These feelings are insane, and I should be committed.

He shifts, spreading his legs a little, and his thigh touches mine. My gaze shifts toward him, and he's locked in on the movie. This is all in my head. That was an accident. I move over a cushion and curl my legs up underneath me, trying to focus on the movie and my brother.

After thirty minutes, Cody looks like he's beginning to nod off. "You ready for bed, bud?" I ask.

He begins swiping on the screen, and then after a few seconds a "Yes" comes through the device speakers.

"I'm just going to get him ready for bed, and then I'll be back," I say, pausing the movie.

"Do you need help?" Tanner asks.

"Maybe when I'm ready to get him into bed, but I can handle the rest."

"Just holler," Tanner says.

Cody begins to type again, and I wait for him to finish before helping him move his wheelchair towards his room.

"I like you you should date my sister," he says as I press down on his chair's joystick to move him forward. Tanner coughs out a laugh, and I groan.

"Seriously, dude?" I mutter.

His shoulders shake as a loud cackle erupts from him, and if I didn't love him so much, I'd kill him.

I help my brother through his night routine, and when we're finished, and he's safely sitting in his chair, I call for Tanner.

"I've never lifted anyone," he says, walking into Cody's room.

"It's okay. I'll walk you through it."

His eyes scan the space and land on Cody's Funko Pop! collection. "Are these all yours?" he asks.

Cody nods.

"These are sick dude." He explores the collection for a few minutes. "There's not a Thor one," he points out.

"Oh. Is there not?" I ask, shrugging. "I've never noticed."

"I don't see one."

He continues to peruse the collection and then pauses in front of a canvas hanging on the wall. "This is a cool painting," he says. I swallow hard as he studies it.

"Is that you?" he asks while looking over his shoulder toward my brother and pointing at a redheaded boy in the middle of the painting dressed like a superhero.

Cody nods.

I feel myself blush. Tanner doesn't know I painted it, but it's my favorite thing I've ever created.

"So then that must be me," Tanner says, pointing to Thor.

Cody begins laughing, and I can't help but join in.

"Alright, that's enough, you two. It's time for bed," I say. Tanner joins me next to Cody, and with his help and my instructions, we lift my brother safely into his bed. I tuck the covers tight around him the way I know he likes and place a kiss on his forehead.

"Night, Cody. It was nice to meet you, man," Tanner says, walking towards the door.

"Night, bud. I love you."

Cody signs, "I love you," with his left hand and then closes his eyes.

"Thanks for your help," I say as we walk out of the room, turning off the lights and closing the door softly.

"I keep trying to tell you we make a good team," he says. "Just wish you'd believe me."

I stop in my tracks, not sure how to respond. My eyes find his, and then we both begin to move down the hall.

"Do your parents lift him?" he asks.

"Yeah. Well them or one of his caregivers. He had a lift, but it's broken, and last I heard, the insurance company denied the claim for a new one."

"That's terrible."

"Yeah, well. That's insurance for you." I shake my head. Tanner's eyes dance with an idea. "What's that look?"

"Nothing," he says. "How much do lifts cost?"

"I'm not answering that question because the only reason you would need to know that is if you were going to purchase one."

He chuckles, and the butterflies swoop. Something deep down tells me he's not going to listen to me, and while I would never expect him to help, I know a new lift would be life-changing for my family.

CHAPTER 21: JUST
BE FUCKING COOL
TANNER

I can't help but think about how easy it would be for me to buy Cody a new lift. I mean, I'm fit, but I don't even think I could lift him multiple times a day, seven days a week, without it eventually taking a toll on my body. I'm not sure how her parents are managing.

Wren might be stubborn, but I have a sneaky suspicion that when it comes to Cody, she'd let down her walls. So, I make a mental note to ask Gray about the lift.

"Are your parents art collectors?" I ask, gesturing towards a painting of a house hanging on the wall.

The interior of their house is a bit eclectic, with mismatched furniture, handmade throws, lots of plants, and where there aren't family pictures hanging, there's art. Some of the pieces are more traditional, like this one in the hall, but others are like the one in Cody's room—whimsical and fun.

"If collecting *my* art makes them art collectors, then I guess you could call them that," she says with a laugh.

"You painted that?" I ask.

"Yeah." She shrugs. "I painted all of it."

"You painted all of it? Even the superhero piece in Cody's room?"

"Yep, that one is my favorite, and he obviously loves it too." She checks the time on her phone. "Do you want to finish the movie? I'm sure my parents will be back soon."

"Oh, um…sure." I run my hands through my hair.

We walk back into the living room, and I take a moment to really look at the art. Painted wildflowers, a beach scene, a portrait of her parents, and even a Christmas tree are all painted on various size canvases and hung around the house. Each one is unique, and it's clear she's incredibly talented.

One catches my attention more than the others. It's a small canvas, simple black and white. It's of a girl curled up in the corner of a room crying. It's heartbreakingly beautiful.

"I knew you said you painted, but I didn't know you painted like this," I point to the small canvas.

"It's really just a hobby," she says, sitting back on the couch. "That one I painted right after I started therapy. My therapist encouraged me to paint what I was feeling after Cody's fall. It really helped me cope with everything."

"You're incredible." The words tumble with honesty from my mouth. It's safe to say I'm falling hard for her. Not only is she beautiful, but she's kind, patient, funny, nurturing, loving, and smart. She is every good adjective there ever was, and I'm just me.

She swallows hard and sits in the recliner, so I take the couch.

It's clear why someone like her could barely tolerate me for so long. I used to think we could never be more because I'd fuck it up and risk damaging our friend group, but the reality is that she is so far out of my league we aren't even in the same universe. She deserves a smart, successful doctor— someone who has a job that helps people and knows her brother needs his chicken cut up. Not the nepo baby who wishes he could own a bar and likes to party.

No, the best I'm going to be able to do is be her friend, and given how fast she moved away from the couch when our legs brushed earlier, I know she thinks it too. The realization hits me straight in the chest. She's too good for me, and I wish so badly I could be the man she deserves.

"Is art something you get to do a lot in your job?" I ask.

"Not a lot," she says, her face falling a little. "But, as the activities director, I get to do all sorts of things with the residents who live there, and some of that is art." There is no enthusiasm in her voice, no joy. It's such a stark difference to when she told me about the brain injury camps in the car.

"Do you like it?"

"Being the activities director?" She pulls her legs to her chest and covers herself with a chunky, crocheted quilt. "It pays the bills, and helps me save for what I really want to do, so I'm thankful to have a job."

"You don't have to be like that with me?"

"Like what?"

"You don't have to pretend to like your job, or like you have everything together. We're friends. If you hate your job, you can just say it."

"Okay," she hesitates. "I guess the truth is I don't love it, and I wish there was a way I could make my dreams happen sooner. Just not for me, but for my brother too. But there isn't, and as much as that sucks, I know I gotta keep pushing forward, and even if it takes me ten years, I'll get there one day."

"You're incredible."

"You keep saying that."

Her eyes shift to mine. The room is mostly dark, other than the glow from the TV and a couple of lamps.

"Well, it's because you are."

A small smile breaks across her face. "So if we're being truthful...do you really want to be CEO of your family's company?"

I let out a groan, sinking back into the couch, crossing my ankle over the opposite knee.

"No, I told you, so now you have to tell me," she presses.

"I don't know."

"What does that mean?"

I pause for a moment, swallowing hard. "My whole life I've never been good enough for my dad. He had this picture of what the perfect little family would be like—two kids, a boy and a girl. They had my brother first, and Mitch is everything my dad could want in a son. But, then they had me, and I messed up the little perfect family image they were going for. So, they tried for a third baby until they got Bella, and of course she's everything he ever wanted in a daughter. I've just always wanted him to be proud of me being his son, and it's never happened."

"Is that why you're working yourself to death for this job? Because you think that'll make him proud?"

"Yes and no. When he found out Mitch was leaving, he was so pissed. I was planning on telling him that night that I was leaving Austere to buy the bar, but then Mitch and his wife, Farah, said they were moving, and everything went to shit. He told me Mitch was his only choice for CEO, and it hurt."

Wren stands and moves over to the couch. She sits down in the other corner, pulling her legs to her chest.

"Go on," she encourages, her eyes finding mine and putting me a little more at ease.

"I knew they hadn't been including me in meetings, but something about him not even considering me when I'm a Mitchell too...hurt. I challenged him on it, and then the next thing I knew, I was wrapped up in trying to become the next CEO." I shake my head. "I'm so out of my depth with it though, and he makes sure I remember that every chance he gets."

"Then buy the bar, and let your dad appoint someone else. It's taken a lot of therapy for me to realize that, some-times, you have to put yourself first. I still struggle with it, so I get it, but you should do the thing that makes you happy."

"If I leave now, it'll be my fault that the company is no longer run by a Mitchell. I know it sounds dumb, but that's all my great grandfather and my grandfather ever wanted. I always let people down, and I can't do that this time."

She begins to scoot toward me, and I feel my stomach flip with anticipation. Her eyes find mine again.

"What are you doing," I ask.

"Moving closer to you because I want to make sure you hear me. Now give me your hand."

My heart knocks against my ribcage, and it's so loud I wouldn't doubt if she could hear it too. She takes my hand in hers, and I do my best to play it cool, but fuck, it's hard.

Breathe, man. This isn't that big of a deal. It's just your dream girl,who is also your friend, and she's holding your hand. This is cool. You can be cool. JUST BE FUCKING COOL!

"You keep telling me I'm incredible, and I think you need to start telling yourself. I've seen you with Jacks and Logan. Hell, you offered me the spare room for free and filled your apartment pantry with all my favorite snacks. You're an amazing friend, and we're all so lucky to have you in our lives. If your dad can't see that, then it's his loss. You deserve to be happy, Tanner. We all do."

"Wren. Cody. We're home," her mom calls from the door. She releases my hand the minute she hears her name, and I start breathing again.

"We're in here," she yells, popping up from the couch.

Her parents walk into the living room, holding hands. "Thanks again for tonight, honey," her mom says.

"Don't mention it. We had fun. Right, T?"

"Oh, yeah. Cody's awesome. Dinner was great, Charlotte. Thank you."

"Oh, it was nothing." Charlotte smiles. Her dad takes a seat in the recliner, and her mom sits in his lap.

"Here," I offer, standing from the couch. "I can move so that one of you can sit."

"No need," she says, warmly. "We might be getting old, but I can still sit with my husband. You kids take the sofa."

Wren and I both sit down.

"So, Tanner, what are your intentions with my daughter?" Paul asks.

Oh nothing, just to spend the rest of my life wishing I was the man she was meant to be with and that I was worthy of her love.

"Dad!" Wren practically shouts. "We're just roommates. Can you please chill?"

He chuckles loudly. "I'm only joking, sweetheart," he says, smiling in her direction. "But seriously, what are your intentions?" He turns back towards me.

"I promise I only have good intentions." I laugh, putting my arms up in defense. He seems nice enough, but the look he's throwing my way does scare me a little.

"And what do you do for a living?" he asks.

"Dad!" Wren turns her head towards me. "You don't have to answer him. This isn't an interrogation."

"It's fine," I laugh. "I'm an executive vice president at Austere Development Group, so I manage the acquisition and development of properties around the Southeast."

"Impressive. A job like that must bring in quite a bit of money, so why do you need a roommate?"

"Do *not* answer him," Wren says.

"I do make pretty decent money, and technically I don't *need* a roommate, but Wren and I are good friends. I happen to be the guy at fault for her needing a place to live, so I offered her my spare bedroom until she could find a decent place to stay."

Her father studies me, and sweat breaks across my brow.

"Interesting. Well, she means a lot to us, so I hope you can understand my hesitation when it comes to her living with an older man."

"Oh, my god. Mom, make him stop. Dad, Tanner is my friend, and we've been over this. He's not that much older than me. The plan is for me to stay with him for a few months, and then I'll be on my way."

My heart sinks at the mention of her plan again, and I remind myself she deserves more than me and that the plan is what's best for her.

"It's okay," I assure her. "Yes, sir, but I promise, I have nothing but the best intentions. Like Wren said, we're friends. She's welcome to stay with me as long as she needs."

"Good," he says. "She's very special, so—"

"Tanner, are you a baseball fan?" Charlotte asks, cutting off her husband. "Paul is a huge Atlanta fan. Have you ever been to a game?"

"Yes, ma'am. My company actually has box seats. I know we're not in baseball season, but if you ever want to go to a game, I'd be happy to get you the company tickets."

"Really?" Paul asks, a little surprised. "I'd love that. I used to have season tickets, but then Cody had his accident, and it was hard to make it to the stadium. So now I catch every televised game right here in this chair." He pats the leather armrest.

I can't imagine how much their lives have changed over the last few years, and despite it all, they seem so positive, still so in love.

"You just let Wren know, and I'll see what I can do. The box is handicap accessible, so if Cody wanted to join, he'd be more than welcome."

"Oh, he'd love that," Charlotte says through a yawn. She quickly covers her mouth with her hand. "I'm sorry. I'm so tired these days," she explains.

"We probably should head out, anyway. We both have work tomorrow," Wren says, standing to walk over and hug both of her parents. "I put Cody's iPad on the charger, so he'll have it in the morning, and Tanner cleaned the kitchen, so you wouldn't have to worry about it."

"Thank you," her mom says. "And thank you, Tanner. It was really nice to meet you. Wasn't it, honey." She elbows Paul in the chest.

"Oh, yes," he coughs out. "Very nice to meet you."

"Nice to meet y'all too." I shake her dad's hand, and her mom wraps me in a hug.

After we find our shoes and our things, the two of us head out of the house toward the car.

"You want me to drive?" I ask. "You seem tired."

"I can drive," she argues.

"You really are stubborn as hell."

"Am not!"

"Oh yeah, then let me drive you home. You did most of the heavy lifting in there tonight. I don't mind."

"If you insist," she says, tossing me her keys.

"What's this green ribbon for?" I ask, gesturing to the metal keychain hanging off her car key.

"It's for traumatic brain injury awareness," she says as we climb in the car. "March is brain injury awareness month, and every year my family raises money. Last year we sold the keychains. If you look closely, *Team Cody* is engraved on the ribbon."

"That's cool. Do y'all raise a lot of money usually?" I ask, backing out of the driveway.

"It depends on the year, but last year we raised, like, five thousand dollars I think. We sell T-shirts and sweatshirts too, and then we participate in this big stroll and roll walk downtown. It's a lot of fun, and Cody loves it."

"I bet he does."

"He seemed to like you too," she says.

"You think?"

"I haven't heard him laugh that much in a while, which is weird because you aren't even that funny."

I chuckle. "I'm a little funny."

She hums under her breath and takes out her phone. Swiping on the screen, she clicks on her playlist and hits play. "Take A Chance On Me" by ABBA pours through the speakers.

"I know he uses the iPad to talk, but does he also sign?" I ask. "I thought I saw him sign to you when you were tucking him into bed."

"Oh, no, not really. I taught him how to sign 'I love you,' but I think it's the only one he knows."

"That's cool. And the cup, spork, and plate. Why does he use those?"

She giggles.

"Sorry if I shouldn't ask. You can tell me to stop."

"No." She smiles. "I like that you're interested. The cup is called a Nosey cup. The rim of it dips lower on one side and makes a space for his nose, so that when he tips it up, he doesn't have to tip his head back. It makes it safer for him to swallow. The plate is built up on the sides, so that his food doesn't slide off when he's trying to put it on the spork, and the spork's handle is built up, so that it's easier for him to hold."

"I had no idea those were things," I say. *God, I sound like an idiot.*

"Adaptive equipment is really cool, and it allows him to feed himself, which is huge for him and my parents."

"I bet. I really enjoyed hanging out with him tonight. Maybe we could do it again. I was serious about the baseball game. No one ever uses the tickets, so they'd be easy to get."

"I'd like that," she says. "Sorry my dad made it so weird at the end."

"He's just protective. I get it."

"Yeah. The last guy I brought home turned out to be a real ass, so I think he's worried I'll get my heart broken again even though I've told him a dozen times you and I are just friends."

Friends. Fuck, I hate that word.

"What happened?"

"Well, his name was Chad, and he and I met at a ladies' night at a bar near Farrington University. He was charming, said all the right things. We never labeled our relationship, but it felt serious, and I thought I loved him." She cringes.

"Anyway, he was with me when I got the call that Cody had fallen. At first he was really supportive, and that made me fall harder for him, but I quickly became a shell of who I once was. I was juggling helping my parents with Cody, trying to finish school, and my relationship with Chad, and I was so tired all of the time."

"That sounds really hard. I'm sure you were doing your best."

"I was trying, but you can't pour from an empty cup. I didn't see myself doing it at the time, but I was isolating myself, and had pushed all of my friends away. Chad and I stopped having sex, and I was just going through the motions of everything. The day he broke up with me, I had fallen asleep at a red light on the way to his house."

"Did you get hurt?"

"No, thank goodness. By some miracle, my foot stayed on the brake and I didn't wreck, but it shook me pretty hard. I had been running errands all morning for my mom and had stayed up late the night before studying. I was just exhausted."

"So why did y'all break up?"

"Let's see, I think he told me that I was 'a real bummer,' and I was 'bringing down his college experience.'" She makes little air quotes as she talks. "He admitted to cheating on me and said he didn't want to be a shitty person, but he never wanted to be serious with me and was only sticking around because he felt bad about my brother."

My hands tighten on the steering wheel, blood starting to run hot.

"What a fucking dick."

"Oh, it got worse," she says. "He blamed me for the cheating, saying that he had needs and that I was too tired to fuck him, so he had no other choice but to look elsewhere. And when I reminded him that he had told me he loved me, he gaslighted me and convinced me that I was crazy and he had never said those words."

My hands grip the steering wheel tighter.

"What a piece of shit."

"Yeah, it's okay. I realize now that he did me favor that day. While he was an ass, the break up pushed me to start seeing a therapist, and without therapy I would still be living at home, and I would have never met the girls."

"That might be true, but nothing he said was okay."

"Oh, yeah, I know that. I just meant, I'm better off without him. He was a total playboy who didn't believe in serious relationships, and he took advantage of me being overwhelmed by everything I had going on."

A playboy like me.

"And you haven't dated anyone since?"

"Here and there, but nothing serious. I know my parents won't be able to help Cody forever, and one day I'll be his primary caregiver. Well, me and whoever I end up with."

"How do you feel about that?"

"Honored," she says, smiling. "I would do anything in the world for my brother, and I know I have to find someone who feels the same way. Primary caregiver is a big ask for someone who isn't a parent or a sibling, but Cody and I are a package deal. Finding someone who accepts us both is non-negotiable."

"You really are amazing," I say.

"So you've said. Do you have any relationship horror stories?" she asks.

"Oh, um, no," I answer her, suddenly even more unsure of myself. "I guess serious relationships have never been my thing."

The word playboy flashes in my head again.

"They're not for everyone," she says.

"I'm not like him," I say without thinking.

"Like who?"

"Your ex. You called him a playboy, and I know that's how I seem to be, but I would never treat someone the way he treated you." I pull back into the parking lot of the apartment complex and park her car next to mine.

She unbuckles then turns to face me. "I know you're not," she says.

I look at her, a little unsure.

"You promise?"

"Swear it. I'm quickly learning you're one of the good ones," she says. "You're gonna make someone really lucky one day."

I inhale deeply. At least she doesn't think I'm a piece of shit, but it's clear she doesn't think she's that girl, and I can't say that I blame her.

We make our way back to the apartment in silence. She unlocks the door and pushes it open. Dolly jumps off the couch and greets us with a loud meow and a big stretch.

"Do you want to watch a movie or something?" I ask, gesturing towards the TV. "We never did finish *Iron Man*."

"Actually, I think I might get ready for bed and read a little before I fall asleep. I'm wiped."

"Oh, yeah," I fake a yawn and stretch my arms above my head. "Me too."

"You're going to read before bed?"

"Oh, no," I laugh out. "Going to bed sounds like a good plan. Night, roomie." I begin to walk toward my bedroom door.

"Hey, Tanner."

"Yeah?" I stop and look over my shoulder.

"Thanks for coming today. It meant a lot to me."

"Thanks for letting me come," I say as she disappears into her room.

Hey

GRAY:

Hi?

I have a question

GRAY:

Not sure I have an answer, but hit me!

What kind of lift does Wren's brother use

CHAPTER 22: PLEASE WITHHOLD YOUR JUDGMENT
WREN

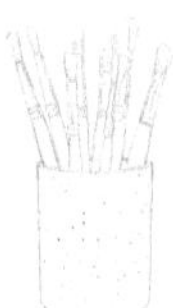

Sorry we missed each other last night. Can't wait for roomie night tonight!
- T

<<Picture of the note attached>>

So what are we doing tonight for roomie night?

TANNER :

Morning roomie

TANNER :

Since we went out last week do you want to just order take-out and chill at the apartment

TANNER 🐴:

Maybe play a game

Perfect!

TANNER 🐴:

Great I'm looking forward to it

Me too!

TANNER 🐴:

If you haven't made your coffee yet try the caramel and the mocha creamer mixed with a dash of amaretto

TANNER 🐴:

Tastes like a chocolate turtle

I open the fridge and pull out all three creamers he suggested as well as the carafe of cold brew. Following his instructions, I craft my drink, give it a stir, and then take a sip.

Damn it's good.

It's delicious!

TANNER 🐴:

Told you

TANNER 🐴:

Gotta go meet with my dad 😋

Good luck! See you later!

———

6:03 pm

TANNER 🐴:

Hey roomie

> Hi! You almost here? I'm hungry.

TANNER 🐴:

Actually I'm still at the office

I check the time.

> Oh!? Is everything okay?

TANNER 🐴:

Great actually

TANNER 🐴:

It's a long story but my dad invited me to dinner tonight which is big and I think I need to go

> Dinner?

TANNER 🐴:

I know we had plans and I promise to make it up to you but can I get a rain check on our roomie night

> Of course! See you later!

TANNER 🐴:

You're the best

Three dots appear and then disappear, and my heart sinks.

I set my phone down and let my head fall back on the sofa. Dolly walks out of my bedroom and the little bell on her collar catches my attention. She pauses to extend her paws forward in a big stretch and then continues to walk towards me.

"Tanner has a work thing, so I guess it's just you and me

tonight," I say, tapping the cushion next to me, encouraging her to join me. "How does a girls' night sound?"

She lets out a small howl and sits.

"What? You don't like my girls' night idea?"

She howls again, but this time it almost sounds more like a long whine, and I let out a giggle.

"That's a new sound. Are you upset that he had to work?"

She meows, almost in response.

"I know. I'm bummed too, baby girl," I say, my breath catching at my own admission.

Her head tips to the right like she's studying me.

"Don't look at me like that. That's not what I meant." I stand and start pacing. "Or is it what I meant? I don't know, Dolls, I just feel like after he met Cody a couple of nights ago, something shifted, and I know that sounds a little crazy, and I know I shouldn't be feeling like this, but if I'm honest, I was really looking forward to hanging out with him tonight."

I look at my cat like she holds all the answers, but she just flops down onto her back and starts to rub against the carpet.

"Goodness, I'm talking to you like you're an actual human and not a cat." I chuckle, running my hands through my hair. "I need to pull myself together."

She meows again.

"Now you say something," I say, shaking my head and giggling.

I wish she did have all the answers, or at least could help me process the feelings I'm having. Because the truth is, I don't know what to think about Tanner anymore. I've only been living here one and a half weeks, and I was sure by now there would have been multiple women to and from his bedroom. But instead, it's been sticky notes, doodles, coffee creamer recipes, comic book collections, and him taking the time to get to know me and my brother. The only woman who's been in this apartment has been me, which is not what I expected at all.

Then there is the problem of the butterflies I've been feeling. The butterflies that have no business making an appearance because I know guys like Tanner. Or at least I thought I did, but now I'm not so sure.

I told him at my parents' that I thought he was incredible, and I wasn't lying. He absolutely blew me away that night, and I know Poppy had a lot to do with how the night with my brother unfolded, but she didn't give that information to him randomly. No, he took the time to seek her out, and all it did was turn me into the human version of the heart-eye emoji.

I really thought I had better control of my emotions, but alas I'm a weak bitch, and it appears that all it takes is one night of him being absolutely amazing for me to melt like a goddamn piece of chocolate.

Since I've met him, he was firmly in the *cute, but a playboy* camp, and now he's crossing lines into the *cute and sweet* camp, and I know I need it to stop before I do something reckless and stupid, but despite it all, I can feel the crush forming, and I'm not sure what to do about any of it.

All day I could feel myself feeling giddy about getting to come back to the apartment, ordering take-out, and spending time with him.

And now I don't know how I feel about the plans changing. I'm not sad, but I'm definitely not happy either. I guess I'm bummed and totally in my head.

I walk into my room and grab the new paperback I started a couple of days ago off my air mattress. A distraction is just what I need. Especially if that distraction is an epic fantasy that has nothing to do with the reality I'm currently living.

Turning to where I left off, I plop back on to the couch and scan the words.

"His long blond hair blew in the wind…"

Tanner immediately pops into my head, and I throw the book to the other side of the room, letting out a little squeal and making Dolly jump. Nope. I'm not about to sit here and dream up images of him as the main character in the book I'm reading.

He's my roommate. Crush or no crush or maybe crush or whatever this is, I should be able to get through a task without thinking about him. It's not that serious.

I consider texting Gray or one of the other girls, but deep down I know they'll just egg this on, and that's not what I need. What I need is a distraction, so I turn on the TV instead and start flipping through the channels.

Wedding Crashers comes into view on the screen, and I breathe out. This is good. This is better. No way a movie this silly will make me think about the roommate I shouldn't be thinking about.

I settle into the couch, trying to relax. The blond male character's face pops up on the screen, and all I can think about is Tanner's smile. *Shit.*

I change the channel.

Fast and the Furious.

And again.

The Princess Bride.

And again.

Barbie.

Does he have some type of subscription to blond actors unlimited on this fucking thing?

The next channel is on a commercial, so I wait a few seconds to see what's playing—and groan when I realize it's *Thor: Ragnarok.*

Is this a fucking joke?

I try one more time and am pleasantly surprised when I stop on a rerun of *New Girl.* This is good. This is just about four roommates and will make me laugh. There are no blond characters in this show.

It takes all of three minutes for me to realize what episode I'm watching, and I quickly turn the channel right as Nick and Jess meet in the hallway and kiss.

"That definitely didn't make me think of kissing my room-mate," I say out loud.

Because a thought like that would be certifiable.

Dolly meows and jumps on to the couch next to me. Her blue eyes pierce through me.

"What? Now you're judging me? I said I'm definitely *not* thinking about kissing Tanner."

She meows again, tilting her head.

"Would you please stop looking at me?"

It's not like I'm thinking about what his lips would feel like or what he would taste like.

I pop off the sofa and move toward my bedroom. Those butterflies return, but this time they aren't in my stomach—they're lower. I breathe out an annoyed breath. No way in hell I'm actually turned on right now.

Slamming my door behind me, I begin to pace my room.

"Just because you're horny doesn't mean it has anything to do with anything other than the fact that it's been a while since you've had an orgasm," I say to myself. Pausing, I try to count the days since I last made myself come. "That's it. This has nothing to do with Tanner and everything to do with the fact that it's been three weeks since I masturbated."

I open the bottom drawer of my nightstand, looking at my toys. I have a few, but I know my wand will get me there the quickest, and then whatever this feeling is will be out of my system.

Checking the time, I climb into bed and pull off my shorts and thong. Tanner won't be back for a while, so I should have no problem finishing without getting caught.

Breathing out, I try to relax and clear my mind. Starting on the lowest vibration, I press the head against my clit.

This is nice. This feels good. This is what I needed.

I up the vibrations a couple of levels and begin to circle my bundle of nerves, applying a little bit more pressure.

Warmth pools low in my belly, and I can feel myself winding tighter by the second.

My head falls back, and my eyes shut, but instead of darkness, all I can see is Tanner. My thoughts begin to run wild, and I couldn't stop them if I wanted to.

I imagine what it would be like for him to touch me. What it would be like for him to watch me pleasuring myself like this. I wonder if he would like it, or if he would join me and want to play with me too.

Tension builds deep in my core with every thought. I imagine his large hands cupping my breasts and his tongue trailing down my body.

God, I want to feel his mouth on me.

I up the vibration one more time, grinding into the head of the toy, thinking about what it would feel like for him to fill me. One hand holds the toy firmly in place against my clit, and my other grips the sheets under me.

I continue to thrust my hips upward, the vibrations threatening to carry me over the edge, and then I find my release, riding out the waves of my orgasm with Tanner's name on my lips.

Fuck. I guess that didn't work the way I had planned.

Tossing the vibrator next to me, I run my hands down my face in a slow movement. This isn't good. I can't believe I…no way I…fuck, I just got off thinking about my roommate who is supposed to be absolutely nothing more than a friend.

I kick my feet and thrash against the mattress, letting out another "fuck" before swinging my feet over the edge and standing.

I get dressed and walk back into the living room, nervously checking my phone. Dolly sits in the corner of the room, and I feel my cheeks heat. There's no way she doesn't know what I just did, and if I thought I wasn't sure what to think before, I definitely don't know what to think now.

"Please withhold your judgment."

She stretches then rolls onto her back, meowing loudly.

My mind is going in three thousand directions as I walk into the kitchen to find some food. I open the pantry and begin digging around, looking for something to make for dinner that doesn't require use of the stove, but the pantry is a mess and it's hard to find anything.

Settling for a bag of tortilla chips and some salsa from the fridge, I begin to snack and try to quiet my mind.

Just because you thought about him doesn't mean you want anything to happen. It just means...well, fuck, I actually I don't know what it means.

Without thinking, I start removing all of the items from the pantry shelves and place them on the counter. I might be a fucking mess, but I'll be damned if I go to bed tonight with the pantry being one too.

CHAPTER 23: YOU'RE GOING TO NEED MORE BUTTER

TANNER

At nine, I pull into my parking spot, and I'm surprised to see lights coming from the apartment. Sliding out of the car, I notice I feel a little lighter, and for the first time since I agreed to be CEO, I don't feel entirely miserable about the idea.

"Wren?" I call, walking through the door. Dolly jumps off the couch to greet me, and some One Direction song is blaring. "Wren? You still up?"

A loud bang comes from the kitchen, and I walk towards the sound, fully expecting to catch her trying to cook again, but instead I'm met with a huge mess and my very disheveled, but adorable, looking roommate. Every inch of the kitchen counters are covered with the entire contents of our pantry.

She's holding a can of corn wearing tiny shorts that show off her toned legs and an oversized T-shirt. Her hair is pulled up into a bun on the top of her head, but it's messier than usual—little bits of her hair sticking out in every direction.

Even like this, she's absolutely stunning.

She sets the can on one of the shelves, mumbles something under her breath, and then pulls it back out and studies it.

I lower the music and clear my throat. Her eyes shift in my direction.

"You okay?" I chuckle.

"Oh, um, yeah. Why?"

"Whatcha doing?"

"Well, I was bored, and so I started organizing the pantry, and at first I thought I should do it alphabetically, but then I thought maybe color-coded made more sense, but now I'm wondering if it should be by category. What do you think?"

"I think you need to step away from the canned goods," I say, walking towards her and grabbing the corn. Our hands brush against each other, causing her eyes to shift upward and her mouth to part slightly. There's a weird moment where the air almost cracks around us, and then she takes a step back, giggling nervously.

"You sure you're okay?" I ask, setting the can down on a pantry shelf.

"Oh, yeah. Definitely good. Cool as a cucumber. Why?"

"Because you appear to be stress-organizing the pantry." My eyes survey the kitchen counters again, and I stop a laugh from breaking free.

"Oh, no. I guess the change of plans just kinda threw me, and I wasn't sure what to do, so I decided to be productive."

"The change of plans threw you?" I lean against the counter top, crossing my arms.

"Well, no, that's not what I meant. I just meant that I wasn't sure what to do since our plans changed."

"I didn't know roomie nights meant that much to you." I smirk.

"They don't...I mean, they're fun, but I'm not stressed about it or anything. I was just bored."

"If you say so." I lift one of my eyebrows, and her brow furrows. "Did you have a good day?"

"It was fine," she says, moving past me and back into the

living room. I follow her and watch as she walks across the room and picks a paperback book off the ground.

"How'd that end up over there?" I ask.

"Oh, um, Dolly must've carried it in here."

"Did Dolly become a large dog while I was at dinner?" I chuckle, leaning up against the wall.

Her cheeks blush, and my heart jumps in my chest at the thought that maybe roomie nights do mean more to her than I thought they did.

She sits down on the couch and opens the book. Wrinkles form across her forehead, and she scrunches her nose.

Man, she's cute when she's flustered.

After a minute, she puts the book down and looks over at me.

"Why are you staring at me?"

"No reason. So, what else did you do tonight?"

Her eyes shift to her open bedroom door and then back to me.

"Just read, watched a little TV, and then tried to organize the pantry."

"Is that all?"

"Yes," she says, panicked. "Why would you think I did anything else?"

"Chill," I say. "You didn't mention dinner. Did you eat?"

"Oh, yeah. I had some chips and salsa."

"That's not dinner."

She shrugs. "I didn't trust myself with the stove."

"Get up," I say.

"What?"

"Get up. *We're* going to make you dinner."

She stands hesitantly then walks toward me. "We are?"

"Yes, I'm going to teach you how to make yourself dinner because chips and salsa are not a meal."

I turn and walk back into the kitchen to start clearing a small space on the counter, so we have a place to work.

"I can do that," she says, following after me.

"We can organize the pantry later. Now, *we* are going to make you a grilled cheese."

"Grilled cheese? Is that supposed to be more nourishing than chips and salsa?"

"Anything would be more nourishing than chips and salsa."

"Not true. Salsa is essentially fruits and vegetables."

"True, but grilled cheese is delicious. Have you ever made one?"

She shakes her head, and her cheeks turn pink.

"Okay, grab some bread, butter, and cheese. The more types of cheese the better," I say, taking out a pan from one of the cabinets, setting it on the stove-top, and turning the burner on. She collects the items and sets them down on the counter. I smile when I see she pulled out cheddar, gouda, and pepper jack.

"What's the first step?" she asks.

"Take out a slice of bread and then put butter on one side."

She follows my instructions, spreading a thin layer of butter over one slice.

I chuckle.

"What?" She smiles.

"You're going to need more butter."

"More?"

I nod. She adds more to the slice, smoothing it over the surface. "Good, now place it butter-side down on the pan, and be careful because the burner is on."

She does, and the butter sizzles against the hot surface. I continue walking her through the steps until the entire sandwich is constructed and it's ready to flip.

"Okay, this is the fun part. Pick up the pan, flick your wrist, and flip the sandwich over to the other side."

"Ha!" she laughs. "You really think I can flip a sandwich in a pan? I'm the world's worst cook."

"What if I help you?"

"What do you mean help—" I move behind her, and she holds her breath. Taking one of her hands, I lead it to the handle of the pan, and we both grab on. She peers over her shoulder, her cherry and vanilla scent filling my senses, and I do my best to play it cool, but on the inside my heart rails against my ribcage.

"We're going to pick up the pan and flick our wrists upward. If we do it right, the sandwich will flip and land on the other side in the pan." I'm trying to keep my breaths steady, and even though I've done this a dozen times, I really hope I don't mess it up and ruin her dinner. "You ready?"

She nods, and we pop the pan upward, flipping the sandwich perfectly.

"Oh, my god! We did it," she squeals.

We set the pan down, and she twirls to face me. There are mere inches between us, and I don't know what I'm doing. She's too good for me, and so, despite the urge to close the space between us, I take a step backward.

"Told you we make a good team," I say, running my hand through my hair and clearing my throat. "So anyway, you let that go for a minute or two, and then it'll be ready to eat."

She nods and turns back around to watch it cook. I move to the kitchen table, trying to shake the feeling that being so close to her left me with.

Pull it together.

"So, how was dinner?" she asks, plating the sandwich.

"Surprisingly, it went well," I explain. "I finally met with my dad today, and he actually liked my new proposal for the Cedar Hill project. He said it had promise, which I never thought I hear him say, and he wanted to go to dinner to talk more about the CEO role."

"That's good." She takes a seat across from me.

"It's really good. I wasn't sure what I was going to do after he bailed last Wednesday, but I think I'm doing the right thing and that he is starting to see that I can be the CEO." I can feel myself smiling as I talk.

"That's amazing. I knew he'd like it."

"I honestly can't believe it. Never in thirty years has he become remotely close to saying he was proud of me, and he said it showed a lot of promise. Which feels kind of like he was proud of me, right?"

"I think so." She blows on the sandwich, and my eyes lock on her lips. My cock twitches below my pants, and I shift in my seat.

She tries a bite, and a smile erupts across her face. "Wow, this is so good."

"Told you. The secret is multiple types of cheese and extra butter."

"Thank you for teaching me how to make it."

"Any time."

She starts to say something but stops herself and takes another bite of her food instead.

"What is it?" I ask.

"I was just thinking about your dad and the dinner." She pauses. "Are you really sure you want to be CEO? Like I know you're feeling good about it after today, but is it going to make you happy?"

"Yeah, I think so. I've waited so long for him to be proud of me, and the fact that I finally did it feels really good. I know my granddad would've wanted this, so it feels like the right move."

"I know. I just can't shake the feeling that you'd be really good at the bar. I'd hate to see you give something like that up."

The Local flickers in the back of my mind, and for a split second I wonder if she's right, if I'd be happier there, but then I push it away.

"How was work?"

"What?" she asks, quirking her head to the side. "Come on. We're not talking about my work. We're talking about you."

"I don't want to talk about me. I'd rather hear about your day."

She exhales. "It was fine, I guess. No one really showed up to my art group, which sucked, but chair yoga had a big crowd, and I had lunch with the girls."

"That's cool y'all are all so close and work together."

"Yeah, sometimes I think they're the only reason I'm still there."

Thoughts about funding her camp idea circle my brain, and I have to stop myself from saying anything. No way she'd ever let me help her.

"You know, *you* could work with people you're close with if you bought the bar," she says.

"Wren..." I pause. "Maybe you're right, but I think today was a turning point, and the CEO gig is the better option."

"If you say so," she says.

I'm surprised when she doesn't say more, and despite the meeting with my dad and the dinner, I'm still not one hundred percent sure I'm making the right choice. What I do know is I'm more sure than I was yesterday, and that has to mean something.

She finishes the rest of her sandwich, and when she's done, she walks her plate to the sink. "I think I'm going to head to bed," she says.

"Okay. Yeah, I'm pretty tired too."

I walk her to her door, and we both pause outside her bedroom. "Thanks again for the cooking lesson," she says. Dolly runs between us and jumps on the bed. My eyes follow the cat and land on Wren's vibrator laying on the mattress.

So, is that what she did while I was gone?

She must see it too, because she quickly moves into her

room, sits on the bed, and throws the blanket over it. Blush covers her face, and she clears her throat. "Okay, well… night."

I hold back a laugh and have to force myself to look away from where I know the toy is sitting. "Night, Wren," I say, turning and moving to my room. I can't help but wonder who she thought about when she made herself come, and how I would give anything in the world to see her fall apart like that.

I run my hand down my face, shutting my door behind me.

While my head seems to know I can't have her, it appears my dick still hasn't gotten the memo.

Looking down, I adjust my erection, and then I do what I know I shouldn't. I move into my bathroom and turn on the shower.

Undressing and stepping inside, the warm water runs over me as I stroke myself to thoughts of my roommate making herself come. The vision is hot as shit, and in no time my cum paints the tile wall in front of me as I find my release and breathe out *her* name.

CHAPTER 24: BEST SEX OF MY LIFE LEVEL LOUD MOANING
WREN

The past week and a half, Tanner and I have fallen into a comfortable rhythm. His work schedule has gotten a little more consistent now that his dad appears to be coming around to him taking over, so most nights we've spent time together cooking and getting to know one another better.

I can feel us growing closer, and despite my one mild lapse of judgment with my vibrator, it feels like he's turning into my best friend, and I feel bad that I judged him so harshly at the beginning of our friendship.

Every so often, though, something deep in my gut makes me think that what's happening is more than just friendship, like missing him when we aren't together or the fact that I've saved every one of his notes and doodles, and they currently are all living in my bedside table drawer.

Both of which I don't have the energy to dissect today because I'm ninety three percent sure my uterus is holding miniature knives and alternating between stabbing itself and my back.

A loud knock on the door causes Dolly to stir and press her paws against my back.

"What?" I groan.

"It's me," Tanner says through the door. "I was wondering if you wanted to come play pickleball with me, Logan, and Enzo. We need a fourth."

"Donovan isn't going?"

"No, he's showing a house. Are you okay? You sound like shit."

"I'm fine, just slowly dying."

"Wait, what?" He pushes the door open without warning, and his face falls when he sees me. "You look pitiful. Are you sick?"

"No, I'll be fine."

He walks in and sits on the edge of the mattress, causing the air to shift under his weight.

"Tanner, what are you—"

"Would you relax? I'm just checking your temperature." He places the back of his hand to my forehead. "You don't feel warm, but you look like you feel terrible. Can I get you anything?"

"Of course I don't feel warm. It's just my period," I say without thinking. My cheeks heat as soon as the words leave my mouth. "Sorry if that was TMI."

He laughs. "I don't care. Why don't I make you some food and then we can hang out the rest of the day?"

"I'm not very hungry, but coffee sounds good, and I think there are a couple more Almond Joys in the pantry."

"It's three o'clock in the afternoon. You sure you just want coffee and chocolate"

"Don't judge my decisions," I scold.

"Coffee and chocolate it is."

"What about your pickleball game?"

"Oh, they'll be fine. It was an odd number anyway, so they can play without me," he smiles.

"I might be a minute," I say.

"Take all the time you need. I'm gonna go call Logan and make your coffee. Do you have a creamer preference?"

"The recipe from Thursday. It tasted like an Almond Joy."

"On it," he says, leaving my room and shutting the door behind him.

Our conversation doesn't completely register until he's disappeared. Him cancelling his game to hang with me is completely normal friend behavior? Right? Right. RIGHT?

I throw the blankets off of me, wincing as I crawl out of the bed towards the bathroom. After brushing through my hair and putting on different sweats, I walk back into my room.

"Shit," I mutter under my breath when I see a little red stain on my sheets. Exhaling, I quickly gather the linens and wad them up in my arms before walking out into the living room. Dolly follows behind me, and I laugh to myself when she runs over and pounces on a little spot of sunlight shining on the floor.

Tanner's on the phone, so I quietly walk by him, heading to the laundry room to start a wash for my sheets.

"Here's your coffee, and there was only one Almond Joy left, but I can order more," he says from the laundry room door a few moments later.

"You don't have to be so nice to me," I say, taking the drink and the little candy bar. I pop the chocolate into my mouth.

"Someone's crabby," he says, chuckling. "I'm never not going to be nice to you. You're one of my favorite people."

"I am?"

His eyes widen. "Yeah, I think you might be becoming my best friend. Just don't tell Logan or Jacks because they'd be really upset to know they've been replaced." One side of his mouth curves into a lazy grin, and my eyes shift nervously, trying to land on anything but him, but I fail.

Of course he meant best friend. What else would that have meant?

"I'm gonna go get my heating pad, and then maybe we can watch a movie?" I ask.

"Sure. What do you want to watch?"

"The Princess Diaries," I say, sheepishly. "It's my comfort movie, and if I had a TV in my room, it's what I would be watching today."

"I've never seen it, but I'm game," he says, turning and walking back towards the TV. I follow him through the kitchen and then head to my room to grab my phone, heating pad, and pillow. Dolly runs in behind me, almost knocking me over, and jumps onto the bed trying to reach a small spot of light shining on the wall behind the mattress.

"Dolly, careful," I snap.

She jumps up and swats at the wall then lands back on the mattress.

"Come on, girl; get down. You're gonna pop it."

She jumps up again, and this time I swear I hear the smallest burst of air when her paws hit the mattress. I gently grab her, put her on the ground, and inspect where she landed. Maybe it was just in my head.

"I got the movie queued up," Tanner yells from the living room.

"Coming," I shout, walking out of my room and closing the door to keep Dolly off my makeshift bed. "Goodness, she's obsessed with those little bits of light. You should've seen her jumping on the air mattress to catch one on the wall in my room."

"When I was a kid, we had a dog that would stare at them." He chuckles.

"Thanks again for the coffee," I say, plugging in the heating pad and then curling up on one end of the couch. "The way I made it was good, but this is delicious." I take a long sip. The chocolate and coconut swirls across my tongue, and I let out a little moan.

"I'm glad you like it," he says, swiping on his phone screen. He sets his phone down and then leans back onto his side of the couch. "Okay, so what is this movie about again?"

"Am I really about to take your *Princess Diaries* virginity?"

"Is that a thing?"

"It's most definitely a thing, and I can't spoil it for you. It's a canon event. You're just going to have to watch and find out what happens."

"And you like to call me insufferable," he laughs.

I kick out my leg and playfully shove him with my foot. "Stop making me laugh. My uterus can't laugh today. It hurts too bad."

"Shhhhh," he teases. "The movie is starting."

Dolly jumps up and curls into the back of my legs right as "Supergirl" begins to play. I do my best to get comfortable, but it's no use. I know it has to be incredibly distracting and annoying, but I can't stop tossing or turning. This fucking couch is really the worst thing in the entire world, and it's exponentially worse with cramps.

"You good over there?" Tanner asks, lifting an eyebrow.

I shift again, and Dolly jumps down. I'm annoying the cat. I definitely have to be annoying him.

"Yeah, sorry. I just can't get comfortable. My back is killing me, and I know I pretended like your couch was great for days when I first moved in, but it's actually terrible."

He lets out a laugh. "So stubborn." He shakes his head. "You slept on my couch for almost a week and refused to sleep in my bed when you were miserable. I knew it."

"No, you didn't."

"It's my couch. I know it sucks, and I'm quickly learning you'd rather be miserable than have someone else be miserable."

It feels like he cut me open with one observation.

"I just didn't want to disrupt your sleep because you took pity on me and let me move in."

"You're confirming my point," he says, smirking.

"Ugh. You're insufferable." I kick out my foot again, catching his thigh. "You are the one who knowingly let me sleep on your uncomfortable couch for almost a week."

He puts his hands up. "Hey, I tried to give you my bed, but you refused more than once. Speaking of beds, where is your new mattress?"

"Ugh, I know. I checked this morning and it's still in transit. I keep hoping it'll just show up and the tracking is wrong." I sit up and shift the heating pad from my stomach to my back. "Goodness, I wish I had two of these things."

He grabs his phone, and taps on the screen.

"What are you doing?"

"Texting Logan. Why?"

"Oh, nothing. Sorry, it's none of my business."

"Is there anything I can do to make it feel better?" he asks, setting his phone back on the arm of the sofa.

"Unless you have some magic cure for back pain, then no, but thanks."

"I could give you a massage," he says.

"*Shut! Up!*" Mia Thermopolis shouts on the television screen, almost in response.

Took the words out of my mouth, Mia.

My head flips toward him, and he's just sitting there with his goofy smile, shrugging.

"What did you say?"

"A massage? I'm not trying to be weird or whatever you're thinking. I just figured a back rub might help you feel better."

"Oh, right, yeah of course that's what you meant. I knew that, but you don't have to."

"Wren, I really don't mind. Come on, let me make you feel

good." His voice is a little gravely—sexy even—and my mind shifts to a place it shouldn't.

"Make me feel good?" I repeat a little breathless as blush creeps up my neck and paints my face.

"Shit, well I just meant, like, massages feel good," he clarifies. "Do you want one or not?"

"Yeah, a massage would be great," I say, turning so I'm facing away from him. I move my hair out of the way and feel his body close in behind me.

His hands squeeze my shoulders and begin to move down my back. "Where does it hurt?" he asks.

"It's my lower back," I say, swallowing hard.

This doesn't feel like a massage from a friend, and, fuck, I should move away. I really should move away, but despite my better judgment, I like the effect it's having, and I don't want him to stop.

"Is this okay?" he asks, his hands gliding downward and across the small of my back, relieving some of the tension that's there.

"Yeah," I say.

"Good…if it's too much or whatever, you can tell me to stop."

"No, it's perfect." I let my body relax, and he continues to rub up and down, applying the perfect amount of pressure. His hands feel huge, and I know there's a sweatshirt between us, but everywhere he touches, my skin ignites. He rubs along my lower back again, and his fingers trail the hem of sweatpants.

I let out a loud moan and immediately cover my mouth with my hand.

Shit. Shit. SHIT.

His hands freeze, and I don't move. He clears his throat and jumps up so quickly that I don't know if I'll ever be able to face him again. His bedroom door closes behind me, and I let my hand fall from my face.

Grabbing for my phone, I swipe up.

The Tortured Therapists Department

I think I fucked up.

LACEY:

What happened?

Have y'all ever gotten a back massage from a friend?

GRAY:

No. Why?

Because I'm on my fucking period and miserable, and Tanner offered to massage my back as a friend, and I agreed, but it felt so good, and then I moaned.

POPPY:

You moaned?

I moaned. Like loud. Like best sex of my life level loud moaning.

GRAY:

I'm dead. 💀

This isn't funny. I'm in the middle of a crisis.

LACEY:

What did he do?

He stopped, and now he's in his room.

Should I knock or something? Or just wait for him to come out?

POPPY:

All the massages Logan gives me have a happy ending, so I guess it depends if you want yours to have a happy ending or not 🙈

I can't sleep with him. It was just a minor lapse of judgment.

LACEY:

Jace just asked if I was okay because I'm laughing so hard.

Don't you dare tell the boys about this.

What do I do?

CHLOE:

Sorry I was changing Ava, but I just caught up.

CHLOE:

Maybe he needed a minute. I'm sure it's fine.

POPPY:

I vote you listen to your body. If you're moaning just from a massage, imagine what else he could do!

GRAY:

Orgasms do help with cramps.

We're done here.

CHAPTER 25: MAGNUM TAMPONS
TANNER

A fucking massage. What was I thinking? I shut my bedroom door behind me and look down at the raging boner pushing against my sweatpants.

Fuck.

I should have stopped it the minute I told her I wanted to make her feel good, but I didn't. She was hurting, and despite telling myself for weeks that she deserves better than me and trying my best to maintain physical distance between us since I fucked my palm to the thought of her pleasuring herself, I just couldn't stop myself from trying to make her pain go away.

She's moaned before, but that moan? That moan changed something in my DNA, and now that I've heard it, I'll never be the same.

I strip my clothes, and my dick springs free. Checking the temperature of the water, I step into the shower. For a split second, I consider using my hand again to put me out of my misery, but when I close my eyes, my brain is flooded with visions of Wren, and I know I shouldn't. Not again. Not now. She probably already thinks I'm a freak for running away like I did. I don't need her accidentally overhearing me jacking off after I was just massaging her. No, that would be terrible. I slam the handle to cold and turn the water to ice.

Quickly, I get dressed again and dry my hair with a towel. When I walk out, she's laying on the couch watching the movie.

"Did you shower?" she asks, confused.

"Oh…yeah." Shit, I didn't think that through at all. "I, uh, I remembered I forgot to take one this morning after the gym, so I took a quick one. Felt like I stunk."

Felt like I stunk? Smooth.

"You're so weird," she laughs. "You want me to rewind the movie?"

"Sure." I join her back on the couch, and she grabs the remote. "Hey, I'm sorry if the massage was too much earlier. I didn't mean to bail like that when you, um…"

"Moaned," she laughs, her cheeks turning a soft shade of pink. "You have no reason to be sorry. The massage was really nice. My moan was weird."

Your moan was hot.

We both laugh nervously, and she lays down on the other side of the couch, beginning to rewind the movie.

"So, we're good?" I ask, trying to relax into the cushions.

"Yeah, we're good."

The movie begins again, and I do my best to focus on the TV, but my mind keeps wandering to places it shouldn't. We are friends. She is my temporary roommate. I shouldn't be staring at her, and I shouldn't have touched her, but damn I liked it.

For the next hour and a half, we watch the movie, and the only sound that fills the apartment is the sound of our laughter.

"I think I might go jump in the shower, see if it makes me feel better," she says once the credits roll.

"That's fine. I'll be out here. You getting hungry?"

"Starving."

"Then we'll eat when you're done." I check my phone, and it looks like the grocery delivery I ordered is five minutes away. While I wait, I move Wren's sheets into the dryer, and then once the groceries have been delivered, I collect the bags from the front step and begin working on our dinner.

I'm blending all of the ingredients together with an immersion blender when I hear her bathroom door open.

"Whatcha cookin'?" she asks, appearing in the entrance to the kitchen a minute later.

"Carrot and ginger soup. I read online that ginger can help cramps, so I figured it might help you feel better."

Her mouth parts in surprise. "You're making me ginger soup to help with my cramps?"

"Well, I don't actually know if it will, but I thought it was worth a shot. Are you feeling any better?"

"Kinda. The shower helped, but I'm still a little crampy." She rubs her hand along her midriff.

Her eyes find the pile of grocery bags on the kitchen table. "What's all this?" she asks, gesturing to them.

"It's all for you. I ordered it at the start of the movie and it was delivered while you were in the shower."

She starts to sort through the bags, and I try to stir the soup, but I can't take my eyes off of her. She's in pink sweats, and her hair is pulled back with one of those clippy things girls wear. She's so pretty.

"You got all of this for me?" she asks, digging through a bag full of Almond Joys, electrolyte packets, and pain medicine.

"Yeah, I wasn't sure what you needed, so I just got everything I could think of or could find online."

She opens a different bag, and a laugh bubbles out of her. "How many tampons do you think I need?" She gestures to the three boxes on the table. "Oh, my god, and they're all super pluses."

"I wasn't sure which ones to buy, so I got the ones with the best rating." I shrug, and my cheeks heat.

I have a sister, but she's younger than me, and I wasn't really raised in the type of household that discussed periods with the boys. It's safe to say I have no idea what I'm doing when it comes to this stuff, but I'm trying.

"Best rating?" she asks.

"Yeah, the store had regular, super, and super plus, so I got you the super plus because they're the best ones right? Like the plus means they're better than super."

"No." She cringes. "It's the size. Super plus means, like, extra-large."

"Oh, like condoms? Did I buy you magnum tampons?" My eyes widen.

"No, not like condoms. I meant the absorption, not the size. You know what, it doesn't matter. Thank you for the tampons." She giggles.

"I got you pads and one of those cup things too."

More laughter erupts from her. "Stop it. This is actually adorable." I beam at her compliment. She digs in another bag and pulls out a heating pad.

"Wait, you knew I already had one of these. Why did you buy another one?"

"When we were on the couch, you said you wished you had two, so I added it to the order."

She places it back on the table and walks over to where I stand.

"Thank you," she says, wrapping her arms around me and squeezing tight. "For taking such good care of me today. I'm not used to being the one who gets taken care of, and it means a lot that you would do all of this for me."

I slowly let go of the spoon and wrap my arms around her too. Inhaling deeply, my nostrils fill with cherries and vanilla, and we both let the hug linger longer than we should. Her head nestles into my chest, and my hands gently rub along her spine.

Dolly pushes herself between our legs, forcing us to break the embrace.

"I think she's jealous," Wren says. "She really likes you."

"Is it so hard to believe that I'm likeable?"

"No, I'd say that it's becoming very easy to believe," she says.

Blush covers both our faces, and as much as I wish I could grab her and kiss her, I know I can't. The timer on the microwave sounds.

"Soup's done," I say.

"Good. I'm so hungry."

We work together cleaning off the table and collecting everything we need for dinner. When we're done, we both sit down.

"What did you think of the movie?" she asks, blowing on a spoonful of soup.

"I loved it."

"You loved it?" she asks.

"Yeah, it was a really good movie. I was surprised too, but I'd watch it again."

Mostly because I was completely distracted by her, and don't remember most of it.

She giggles. "You know there's a sequel?"

"A sequel," I gasp. "Well, I know what we're doing the rest of the night."

She shakes her head and takes another bite of soup. "This is delicious," she says. "Thank you. Soup is just what I needed."

"It's not bad, is it? I was a little nervous about the carrots, but it turned out pretty good."

"It turned out very good."

We both take a couple more bites of food, and my eyes find hers. She's breathtakingly beautiful, and after the massage and that hug, I just want to hold her again, even if it's a bad idea.

"Will you dance with me?" I ask.

"What?" She giggles. "Right now?"

Grabbing my phone, I search for the song I want and tap play. "Miracles Happen" by Myra begins to play over the speaker in the kitchen. "Come on, dance with me? I think I read that exercise was good for cramps, so dancing should help."

I stand and walk towards her. Taking both her hands in mine, I pull her into the standing position.

"Tanner!" She giggles as I start swaying her from side to side with me.

"Please," I beg, giving her big puppy dog eyes. "I danced with you in the Waffle House. The least you can do is dance with me in the privacy of our apartment."

She exhales and starts to dance along to the music. The beat picks up, and I pull her away from the table and twirl her, causing her to squeal. For the next few minutes, we dance. Happiness radiates from her, and everytime she laughs, I do the same.

As the song starts to fade, I twirl her once more and then dip her. Our faces are a hair's breadth apart, and we both hesitate for a split second. The air crackles between us, and then she stands abruptly and steps away from me. Her chest rises and falls with heavy breaths, and I wonder if there is a chance she felt what I did.

I clear my throat. "We should probably finish eating before it gets cold."

"Yeah," she says, nodding. "Right, before it gets cold." We both sit down at the table.

We finish eating and work together cleaning the kitchen mostly in silence, and I wonder what's going through her head. Once we're done, she runs to the bathroom, and I get the movie set up.

"You're gonna love this one," she says, walking back into the living room.

"More than the first one?" I question.

"I think it's really good." She sits on the other side of the couch, and I hit play. She immediately begins to fidget, and I can tell she isn't comfortable again.

"You hurting?" I ask about a quarter way through the movie.

"Oh, um, yeah. More cramps, but it's fine. I think I've just been in the same place for too long."

I grab a throw pillow and set it next to me.

"You want to try turning around, maybe laying this way?"

"Would you mind?"

"No," I say, fluffing the pillow. She turns, removes the clip from her hair, and lays down, the top of her head barely touching the outside of my thigh. Within minutes, she sits up.

"Is it not comfortable?"

"Would it be weird if I put the pillow in your lap, so I could stretch out a little bit more?"

It's just her head on your lap. It's not her head near your dick.

"Oh, um, sure."

She moves the pillow, and lays her head in my lap.

Calm the fuck down and don't ruin this for yourself. I inhale deeply, trying to regain control of my body.

"You sure this is okay?" she asks, nuzzling against the back of the couch and pulling a blanket over her.

If I didn't know better, I'd think she might be trying to kill me.

"Yep. You good?"

"It's so much better. Thank you."

I try to find a place for my hands, but my options are limited—the back of the couch or her ass. I settle for the back of the couch and continue to try to control my breathing and my cock.

———

"Your Crowning Glory" startles me awake, and when I look around the living room, I realize the movie is over, Wren is asleep in my lap, and my hand found its way to her ass. I carefully stand, trying my best not to wake her as she nestles into the spot where I was just sitting. She's sleeping hard, and I consider for a minute leaving her where she is, but decide a night on my couch with her cramps will just make her feel worse tomorrow.

I gather her sheets out of the dryer and quietly tiptoe across the apartment to her room. Dolly trails at my heels, and when I push the door open, she runs in and jumps on the bed. The whole thing buckles under the small cat's weight, and it's clear it's deflated.

I grab the air pump, and start to try to inflate it. It's working, but it's slow, and I have a bad feeling there's a leak somewhere.

Shit.

I leave the sheets and return to the living room. Carefully picking Wren up, I carry her into my room and lay her in my bed. She surprisingly doesn't stir, and I send a silent thank you to the universe because I know if she woke up, there's no way she'd let me take the couch tonight.

I tuck her in gently, stopping myself from placing a kiss on her forehead. Returning to the couch, I lay down, make sure my alarm is set, and then pull the blanket over me.

Today was a good day. A really fucking good day.

CHAPTER 26: WE DIDN'T CUDDLE
WREN

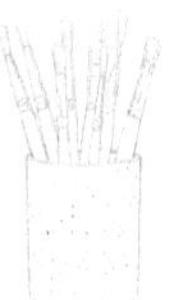

An alarm starts to ring, waking me up. I squint my eyes open and grab for my phone, but there's no sound coming from it. Gosh, is Tanner's alarm really that loud? I let out a groan and nuzzle deeper into the buttery soft comforter covering me. I'm a little surprised by how good I slept last night. I guess when you're tired enough, even an air mattress doesn't suck.

I shoot up in the bed—I'm not on the air mattress.

Blinking, I try to take in my surroundings in the dark room. I'm not in my room. I'm not on the couch. I'm sitting in Tanner's bed. My head flips to the other pillow, but I'm alone and the alarm starts ringing again.

Confused, I get out of his bed and follow the sound.

"Tanner, can you turn that off?" I yell toward my bedroom, still a little disoriented from waking up in his room.

"Morning," he says from the couch, startling me.

"Oh, morning." I flip around. "It sounded like it was coming from my room for a second. I think I'm still half-asleep."

"How'd you sleep?" he asks, rolling his neck from side to

side. He's shirtless, and I try to redirect my gaze, but it's no use. My eyes are drawn to him like moths to a very hot flame.

"Great, actually," my eyes dip down to his abs, and I swear he flexes his muscles just for me. "Why are you on the couch?"

"We both fell asleep before the movie was over. I tried carrying you to your bed, but it was deflated."

"Deflated?" I question.

"Yeah, Dolly jumped on it when I went in to make it, and it folded like a pancake."

"She must have popped it yesterday when she was trying to catch the light. I thought I heard something weird, but I didn't see a hole," I say, yawning and rubbing my eyes. "Goodness, what time is it?"

"Four-thirty," he says.

"Four-thirty?" I groan.

"Yeah, I gotta go to the gym before fighting the Atlanta traffic to get to work."

"Sounds terrible."

"You're welcome to go back to sleep in my room," he offers. "You really can't catch a break with your bed."

"That's okay, I'm up now, so I might as well stay awake."

"Well, if you want to take my bed until the new mattress arrives, you can," he offers.

Now that I've slept in it, it's tempting. His mattress is the perfect firmness. It's not too hot or too cold. The comforter feels expensive, and last night was admittedly the best sleep I've had in a long time. I can't take his bed though. I have yet to repay him for letting me stay here, and stealing his room doesn't exactly scream that I'm thankful for his kindness. "No, I'll figure out the air mattress. Thank you though."

He stands and begins to walk toward his room, invading my space. "You feeling better today?" he asks, stopping right in front of me.

"Much better," I say, smiling up at him. "I think that soup really did the trick."

There's a pause, and tension ripples through the air.

"I'm gonna go get ready to leave," he says, nodding his head in the direction of his door.

"Me too." We start moving toward our rooms at the same time, both taking a step to my right. My body crashes against his bare chest, and I stumble trying to gain control of my footing.

"Shit, sorry," I say, trying to switch directions, but this time we both go left, and our bodies tangle again.

"You trying to run into me, roomie?" He smirks.

"No, uh, I'm—" I try again to move around him, but this time he intentionally steps in my way, laughing. "Tanner! Move!" I yell, and he lets out a loud chuckle as he picks me up and spins me around, placing me on the other side of him. A spark ignites between us, and for a moment we both freeze. His eyes lock on mine, and I swallow hard. He takes a step towards me, causing my breath to catch. My heart rate quickens because, for a split second, it feels like he might kiss me.

The alarm on his phone starts ringing again, interrupting whatever the hell this is.

Kiss me? He was about to kiss me and I wanted him to.

He clears his throat and then takes a couple steps backwards towards his room.

"I'm gonna be late," he says.

"Yeah, me too."

"No, you're not." He laughs. "It's not even five yet, remember?"

"Oh, yeah, right. Thanks again for letting me sleep in your bed last night," I say, awkwardly, trying to look anywhere but the cut lines of his perfectly sculpted abs and think about anything but the almost kiss.

"Any time," he says. His voice is doing that gravely thing again.

"Any time?" I quirk my head. Blush creeps up his cheeks.

"I just meant, like, if you were uncomfortable, then I could sleep on the couch again. Or, like, if the air mattress doesn't work out or whatever."

I giggle.

"You know what? Ignore me. I'm gonna go get ready for the gym." He stumbles over his words and then turns to go get ready, and I go to my room because I don't know what else to do with myself.

What in the actual fuck is going on?

I begin to pace the minute my door shuts behind me. I thought I had gotten things under control, but it appears I have not. Two almost kisses in less than twenty-four hours.

Does that mean he likes me too?

No, that's impossible. Maybe it's just flirting or something else. I don't know, but I do know that it's hot.

Shit.

Need pulses through my body, and those fucking butterflies return between my legs, so I wait until the front door closes, grab my wand, and I repeat what I did a week and a half ago because, god dammit, how else is a girl supposed to pass the time or process her feelings?

———

On my drive to work, I replay yesterday and this morning, and I don't know what to make of any of it. When I got into the kitchen, there was another post-it note and doodle stuck to the fridge. In the doodle, the animals were wearing crowns —no doubt a nod to the movies we watched yesterday.

Glad you got some rest. See you tonight.
— T.

I must be temporarily insane because I have no idea what we're doing—or rather what I'm doing. He's just being himself—his flirty, goofy self—and I can feel myself crushing harder by the minute. I try to shake the thought as I walk into Dogwood Manor, but it's no use.

I quickly move to my office, shutting the door behind me. I need to talk to someone and process what the hell is going on.

The Tortured Therapists Department

SOS! Are any of you not working yet?

POPPY:

I'm just walking in. What's up?

I need advice. Can you come to my office?

POPPY:

On my way!

LACEY:

Advice on what?

GRAY:

Yeah, everything okay?

Tanner 🙈

CHLOE:

Tanner?

LACEY:

Tanner?

GRAY:

Tanner?

Y'all are hilarious.

There's a small tap on my door, and Poppy appears holding an extra large cup of coffee. "What's up, babe?" she asks, walking in.

"I don't know." I let my face fall into my hands.

"Did he do something?" she asks, hesitantly.

"Oh, no. I mean yes, but nothing bad. It's all really sweet."

"What do you mean?"

"Let's see, yesterday I felt like actual garbage."

"Right. You texted. He massaged your back. You moaned. Oh, my god, did you sleep with him?"

"No. He just hung out with me all afternoon watching *The Princess Diaries*. And then he bought me all of these period supplies, cooked me dinner, and then when I fell asleep in his lap, he carried me to his bed, and he slept on the couch."

"Is that all?" she asks, giggling.

"Oh, and he danced with me. I forgot that one."

She giggles again.

"It's confusing right?"

"What's confusing? It sounds like he's being really sweet, and you like one another."

"Because I'm all up in my feelings about it and he keeps not wearing his shirt and we almost kissed last night and then again this morning."

"He almost kissed you?" She plops down into one of the chairs in front of my desk. "Twice?"

"Yes."

"And how do you feel about that?"

Blush covers my cheeks as I think back to how I used by vibrator this morning.

"Why are you blushing?"

"If I tell you, it has to stay between us."

"I'm listening." She leans forward, propping her chin on her fist.

"I may have…" My voice drops to a barely whisper. "I may have used my vibrator after."

Her coffee almost sprays from her mouth.

"Stop!" I whine. "I feel like I'm teetering on the edge and playing with fire. I said I wouldn't fall for him, and here I am melting and thinking about him every time I make myself come."

"Oh, fuck. You do like him."

"He's our friend. Of course I like him."

"No, that's not what I meant. Like, you want to fuck him."

"I do not."

"I think your vibrator would have a different opinion."

"I don't know. Yes. No. Maybe. That's absurd. We're roommates, and I'm just falling for his playboy charm, right?" I sip my iced coffee.

She shrugs. "Sounds like it's more than just playboy charm. That's what gets a girl into bed for a one night stand, and that is not what is happening here. He's buying you period supplies, cuddling you on the couch, and cooking you dinner. It's charming, but I don't think that's his playboy charm. I think it's really sweet, and he really likes you."

"We didn't cuddle. He just let me lay on his lap because I couldn't get comfortable."

"Right, and Logan just lets me suck his dick because I like the way it feels on my tongue." She giggles.

"Jesus, Poppy, we're at work."

"No one can hear me." She sips her coffee and looks over her shoulder to see if anyone is nearby. "I'm just saying that men don't usually let their friends lay in their lap, and I'm not grabbing my vibrator and thinking about any of our friends while I use it."

My phone chimes again.

LACEY:

Hello?????

GRAY:

Do not leave us hanging like this.

CHLOE:

What's going on with Tanner?

"Would it be so bad if something happened between you two?" she asks.

"I don't know, but the last time I let myself fall for someone, it ended so badly. And I know he's not Chad, but I don't want to be hurt again. He's being nice, and that's what friends do. Maybe it's just my hormones and the fact that I haven't had sex in awhile."

"Maybe, but he's never done any of that nice stuff for any of us."

"True, but y'all have never lived with him. Ugh. What am I going to do?"

"Do you want Logan to talk to him and see where his head is at?"

"No. I don't need the boys knowing. I'll figure it out. I'm sure I'm just overthinking it."

"I personally think y'all would make a really cute couple."

A cute couple?

My face heats and I divert my eyes away from my friend.

"You do like him," she says. "You're blushing again. It's okay to admit it."

"But is it crazy? I haven't even been living with him for a month."

She shrugs. "Things happened fast for Logan and me too. I think you had a certain image of him in your head, and he's proving you wrong. Has he had a girl over since you moved in?"

"No."

"I don't know how he's feeling, but you should stop freaking out. Just see where things go, and have fun."

"Maybe you're right."

"I usually am," she teases, standing. "I hope I helped. I think it's all going to work out, and if you change your mind, I know Logan wouldn't mind chatting with him."

"Thanks, girl!" I say, as she turns and disappears into the hall.

Exhaling, I sip the last bit of my iced coffee. Maybe Poppy's right. Maybe I'm not misreading things, and he likes me too.

My heart rate quickens at the thought, and I nervously suck on the straw making the little remaining liquid bubble around the ice at the bottom of the cup.

Now, if only I had the courage to tell him how I was feeling.

CHAPTER 27: OH SHIT!
IT HAPPENED AGAIN
TANNER

"Wren, you here?" I call from the door, carrying two large pies from Bruno's Pizzeria. Tonight is our one month roomie-versary, so we decided to move our usual weekly roomie night to Monday.

The past week I've been working late, and she's been busy, so our hangouts were rare. I've missed spending time with her, but I've also been in my head about what I think were two almost kisses.

On the one hand, it felt like she wanted me to kiss her. But, on the other hand, it's me and her, and if I did read that situation correctly, I must've entered into the twilight zone.

When we did see each other over the last week, she felt a little distant, so I also don't know what to make of that.

"In here," she calls from her room.

I set the pizza on the coffee table and walk to her door. "Can I come in?" I ask, knocking gently.

"Sure," she says.

I open the door and find her on all fours on top of her deflated mattress. Her ass is pushed into the air, and I have to divert my gaze.

"What are you doing?" I ask.

"The mattress deflated again, so I'm just replacing the tape."

"Replacing the tape?"

She looks over her shoulder. "Yeah, I found the hole, so I put a piece of tape over it last Monday, and it was working, but then this morning I woke up and it was deflated again, so I'm fixing it."

"You've been sleeping on a deflated mattress that you fixed with tape for a week?"

She turns back around and rips a piece of tape with her teeth, carefully pressing it over the plastic mattress.

"Yep. I haven't been on the couch. Did you think I was sleeping on the floor?" She stands, setting the tape on her bedside table.

"No, I thought you bought another air mattress."

"Why would I have done that?"

I rub my temples. "Because it popped, and they're not that expensive."

"Just because something isn't expensive doesn't mean you should spend money on it," she chimes, pushing past me and out of her room. "Come on. I'm starving!"

"If I had known you were sleeping on a damaged mattress, I would have—" I begin following her back into the living room.

"Would've what? Bought me one?" she asks, shaking her head. "I'm the one who owes you. I don't need you to buy me a mattress. The real one arrived at a different shipping facility today, so I think it's finally starting to move and will be here soon. The tape is fine until it gets here."

I shake my head and rub my hand down my face. I wish she would just let me help her.

"So, what's the game plan for our roomie-versary?" she asks, grabbing a slice of pizza.

"Well, I thought I'd make us a little cocktail and then we could watch a movie."

"I'm cool with that. What do you want to watch?"

"Maybe something for Halloween," I suggest.

"Okay, but not too scary. I don't do super scary movies."

"Have you ever seen *Zombieland?*" I grab the remote and toss it towards her. "It's not scary. It's funny, and the zombies kinda fit the October vibe."

"Okay." She grabs the remote with her free hand. "What streaming service is it on?"

"Oh, you don't have to worry about that. Just click on the Moviez4Zer0 app, and you can literally watch anything you want."

"Moviez4zer0 app?"

"Yeah." She turns the TV on. "You haven't been using it?"

"No, I typically just watch cable."

"Oh, well it's the first one right there," I say, pointing.

"Oh, my god! You pirate movies?"

"Huh?"

She puts down her slice of pizza on top of the box and turns to face me. "This is an app for pirated movies. Is it not?"

I shrug. "I guess, but it's free and they literally have anything and everything you could want on there."

"Tanner, this is so bad. It's stealing."

"Is it?"

"Yes."

"I've never really thought about it. It's free, and those streaming apps really add up." I try to explain, but even I can hear how bad it sounds.

She rubs her eyes. "You were just giving me so much shit for taping my air mattress, and you're over here with this seventy-five inch, high definition, fancy ass TV and a trust fund, and you can't be bothered to pay for a movie." She bursts out laughing. "God, the irony."

"You didn't seem to care the other day when we watched your movies on it."

"Because I didn't know!"

"How about this? If you buy a new air mattress, then I will look into paying for one or two apps and delete the free one."

She rolls her eyes. "And what about tonight?" she asks.

"Are you sleeping on the taped up mattress tonight or are you going to take my bed and let me sleep on the couch?"

"I'm sleeping in my room. Also, my mattress and your thievery are two totally different things," she quips.

"My thievery?"

"Yes, I can't believe I'm living with a common criminal. You think you know a person, and then he shocks you with some horrible admission. I could have you arrested for this."

"You want to see me in handcuffs, Wren? Because I think we could arrange that without calling the police." I lean my shoulder against the wall, tipping my lips up to a smirk.

Fuck, what am I doing? And is it just me, or does that look on her face mean she's thinking about it?

My cock strains below my boxers at the thought of her locking me up and having her way with me.

"Insufferable," she teases.

"One more movie, and then I promise I'll put all my bad boy ways behind me."

"Fine, but I'm not going to like it."

"What, me being a good boy? Or the movie?" I flirt, testing the waters to see where she goes with it.

"The movie," she deadpans, scrolling through the app and obviously not interested.

Damn. I'm definitely misreading all this and I need to stop because of course this is all in my head.

When she gets to *Zombieland*, she selects the movie and then pauses the start of it. "So what cocktail are we having tonight?"

"I'll come up with something," I say, popping off the wall and moving into the kitchen. I gather cranberry juice, Grand Marnier, cream of coconut, a lime, some coconut shavings, and marshmallow fluff. "You like coconut rum?" I ask.

"Yeah, that sounds good," she calls back.

After I rim our glasses with marshmallow fluff and coconut flakes, I fill a shaker with each ingredient. I can't help but notice how at ease I feel. I wish the job at Austere allowed me to be a little creative. The Local flashes in my head, and I remind myself I really should call Jerry. Putting it off any longer isn't going to make it easier, and he's been kind enough to give me more than enough time to make a decision. I pour the light pink mixture over some crushed ice and carry them out into the living room. For something I made on the fly, I'm pretty proud of it.

"That's pretty," she says, standing to meet me. "What is it?"

"I'm calling it a sno-ball," I say, handing her one. "It's a nod to one of my favorite scenes in the movie."

"The stolen movie?"

"Stop, I'm actually starting to feel bad."

"Good," she says, nudging me with her elbow. We both sit on the couch, and I grab a slice of pizza. The movie starts, and I honestly forgot how gory it was, but thankfully she doesn't seem to mind.

"You excited for Halloween next week?" I ask. "Feels like forever since the whole group has been together. It should be fun."

"Definitely." She sips her drink. "Wow, this is delicious."

"The recipe was easy. I can teach you how to make it if you want?"

"I'd like that," she says, her lips curling upward. "So what did you decide to dress up as?"

"It's a surprise."

She tilts her head. "Come on. I'll tell you what I'm wearing, if you tell me what you're wearing."

"Not a chance," I tease. "But you could tell me yours?"

"No way I'm telling you mine." She shakes her head. "Fair's fair."

"Can I get a hint?"

"Can I?" she asks, tipping the corner of her mouth into a sexy grin.

"No."

"Then no." She turns back to the TV and laughs at the movie.

We both sit there in silence, watching the screen. It's a good movie, funnier than I remember it being, but my mind keeps wandering to The Local, and I wish it would stop.

"I've been thinking about the camps you want to open." I say, catching her attention. "Will you tell me more about them?"

Maybe hearing more about her dreams will distract me from mine.

She breathes out a long breath, pulling one of her knees to her chest. "Oh, gosh. They seem like such a far off dream. Right now I'm just focusing on saving money. I'll be lucky if I have them up and running a decade from now."

"You don't think you could do it sooner?"

"I mean, I don't see how. My old landlord was discounting my rent, so I was able to put a little extra money away, and you've been kind enough to let me live here for free, so that's helping me save, but it's still slow."

"Well, you also have all the money you saved from taping your air mattress back together."

She shakes her head.

"Have you ever thought about starting smaller?"

"Not really," she says. "I'd rather it take ten years, and I do it right, then try to do it with less money, and fail. I mean, it's a huge undertaking, and there are so many moving parts and people needed to make something like that work."

"I get that, but what if you started with an art class, and then eventually grew it to an art camp, and then from there you could expand to the overnight camps or whatever you want."

"I hadn't thought of that. It's a good idea, but I don't even know where I'd do an art class." She shrugs. "I'm sure that would take money too. I don't know."

"You're scared?"

"What?" She looks at me. "No, I'm scared of heights. I'm not scared of living out my dreams. I'm just a realist, and I know something like this doesn't happen overnight or with the little bit sitting in my savings account."

My mind starts racing with ideas of how I might be able to help her. I know she'd never take my money, but there might be another way.

"I'll figure it out one day," she says, pushing off the conversation, and I take the hint.

"Did you say you're scared of heights?" I ask.

"Yeah, ever since my brothers fall, I don't go up high."

I internally cringe; of course she's scared of heights. I should've put that together.

"Sorry. I should've known."

"No, don't be sorry. Sometimes it feels irrational because the bad thing didn't happen to me. It happened to him, but I'm just so terrified that I'd fall and get hurt too."

"I think if that had happened to Mitch or Bella, I'd feel the same way."

"I bet you're not scared of anything."

"Spiders," I say, chuckling.

"You—the big, tall, Thor-like man—are scared of spiders?"

"Terrified. Anything creepy crawly really."

"But they're small. How could you be scared of something so tiny?"

"Are you saying you're not scared of spiders?"

"Yes."

I look at her, shocked, and my face heats.

"I don't think I've ever met another human who isn't

afraid of them. You should've seen Jacks and me trying to kill one when he was living here. We ended up trapping it under a bowl and scooting it all the way across the apartment until we got to the door. I swung the door open, and he kicked the bowl outside, and we didn't bring it in for, like, three days."

"Men are such babies," she laughs. "I promise to take care of all the spiders. Just call my name, and I'll protect you."

"I'm going to hold you to that."

A loud moan comes from the TV, catching both of our attention.

Two people, who are definitely not actors in the movie, are on the screen. The man is leaned up against a wall, and the woman is on her knees, completely naked, sucking his dick.

"Oh, shit, it happened again," I laugh.

"Happened again?" She cuts her eyes in my direction. "What do you mean it happened again?"

"Yeah, occasionally something like this will pop up in the middle of a movie on this app. I guess it's the price you pay for it being free." I begin to search the couch for the remote, but I don't see it.

"Something like this? Tanner, this is fucking porn."

"Well, yeah." I shrug. "Do you see the remote?"

"No, I gave it to you."

The camera angle zooms in on the woman's red lips wrapped around the man's cock.

"*That's it, baby; suck my fat cock,*" the actor on the TV says.

"Oh, my god—turn it off," Wren squeals.

"I'm trying, but it would help if you looked for the remote."

She lets out a frustrated huff and starts tossing pillows and blankets onto the floor. "How did you manage to lose the remote?" she shrieks, right as the woman on the screen moans again.

"I didn't lose the remote; you did."

"Not true."

The actors switch positions, so that they're now fucking, and I pause my search.

"Are you watching it?" she shrieks.

"It's actually not that bad. I mean, it's definitely low budget, but I've seen worse."

She lets out another exacerbated breath. "Turn it off!"

I walk over to the TV and search the edge for the power button. "I'm trying, but I can't find the switch."

"Four thousand dollar television and you can't find the power button. Useless. Come help me look."

"*Oh yeah…that's it…*" the woman moans.

I turn and catch Wren watching the TV. "You're giving me shit, but you're into it."

"Am not!"

"You can't look away!" I laugh.

"Not true." She flips back around and throws a couch cushion to the floor, causing Dolly to jump down. "I'm over here sweating and looking for the remote, and you're the one acting like it's just another normal Monday."

"It is a normal Monday."

"There is nothing normal about this."

The moans and slapping of flesh against flesh start to get louder. "Is it getting louder or is it just me?" I ask. Flipping around, I watch as the volume control bar climbs to seventy.

Another moan.

"It's definitely getting louder. I must have thrown a cushion on top of it," she says, frantically moving the cushions spread all over the floor. Dolly lays down, looking upon the chaos unfolding around the living room, completely unbothered.

The volume continues to get louder, not stopping until it hits one hundred.

"Are you stepping on it?" I shout.

"I'd think I'd know if I was stepping on it," she shouts back. "Fuck, is it broken?"

More moans come from the TV, and Wren turns around again and stares.

"You little nympho. You do like it. If you want we could just watch it. I'm sure it's almost over," I say because apparently I can't help myself.

Blush crawls up her neck. "You're unbearable!" she yells.

"There is no shame in liking porn," I yell over the TV.

A loud banging comes from the apartment above us.

"Shit, you think the neighbors think we're doing it?" I laugh.

"No, I don't think they think we're doing it."

There's another loud moan, and then more banging from upstairs.

"They totally think we're doing it," I say, smirking. She chunks a pillow at my head.

"God, where is the fucking remote?" she shouts, grabbing a blanket and tossing it across the room, barely missing Dolly, who jumps out of the way.

The sounds of clapping skin echoes through the apartment.

I bend down on all fours to look under the coffee table, and see something on the other side. Crawling around the base of the table, I continue to check, but Wren must not see that I'm on the ground. At the same time that I reach under the table to grab for what I think is the remote, she steps backwards and trips over my body. I grab for the object, but it's just a cat toy.

"Shit," she yells, as she tumbles to the floor, causing me to lose my balance and fall with her. We both roll to our backs and burst out laughing as another dramatic moan comes through the TV.

"Are you okay?" I ask, turning to face her. There's only a few inches between us, and she looks adorably annoyed with me and the situation. She turns toward me, and her hair covers her face. Without thinking, I move it behind her ear, and her breath catches. Alarm bells start going off in my head, and I'm certain that the look she's giving me is the look of a woman who wants to be kissed.

My body takes over, and I begin to close the gap between us, but before my lips can find hers, she rolls onto her back, and my heart deflates.

"I'm fine," she says, smiling. "This is absurd."

"I think it's pretty funny," I say, trying to shake the feelings I'm having. We both sit up. "Honestly, you have to give it to them. They're still going at it," I laugh again and gesture toward the TV with my hand.

She stands, frustrated, and starts flipping over pillows again. "It has to be here somewhere."

I stand, and grab the blanket. "Found it!" I yell, picking it up and laughing hard.

"I'm coming," the woman says, as the man pumps into her harder.

"For the love of god, use it then," Wren screams. I click the TV off, right as they both climax.

Laughter bubbles out of both of us. "It's a mess in here," she says, looking around the space.

"Hey, at least we found the remote," I shake it in the air and then set it on the table.

"Watching a porno with you tonight was not on my BINGO card," she says, laughing.

"Mine either, but you have to admit it was funny. Do you want to try a different movie?"

"And risk being assaulted by another seventy-five inch dick? No, thank you."

"His dick didn't take up the whole TV."

"Regardless, I've seen enough. Maybe we can just hang out until bed," she says as she giggles.

"I'd like that. Want another drink?"

"Definitely." She hands me her glass, and I stand to walk back into the kitchen as she begins to pick up the living room.

While I craft the drinks, I do my best to sort out all of the mixed signals and conflicted feelings I'm having, but it's no use. My head is telling me I'm not good enough. My heart is so fucking gone for her that I feel pathetic. And my dick gets hard every time I see her.

Finishing the cocktails, I decide it's best to listen to my head because it's not about what I want. It's about what she wants, and what's best for her—*and that's not me.*

The couch is put back together when I emerge from the kitchen. Sitting down next to her, I hand her one of the cocktails and then take a long pull from mine.

"So, where were we before we got interrupted?"

"I was promising to rescue you from any spiders that might find their way into the apartment."

"That's right. What am I ever going to do without you when you move out?" I chuckle.

"Oh, um, I've been meaning to mention that. I haven't started looking for a new place, so I might be here a little longer than I initially planned."

She doesn't look at me when she says it, and hope expands in my chest. I mean, she keeps saying this is temporary, so I fully expected her to pull out a list of potential apartments when I asked that question, but she didn't.

The almost kisses and the shared dances pop back into my head, and my heart rate quickens.

"You haven't?" I ask, a little too excited.

Her eyes find mine, and I want so badly to know what she's thinking.

She opens her mouth to say something but then sips her drink. Our eyes stay locked on each other, and then she clears her throat.

"I've just been busy," she says. "So, I know I was hoping to be out in three months, but it might be closer to six." She shrugs. "I hope that's okay."

"Yeah, of course. You know you're welcome to stay as long as you need."

Busy. Of course it's just because she's busy.

She offers me a hesitant smile. "You want to watch TV? Just regular cable this time, though."

"Sure," I say, grabbing for the remote. "This okay?" I gesture toward the screen where a rerun of *The Office* is playing.

"Perfect," she says, setting her drink down and tucking her knees to her chest.

For the rest of the evening, we watch TV, and I wonder if a universe exists where I'm worthy of her choosing me.

CHAPTER 28: BEST FRIENDS...
TANNER

Today was weird. My dad called around ten this morning to cancel the meeting we were supposed to have. Apparently, golfing with a client was more pressing. He promised to call me after, but I couldn't help but feel uneasy about the whole situation.

Things have been going well the past few weeks since our dinner, but I don't know. Something in his voice made my heart drop, and I haven't been able to shake it all day.

Thank goodness Halloween is tonight, and I get to spend time with Wren and the rest of our friends. A group hangout sounds like just what the doctor ordered, and I'm really looking forward to it.

Closing the door behind me, I walk into the apartment. Dolly runs to greet me, and I bend down to scratch between her ears.

"Is your mama here?" I ask.

She lets out a loud meow then runs toward the kitchen, so I follow her.

"I thought you'd already be with Chloe," I say, as I round the corner to find Wren filling up a glass with water.

"Oh, good—you're here," she chimes. "My mom texted

me half an hour ago and asked that we Facetime them together when you got here, so I've been waiting for you."

"Really?"

"Yeah," she shrugs. "I don't know. Maybe Cody wants to show us his costume or something."

My heart rate picks up as she swipes on the screen of her phone. He definitely wants to show us something, but it's not his costume. I was so distracted by my dad today, that I didn't realize it had been delivered, and I definitely planned on Wren finding out a little differently.

Fuck.

"Hey before you call can we—" I try.

"Hi, sweetheart," Charlotte's voice comes through the phone.

Shit. This is fine. She's not going to be mad.

"Hey, Mom. I've got Tanner with me. What did Cody want to show us?"

I walk over and offer Charlotte a wave over Wren's shoulder.

"Tanner," she smiles. "Oh, good. Let me grab Paul and Cody."

"Mom, what's going on?"

"You don't know?" her mom asks.

"Know what?" Wren's eyes shift to me and then back to the phone screen.

Charlotte flips the camera around. Cody is in his wheelchair with a big grin spread across his face. Next to him is the brand new lift I ordered a month ago. Wren's eyes flare, and Cody begins to type on his speech device.

After a few moments, "Thank you Tanner" comes through the device, and Wren drops the phone.

Without thinking, I pick it up off the floor and smile. "You're welcome, man. Glad it made it."

"You…um…what…" Wren can barely form a sentence as she continues to stare at me completely stunned.

"This was so kind of you," Charlotte says, ignoring Wren's reaction.

"Yes," Paul adds. "I know these things cost a pretty penny, so thank you for this."

"It's my pleasure," I say. "Wren told me the insurance company was giving you a hard time, and I talked to our friend, Gray, who's a PT, so it should be the right one."

"It is," Charlotte says. "We'd love to have you over for dinner to say thank you. Wren, you let me know when you two are free and we'll get it on the calendar. This is just…well, I'm speechless."

"Okay," Wren says, breathless.

"Really, it was nothing. I look forward to dinner. We'll talk soon?" I say.

They nod, and we say our goodbyes. When the call ends, I set the phone down and turn to face Wren.

"Look, I know you probably think I over—" I begin, but she throws her arms around me and squeezes me tight.

"Thank you," she says, her voice cracking. Pulling her into me, I breathe a sigh of relief.

"You aren't mad?"

She pulls away. "Mad? How could I ever be mad at you for such a generous gift. I mean, I know they cost a fortune, but are you kidding me right now?" She wipes the tears running down her cheeks. "I don't know how I'll ever repay you, but I'll try. Thank you." Her arms wrap back around my waist and she nuzzles into my chest.

"You don't have to repay me," I say, hugging her.

She begins to laugh. "No, my mom said dinner and she'll be holding us to that, but I'll think of something. God, you're incredible." Her whole face lights up as she pulls back and looks up at me.

My phone starts to ring, and I pull it out of my pocket. My dad's name flashes across the screen.

"Take it," she says, when I hesitate to answer. "I need to get over to Chloe's anyway. I'll see you at the fair."

"You sure?"

She nods.

Swiping up on the screen, I walk into my room. "Hey, Dad. How was golf?"

"Great. Sorry about the meeting."

"It's fine," I say, the uneasiness I felt earlier returning.

"I actually ran into Stuart Barton today at the club."

"Stuart Barton?"

"Mitch's friend from college."

I know who he is, I'm just confused why he's telling me about it and not Mitch.

"Right. How's Stuart?"

"He's doing well. He's married and his wife is pregnant with their first. He's been up in Chicago for the last few years, but they're planning on moving to Atlanta to be closer to his family."

"That's good, but what's that got to do with me?"

"He's looking for a job, and he approached me today at the club about coming to work for Austere."

"Oh, yeah. I think he'd be a great addition to the team. If he's in town, maybe he can come by tomorrow. I'd love to talk to him. Once I take over as CEO, we will need to fill my position. It could be a good fit."

My dad chuckles. "I agree he'd be a good addition, but I was thinking he may be better suited for CEO."

I physically feel the blood drain from my face. The room starts to spin, and I have to brace myself against my dresser so I don't fall. I set the phone down and hit the speaker button.

"You want Stuart to be CEO?"

"Now before you get all emotional, I know you've been working hard, but I've been thinking a lot lately, and I've had some employee concerns come to my attention about you taking over. The company needs someone who our employees can trust. We are a family company, and Stuart is a family man. He has the experience, and he fits the image that we're known for. I think he's an excellent candidate for the position, and I know this is hard for you to hear, but if you put your feelings aside, I think you'll agree this is for the best."

"I'm responsible." It's a pathetic argument, but it's all I have.

"Our employees need to be able to trust the man leading the company, and it's hard for people to trust someone who is thirty, still single, and has your reputation."

"I've been killing myself trying to earn this position, and you're just gonna give it to the first guy who approaches you at the golf club?"

"Stuart is not some random person. His resume is phenomenal. He's just like your brother, but he will be living in Atlanta."

Just like your brother. My heart sinks into my stomach. How could I be so dense and think he'd ever pick me?

"Okay, I understand."

"Good. Stuart will be coming by tomorrow. I'd like you to be there to meet with him."

"Got it."

He hangs up the phone, and I stumble backward. The back of my knees hit the foot of my bed, and I crumble.

WREN

I didn't mean to eavesdrop on the call, but Tanner's door is wide open, and the apartment isn't very big. My heart breaks for him, and I know he has to be devastated. I wish his dad could see the man I see. The man who continues to blow me away with his kindness.

"Can I come in?" I ask, tapping my fist against the door frame.

"Oh, um, sure," he says. "I thought you were leaving."

"I was going to, but it sounded like you might need me to stay."

His face is painted with disappointment, and all the joy that radiated off of him before the call is gone. He doesn't even look like himself, and I want so badly to make him feel happy. To make him feel seen.

"Dance with me," I say, reaching out and taking his hands.

"I don't want to dance."

"It'll make you feel better. Come on, please." His hands fall out of mine, and his shoulders slump. Grabbing my phone, I swipe through my playlist and put on "Boogie Shoes" by KC And The Sunshine Band. "Come on, dance with me, or I'm going to make you talk about your feelings, which I know you hate." I put my hand out again, and to my surprise, he takes it.

Pulling him to stand, I start swinging his arm, twirling myself underneath it. He shakes his head, and his lips turn slightly upward. He begins to move his feet, and we move around his room. By the end of the song, we're both out of breath, and his smile is back.

"Feel better?" I say, nudging him with my elbow.

"A little," he says. "Thank you." We both sit on the edge of this bed.

"Do you want to talk about it?"

"How much did you hear?" he asks.

"Most of it," I say. "Sorry. I wasn't trying to listen, but then you put it on speaker."

"It's okay…so I guess you heard he's going with someone else?"

"I did." I try thinking of the right words to say, but I don't know what will make it better. "For what it's worth, I think you'd make a good CEO, and I think you're responsible."

He laughs. "You say that to the thirty year old who's never had a serious girlfriend. I should've known this would happen. He's never agreed with my lifestyle choices. Single guy with a playboy reputation doesn't really scream leader of a family-owned company, but I doubt there's anything I could do to change his mind."

"I wish you wouldn't be so hard on yourself."

"How can I not be? I've literally been busting my ass for almost two months. I thought I was finally doing a good job, and then he just pulls the rug out from under me like that. Like I don't matter to him at all. He told me the new guy was just like my brother. Who says that shit to their other son?"

"He shouldn't have said that. It's not fair to compare you to Mitch."

"No, but that's Dad. My whole life I've looked up to both of them and just wanted them to include me, and they never have, and then he invited me to that dinner. He complimented my work, and I know it sounds pathetic, but I thought I'd finally started to earn my seat at the table."

I grab his hands, and his eyes find mine. There's so much sadness behind his baby blues that my heart cracks.

"After Cody's accident, I was really hard on myself too. I would beat myself up for not being able to do it all. Balancing everything and everyone was overwhelming, and no matter how hard I tried, I always came up short somewhere. The guilt tore me apart.

"After Chad dumped me, I started therapy, and it took me a while, but I started to realize I couldn't be the sister, or daughter, or friend I wanted to be if I didn't take care of myself. I know our situations are different, but you're putting all this pressure on yourself to make someone else proud of you, and I don't think it's fair to you. You're incredible, Tanner. I mean, people don't just buy lifts for people they barely know."

"I know you," he says, his eyes finding mine again, causing my stomach to bottom out.

"But you don't know Cody that well, and the lift was for him. Don't sell yourself short. Your dad fucked up, but maybe it needed to happen to set you free from whatever family obligation you keep trying to convince yourself you have."

"God, maybe I need therapy," he says.

"There is no shame in asking for help, and I think it would do you good to talk to someone who can help you see yourself the way all of us see you."

"You're right."

I squeeze his hand.

"I'll look into it," he agrees.

"Good. For what it's worth I'm proud of you."

A small smile breaks across his face. "You're a really good friend. Maybe the best ever," he says. "Thanks for trying to cheer me up and listening."

Fuck, I don't want to be friends. I want to pull him to my arms, kiss him, and tell him it's all going to be okay. But it's obvious he doesn't feel the same.

"Best friends," I smile. "Just like the cheetah and the dog." My phone vibrates, stealing my attention. "That's Chloe wondering where I am."

"Yeah," he says, checking the time on his phone. "You should go meet her. I'll see you at the fairgrounds."

"You sure? I can tell her you and I are going together. She'll understand."

"No, I'm going to take a shower and clear my head. Go have fun with her and Ava. I'll be there; don't worry."

We both stand, and I wrap my arms around him, breathing in the mix of woods and amber. Pulling away, I try to shake what I'm feeling, but I can't because no matter how hard I try, it doesn't change the fact that I've fallen hard for Tanner Mitchell.

"You sure you're good?"
"Yeah," he assures me.

267

CHAPTER 29: ARE YOU A SAILOR?
TANNER

I was so close to telling Wren how I felt about her when she grabbed my hands and looked me in the eyes, but I was so afraid that she'd reject me just like my dad did, so like a coward, I didn't say a word. Instead, I told her she was a good friend, and while she is, I want to be so much more than that with her.

The minute she left the apartment, I knew I had made a mistake because she's right. I might think I'm not worth a shit because of my dad, but I think I might mean something to her.

I pull into the fairground parking lot, and it's packed with people there for the event. I almost didn't come because I wasn't sure how I'd push away the feelings my dad left me with, but I know Wren will be here, and I want to be where she is.

Are you here

WREN 🐾:

Almost!

S·H·I·E·L·D·

Here

LOGAN:

We're by the funnel cake stand.

I slide out of my car and head towards the front gate.

"Oh, and a man in uniform," the middle-aged woman running the admission booth says when I walk up to her window. "Are you a sailor?"

"A seaman." I smile, handing her my card and taking my wrist band.

She chuckles. "The wristband gives you unlimited rides all night and admission into the haunted house," she explains, handing back my card.

"Thanks." I scan the crowd, finding the bright yellow funnel cake stand about a hundred yards to my right. Pushing through groups of people dressed in costumes, I quickly move over to where my friends are. Logan is dressed like Clark Kent and is standing next to Poppy, who is dressed like Lois Lane. His shirt is unbuttoned halfway, revealing the Superman logo on his T-shirt. Jacks and Lacey are dressed like Bixito parrots, the bird Jacks re-discovered earlier this year. Their costumes are bright purple and covered in feathers. They look like they're going to Carnival in Brazil. Donovan and Enzo are both dressed in neon roller skating get-ups minus the roller skates.

"I see everyone did a couple's costume," I say, walking up to where they stand. "Who are you two supposed to be?" I ask Enzo.

"We're Ken and Ken," he laughs. "I wanted to wear roller skates, but my husband didn't think they'd let us in."

"Are you a sailor?" Lacey asks, eyeing my costume.

"I'm a seaman. Get it?" I smirk. "Like semen."

"Oh, I get it," she deadpans.

"Did you and Wren coordinate costumes?" Poppy asks.

"No, we kept our costumes a secret from one another," I say. "Why?"

"Oh, I'm not giving away the surprise," she giggles. "She should be here any minute and you can see for yourself."

I nod, looking around the colorful fair. There's a ferris wheel with multi-colored bucket-seats, a tilt-o-whirl, a swing ride, bumper cars, and half a dozen other attractions all adorned with bright lights and colors.

The air smells like fried food and sugar. Music being fed through a speaker competes with screams from the fair goers as the rides flip and drop.

The crowd parts, and Wren appears, dressed like a mermaid. Time seems to still. Her red hair is wavy and falls around her shoulders. She's wearing a shiny green, flowy skirt that looks like a fin, and a purple corset top hugs her figure. The light catches on blue and green jewels on either side of her eyes. She looks stunning.

Any remaining negativity I had from earlier melts away, and as far as I'm concerned, it's just me and her in the world.

She smiles when our eyes meet, and I lift my hand in a wave. Time speeds up again, and she begins to move towards us. She greets the girls first and then stops in front of me.

"You okay?" she asks.

"Much better now," I say. "Ready to have some fun."

A wide grin spreads across her face. She wraps her arms around me, and I pull her close, breathing in the scent of her hair. Her body fits perfectly against mine, just like it did earlier tonight. We stay wrapped up in each other for a few long moments.

Logan clears his throat, causing Wren to pull away. I cut my eyes in his direction, and he gives me a questioning look that says, "*What the fuck was that?*"

"What do y'all want to do first?" Wren asks, turning to face the group.

"Logan said he was gonna win me one of those big stuffed

animals," Poppy says, leaning into her boyfriend. "Y'all want to go play some games?"

"We're in," Jacks says, grabbing Lacey's hand.

"Y'all want to make it more interesting?" I ask.

"What did you have in mind, T?" Donovan asks.

"First person to win a stuffed animal gets to pick what we do next."

"That sounds like fun," Wren says, giggling. "I'm in."

"You know I'm always up for a little friendly competition," Logan says.

"Are there rules?" Lacey asks.

"Let's keep it simple. First one to win a stuffed animal wins. Time starts now," I yell, turning and running toward the row of brightly colored game booths.

"Tanner!" all three girls shout. I look over my shoulder and see all of my friends start sprinting after me. Wren catches up with me first.

"You're going down, roomie," she says. I slow my pace, and she shoots by me, heading straight for the milk jug ring toss. Poppy, Logan, Jace, and Lacey stop at the water gun run. Donovan and Enzo opt to pop balloons with darts at the balloon-a-rama booth. Wren is collecting her rings when I run up next to her.

"You playing?" the carnival game worker asks.

"Yep," I say. He hands me a stack of rings, and Wren cuts her eyes in my direction.

"What are you doing?" she asks.

"Thought you could use some friendly competition."

"Don't you dare distract me," she warns, taking her time setting up her aim for one of the glass milk jugs. "I really want to ride the bumper cars next, and I'm not going to let you keep me from winning."

"Can't perform with an audience?" I ask, right as the ring leaves her hand. It bounces off a bottle and clatters to the ground.

"Stop it," she says, flipping toward me, placing her hands on her hips.

"You see, I really want to ride the pirate ship, so I think I'm going to have to show you how it's done." I confidently throw a ring towards the bottles, and it ricochets off the glass and bounces back towards where we stand.

"Is *that* how it's done?" she asks, giggling. "Because I thought the point was to get the ring on the bottle."

"Ha! It's harder than it looks," I say, throwing another ring, but I miss again. "I'm just warming up. I'll get it."

"Oh, right. I was just warming up too," she says, trying to toss another ring. She comes close, but doesn't make it. "Shit, maybe we should have picked a different game."

"Quitting already," I tease.

"Never," she says.

Ring after ring, we both attempt to hit our target and fail. I'm down to three rings, and it looks like Wren only has two left. I glance toward our friends, and it doesn't look like anyone has lucked into a prize, so there's still time. We both toss a ring at the same time, and they bounce off.

"Dammit," she curses. I watch as she moves her feet and attempts to get into the perfect ring tossing stance. She carefully aims for a bottle in the front and misses.

"Better luck next time," the booth worker says. "Want to play again?"

"No," she says, disappointed. "I think I'm gonna go try the balloon-a-rama game with Donovan and Enzo. Want to come?" She looks at me.

"You aren't gonna watch me win?" I ask. "I have two more rings."

"You could have fifty more rings, and there is no way you'd win," she taunts. "I'm pretty sure it's rigged so that no one wins."

The worker behind the booth snickers at her statement.

"Come on, have a little faith ," I say, throwing a ring. It circles the rim of the jug, and then bounces off.

"See. It's impossible," she says. "Let's go play something else."

"Which one is your favorite?" I ask as she turns to walk away.

"What?" she asks, looking over her shoulder.

"Which stuffed animal is your favorite?" I glance up at the rows of stuffed animals and toys lining the ceiling of the booth.

"What does that matter?" she asks.

"I'm just wondering. Indulge me."

"Um…" She looks up at the display of prizes. "I guess the unicorn or, no, the cheetah," she says, pointing to a little yellow cheetah hanging from the top of the booth. "Yeah, I like her."

Rocking back and forth, I extend my arm in a practicing motion, lining up my aim. I toss the ring, and it connects with the bottle, slipping around the neck.

"No way!" she exclaims. "You won!"

"Winner!" the operator yells, ringing a loud bell.

"I'll take the cheetah," I say, pointing to the one Wren liked. He grabs it down with a long hook and hands it to me.

"Here you go," I say, putting my arm out to hand it to her.

"You won me the cheetah?" she smiles. "Now I feel like I should win you a dog."

"Well, you did say you liked it." I flash her grin, and she takes it from me.

"Thank you."

"What are you going to name her?"

"Goldie."

"Perfect." I smile, slinging my arm around her shoulders. "Come on, I need to gloat that I won the bet, and we have bumper cars to ride."

CHAPTER 30: ARACHNOPHOBIA
WREN

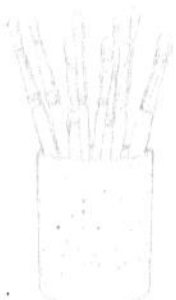

Earlier at the apartment, Tanner called me his friend, but then he won me the little cheetah and picked the bumper cars over the pirate ship. The mixed signals have my head spinning, and the ambiance of the fair is making it worse.

"Y'all want to do the haunted house?" Lacey asks.

"Of course you want to go to the haunted house next," Poppy says. Logan wraps her up in a hug from behind and kisses her on the cheek.

"Come on, Chatterbox, I'll keep you safe," Logan says.

"We're in," Donovan says, grabbing Enzo's hand.

"I'm in," Jacks says, throwing an arm over Lacey's shoulder, pulling her into his side.

"Tanner? Wren? Y'all coming?" Lacey asks, smiling.

I rock back on my heels nervously and look over at Tanner. Haunted houses are kinda like scary movies—I usually do my best to skip them. I'm hoping Tanner remembers our conversation from the other night and will help me bail.

"I'll do it, if you do it," he says, smirking. "Come on, roomie. Let's go."

Asshole. Hot, sweet, incredibly wonderful asshole, but still an asshole.

"I might sit this one out," I say, clutching the cheetah stuffie in my arms.

"Nope," Poppy says. "If my anxious ass has to go in this thing, we're all doing it."

"She makes a fair point," Tanner says, popping cotton candy into his mouth. "Come on. Goldie and I will keep you safe."

"Fine, but the first sighting of a clown with a chainsaw and I'm out."

"Deal," he says. "I doubt it'll be that bad. This is a family fair." He gestures toward a young family with small kids.

Our group begins to head towards the haunted house which is positioned in the back of the fairgrounds. It's a bit of a walk, and we all do our best to maneuver through the crowds and stay together, but it's difficult with the amount of people.

Everyone is paired off, so Tanner hangs back with me. "Cotton candy?" he asks, holding the bag out in my direction.

"Thanks," I say, grabbing a handful.

"Tonight has been fun," he says. "I'm glad we got to hang out. After today, I really needed a fun night."

"I know you did."

The thought of holding his hand crosses my mind as our fingers brush. My eyes find his, and his are looking down at the spot where our hands are barely touching.

"Any ideas of what we should do after the haunted house?" he asks, moving his hand to grab more cotton candy.

"I've been craving a funnel cake since I walked in." I shrug.

"Me too," he agrees. "Is there anything better than fair food?"

"Oh, my god! I love y'all's couple costumes," a girl

around our age, dressed like a cowgirl, says, stopping me with her hand.

"I'm sorry?" I say, a little confused.

"You and your boyfriend," she says, pointing to Tanner. "A mermaid and a sailor is such a cute idea!" she chimes. "Babe, we should have done something like them." She looks toward the man dressed like a cowboy.

"Oh no...this...we're..." I try to explain, but the cowgirl has already gone back to talking to another girl dressed like a witch.

"I guess we do kinda look like a couple," Tanner laughs, giving me a little nudge. My stomach does a somersault. He takes another bite of cotton candy and offers me the bag.

"So, who told you I was going to be a mermaid?" I ask.

"What?"

"The girls knew what my costume was going to be. Which one of them told you?"

"They didn't tell me."

"So, you just happened to be a sailor all on your own?" I question, quirking one of my eyebrows upward.

"First of all, I'm not a sailor. I'm a seaman," he explains. "And, second of all, did you ever consider that maybe we do make a great team, and us unknowingly matching tonight proves it." He smirks.

"They really didn't tell you?"

"Swear it!"

"I guess you're right," I surrender. "Can I ask you a question?"

"Go for it."

"Why didn't you pick the pirate ship ride after you won Goldie?"

"Because I know you're scared of heights, and you said you wanted to do the bumper cars."

I stop walking.

"Why do you keep doing nice things for me?"

"Because you mean a lot to me, and I like doing nice things for you."

My stomach does a swoop, and my heart bangs against my chest. I stare at him, unsure how to respond.

"You can pick your jaw up off the floor," he says. "I know you aren't that surprised. You called me incredible earlier, and I kinda am. That's why I'm forcing you to go into the haunted house with me."

A giggle burst out of me. "Oh? Now you're cocky!"

"Yes. So come on, scaredy cat; let's do it so we can go get a funnel cake."

"I really hate haunted houses," I admit, looking ahead to see that we've been left behind, and our friends are nowhere to be found.

"They're not that bad. Just a bunch of actors dressed up," he assures me.

After a few more yards, we've finished off the cotton candy and the haunted house comes into view.

"Fuck that!" he says, causing a few people to look in our direction.

In front of us is a fifteen foot tall spider at the entrance of the haunted house. Its long legs are sprawled out, and its body is covered in fur and creepy little eyes. Two large fangs jut out of its mouth.

I can't help but burst out laughing.

"I'm not walking under that thing," he says in a panic. "When I heard haunted house, I thought it would be ghosts or zombies. The whole fucking thing is themed to be spiders." He points at the wooden sign to our left. Big, bold letters that read *Arachnophobia* arch over a painting of a man wrapped up in a spider's web. His face is contorted into a scream, and a large hairy spider with fangs sits a few inches away from him on the web ready to make him her prey. It looks like one of those 1950s retro movie posters, and another laugh bubbles out of me.

Haunted house full of ghosts or zombies: No, thank you. I'll pass.

Haunted house full of clowns with chainsaws: Not no, but hell no.

Haunted house full of bugs: Please! I'm sure I've seen scarier things at Dogwood Manor.

"Come on. It won't be that bad," I say. "It's just a bunch of fake bugs and actors dressed up, right?"

"No, it's a bunch of spiders, and I'm not going in."

"You had no problem forcing me to go in there when you thought it could be clowns. You're going in."

"You're right. I was being a total ass. You didn't want to go in, so maybe we should just skip it and go get that funnel cake," he tries.

A group of kids skip by us, laughing and yelling.

"Tanner, those children just went in. Let's go meet up with the rest of the group. Come on."

"Over my dead body am I walking through a spider themed haunted house. You go ahead. I'll be out here when you're all done." He begins to turn to walk away, but I reach out, connecting my hand with his.

"Please come in with me," I beg. "You told me you and Goldie would keep me safe." I wiggle the little yellow cheetah in his direction.

"That was before I knew it was spiders. I wasn't lying when I said I was afraid of them the other night. You wanted to skip, so let's skip it."

"What if I hold your hand the whole time?" I tug him closer, weaving our fingers together.

There must be a part of him that likes my offer because I swear I can see the gears turning in his head as he weighs his options.

"The whole time?" he questions.

"Yes," I say, squeezing his hand gently. "Now, let's go." I begin to pull him towards the door, and he slams his eyes shut as we walk under the giant spider and then into a very dark room.

"I think I'm just going to keep my eyes shut the whole time. You lead the way," he says.

"There's nothing in the room but a black light. You can open your eyes."

"Are you sure?" he asks at the exact moment a brown tarantula looking creature pops out of a hole in the wall, causing me to jump.

"FUCK!" he yells. "That's it. I'm done. Let's turn around."

I squeeze his hand again, and pull him close to me. "I'm right here," I assure him. "And that was just a puppet. Nothing in here is real," I say calmly.

Something falls from the ceiling, and he screams again. "God dammit!" He lunges forward, letting go of my hand, and wraps his arms around me from behind.

"It's just a fake spider," I say, giggling and swatting at the legs hanging from the ceiling. "You can do this. I'm right here."

"You keep saying that, but this is my worst nightmare."

His breaths are panicked, and I know he's scared, but I like the way he feels around my body, and selfishly I don't want him to let me go. I grab both of his arms, and squeeze them around me. "Do I need to hold you?"

"No, but this is nice though. Maybe we can stay like this until we're done."

I shake my head, and my stomach bottoms out. "If it's helping, then I guess it's okay, but I will not be giving you a piggyback ride, so you better keep your feet on the floor."

Another spider jumps through a hole in the wall, causing both of us to jump. "Deal," he says.

I push the next door open, and we enter into a hallway. The black walls are only illuminated by a sporadic strobe light. The sound of bugs crawling is being piped in from every direction. It's disorienting, and I brace myself for the next jumpscare. Tanner tugs me against his chest, and goose-bumps break out down my arms.

"This is creepy as shit," he says as more bug noises start. It's a symphony of clicking and gnawing, and the rubbing of little legs. A group of kids runs past us down the hall, and Tanner screams again, pulling me tighter against him.

"I know you're scared, but I need to be able to walk," I say, giggling. "Can you loosen your grip, scaredy cat?"

"Oh, sorry," he says, letting go of me a little. We finish moving down the hall, and I push open the next door. We enter a dark room that looks like some type of laboratory. Lining the shelves are little jars full of bugs covered in cobwebs and dust.

In the middle of the room stands an actor in a white lab coat, looking at something covered with a sheet on the metal exam table.

"It's alive!" the actor yells, and at the same time, the thing on the table sits up and jumps in our direction. The lights flash, and the sounds being filtered into the room are border-line deranged. Before I can react, Tanner picks me up and throws me over his shoulder. He runs through the next two doors, not stopping until the fair comes back into view.

"Tanner!" I shriek. "Put me down."

"What the fuck was that thing?" he yells, breathing rapidly.

"It was like a Frankenstein bug thing," I get out between laughs. "Are you okay?"

"No. I'm not okay. That was terrible."

"But you did it," I say. "We're outside now. It's over. We can go get that funnel cake we wanted."

He bends over into his knees, trying to catch his breath. "I think I might be sick. I can't eat right now."

"You okay, T?" Jacks asks. I look over and spot all of our friends standing to our right.

"No, I'm not okay. That was fucking awful. Y'all know I don't do bugs."

The group bursts out laughing, and I try to stifle my laughs, but his hair is a little disheveled, and I can't help but notice how adorable it is when he gets flustered.

"It's not fucking funny."

"It's a little funny," I say. "Come on, let's go get the funnel cake or do something fun. You can pick the next thing."

He looks around the fair, scanning each of our options. My stomach sinks when his eyes land on one of the rides.

"Ride the ferris wheel with me," he says.

"No, you know I don't do heights. Let's go do the bumper cars again."

"Oh, no, Wren Dawson. You forced me to face my fears tonight. It's your turn."

"That's not how this works," I argue.

"That's exactly how this works," he quips.

"Look, I'll even hold your hand the whole time," he says, reaching for me. "You owe me after putting me through that. I almost had a heart attack."

I look over toward Poppy and Lacey, who both shrug.

"It's not that high, babe," Lacey says. "You got this."

I look back at him, and he does the pouty, puppy dog face. "Please ride it with me," he begs.

I breathe out and then take his hand. "Fine."

"Have fun you two," Poppy calls behind us, smirking.

"Wait, y'all aren't coming?" I question.

"No, I think we're gonna hang down here," Logan yells behind us as we disappear toward the ferris wheel.

The line is short, so we walk right up to board. Tanner pulls the lap bar down, and the wheel begins to move, taking us higher.

I move closer to him, shutting my eyes.

I'm not going to die. I'm not going to die. I'm not going to die.

"You're safe," he says "Open your eyes. The view is beautiful."

My chest is tight with anxiety, and I'm doing my best to control my breathing, but I'm terrified. I squint my eyes open and find Tanner staring at me. Not the fair. *Me.*

"You're safe," he repeats.

"This is terrifying," I say. "What if it gets stuck?"

"It's not going to get stuck," he says. "You can release the death grip on the cheetah. Goldie didn't force you on here."

I release my grip a little and set the stuffed cheetah in my lap. Breathing out, I scoot a little closer to where he sits. The wheel moves down and around and then starts to climb again.

"We're going around again?"

"Yeah, a few times, but you're okay." He settles his arm around my shoulders.

"I think I'm just going to look at you because if I look out or down, I'm afraid I'm going to get sick."

"That's fine," he chuckles, fixing his gaze back on me. "Would it help if we talked about something else," he offers.

"No."

"Okay," he says with a laugh.

The wheel continues to move, and we sit in silence, staring into each other's eyes. He attempts a funny face, and I let out a little giggle. My stomach begins to flip, and I'm not sure if it's our proximity, or him being so nice, but I know I don't hate it. In fact, I really like being close to him.

The wheel makes another round, and my heart drops as we make it back to the top. Then, it stops.

"Why did it stop?" I shout.

"Relax, I think it's supposed to," he says.

"You think?"

"Well it's been a while since I've ridden a ferris wheel, but I think they usually stop at the top at least once. It'll start moving again soon."

I fidget with Goldie, accidentally letting my gaze drop. I realize how high up we are, and I immediately panic.

"Tanner, it's not moving." I shift closer to him, and the seat begins to rock. "Tanner, I'm, like, really freaking the fuck out. It needs to start moving. Why isn't it moving?" I bury my head into his chest and try to slow my breathing.

His hand finds my back, and he starts to rub slow, calming circles around my spine. "It'll start moving in a minute."

"Attention folks! Looks like it's stuck. Please remain seated, and we'll get y'all down as soon as possible," the operator calls through a megaphone.

"It's going to be okay," he assures me.

"Did he say we're stuck?" I ask, panicked. "Oh, my god! What if they can't get us down?"

I'm going to die. I'm going to die. I'm going to die.

"Yes, he said we are stuck, but it's okay. Focus on me. Nothing bad is going to happen. I'm here. It's fine. We're fine. You're fine." He turns towards me more.

"I'm not fine." My voice starts to rise, and I just want my feet to touch the ground. I nuzzle my head harder against his chest.

"Wren," he says, a little breathlessly. "It's okay. Look at me."

I peer upward and let my eyes land on his. "You're okay. They're going to get it moving any minute, and then we will be back on the ground."

Sitting up a little straighter, I nod my head and try to hold back tears.

"Breathe," he urges. Reaching out, he pushes a piece of my hair behind my ear. A gust of wind blows, and our seat begins to rock again. I let out a scream, and he cups my face with both of his hands, causing my breath to catch.

"Breathe," he says, staring into my eyes.

"I'm really fucking scared," I say, biting my lip. "I need you to distract me."

"Distract you?"

"Yes, say something. Do something. I don't—"

Without warning, his lips find mine, and he kisses me so damn hard, my head scrambles. His lips are soft, and his rough beard scratches against my skin. His tongue presses forward as he continues to kiss me, and I open, letting him in. He tastes like cotton candy, and I melt into him. Our tongues twist, and his hands move through my hair. Goosebumps erupt down my arms. The kiss is everything I've ever wanted and didn't know I needed.

The ferris wheel begins to move, and as he pulls away, it hits me—*I was just kissing Tanner Mitchell.*

Confusion takes over, and I don't know what to make of the moment we just shared. We both sit there a little stunned.

"Wren—" he begins, but we're back on the ground, and I need to get off this thing. The operator removes the lap bar, and I pop off, moving away from him. Trying to get a grasp on my emotions, I bypass our friends, ignoring them calling my name.

"Wren, wait!" he calls behind me, but I don't stop. My fingers find my lips, and I can still taste him. I can still feel him, and it's confusing. It doesn't make any sense why he would kiss me, and I need to find somewhere quiet to process it all.

I turn a corner and stop when I find a secluded place on the other side of one of the small buildings. Leaning up against the wall, I try to regain control of my emotions.

"Wren!" he yells, turning the corner after me.

"What the fuck was that?" I yell, a little too loud. "I told you to distract me. Not kiss me."

"Look, I'm sorry. You were just so scared, and you said to do something, so I did the one thing I can't stop thinking about doing."

"No, you don't get to say that kissing me is all you've been thinking about." I point at him. "What am I supposed to do with that, Tanner? A few hours ago you were calling me your friend, and now you're kissing me on top of the ferris wheel like you're some character in *The Notebook*."

"Just let me explain," he begs.

"No. I'm going back to the apartment. I don't want to do this here, around all of our friends, and especially not dressed like a mermaid." I walk away, and don't stop until I'm in my car.

CHAPTER 31: SHARE IT?
WREN

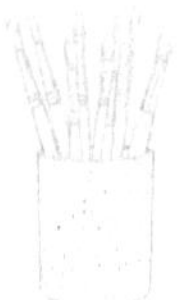

My head spins with thoughts of the kiss the whole way to the apartment, and I can't make sense of any of it. Fuck, that was a good kiss. Maybe the best, but it's him and it's me and we're roommates and he made it clear earlier that he saw me as a friend.

I make my way out of my car and into the apartment, still holding the little cheetah he won me. I place Goldie on the bedside table, and it's not until my clothes are changed and my face is washed that I realize that I still haven't picked up a new mattress. So, it's either the couch or the floor because as of last night, the hole is too big to be taped. *How fucking perfect.*

Walking back into the living room, I throw my pillow and a blanket on to the couch and then head to the kitchen to get something to drink.

I'm filling a glass with water when I hear the door click open.

"Wren, you here?" he asks, closing the door behind him. Taking the glass of water with me, I walk into the living room and sit on the couch.

"Wait, why is your pillow out here?" he asks.

"Because my bed is still deflated, and I don't want to sleep on the floor again."

"You're kidding," he deadpans.

"No, I'm not. It's fine."

"Just go sleep in my room, and I'll sleep on the couch."

"No."

He breathes out a long frustrated breath. "Fine. I don't want to fight with you." He begins to walk towards his room, and I know I'm not going to sleep if we don't talk.

"Why did you kiss me?" I ask.

"What?"

"Why did you kiss me?" I repeat the question.

"Because it's all I've wanted to do since the first time I saw you."

His admission knocks the breath out of me.

"Then why not just ask me out, or tell me how you were feeling? Why act like we were just friends?"

"Because you deserve so much more than me," he says. "You deserve someone who can make you proud to be with him. I can't even make my own family proud of me." He shakes his head. "How could I ever live up to what you deserve?"

"No. You don't get to decide what I deserve," I argue. "You don't get to pretend that you aren't good enough for me because you're in your feelings about your family and this job shit. A job that you don't even want. No. I'm not your dad, and I'm not your brother. That's not fair." Dolly jumps on my lap and nudges the hand that's holding the cup of water.

"But you know it's true. I'm me. The fuck around, have good time playboy who doesn't commit because I will somehow inevitably fuck it up. I always do."

"We're not having this discussion if you're going to talk about yourself like that. I'm going to bed," I snap, fluffing my pillow one handed. "I want to talk to you about this, but I'm not going to let you continue to berate yourself."

"Then go to bed." He gestures towards the pillow.

"Good night, Tanner," I say, but Dolly nudges my hand again, and the glass tumbles out, covering the couch with water. "Shit!"

Tanner chuckles under his breath. "Where you gonna sleep now?" He smirks.

"I'll just sleep on the floor." I stand to walk back into the kitchen to grab a towel to clean it up.

"God, you're so fucking stubborn."

"I'm stubborn?"

"Yes."

"Where do you propose I sleep?" I ask, drying the couch with some paper towels, then walking them to the trash can.

"My room."

"No," I say, walking back into the living room.

"See. Stubborn," he jabs.

"I'm not sleeping in your bed and making you sleep on the floor."

"Then share it with me," he says.

"Share it?"

"Yes. Put pillows down the middle if you must, but stop forcing yourself to be uncomfortable because of me."

"Fine."

"Thank god."

"Ugh." I grab my pillow and blanket off the couch.

"After you…" He puts out his hand and follows me into his room.

I climb into his bed, watching as he starts to take off his costume. "Are you kidding?" I ask.

"It's my room. Don't look if you don't want to see something."

He undresses down to his boxer briefs. I do my best to divert my gaze, but I fail—miserably—and he catches me staring.

"Like the show?" he asks, grabbing a pair of sweats off the top of his dresser.

"Shut up," I say, turning over and facing the wall. He chuckles, and then I hear him disappear into the bathroom. A couple minutes later, the bathroom door clicks open, the lights turn out, and the mattress shifts slightly under his weight.

"Night," he says, tugging on the comforter.

"Night," I say, rolling to my back to try to get comfortable, but I don't even know how we got here, and he's so damn close to me. The kiss replays in my head, and need builds low in my belly. I shift again, this time causing my foot accidentally to brush against his leg.

"Wren," he warns.

"What?" I ask, playfully grazing him again with my foot.

"If you don't stop touching me, then—"

"Then what?"

I hear him turn over, so I flip to face him too. I can barely make out the curves of his face in the dark room, but I know we're facing each other. His breaths are steady, and I'm trying to maintain my distance, but I'm laying in bed with the gorgeous man who kissed me on top of the ferris wheel, and it's hard.

"What will you do if I touch you again?" I ask.

I hear him take a deep breath. "You're playing with fire here," he says.

"What if I want to play with fire?"

He lets out a low groan as I move my foot up and down his calf.

"For the record," I begin. "I think I deserve someone who will teach me how to cook dinner. Someone who will go above and beyond to understand my brother's needs. Someone who will drop everything to take care of me when I don't feel good." I reach out and connect my hand with his arm, running my fingers along the veins in his forearm.

"Someone who will stock the pantry with all my favorite things, will leave me notes in the morning, and will kiss me like his life depends on it when I'm scared."

"Wren," he breathes out.

"You may think you're not good enough for me, but maybe if you stopped and asked me what I wanted…you'd know I want you."

"You don't mean that," he says.

"I do mean that, and I'd like to know what you meant when you warned me to stop touching you."

"Wren," he warns again.

"Tell me what you meant," I breathe out. "Please, don't start with that self deprecating bull—"

"Fuck it," he says, reaching out and pulling me flush against his body. His lips find mine, and he kisses me just like he did at the top of the ferris wheel. It's slow, and passionate, and everything I've ever wanted.

My hands find his hair, and I tug gently, causing him to moan against me. His lips part, letting me in. Our tongues tangle and our teeth clash. His hands move down my back and find my ass, pulling me in tighter. Hooking my leg over his, I bring us even closer, thrusting my hips forward. His length pushes into me, and heat builds between my legs.

"Are you sure this is what you want?" he asks, pulling away.

"Yes," I say, rocking my hips forward again. He flips to his back, carrying me with him, and our mouths meet again in a long kiss.

My hips continue to rock against him and he pushes up into me, causing the perfect friction against my clit. His hands explore my body, and my hands tangle in his hair.

His lips find my pulse point, and he sucks gently. "Oh, fuck," I let out.

"You like that?" he asks, finding the spot again.

"Yes," I breathe out, grinding my hips against him.

He sits up, positioning me so that I'm sitting in his lap. Wrapping my legs around his waist and my arms around his neck, I pull him into me, and our lips meet in another needy kiss.

"I like kissing you," he says, pulling away.

"So kiss me," I say, shifting in his lap.

"I want to make sure you're comfortable with this," he says, moving my hair behind my ear. "Because it's taking all of my control not to take this further, but I can't go all the way with you and it just be sex. Losing you would break me, and I know this is a lot to throw out there, and I'm not saying you have to promise me forever, but I've been falling for you since I saw you, and I don't want to fuck it up by being reckless tonight."

I lean down, cup his face, and kiss him softly. "This isn't just sex. This is real. I promise I want you." He rolls me to my back. "Now, kiss me."

Leaning over me, he lowers himself to my mouth and then begins to trail kisses down the side of my neck. Every spot he touches ignites, and I thrust my hips forward.

"Is it okay if I kiss you here?" he asks, removing the strap of my tank top, pulling the fabric down, and kissing me tenderly along the curve of my breasts.

"Yes," I say.

"And what about here?" He moves down my body and raises up the base of my shirt, kissing my abdomen.

"Yes," I say, swallowing hard. His eyes find mine, and he continues to move, hooking my pajama pants with his fingers, pulling them down slightly.

"What about here?" he asks, placing a kiss along my right hip bone.

"Yes…" I begin to squirm. "Tanner, please kiss me."

"I am kissing you," he says. "And I'm going to take my time because this is all I've wanted to do for months, and now that I'm getting the chance, I'm going to kiss every inch of your perfect body." He moves over to my left hip bone, kissing me again.

"Can I take these off of you?"

"Please," I beg. He begins tugging my pants down my legs, revealing my red lace thong.

"Have you been wearing this the whole night?"

I nod, and he bends down and places kisses up my thigh. His beard tickles against the sensitive skin between my legs, and my breath quickens as he nears my center.

"Can I touch you?" he asks, running his fingers along the band of my panties.

"Please," I beg, desperately, causing him to chuckle. He moves the red lace to the side and swipes his finger through my wet center.

"So fucking wet for me," he says. My head falls back, and my eyes shut as he draws slow, purposeful circles against my clit.

"Eyes on me," he says, causing mine to shoot open. He dips down again, tracing his tongue up my inner thigh, and he doesn't break eye contact.

"Can I kiss you here?" he asks, rubbing his thumb over my clit on the outside of my thong, eyes locked firmly on mine.

I nod my head, and bite my lip. "Please, kiss me there."

He slowly removes my thong and presses kisses up my leg starting at my ankle. Each kiss is purposeful, and tender, and nothing like what I thought sleeping with him would be. When he makes it to my upper thigh, his rough beard creates a sweet friction that causes liquid to pool between my legs. His mouth finds my clit, and he spreads my thighs wide apart, exposing all of me to him. I let out a long moan.

I watch him work between my thighs, and I don't know if I ever witnessed anything hotter. My whole body heats as he strokes my pussy with his tongue, and my hands grip the soft sheets, trying to hang on as long as I can.

"You taste so fucking sweet," he says against me, his eyes finding mine. "You like watching me devour you?"

I nod.

"Good, keep watching, and when you're ready, don't hold back. I want you to soak my face. You think you can do that?"

"Yes," I breathe out, rocking my hips forward. He continues to work me with his mouth, and the pressure in my core winds tighter with every lick and flick of his tongue. He moves his head and presses a finger inside of me.

"Tanner…fuck…yes…more…" I call out.

He adds a second finger, and his eyes find mine. "You still watching, pretty girl?"

"Yes…but…fuck…I…" My head lolls back. The feeling is overwhelming, and I'm on the edge of my release.

"That's it, Wren. Let go for me." His tongue finds my clit, and he spends extra time sucking and playing with the bundle of nerves, his fingers working in the perfect tandem with his tongue. He curls his fingers in me, and that's all it takes. I completely uncoil. Liquid floods between my legs, and I watch as he continues to work me through the waves of my orgasm, drinking me in like he's stranded on a desert island, and I'm the first drops of water he's seen in days.

CHAPTER 32: JUST MAKING SURE THIS ISN'T A DREAM
TANNER

I sit up on my knees and take her in. Her chest rises and falls with heavy breaths as she pushes up on her elbows. A sexy smile spreads across her face. Her hair falls around her shoulders, and she moves a piece of it behind her ear. Wren is always beautiful, but Wren, laying here after I've made her squirt, is a goddamn goddess.

"Did I just—"

"Squirt?" I ask.

"I've never…fuck…" she breathes out, and my dick throbs below my pants. I slap at my face with both hands, and she giggles.

"What are you doing?"

"Just making sure this isn't a dream."

I move next to her, and she rolls to meet me, placing her leg over mine. She runs a hand through my hair and then leans in to kiss me. Our tongues swirl around each other, and she lets out a little moan, making my cock harder. "Well, if it is a dream. I really hope it's not over yet," she teases, snaking her hand down my chest and abs. Everywhere she touches erupts with heat.

"Can I touch you?" she asks, her hand finding the waist-band of my sweatpants.

"I thought you'd never ask," I say, swallowing hard.

Her hand wraps around my shaft and begins to move up and down. Her touch threatens to take me over the edge, and a sound escapes me that's borderline primal.

"Fuck, you're huge," she says, rolling her palm down my length and then pausing to play with the tip.

My whole body shudders under her touch, and I try to come up with a hot comeback, but I'm too distracted by her hand on my dick.

"If you keep touching me like that, you're going to make me come fully clothed," I breathe out.

She giggles against me, and then her lips crash into mine. She works my cock in her hand and begins to rock against my leg. Our mouths stay locked on each other, and my hands find her back and pull her in closer.

"Wren," I breathe out. "I really want to fuck you, and I haven't been with anyone since April, so if you keep it up, this is gonna be over too soon."

She rolls back and stares at me. "You haven't been with anyone since April?"

"No."

"Are you serious? But I saw you with that blonde at The Local a couple months ago."

"What blonde?"

"I don't know, but it was ladies night and you were there kissing her by the door, and then you left."

That night replays in my head.

"You were there?"

"Yeah, Gray and I went out for drinks."

I chuckle. "I could've sworn I saw you that night, and I convinced myself my mind was playing tricks on me. The blonde kissed me, and I turned her down. I haven't been with anyone since my birthday."

"Why?" she asks.

I hesitate before answering her because I don't want to freak her out, but she deserves the truth. "Because the minute I saw you, I only wanted you, and no one else compared."

Her breath hitches.

"I bet you think I'm crazy."

"You are crazy, but not for saying that." She moves closer. "All this time you've been feeling this way, and didn't say anything."

"I just thought you deserved more than me, and I guess I convinced myself that if the best I could do was be your friend, then that was enough because it meant I got to be around you."

Our lips meet in a soft kiss.

"I wish you could see yourself the way I see you," she says, kissing me again softly. "You are incredible, and I hate that it took me so long to figure it out."

Our tongues tangle again, and this time, it's full of passion and heat. She grabs at the waistband of my pants, shoving them down, and I kick them off. I roll over, grab a condom from the bedside table drawer, and we both pull off our shirts.

"You sure you want to do this?" I ask.

"Give me that," she says, snatching the foil packet from my hand. She pushes me back against the pillows, rips it open with her teeth, and then rolls it down my cock.

Holy fuck, she's hot when she takes what she wants.

She hesitates for a moment once it's on.

"What is it?" I ask.

"I've just never been with anyone as big as you, and I'm worried it's not going to fit."

"We'll make it fit," I say. "Now come here. You get on top, so you're in control. If it's too much, we can stop."

She nods and moves to straddle me. After lining me up between her legs, she begins slowly to sink down on my cock.

She's so fucking tight, and I can feel myself stretching her, but she doesn't stop. "Fuck...it...feels...so..." she breathes out, punctuating each word with a small moan.

"Look at you taking me so well," I say. "It's like you were made for me."

She carefully continues to move down my shaft until she's taken me all the way to the hilt.

"Move," she calls out. "Fuck, I need you to move."

We both begin to rock in sync, and pressure immediately begins to build in the base of my spine. I do my best to push it away, but I've been on the fucking edge since the kiss, and I haven't had sex in six months, so I know I don't have much longer.

"Lean back," I say, and she does. She continues to ride me, and my thumb begins to circle her clit. God, the view of her on top of me, tits bouncing slightly as she moves up and down, is a fucking fantasy.

"I'm close, and I want you to come with me. You think you can do that?" I ask.

"Yeah," she says with a moan.

I continue to work her clit, rocking my hips into her. "Fuck...it's so fucking good," she says as she continues to move against me.

"That's it, pretty girl—take what you need. I want to feel you come apart for me."

With my spare hand, I grab her ass, tugging her tighter against me, and she falls. Her pussy tightens around my dick, and she falls forward, covering my face with her hair.

"Tanner," she screams, and it's all I need. I find my release as well. Her mouth finds mine, silencing us both. Our bodies continue to rock together, until we both are completely unraveled.

"Fuck," I say when she rolls off the top of me. "You are absolutely amazing."

She climbs out of bed, and I watch as her bare ass sways in

the dim light. "You were alright," she teases, glancing over her shoulder.

I jump out of bed and run up behind her, grabbing her and pulling her into me. "Just alright?" I ask, tickling her sides.

"Stop, you know I'm just teasing you. I need to pee." She laughs. "And you're still wearing the condom."

I kiss the side of her head and move past her into the bathroom, discarding the rubber into the trash.

Once we've both cleaned up and dressed in nothing but our underwear, she climbs back into bed, and I walk out to get us both some water.

"Thank you," she says, taking the glass from me. She takes a sip then places it back on the nightstand. I crawl into bed, and her body relaxes against mine.

"I hope you like being the big spoon," she says, nestling in closer. "Because I like being the little spoon."

"I'll be your big spoon any time."

"Maybe we do make a good team," she says.

"I've been trying to tell you, but you wouldn't listen." I lay a kiss against the side of her face. "Did that really just happen?" I ask, replaying our night.

"Yes," she says. "And I'm really happy it did."

"I'm pretty sure you've made me the happiest man on the planet," I say.

"I know serious relationships aren't really your thing," she begins, her tone shifting to nervousness. "But what does all this mean? Are we together now? Is it casual?"

"I meant what I said. I don't want it to be just sex. I like you a lot, Wren, and if you don't want to label it, I can be cool with that, but I'd like to see where it goes. I'd like to take you on dates. I'd like to be able to kiss you whenever I want. I don't want to hide this from our friends. God, I want to tell everyone you're mine, if you'll have me."

"I'd like all that too," she says. "And I'm not opposed to labels."

"I've never asked a girl to be my girlfriend before," I admit nervously, my heart beginning to race.

"Ever? Not even when you were in middle or high school?"

"No. I've dated a lot of women, but never have been exclusive. Does that weird you out?"

"No. I mean maybe it should, and if you asked me a couple months ago maybe it would have, but then I got to know you, and despite you being insufferable, I couldn't help but fall for you."

"So, how does this work? Do I ask, or do we just kinda agree to be in a relationship?"

My cheeks heat, and I've never been more thankful that the room was dark. I'm thirty. I should know how to ask a woman out. How fucking embarrassing.

"You should definitely ask," she says. "And we've kind of done it all out of order, but I'll let that slide."

My heart rate picks up, and nerves pulse through me.

"Okay, well then…will you be my girlfriend?"

"Umm, I might need to think about it," she says, giggling.

"That's not funny," I say. She pauses for an extra moment. "Wren, will you be my girlfriend?"

"Yeah, I'll be your girlfriend."

My heart swells, and she turns to face me, placing another kiss on my lips. "The group's going to freak," she says.

"Not gonna lie, I'm freaking out. Don't you dare break my heart, Wren Dawson."

She kisses me hard. "I won't, but that goes for you too."

"Never."

I lay there for a few long minutes until her breaths start to even out, and I know she's asleep. Reflecting on my day, I'm still not sure about a lot of things, but I know this, *us*, is right.

CHAPTER 33: PLAYING HOOKY
WREN

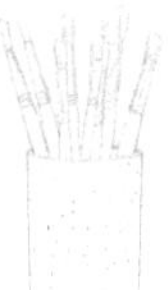

Tanner's alarm sounds, and I let out a grumble. We stayed up far too late last night, and I'm exhausted.

"Five more minutes," Tanner groans, turning the alarm off and pulling me into him. His body is warm and completely envelopes mine. His bed is so damn cozy that I would stay curled up like this forever if I could.

I scoot further into the crook of his body, and his erection presses into my ass. "You're really making it hard to sleep," he says, burying his face into my neck.

"I wish we could skip work today and stay in bed," I joke, wiggling my ass into him.

"Then let's call out," he says.

"We can't do that," I whine.

"Why not?" he asks, his lips finding my neck, and he places soft kisses across the top of my shoulders.

"I've never called out before," I say.

"That doesn't surprise me," he teases. "I've called out dozens of times. Perks of working for your dad."

"Well, not everyone has that luxury."

"It's only one day," he says. "Do you have a lot on your schedule?"

I think through my usual Friday. "Um, not really…there is a book club meeting, BINGO, and a sittercize class, but most of those can be run by other people."

"Sounds like you won't be missed," he says, laying more kisses down my neck. "Stay home with me, please."

"And what will we do if I stay here?"

"Well, after we repeat last night, then I'll cook you waffles, and then we can repeat last night again."

"That does sound much better than BINGO." I laugh. "Ugh. What if they find out I'm not sick and fire me."

"You're allowed to take a day off." He kisses me again, and my whole body erupts with goosebumps. "Your body is practically begging for you to stay with me." He runs his hand up my leg, and his fingers dip below my underwear. "You're soaked."

"Tanner," I warn.

"Call your boss and tell him you're taking a mental health day. I promise to make it worth your while."

"You're a terrible influence," I say as his finger circles my clit and my breath catches.

"Please stay with me," he says.

"Fine, but you're going to have to stop playing with me long enough for me to let him know I'm not coming in." I roll away from him and begin to look for my phone on the bedside table, but it's not there. "I'll be right back," I say, walking toward the door.

"Hurry back," he says.

I find my phone still in my purse. I swipe it open to discover an endless stream of missed calls and texts from my friends.

The Tortured Therapists Department

LACEY

Are you okay? You looked so upset when you left.

POPPY:

Text us back. We're worried about you.

GRAY:

I just tried calling and no answer. Wren, are you okay?

LACEY:

Tanner isn't messaging Jace back either. Do y'all think they're together?

POPPY:

Logan said the same thing. Maybe 🐧

CHLOE:

Her location says she's at their apartment, so I'm sure she's okay. Maybe sleeping.

LACEY:

Wren, we really wish you'd just let us know what happened.

POPPY:

Yeah, we're here if you need us.

I swipe out of the message chain to click on Daryl's name.

Hey, Daryl. I hate to do this, but I'm going to have to call out today. Robin knows the schedule and has helped me when I was out sick before. If you need anything, feel free to text.

Clicking back into the group text, I take a deep breath before responding.

The Tortured Therapists Department

I'm alive! Thanks for all the concern.

Poppy: What the hell happened last night?

So much happened last night.

"DID YOU CALL OUT?" TANNER ASKS, PEEKING HIS HEAD INTO MY
room.

"I did, but he hasn't responded yet. Just give me another minute. I missed like one hundred texts and calls from the girls last night, so I'm responding."

He chuckles. "Yeah, the guys blew up my phone too."

"Did you tell them?" I ask, looking toward him.

"I haven't responded yet. I wasn't sure if you wanted to tell everyone together, or if it was cool for me to say something."

"I was about to tell the girls."

"I have an idea." He grabs my phone and pulls me next to him. "Smile," he says, kissing my cheek. He snaps a selfie of us then begins tapping on my screen.

"Tanner, I'm topless," I shriek.

"You can't see anything," he assures me, handing my phone back. "I zoomed in on the photo, so it's just our faces."

<<Selfie photo attached>> Consider this our hard launch!

"You texted the entire group a selfie of us in one huge group chat!" I giggle. Texts start to pour in, and my phone vibrates uncontrollably.

"I figured this way no one could complain that they weren't the first to know."

He leans forward with both hands on the top of the door frame, and a grin spreads across his face as he looks at me. For the first time since I moved in, I don't try to divert my gaze. Instead, I rake my eyes down his bare chest, following his perfectly manicured abs straight down to where his cock protrudes behind his boxer briefs.

My phone continues to vibrate, stealing my attention. He plucks it from my hand and tosses it onto the deflated air mattress, then goes back to leaning on the top of the door frame.

"We'll text them later," he says. "Right now I have other plans."

He lets go from above, gently turning me so my back is flush with the molding. Propping himself over me with one arm, he leans down, grabs the back of my head with the other hand, and then takes my mouth in an all-consuming kiss.

I wrap my arms around his waist, pulling him to me. His back muscles flex under my grip, and I allow myself to melt into him.

"That was really hot," I say as he pulls away.

He leans forward again, but this time instead of kissing me, he kisses the top of my shoulder.

"Did you know that I think your freckles are one of the sexiest things about you?"

"I've always been a little self-conscious about them," I admit.

"No," he says. "I've been dying to kiss every single one of them, and last night it was dark, and they were hard to see. But right here, there's the perfect amount of light." He moves to the other side of my neck.

"You aren't going to take me back to bed?" I ask.

"Patience, pretty girl," he says. "We'll get there. We have all day, and I want to take care of you right here first."

He continues to plant kisses across my neck and shoulders. His hand moves from the back of my head, trailing down my body until it finds the lace of my underwear.

I shudder under his touch, and my breaths quicken. Kissing him in the dark was hot, but watching him with every light on is a whole other experience. Every kiss is placed with purpose, and he smiles every time I react to his touch.

He dips a finger under the lace of my underwear and swipes it up my center, only stopping to draw circles on my small bundle of nerves. My knees threaten to buckle, but I manage to stay upright, and a grin spreads across his face.

"What do you like?" he asks.

"This," I say, breathless. "I like this. And I like when you curl your fingers inside of me."

He pushes one finger inside, and I buck my hips forward.

"Like this?" he asks.

I nod. "Mmhmm, but I can take more," I say, almost on a whimper.

His lips find mine as he pushes in another finger, and I rock my hips again. Pressure begins to build low in my belly as his fingers pump in and out of me, and his thumb continues to circle my clit in perfect rhythm.

"What else do you like?" he asks.

"I like when the other person takes control."

His lips find my neck again, and he sucks gently on the sensitive skin. He removes his fingers and brings them to my mouth.

"Open," he commands. "I want you to taste how sweet you are."

My lips part, and he pushes his fingers into my mouth. My tongue swirls around them, cleaning me off of him.

"So fucking pretty when you taste yourself," he says, removing his fingers. His mouth meets mine in a filthy kiss, one that causes my legs to wobble.

He drops to his knees and begins tugging down my underwear. "It's my turn to taste you," he says. He works the lace down my legs, and when it gets to my ankle, I fling it across the room and hook my leg across his back.

"Fuck," I let out as his tongue finds my center in a long, slow lick. My head lolls back against the wood of the frame, and my hands tangle into his hair.

Pushing my hips forward, I grind against his face, and he groans against me. His hands dig into my hips as I continue to rock against him. Stroke after stroke, I watch him devour me like his last fucking meal, and my core tightens with every flick of his tongue.

"Oh…my…fucking…Tanner!" I scream out his name as he pushes two fingers deep inside me and curls them against my most sensitive spot.

His fingers apply the perfect amount of pressure, his tongue still circling my clit, and I bury my heel into his back as my hips rock back and forth taking everything he'll give me.

"Let go, pretty girl," he says against me, and I snap, falling so hard the room spins.

He sees me through the aftershocks of my orgasm. Standing, he kisses me hard, then picks me up and throws me over his shoulder.

"Tanner," I yell, as he carries me across the apartment. "Put me down."

He chuckles and sets me down at the foot of his bed. "Is it my turn?" I ask, sinking to my knees.

"You want my cock in that pretty mouth of yours?" he asks.

I nod my head slowly and begin pulling down his underwear. His dick springs free. I bite my lip remembering how big he actually is.

Peering up at him, I wrap my hand around his shaft and begin to pump up and down. "Do you like that?" I ask.

"Yes," he grits out, his head falling back.

"And do you like this?" I tease, running my tongue up the length of him.

"Fuckkkk yes," he says.

The tip of his cock is already glistening with precum, and need starts building low in my belly again. Continuing to stroke the base of his cock, I bend forward, taking him into my mouth.

"That's it," he says. "Fuck, your mouth feels so good."

My mouth moves down his shaft until the tip hits the back of my throat, causing me to gag.

"You okay?" he asks.

"Mmhmm."

I've never been with a guy as big as him, but I do my best to breathe through my nose so I can take him as deep into my throat as I possibly can. Over and over, I work him with my mouth and hand. His hands find my hair, holding me steady, and he pumps his hips forward.

Saltiness swims across my tongue as his cock begins to leak, and I pull away, sucking on the tip.

Making eye contact with him, I flick my tongue against the head, drinking up the little bit he's given me, desperate for more.

"Fuck," he says. "You look so fucking pretty on your knees for me."

I smile at his praise and then wrap my lips around his shaft. One hand still stroking his cock, my other finds his balls, and I begin to gently play with him.

"Shit...fuck...yes..." he says, his hand tightening in my hair. He continues to pump into my mouth, and lust courses through my body. I like pleasuring him. I like turning him on like this. Fuck, it's hot.

"I'm close," he warns, and I hollow out my cheeks, taking him as deep as I can. His movements become frantic, and I let him take what he needs from me.

A moan escapes as he finds his release, and he spills into

my mouth. I continue to suck his cock through the aftershocks of his orgasm, and when I'm sure he has nothing else to give me, I sit back and look up at him. My lips wet, my face flushed, and my breaths heavy.

Pulling me to stand, he wraps me in his arms. "You are incredible," he says, and a mischievous grin flashes across my face at his compliment.

Wren on her knees for me is a sight that I never thought I'd see anywhere but my wildest fantasies. Fuck, she was pretty taking my cock, and given the look on her face, I'd say she actually liked giving me head.

"Come on. Let's jump in the shower. I've got an idea of what we can do today," I say.

She runs to her bathroom to grab her shampoo and soap. I turn on the water, and when she returns, she sets the soap inside and then wraps her arms around me. I hold her against my chest, breathe her in, and wonder if she's falling for me as hard as I'm falling for her.

Stepping into the shower, the steam from the hot water fogs the glass. I help her in after me, and she moves under the stream of warm water, wetting her hair.

"Is it too hot?"

"It's perfect," she says, grabbing for her shampoo.

"May I?" I ask, taking the bottle and squirting a small amount of soap onto my palm.

She nods, and I work my hands through her hair, massaging her scalp. I rinse it with water and then grab her conditioner, repeating the steps I just completed. The shower fills with the scent of cherries and vanilla that I've grown to love.

"Aren't you cold?" she asks. "I'm hogging all the water."

"I'm fine," I say, grabbing the soap, lathering it in my hands. I take my time rubbing my hands all over her body. She shudders under my touch, and her head falls back when my fingers graze her nipples.

"Tanner, stop," she teases. "You're going to make me want to have shower sex, and I'm really hungry."

"I'm not opposed to shower sex," I say.

"I'm sure you're not, but if we're going to be having sex all day, I'm going to need food."

"Fine," I grumble, moving my hands down her body until they both find her ass. I pull her into me, kissing her deeply. The water pours over us, and her hips rock against me. "You sure you want breakfast? Seems like you kind of want to do something else."

She shakes her head. "Yes, I'm getting out before my waffles get delayed any further." She slides past me, opens the door, and grabs for a towel. My hand finds her ass in a playful slap, and she lets out a little squeak. Glancing back over her shoulder, she rolls her eyes and then the shower door closes behind her.

Quickly, I finish my own shower and then throw on pants. When I walk out of my room, she's sitting on the couch, drinking iced coffee with her phone in her hand.

"Did your boss get back to you?" I ask.

"Yeah, but I think he's mad," she says, flipping her phone around.

DARYL:

Okay. – Daryl

"You just think that because he used a period. How old is he?"

"I don't know. Maybe in his fifties…" She shrugs. "Should I respond?"

"Nah. I don't think it means he's mad. I think he just doesn't know how to text. Periods make everyone sound mad. I mean, he signed his name." I chuckle. "I wouldn't worry about it."

"You're right." She sets the phone down on the table, and it immediately begins to vibrate. "Are the girls still texting you?"

"Yes," she tells me, giggling. "They're freaking out that I called you my boyfriend."

Her eyes find mine, and her lips form a small smile.

"What is it?"

"Nothing, it's just…I don't know. I'm really happy, and I feel like a teenager whose crush finally asked her out."

A big smile spreads across my face, and she stands to meet me. "Stop looking at me like that," she says.

"Like what?" I pull her into me, and my lips find hers.

"Like you're thinking about skipping the breakfast I was promised."

I chuckle against her. "Alright, alright. I'll make you waffles." I pick her up, and she wraps her legs around my waist and her arms around my neck.

"Wait," she says. "I need my coffee."

I bend down, grabbing the glass, and then walk her into the kitchen. She nestles her face into my neck as I move.

"You know I can't help. I burn everything I try to cook," she says as I set her on the counter and hand her her coffee.

"Not true. You didn't burn the grilled cheese, but I don't want your help. Just your company." I kiss the tip of her nose and then begin to move around the kitchen to collect everything I need to make the waffles. She sits on the counter, watching me.

"What do you want to do today?" she asks.

"Have you ever done an escape room?"

"No, but it sounds like fun."

"Yeah, I've never done one either," I say, mixing the dry ingredients in a large bowl.

"I'd really like that," she says. "Did you tell your dad you weren't coming in today?"

"No," I say, combining the wet ingredients.

"Weren't you supposed to meet with the new guy?"

I shrug, "I guess, but I can't go in there. I'm sure I'll get an earful on Monday, but I don't care. Today, I want to spend time with my girlfriend."

"I'm really sorry about everything."

"It'll be fine. It's not what my grandfather would have wanted, but I'm sure Stuart will be a decent boss, and I don't mind my current role. "

"What about the bar?"

"What about it? I essentially ghosted Jerry." My stomach turns. I could kick myself for not talking to him and letting it fall through my fingers. "I'm sure he's found someone else by now."

"You don't know that. Maybe you could talk to him, see if it's still available."

"I don't know." I whisk the ingredients together, adding a little extra vanilla to the batter for good measure.

"They already smell so good. Can I taste it?" she asks.

I dip a finger in and walk over to where she sits.

"Say it," she says.

"Say what?" I laugh.

"Tell me to open."

My whole face heats, and my dick twitches. "If I didn't know any better, I'd think you were one trying to make me forget all about breakfast."

She giggles. "Say it." The corner of her mouth tips up.

"Open," I command, and she does. She sucks my finger into her mouth and swirls her tongue around it, cleaning off all the batter. My dick throbs below my sweats, and I replace my finger with my mouth. Her lips part, and she tastes like vanilla. "And you say I'm a bad influence," I tease, pulling away.

"I never said I was a good one. And I can't help it. I like it when you're a little bossy."

I let out a loud laugh and move away, continuing to prepare the waffles.

"I just want you to be happy," she says, returning to the work conversation. "So, if that means you stay at Austere then I'll support you, but if you aren't happy there, then I think you should try talking to Jerry again."

"Maybe. I'll think about it."

"What does your mom think?" she asks, sipping her coffee.

I pour the batter into the waffle iron and close the lid.

"I don't know. I think she was part of the reason he even entertained me becoming CEO, but she's so wrapped up with my little sister and work that we don't talk about this kind of stuff."

"Have you tried?"

"No," I shake my head. "I love my parents, but they aren't really the kind that you talk to about how you're feeling."

"I hate that," she says. "What about your sister?"

"Bella is young. She's only sixteen."

"I didn't realize she was still in high school."

"Yep, my mom struggled to get pregnant after me. I was almost fourteen when she was born."

"That's crazy. I can't imagine having a sibling that much younger than me. Growing up, Cody and I were inseparable. He's only a year younger than me, so most of the time people thought we were twins. Was it hard to have that big of an age gap?"

"Mitch and I were always really protective of her and loved spoiling her when we were still at home, but then I moved out for school, and she has her own life. She's cheerleading captain and trying to decide where she wants to go to college. You remember what it was like being that young. I don't want to weigh her down with the drama between my dad, brother, and me. I know it's always bothered her."

She nods, and I remove a waffle from the iron before pouring in more batter.

"Your family seems great," I say.

"Ha!" she laughs. "They are pretty great, but I think every family has their stuff. After Cody's accident, we all did a lot of family counseling and therapy. It made us a much stronger unit, but they still don't understand why it's so important for me to save for the camps. I think they'd rather me live in a super nice apartment than save."

"I think the camps are an incredible idea," I say. "I went to sleep away camp every summer as a kid, and those are some of my favorite memories."

"Cody and I did sleep away camp too." She smiles.

"Did y'all's have a talent show? That was always my favorite part."

"Did we have a talent show?" she asks, dramatically, grasping her chest. "Cody and I were talent show champions for three summers in a row. We were so good that someone actually tried to go to the director of the camp and say we shouldn't be able to perform together because we were in different age groups." She laughs.

"What was your talent?" I ask, removing another waffle and pouring more batter into the iron.

"Magic and comedy," she says, laughing. "We'd practice for months leading up to camp, and the whole routine was so silly. We were the world's worst magicians, so we made it part of the bit, and it killed every time. Cody's timing was hilarious."

I chuckle. "I wish I could have seen it."

"It was so good. I wonder if I could find a video. I'm sure there's one somewhere. What was your talent?"

"Yodeling."

A laugh bubbles out of her. "You're joking."

"I'm dead serious."

"You yodel? Did you have one of the little costumes? What is it called?"

"Lederhosen."

"Oh, my gosh, yes. It's like little short shorts and suspenders."

I nod.

"Can you still yodel?"

"I mean I haven't done it in years, but I'm sure I can."

She pops off the counter and grabs her phone.

"What are you doing?" I ask, shaking my head.

"Preparing myself. If my boyfriend is about to start yodeling, I need to have this on video."

"I'm not yodeling?"

"Yes, you are," she says. "Pretty please?" She pouts her lips, looking up at me with big eyes.

"Fine," I say, clearing my throat. "But this video is just for you."

"I won't show anyone; I promise." She continues to giggle and holds the phone up so that the camera is facing me.

"Yodel-Ay-Ee-Oooo," I begin to sing, and she erupts in more giggles. I continue for a few seconds, moving my voice up and down, and then stop. "Okay, I think that's enough."

"But it's so cute," she says, walking towards me. "Maybe next time you could wear the little shorts. I bet they make your ass look great."

"Very funny," I deadpan. "You better send me that video."

"I'll just air drop it," she says, grabbing my phone off the counter. She taps on her phone, and I hear mine buzz. Her eyes find mine.

"What is it?" I ask.

"You have a cheetah emoji by my name?"

"Yeah." I shrug. "Added it after you came over for dinner that night."

She turns her phone around to show me my contact. Next to my name is a little yellow dog emoji. "I changed yours after you left me the first doodle," she says.

"Great minds," I say, pulling her into me and kissing her forehead. "You ready to eat?"

"I'm famished," she says.

I pull away and plate the waffles, adding a handful of mini marshmallows on the top of both of our stacks. We move to the table and begin eating.

"I could get used to this," she says, taking a bite of her food.

"The waffles?" I ask.

"No, I could get used to playing hooky with you."

"Me too."

Honestly, I might never work again because lazy mornings with Wren are quickly becoming my favorite thing.

CHAPTER 35: KLEPTOMANIAC
WREN

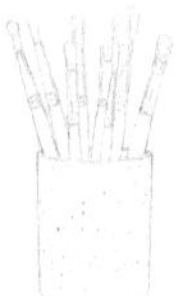

"**Y**ou ready to become world class art thieves?" Tanner asks, pulling into the parking lot of Lock and Key Escape Rooms.

"I didn't realize you were such a kleptomaniac," I tease.

"Me?"

"Yeah, first it was movies, then my heart, and now art."

"Hey! I'll have you know that I officially subscribed to multiple streaming services after the whole porn debacle, the art we are about to steal isn't real, and I'm going to let your bad joke slide because it makes me really insanely happy to hear you say I stole your heart." His hand squeezes my thigh where it's been resting for the entire drive.

"Well, you did." I look over at him, my heart skipping a beat.

He parks the car then leans towards me, peppering my face with kisses and making me giggle. "Now come on. We need to get in the right headspace for what we're about to do," he coaches me.

"The right headspace for an escape room?"

"Yes, the art heist one was labeled as 'challenging' on the website, and we'll only have an hour."

"I should've known you were going to treat this like a sport. Let's just go have fun. If we don't beat it, it's okay. I'm just glad we're trying something new together."

We climb out of the car and walk into the seemingly boring brick building, hand in hand. The man behind the counter has a mustache that is as scrawny as his build. He's wearing glasses and a branded polo. His name tag reads: *Ted*.

"How can I help you?" Ted asks, as Tanner and I approach the front desk.

"I called earlier about the art heist escape room," Tanner says.

"Is it just you two?" he asks.

"Yep, is that a problem?"

"Nah. Usually I'd pair you with another couple, but it's been a slow day. Y'all ready to get started?"

"Yes," I say, squeezing Tanner's hand, bouncing up and down a little. We follow Ted to a set of lockers outside of an unmarked door.

"Y'all can put all of your belongings in here. No phones or cameras are allowed in the room. You just enter a pin, and then when you're done with the game you use the same number to open the locker and retrieve your items."

Tanner and I place our phones inside, and then he locks the door.

"You can bring in one piece of paper and a pencil," he says, handing the materials to Tanner. "Are you ready to begin?"

We both nod.

"Alright," he says, reading from a laminated piece of paper. "You are now underground art dealers, and your new client is none other than the extremely dangerous, Italian mob boss, Lorenzo Marino. He has his eye set on the Mona Lisa for his personal art collection, and he wants you to steal it," Ted continues to read from the piece of paper with as much enthusiasm as a dry piece of toast.

Tanner nudges me, wiggling his eyebrows, and I stifle a little giggle.

"Unfortunately, a mole has made the police aware of your plans, and the museum has taken extra precautions to ensure the painting remains safe, hiding it somewhere within the museum. You've received special intel that it's somewhere in the head curator's office. You have one hour to find the painting and get out before the police arrive, or you'll have to answer to Lorenzo, and he rarely lets people walk away alive."

He glances up from the script. "Do you have any questions?"

"Are we really going to be locked in?" I ask.

"No, but if you open the door without the code, then the game will end and you'll lose. I can see and hear your room from the front desk, so if you need something just holler."

He opens the door, and Tanner leads me into a long, white hallway, still holding my hand. The door clicks closed, and sixty-minutes appears on the countdown clock by the door.

"Alright, it's game time," Tanner says, looking around the space. The hall is set up to look like an art gallery. Five framed canvases line each side of the hallway along the walls, and small plaques describing the art are situated to the left of each painting. At the end of the hall is a door with a coded lock, a placard next to it reading: Luigi Albertini, Museum Curator.

"That must be the office door," I say, pointing. "I think we need to figure out a code to open it." Letting go of his hand, I walk across the room. "It's a four digit number."

"Makes sense to me, but how do we figure it out?"

"I'm not sure. You think the numbers are hidden in the paintings?"

"That's a good thought," he says, walking over and studying one of the paintings hung on the wall. "Do you see any hidden numbers? Because this one has nothing."

"There's ten paintings and only four numbers, so maybe

they don't all have hidden numbers," I say, looking at a different painting. "Nothing here either."

He bends down and reads one of the plaques. "All the letters on this one are lowercase, except for one. You think it's a secret code."

I check the plaque in front of me and then another. "Yes! That's it. Quick write down the letters." Tanner begins to scribble them down as I read them out loud.

We both stare at the ten letters on the piece of paper: I B T E C O L I T L

"What the fuck does that mean?" Tanner says, laughing.

"I think we have to unscramble them."

"LITTLE BICO? Is that the name of one of the paintings."

"No," I say, shaking my head. I study the letters, then look back at the paintings, but nothing makes sense. "Could it be in another language?"

"Maybe Italian? That seems to be the theme of this game."

"Wait, I think it's a name. Go read me the names of the artists, and I'll see if any of the letters match up."

"Michaelangelo. Raphael. Donatello. Aren't these all Ninja Turtles?"

I giggle. "Yes, you didn't know the Ninja Turtles were named after famous Italian artists?"

"Wait, really?"

"Yes, now keep reading. We need one with a B."

Tanner walks around the room looking at the plaques. "Botticelli?"

"That's it. Is there a number on the plaque?"

"There's a year. 1485." I jump up from the floor and run over to the keypad lock. Carefully, I type in each number of the year, and the door clicks open. "We did it," I squeal. Tanner runs at me full force, picks me up, and spins me around. "Hell yeah! Come on; let's keep going."

"How much time do we have left?" I ask, as he sets me back down and places a kiss against my forehead.

"Forty-three minutes."

We walk into the next room, and it's an office. In the middle of the room is a large desk. A bookshelf lines one of the walls, and curtains frame each of the fake windows. There's another door, and the remaining wall space is covered with art.

"Now what?" Tanner asks.

I scan the room. "I think we need to open that door," I say, pointing to a closed door with another keypad lock. "Look for something that could be a puzzle."

Tanner walks over to the desk and starts shuffling through the papers that cover the top.

"Anything?" I ask, checking out one of the canvases.

"Just a bunch of museum blueprints, information on different pieces of art, and instructions for a fake art finder." He shrugs, setting the papers back where he found them. "Nothing is popping out at me like the letters did."

"It's another four digit number code, so maybe another date," I suggest, looking through a stack of books on top of a side table. Time continues to tick down and, despite our trying, we're not making any progress.

Forty minutes remaining.

Thirty-five minutes remaining.

Thirty minutes remaining.

"Goodness, this is stressful," I say. "We need to focus and find the code."

Tanner chuckles.

"What?"

"I thought we were just here having fun."

"We are, but now I want to win."

"Then let's win. We can do this. Do you think it's the books? Are there numbers on the spines?"

We both walk over, and start scanning the white, black, and gray books lining each shelf. "Wait, they're in a pattern," I note. "Gray, black, white, gray, black, white." I continue to say the pattern out loud moving down each shelf. "Gray, black, black."

"That's not the pattern," Tanner says. "It's out of place."

I slowly pull the book from the shelf, and the whole wall begins to move. "You've got to be kidding me," Tanner says. "We've been looking for a four digit number, and we could have just found the hidden lever." Laughter bubbles out of both of us as he grabs my hand and pulls me into the secret room.

"Kiss me," he says, spinning me toward the wall.

"We can't do anything in here. That guy's watching," I whisper, my cheeks heating. "Plus, we have less than thirty minutes."

"Kiss me," he says, pushing his hands into my hair. "You're so fucking sexy when you solve the puzzles, and I'm dying to kiss you." I shiver under his touch, and his lips find mine. He kisses me hard, gently tugging on my hair. My lips part, and his tongue dips into my mouth. It feels forbidden, and need builds between my legs. My hips rock forward against him, and for a moment I forget where we are.

"There's no PDA allowed in the game rooms," Ted says flatly over a speaker, ruining our moment.

Tanner pulls away and he pushes a piece of my hair behind my ear.

"Consider that your one warning," Ted says.

"Got it!" we both yell, laughing.

"You ready to win this?"

"Yes," I say, still a little breathless from the kiss. "Let's win it."

Moving apart, we take in our surroundings. There are five Mona Lisas on one wall, and a small black box with a key lock hangs on the wall opposite the door.

"I think we need to figure out which one is the real one," Tanner says.

"But they look exactly the same."

"Maybe we have to get closer. You start on your end, and I'll start over here."

We both move from painting to painting, but it's no use—they're all identical.

Eighteen minutes remaining.

"Do you think we missed a clue in the office room?" I ask.

"That's it," he says. He begins to jog back to the office. As he passes, he lays a chaste kiss against my lips, and yells, "Sorry, Ted."

"Where are you going?"

"You'll see."

He returns a couple minutes later holding a piece of paper and a small black device.

"What's that?" I ask.

"It's how we win. I found it in one of the desk drawers earlier." He hands me the piece of paper, and on it is a small picture of the thing Tanner is holding. Across the top reads: *Fake Art Finder*. Under the photo are instructions. "Read me what it says."

"Okay, place the black box in the center of the painting. If it beeps, it's fake, and if there's no beep it's real."

Tanner quickly starts to move from painting to painting.

Beep.

Beep.

Beep.

Beep.

No beep. Of course the last painting is the one we need. He lifts it off the wall and turns it around. Hanging off the back is a key. He grabs it and runs over to the black box. The minute he unlocks it, a dozen white and orange ping-pong balls fall onto the floor.

"Looks like another puzzle," he says.

Eleven more minutes.

"We're going to have to hurry."

"We got this," he assures me, starting to turn over the little balls. All but three are blank. On those, the letters X, L, and V are written in black sharpie.

"Another word?" he asks.

"It can't be. There's only consonants. Is there a letter lock somewhere?"

"I haven't seen one."

"Do you think by some miracle they coordinate with the code to get out?"

Six more minutes remaining.

Police sirens and lights start to be piped into the room, and even though I know it's not real, my heart rate soars. We both stare blankly at the balls.

"Fuck, we're almost out of time," he says. "I think we assume it's the code to get out and try."

"Are they Roman numerals?" I ask. "L is a Roman numeral, right?"

Three more minutes remaining.

"God, you're so fucking hot when you figure this shit out," he says, grinning. "L is the Roman numeral for fifty."

"That's right. And X is ten and V is five. That's technically five numbers if you line them up."

"Okay, yeah, but what order do we put them in? Biggest to smallest?" he asks.

"I was going to say alphabetical."

"Okay, let's try that. So the code would be 5-0-5-1-0." We both take off towards the door we entered through at the beginning, and Tanner sings the five numbers over and over again like a chant.

One minute and thirty seconds remaining.

I press the numbers into the keypad as Tanner repeats them slowly. The door clicks, and the light turns green. We did it.

"Hell yes!" he shouts, grabbing and spinning me around. "You're amazing."

"I'd say we make a pretty good team."

His lips find mine, and he slowly lowers me down his body until my feet touch the floor. "Yeah, we do!" he says, kissing me again.

CHAPTER 36: THE L-WORD
WREN

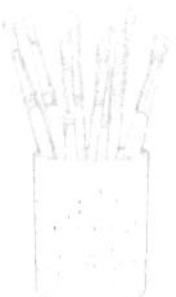

"Where are you taking me now," I ask as Tanner pulls out of the escape room parking lot.

"I needed to run an errand, and then I thought we could go grab a bite to eat."

"What kind of errand?"

"You'll see." He smirks, grabbing my upper thigh with his right hand. I place my hand over his and link our fingers.

"Today has been a really good day," I say. "I can't believe we made it out with time still on the clock. I was so nervous we weren't going to make it."

"With you I think anything is possible, so I wasn't surprised. I can't believe Ted cock-blocked me in that secret room," he chuckles.

"I promise to make it up to you later."

"Oh, do you?"

"Yes."

He continues to drive, and we both sing along to the music playing through the speakers. I mindlessly scroll on my phone.

"Anything else from your boss?" he asks.

"No, they must be surviving without me. Did your dad reach out?"

"Of course not," he says, merging into a turn lane.

I click on my email and scroll through the new messages. Four messages from the top, I have one from the mattress company that reads: *Shipping Update*. Clicking on it, I scan the contents. "You've got to be kidding me." I laugh.

"What?"

"It looks like my mattress got delayed again. Something about a cargo ship overturning. I guess my mattress is currently sinking to the bottom of the Pacific Ocean."

"Well it's a good thing you don't need one for a while."

A while. The plan was for me to only stay with him a few months, and I know we're dating now, but we haven't talked about whether or not I should look for a different place to stay. While being exclusive was a no brainer, living together officially seems like such a bigger decision. I make a mental note to look into alternative places to stay when I have time. We're already burning pretty hot—I don't want us rushing into something more serious too quickly and fizzling out.

"Yeah. I just can't believe I've hit another issue with this mattress. I guess I can go back to sleeping on the—"

"If you finish that sentence, I'm going to take you home and teach that pretty mouth of yours a lesson. Now that you've been in my bed, you will only be sleeping curled up in my arms."

"So bossy," I tease.

"You like it."

And he's right. I do like it.

"So, what were you thinking for food?"

"I've got an idea, but if you were craving something different, we could eat whatever you wanted."

"Why don't we say it on three?"

"Okay. One. Two. Three," he counts.

"Italian," we say at the same time.

"Thank god. I've been craving that since Ted said it in his little spiel." I giggle.

"Me too," he says, parking the car in front of a building I've never seen before.

"Where are we?"

"Logan's mom, Gwen's, art studio."

"Why?" I look at him a little confused. I knew Logan's mom was an artist. I met her at Donovan and Enzo's wedding in July, but I've never been to her studio before, and Tanner didn't mention anything about Logan today.

"Do you trust me?" he asks, grabbing both of my hands.

"Yes. Wait, what's going on?"

"Do you remember when I mentioned starting small with art classes and working your way up to full-blown camps?"

"What did you do?"

"Well, you said that you didn't know where you would host classes like that, and so it got me thinking that Gwen owns an art studio."

I stare at him blankly, trying to process what he's saying.

"I wasn't sure about how accessible it was, so I came down the other day and toured it, and I don't know much, but I think it might be perfect, and Gwen seemed really excited about the idea."

"You didn't have to do that. I told you I'd figure it out."

"I know, and I'm not trying to overstep. You are completely capable of doing this camp thing on your own, and if you hate this idea, we can leave and go carb load on pasta, breadsticks, and wine. But I also know that you're stubborn, and you're a little scared to take the leap because you don't want to fail, and I get it. I understand being scared of failing, so I thought maybe if I gave you a little friendly push, you could finally have a piece of your dream. I know it's not the whole camp plan, but I think it's a really good start."

I lean forward and press my lips against his. "Thank you,"

I say, tears filling my eyes. "You have no idea how much this means to me."

The L-word pops into my head, and my stomach flips. This seems too fast for love. I mean, fuck, it's only been a day, but damn if I'm not falling harder for him by the second.

"You want to go see it and talk to Gwen?"

"Yes." I smile and nod my head. "Let's go."

We climb out of the car, and I follow him down the side-walk to a door about a block from where we parked. He doesn't let go of my hand, and I smile at the thought that, since we started this thing, he hasn't let many moments go by that he wasn't touching me in some way.

"Okay, so there are three handicap parking spots right here," he says, pointing to three spaces up ahead of us.

"That's great."

"And there's no stairs to enter the building, which I thought would be good because I've been reading, and I know a lot of times people with brain injuries can have trouble with balance, and I know Cody uses a wheelchair."

"You've been reading?"

"Yeah, I know it's important to you, so I want to know more about it."

I stop right before we reach the door of the studio, and he turns to face me. Tears fill my eyes, and his face falls. "What's wrong?"

"It's just..." I say, my face breaking out into a smile. "I don't understand how you ever thought I deserved more than you. This whole day has felt magical, and now we're here and you've taken your time to learn about something so close to my heart. Tanner, you're incredible, and I feel like the luckiest girl in the world."

I step towards him and wrap my arms around his neck. Pressing my lips to his, he pulls me against him. Butterflies dip and swoop in my stomach.

"For what it's worth," he says, breaking our kiss but still

holding me close, "today was easily the second best day of my life."

"The second?"

"Yep, the best was the day I met you." He leans forward and kisses the tip of my nose. "Now let's go make your dream a reality."

He takes my hand again and opens the door. We walk into the studio space. It's large and spacious with lots of natural light. Gwen walks out from the back wearing loose overalls covered by an apron splattered with paint. Her light brown hair is pulled back out of her face using a clip.

"Hi, you two. Thanks for stopping by." She smiles at both of us warmly.

"It's so nice to see you again," I say.

"Yeah, thanks for meeting with us," Tanner says, letting go of my hand long enough to wrap Gwen up in a hug.

"Tanner tells me you're looking for a place to hold art classes," she says. "Would you like a tour of the studio?"

"I'd love that."

Her studio is incredible. There's a private studio where she paints most of her pieces, a splatter paint room, and a small gallery of her paintings.

"Are the tables adjustable?" I ask when she shows me the classroom space in the back. It's lined with long, counter-high tables and barstools, and while I'm sure the current set-up meets the needs of her usual clients, my students would require a more accessible set-up.

"They aren't," she says. "Would they need to be?"

"Yeah, the barstools might work for some people, but it would be safer if we could use chairs and then if someone is in a wheelchair, like my brother, we would need to lower the table so he could use it."

"Hmmm, well if you want to bring in adjustable tables, I wouldn't be opposed to that," Gwen says.

"That might be doable. I'd just need to look into how

much they cost. How much were you thinking you'd charge me to use the space? I'd probably start out with one class a month. If the turn out is good, then I might want to add more down the line."

"Oh, honey. You don't have to pay me. We'll just need to work it around my current schedule which shouldn't be that hard."

"Are you sure?"

"I'm positive. You two are friends with Logan and Poppy, so that makes you family."

"Well thank you. Your studio is great, and I'm so excited to get this started. You have no idea how much this means to me. I'll look into the tables, and then maybe we can meet again soon and get a plan together for the first class."

"Sounds perfect. I'm happy to help in any way I can."

"Gwen, do you mind if I use the bathroom before we head out?" Tanner asks.

"Nope, through the door on the left."

"Thanks. I'll be right back," he says, kissing me on the side of the head and then walking away.

"It's so nice to see two young people in love," Gwen muses, sitting on one of the barstools.

"I'm sorry?" I ask. "No, we just started dating last night. It's too soon for love, but maybe one day."

"Hmm," she hums. "I know love when I see it, and that boy loves you very much. He wouldn't have called me if he didn't. And I recognize the look on your face. It's the same one Poppy makes when she's around my son."

"You ready to go?" Tanner asks, walking back in from the bathroom.

"Oh, uh, yep. Thanks again, Gwen. I'll be in touch really soon."

"I look forward to it. I'm so glad y'all stopped by."

We walk out of the studio, and a cool breeze sends a shiver through me. "Goodness, it's getting colder."

"Hold on," Tanner says, removing his jacket. He wraps it around my shoulders and pulls me into his side, rubbing my arm with his hand. "Is that better?"

"Much better."

"What were you two talking about when I went to the bathroom?"

The L-word pops into my head again, and my heart rate spikes.

"Just art class stuff," I lie, and my stomach sinks. An unwanted memory of my breakup with Chad pops into my head, and I realize I'm terrified of the word love. I'm terrified that I'll eventually put myself out there and it won't be returned. Or worse, he'll say it and won't mean it.

CHAPTER 37: GOOD LUCK WITH THAT

WREN

I stick the Post-it note that Tanner left me this morning on the bulletin board in my office. It's his normal doodle of a dog and a cheetah, but this time he's drawn a little heart in the middle above their heads.

"Did one of the resident's grandkids draw you a picture?" Gray asks, walking into my office with her lunch box.

"Huh?"

"The Post-it?"

"Oh, no, it's the doodle Tanner left me this morning," I say, smiling. "He's not the best artist in the world, but I like it."

"Doodle Tanner left?" she asks, confused. "What's it

supposed to be?" She cocks her head to the side and studies the drawing.

"Oh, it's a dog and a cheetah."

"I can kinda see it. Care to explain what it means and why I'm just now learning he's been leaving you doodles?" she asks, sitting in one of the chairs in front of my desk and pulling out a salad.

"It's our thing I guess." I shrug, sitting in my chair and grabbing for my lunch. "When I went over to tour his place for the first time, he told me this story about how at the San Diego Zoo, they pair cheetahs with dogs to help the cats feel less nervous. I misunderstood, and thought he was trying to give me this dramatic metaphor about us moving in together, and it stuck. The doodles started the first morning I was living with him, and I get one every day. I'm not sure why I haven't mentioned it, but I've saved every single one."

"Do they always have a heart?"

"No, that's new." My stomach does the swoopy thing that it does every time I think about the man who continues to surprise me in the best ways. "Most of the time they reference something that happened or that we talked about."

"That's really sweet," she says. "So, spill. I know you've been holding back in the group text, and I want every last detail about your slutty little three day staycation with your new boyfriend."

"It was amazing. We spent most of it in his bed, but when we weren't there, he cooked for me, took me to an escape room, we went on a couple walks, and on Friday he surprised me by taking me to Logan's mom's studio."

"Girl, you texted us about that. I need to know the dirty, filthy details of this weekend."

My face heats, and I take a bite of my sandwich. "Close the door."

She jumps up and quickly shuts the door and spins around. "Spill."

"It's hands down the best sex I've ever had, and I know I haven't had sex with a ton of people, but holy shit, I didn't know it could be like this."

"No, you're gonna have to do better than that."

"Fine," I whisper. "The man eats like I'm his last fucking meal. The first time he went down on me, I squirted. Which isn't even something I knew my body could do. We literally cannot get enough of each other. It's mind-blowing."

"That's what I'm talking about." She laughs. "So, you're having mind-blowing sex with Tanner?"

"It's so good, girl. Like, maybe the best ever."

"Well I won't pretend like I'm not a little jealous. Not of Tanner, but of the sex."

"How's pelvic floor PT going?"

"Slow, but I'm seeing progress. I just hope one day I'll have what you, Poppy, and Lacey have found and that I'll actually maybe enjoy penetrative sex again." She breathes out.

"I know this is going to sound insane, but it feels like my body and Tanner's were made for one another. Maybe you just have to find the right person who's willing to be patient and gentle."

"Maybe. You sound like your feelings are getting serious though."

"You think it's too fast?"

"I mean, you've known him since May. I don't think it's fast."

I take another bite of my sandwich. "Logan's mom thought we were in love."

"Are you?" Her eyes go wide.

"No, we've only been together a few days, but when I think about it, I can see us ending up there."

"Does that mean your plan to move out after a few months is on hold? Or are you still going to look for another place to stay?"

"I don't know. I know serious relationships have never been his thing, and I don't want to be the type of girlfriend who doesn't give him space or comes off as clingy. I haven't looked for another place yet, but we also haven't talked about it."

"I mean he's drawing you pictures and fucking you're brains out. It sounds like he really likes you too." She laughs.

My office phone begins to ring, and I grab the receiver. "Hello, this is Wren."

"Hey, Wren. This is Johnny, the pickleball instructor. I've got a mad cold, and I don't want to get any of your people sick, so I'm going to have to cancel our lesson today. You're welcome to still use the court, but I won't be there."

"I understand. Feel better," I say, massaging my temple. "Thanks for calling and we'll see you Wednesday if you're up to it."

"Who was that?" Gray asks once I've hung up the phone.

"The guy who volunteers to give pickleball lessons. He's sick, so it looks like I'm going to have to cancel the outing. God, I can already hear Ethel and Clara complaining."

Gray laughs. "If only you were dating someone who loves pickleball," she jokes. "Then maybe he could come help you."

"It's a good idea, but I don't know if he can come. Things are really weird at his job, and he's at the office today. We texted a little this morning, but he mentioned having a lot of meetings."

"You never know."

I pull out my cell phone and click on his name.

Whatcha doing?

TANNER:

Missing you

I might have an idea of how you can see me before tonight.

TANNER 🐴:

I'm listening

Any chance you want to help me teach a pickleball lesson this afternoon? The usual instructor is sick and if I don't do it, the residents are going to revolt against me.

TANNER 🐴:

I'm there

TANNER 🐴:

Send me the address and the time

You sure? I know you're at the office today.

TANNER 🐴:

I'm done with my meetings and my dad left early to check out a new project

TANNER 🐴:

I want to see you

Good! We should get there around 3. Here's the address.

"Look at you smiling," Gray says. "I guess that means he's coming."

"Yeah, he said he'd help me."

"What's going on with his job?"

"It's a whole mess, but I'm not sure it's my story to tell."

"I get that. Is there anything we can do to help?"

Ever since Tanner brought me to Gwen's studio, I've been trying to think of a way to help him. He told me that he understood what it was like to be scared to fail and that he thought I could use a friendly push.

"Actually, now that you mention it, can you help me get everyone to The Local on Friday?"

"That should be easy. Why though?"

"I have an idea, and I think having everyone there will

help. I still have to work out some things, but if you can get everyone to come that would be a good start."

"You got it. Oh, shoot—what time is it?" she asks, turning and looking at the clock on my wall.

"Twelve twenty-seven."

"Fuck, the orthotist is coming today at twelve-thirty to measure Mr. Benson for his AFO and I completely forgot. I guess I'll be finishing my lunch later."

"Oh, no. I'll actually walk with you if you don't mind. I need to talk to Margaret about something."

"You don't want to finish eating?"

"I'm done. I really should try to convince Tanner to pack my lunches. There is only so much turkey and bread a person can eat." We both stand and head out of my office and toward the therapy gym.

"Hey, Wren, what brings you to our neck of the woods," Jasmine, the physical therapy assistant asks when we walk in.

"I came to talk to Margaret about Thanksgiving for the residents. Is she in her office?"

"No, you just missed her. I think she had a doctor's appointment or something," Jasmine explains, walking by us and out of the room.

"Hey, y'all," Poppy says, walking into the gym. "Sorry I missed lunch. Chloe and I are swamped."

"It's fine. We actually had to cut it short because I forgot the orthotist was coming today," Gray says. "You did miss all the good gossip about Wren and Tanner though."

"No way. That's not fair."

"What's not fair?" Lacey asks, joining us.

"Wren gave Gray all the dirty details about her new relationship and we missed it," Poppy says.

"Yeah, sounds like you were wrong, Lace, and Tanner is far from mediocre in bed" Gray laughs, and my cheeks blush.

"Way to make it weird," I deadpan.

"Ha!" Lacey laughs. "It's not weird. Look, he and I were

both drunk and obviously had no connection. I'm happy for you both. It's crazy how good sex can be when you're doing it with the right person, and it sounds like Tanner is yours and Jace is definitely mine." She wiggles her eyes at me.

"You're so right," I say, thinking back to my weekend.

"Excuse me, I'm looking for the physical therapist," a deep voice says, in an accent I can't place, causing all of us to turn toward the door and stare.

The man standing before us is tall, and if I had to guess, he's around Tanner's age. He has dark hair and a beard. He's wearing blue scrubs and glasses.

"Cal?" Gray says, staring stunned at the man still standing in the doorway. "What are you doing here?"

He chuckles, "Grayson Arceneaux? Is that really you?" He moves into the room and wraps her up in a hug. "Your brother said you lived outside Atlanta and that I should reach out, and I just haven't had the time. It's really good to see you."

"Yeah, same. I'm guessing since you're here looking for the PT that you're the orthotist I'm meeting?"

"I guess I am."

Lacey clears her throat, and Gray turns to see all three of us staring at her.

"Oh, I'm sorry. These are my friends, Lacey, Poppy, and Wren." She points to each of us as she says our names. "Girls, this is Cal. He's my older brother, Torren's, best friend.

"What a small world," I say, looking at Gray, who fidgets nervously.

"It really is. Okay, well Mr. Benson is in his room. If you follow me, I'll take you down there so you can get him measured."

"It was nice to meet you," he says. "Maybe I'll see you all around."

"Nice to meet you," I say. Lacey and Poppy offer him a wave.

We all smile, and the two of them disappear down the hall.

"Was it just me or did she seem a little nervous?" Lacey asks, once they're out of ear shot.

"Oh, she definitely did," Poppy says. "He was cute too."

"You think there's a history there?" I ask.

Poppy shrugs. "I'm not sure, but we should ask her."

"I told Gray earlier that I was thinking we could all go to The Local on Friday…maybe we can convince her to invite him."

"Yes," Lacey says. "I like that idea."

"I'm in, and I'm sure Logan will be too," Poppy says, glancing at her watch. "Ugh, I gotta go. My productivity is going to be shit today."

"Same," Lacey says.

"When is your productivity not shit?" Poppy teases as the three of us walk back into the hall.

"That's not true. Margaret hasn't talked to me about it in over a month," Lacey quips. "What do you have the rest of the day, Wren?"

"Book club, and then Tanner is meeting me at the pickle-ball courts. He's helping me with lessons because the normal guy is sick."

"You're really going to bring him around Clara and Ethel?" Lacey's eyes go wide. "Good luck with that!"

CHAPTER 38: STOP DEFLECTING
TANNER

I pull into the parking lot of the pickleball courts and grab my paddle and water bottle. I'm not exactly sure what Wren needs me to do, but I knew coming meant I got to see her, and I will jump at that opportunity every chance I get.

"Hi!" Wren says, waving in my direction. Her whole face breaks into a wide grin when she sees me. She's standing with a small group of men and women. Each one is over eighty and dressed in tracksuits.

I quicken my pace, jogging across the grass and through the metal gate. Scooping her up, I spin her around and then set her down slowly. Pushing her hair behind her ear, my eyes find hers. "Am I allowed to kiss you?" I ask.

"Maybe a quick peck," she says, rising up on her toes. Her lips find mine in a chaste kiss.

"You got to kiss her better than that, honey," a woman with gray hair says.

"Yeah, kiss her like you mean it," the woman with white hair and a walker says.

"I think we should give the people what they want," I say, smirking.

"Not at my job," she says, giggling and swatting me away. "Tanner, this is Mr. Eugene, Mr. Silas, and Mr. Morton."

"It's nice to meet y'all," I say. "And who are these two beautiful ladies?"

Both women blush. "I'm Clara, and this is Ethel."

"It's a pleasure," I say, laying on the charm thick.

"He's very cute," Clara says.

"Looks like I might have some competition," Eugene chuckles.

"You know I only have eyes for you," Clara says.

"Ms. Clara and Mr. Eugene are dating," Wren explains.

Ethel moves toward me and starts to study me. "He's much cuter than that Johnny," she says. "See, Wren, this is what we meant by eye candy. You should bring him around Dogwood Manor more often. You're a very lucky girl."

"I like to think I'm the lucky one," I say, putting my hand around Wren's shoulders, tugging her a little closer. She looks up at me and smiles.

"Alright," she says. "We need to get started or we're going to be late for dinner. Tanner, Ms. Ethel and Ms. Clara like to watch, so I'll sit over here with them. Usually, Johnny takes the men out and they do some easy drills and then play a doubles game."

"Sounds easy enough," I say. "Gentleman, shall we?"

The men join me on the court.

"Why don't we start by warming up. Arms out, and let's do some stretches. All three men put their arms out to the side. Following my lead, they begin to do arm circles.

"Good. Alright take your right arm across your body." I demonstrate and they copy me. "That's right, and now your left." We finish stretching our arms. "Alright fellas, we're gonna do a couple lunges."

Silas seems to be struggling, so I walk over and attempt to help him.

"Step back with your left foot, and lean forward on to

your right, bending your knee a little." I step behind him, helping him keep his balance.

"If I knew there was an opportunity for you to help me stretch, then I would have volunteered to play," Ethel says.

I let out a laugh and shake my head. These women are a little spicy, and it's not what I expected. We finish our stretches, and then each takes a spot on the court. For old guys, all three men are actually pretty good at the sport. We play half a game and then break for water.

"Do you ever play?" I ask, sitting next to Wren.

"Johnny usually handles it," she says.

"We've been trying to convince her to play with us," Morton says. "But she never says yes."

"Why don't we switch," I say. "I'll sit here with the ladies and you go show the men how it's done."

She looks at me.

"Go and play," Clara says. "Let us spend some time with this man of yours."

"Go. I could use a break. Morton's got quite the swing." I chuckle.

She walks out onto the court, and I move closer to Clara on the bench. "So, how long have you loved our Wren?" she asks, as soon as Wren's out of earshot.

"Woah," I laugh. "You ladies don't waste any time do you?"

"Silas and Morton can never last a full game," Clara explains. "Stop deflecting and answer my question."

"We've only been together a few days," I say.

"Oh, please, you have love written all over your face," she says.

I glance toward Wren. Her ponytail swings behind her as she swings the paddle, hitting the ball back over the net. Silas hits it back towards her, and she misses it. He shouts something at her, and she bursts into a fit of giggles. She looks over at me, so I throw her a wink, and she winks back.

"It's true," Ethel agrees. "It's radiating off of the both of you."

The both of you. I know without a doubt they're right about me, and I hope that maybe they're right about her too.

Wren and the men walk over once the game is finished. "Last time we ask you to play with us," Silas says, patting Wren on the arm. "You've been holding back, sweetheart. You're a tough pickleball player."

"I don't know about that," she says. "You two gave Eugene and me here a run for our money."

"You flatter us," Morton says. "But he's right. You're very good."

"Ladies, y'all sure you don't want to play?" I ask.

"Oh, no, honey," Clara says. "You put Ethel and me out there and we'd both be catching a ride back to Dogwood Manor in an ambulance instead of the bus."

"She's right!" Ethel laughs. "We just come to watch the athletes do their thing."

Wren giggles. "Okay, everyone. Time to go home."

We all make our way over to the bus, and I help Ethel and Clara up the stairs and to their seats. Eugene sits next to Clara and immediately finds her hand. "Thank you for helping my girl," he says.

"It was my pleasure."

"Tanner, you sure you don't want to come back with us?" Ethel asks.

"I'll have to stop by some other time," I say. "It was nice meeting you all."

Wren and I walk back off the bus together and stop at the bottom of the stairs. "Thanks again for today," she says. "You were a real lifesaver."

"I'll always come when you call," I assure her. "Today was fun. The ladies are a hoot."

"Oh, yeah, they're two of my favorites."

I lean down and cup her face, kissing her gently. Her lips

part slightly, and I push my tongue forward. Our tongues tangle, and when she pulls away, her cheeks are tinted pink.

"I'm going to get them back and then I'll be done for the day. I'll see you at the apartment."

"Sounds good." She wraps her arms around me, and I kiss the top of her head. I watch as she walks up the stairs. "Now, that was a kiss!" Ethel yells, before the doors close.

CHAPTER 39: HEY, BARTENDER
TANNER

Wren insisted that she and I go out with our friends tonight, and while I enjoy everyone's company, the idea of staying in with Wren was tempting as shit. She only convinced me by promising a dance and a night of barely sleeping once we're home.

I'm convinced that no one is better together than we are. The conversation with Ethel and Clara from Monday has continuously replayed in my head this week, and I keep having the urge to tell her how I feel, but I don't want to scare her.

We make our way inside, and as we walk past the bar, she greets Tony and Frank, the bartenders, by name.

"You know the guys?" I ask.

"Everyone knows Tony and Frank," she says.

I shoot her a questioning look. "I'm certain you've never known their names before."

"Oh, look there's the group," she says, smiling and pulling me towards the table.

"Who's the new guy?" Sitting next to Gray is a man I've never seen before.

"Oh, good! She invited him. That's Cal."

Who the hell is Cal? We arrive at the table and I greet our friends. "I'm Tanner," I say, reaching out my hand and shaking the stranger's hand.

"Cal," he says. "Grayson—I mean Gray—and I knew each other as kids. I'm good friends with one of her older brothers."

"It's nice to meet you. What brings you to town?"

"I just transferred to Atlanta for work."

"What do you do?" Logan asks him.

"I'm an orthotist, so I make braces and splints for individuals with physical disabilities."

"Yeah, it's so crazy because I had contacted his office for one of our residents, and I had no idea he worked there. He walked in on Monday," Gray explains.

"Well, we're glad you could make it, man," I say. "Maybe you and Gray can play me and Wren in ping-pong in a bit." I nod my head toward the table.

"Why would we do that?" Gray says, panicked.

"It could be fun," Cal says.

Lacey, Poppy, and Wren all giggle.

"Just tell us when y'all are ready," I say.

Gray's whole face turns beat red, and she throws me a look that makes me fear for my life.

"Or not. So, what's everyone drinking? It's on me."

"No," Jacks argues. "I'll open a tab."

"Respectfully, I'm out with my girl for the first time since we got together." I pull Wren into me, and wrap my arms around her, kissing the side of my head. "We're celebrating, so let me."

Jacks shakes his head. "Fine, but you have to let us next time."

"Are Donovan and Enzo coming?" I ask.

"No, they had a family thing," Chloe says.

"Alright, is everyone drinking their usuals?" I ask.

My friends nod. "Cal, what are you drinking?"

"I'll just have a beer."

"Got it."

"I'll help you with the drinks," Wren says. We make our way to the bar. There's a moderate crowd, and we push our way to the front, catching Tony's attention.

"Give me a second, y'all," he says. "Frank had to leave, so I'm back here by myself." His eyes shift to Wren.

"Babe, you should help him," she suggests.

"What?"

"You know how to make drinks. Look how swamped he is; I'm sure he could use the help."

"I can't do that. Can I?" I chuckle.

"Actually, if you wouldn't mind." Tony says, looking toward the people gathering next to the bar.

"Y'all are both serious?"

"It's fine," Wren says. "Jump back there. And I'll go get the girls to help me carry the drinks," she encourages.

"But I was looking forward to dancing with you," I whine.

"Just help him through the rush, and then you can pick the song." She winks, and I let out a chuckle.

Something tells me I'm missing something, but Tony's a friend, and the bar is packed. Wren disappears into the crowd, and I run around, joining him on the other side of the bar. "Tell me what you need me to do," I say.

"I'll take over here, and you can take over there." I nod then head to the opposite side.

I work nonstop, taking orders, making drinks, and talking to the bar goers. Tony and I work in tandem, and while it's hard work, it feels more like play, and outside of the past week with Wren, it's the most fun I've had in a long time.

Wren finds me from across the bar and smiles wide, giving me a thumbs up. I shake my head, topping off a vodka soda with carbonated water and then handing it to the man in front of me.

"What can I get you?" I ask the next man waiting to order.

"Two beers and a dirty Shirley," he says.

I flip around to grab the beer from the cooler, and someone catches my eye, but it's not Wren. Leaned up against the bar, watching me work, is Jerry. He nods in my direction, and I nod back, grabbing the beers, and then getting started on the cocktail.

"Hey, bartender," Wren says, bouncing over to the bar.

I chuckle. "Do you need a refill?"

"Please," she says. "Gray also needs another martini."

"You got it."

I prepare a cosmo and dirty martini then slide them towards her. "Are you having fun?" she asks, taking the drinks.

"I actually am." My mouth spreads into a grin. "I mean, I'm looking forward to our dance later, and I wish you were back here with me, but this feels good."

"Good," she says. Reaching forward, she fists my shirt and pulls me into a kiss.

"What was that for?" I ask.

"Those girls over there have been eyeing you since you jumped back here. I wanted to make sure they knew you were mine."

She turns her head and throws them a borderline evil smile.

"Come find me when you're done," she says, disappearing into the crowd with both drinks.

Tony and I continue to work, and the crowd slowly dies down. I'm halfway through making an order of four espresso martinis when I hear someone clear their throat. I look up to find Jerry standing before me.

"Tony," he yells. "Take over this order for Tanner. He and I need to talk." Tony nods and walks over to begin making the remaining two drinks.

I dry my hands, round the bar, and then follow him to his

office. He leads me through the door and leans up against the edge of his desk.

"You're a natural," he says, crossing his arms.

"It's not that hard," I say.

"No, but it's not easy. Why did you never call me about the bar?"

I shrug. "Honestly, I'm not sure. I had an opportunity to impress my dad, and I took it even though, deep down, I never really wanted it, and I kept hoping I could do both, and then it felt too late."

"That's what that girlfriend of yours said."

"You talked to Wren?"

"I did. She called up here the other day and left a message for me to call her back. Told me she had a potential buyer for the bar."

I chuckle. "Did she?"

"Yes, so you can imagine my surprise when she said you were the potential buyer. Especially since I hadn't heard from you."

"I've been regretting that lately," I say, honestly. "I'm sorry."

"She told me that too." He smiles.

"Of course she did."

"Well," he says, "I love this bar, and I'm not going to sell it to just anyone. When I offered it to you in August, it was because you are currently the only person I trust enough to take it over. And after watching you help out Tony tonight, I've never been more sure. The bar was yours three months ago, it's yours today, and while I hope you make a decision sooner, it'll still be yours a year from now."

"You haven't looked for other potential buyers?"

"No, because I've learned to trust my gut, and my gut was telling me you'd call me. I know you want this, and nothing would make me prouder than having you take over my legacy."

"I'm sorry," I say, rubbing the back of my neck. "I'm honestly at a loss of words. I was sure I had missed my chance."

He shakes his head. "So what will it be? You want it, or are you going to make me lose a year of my retirement while I wait on you to make a decision."

My shoulders shake with laughter, and I turn over his offer for a short moment, knowing without a doubt what my answer should be. "You have yourself a deal," I say, putting out my hand and shaking his.

"We were hoping you'd say that," Wren says from the door.

"What are you doing back there?" I ask, surprised.

"Well, I saw you two sneak away, and selfishly I wanted to be here for the moment you said yes."

"Come here." She joins us in the office, and I wrap my arms around her.

"I'll contact my lawyer to begin the paperwork, and I'll be in touch next week," Jerry says.

"I look forward to it."

We follow him out of the office, and he closes and locks the door behind us. "Y'all enjoy the rest of your night. I'm going home to my wife."

"Thanks again," I say, shaking his hand once more.

"Don't thank me," he says, looking at Wren. He turns and heads to the back door. I grab her hand and begin dragging her towards the front of the building.

"Where are we going?" she calls, giggling and squeezing my hand tighter.

I don't stop until we're outside, and then I push her up against the bricks and take her mouth in mine.

"You are amazing," I say, pulling away from her. "Thank you for tonight."

"I thought you might need a gentle push too," she says.

"I did."

She wraps her hands around my neck and brings her lips to mine. For the next few minutes I lose myself in her kiss and we make out like two teenagers. She tastes like the cosmos she's been drinking, and when she pulls away, I feel drunk off of her kiss.

"Want to head out?" I ask, trying to catch my breath.

"Soon, but not yet." She places a chaste kiss against my lips. "What are you going to do about Austere?"

"I'm going to tell my dad the truth. I'll stay on through his retirement party, but then I'll back out gracefully and focus on doing something I know will bring me joy."

"That sounds like a good plan," she says. "When is that?"

"Next Friday. I was actually thinking about skipping it because they'll be announcing the new CEO, and I didn't think I could stomach going, but maybe if you come with me, I can hang on a little while longer. I think it's the right thing to do, and I know agreeing to attend will soften the blow."

"It would be an honor to be the girl on your arm," she says.

"You'd have to meet my parents."

"I'd like that."

"You sure? They can be a lot."

"I know, and I'll be by your side the entire night."

I lean down, kissing the tip of her nose. "Thank you." The door to our left swings open, and Lacey appears. "So, are we celebrating?" she asks.

"They all know, don't they?" I ask.

"Well, I figured tonight would be a big deal, and you'd want them here."

"We're celebrating," I say, smiling.

"Yes!" Lacey squeals. "I'll go order a round of shots, and I'll see you two at the table." She spins and disappears back into the bar.

Wren and I follow behind her, heading to the table.

"So, T, what are you going to call it once it's yours?" Logan asks once we're all back together.

"Yeah, are you going to keep the name or change it?" Poppy asks.

"I was thinking I'd change it," I say. *"Tanner's: The Local Spot* has a nice ring to it."

"It's perfect," Wren says.

Lacey returns with a tray full of tequila shots and limes.

"Not fucking tequila," Logan groans.

"Stop being a baby, Peterson," Lacey quips. "Everyone grab a shot."

"To Tanner's!" Wren yells.

"To Tanner's!" the rest of us repeat, clinking our glasses together. I bring mine to the table, tapping it against the wood, and shoot it back, chasing it with a lime. Grabbing Wren, I dip her into a kiss.

"Come on, pretty girl. You owe me a dance."

She takes my hand and leads me toward the dance floor. We stop in the middle of the floor, and I jog over to the DJ to request a song.

"You Make My Dreams (Come True)" by Hall and Oates begins to play, and I spin around. Her mouth spreads into a wide grin, and once again, we get lost in each other, dancing around the bar that will soon be *mine*.

CHAPTER 40: MY WILD GIRL
TANNER

Tonight meant more to me than Wren will ever know. We're laying in bed, and she's curled up in my arms. My mind is bouncing between thoughts of the bar and telling her I love her, but I've never said those words to anyone before, and it's scary as hell. I think I probably need to take her on a few more dates, and then if I can muster the courage, I'll tell her when the timing is right.

"You still awake?" I ask.

"Yeah."

"What's something you've always wanted to try but have never gotten the chance to do?"

"Um, like sexually?" she asks, and even though that's not what I meant, I love that's where her head went.

"I meant like a non-sexual activity." I chuckle. "I was just thinking about our next date, but now I want to know what popped into that head of yours."

"Oh, oops," she says. "No, forget I said that. I've always wanted to take a pottery class."

"No, you're thinking about something, and I must know what it is."

"Yeah, a pottery class," she says.

"No, you're thinking about a sex activity. What is it?"

"It's silly."

"I doubt it. Come on—I'll tell you my sexual fantasy if you tell me yours."

She hesitates again.

"I'm gonna start guessing," I warn.

"Don't you dare."

"Is it me in bat wings like that book you like?"

"No." She giggles. "Although, now that you mention it, that might be added to the list."

"Come on, tell me. This is a judgment free zone."

"Okay, well I've always wanted a guy to, um, fuck my mouth." She turns her head away from me, and buries it in her hands.

"Like a blow job?" I question, confused, because she literally gave me one an hour ago.

"Well, yeah, but not like a normal blow job. Like I've always wanted to try the thing where I hang my head off the side of the bed and the guy fucks my mouth."

"Consider it done," I say, jumping out of bed, pulling her towards the edge.

"I didn't mean right now, you psycho," she says, laughing hard. "You have to tell me yours first."

She sits up, and I climb back into the bed. "That wasn't on my list of things I wanted to try, but it sounds hot as fuck, and I'll gladly fuck that pretty mouth of yours anytime you want."

"Good to know," she says, kissing me. "Now tell me yours."

"Butt stuff," I say, quickly.

"Okay," she says. "You're gonna need to elaborate. Like do you want me to use a finger or are we talking full blown pegging, because I've never done either before, but I could research how."

"What? No," I say, starting to panic a little. "I didn't mean my butt. I meant yours."

"Oh!" She laughs. "Well, you need to be more specific. So, are we talking just a finger or anal? Because I'm not opposed to anal, but your dick is really big, and I think we'd really have to work up to that."

Her statement shocks me a little, and I'm surprised how easy this conversation feels.

"I didn't mean anal. Have you ever used a plug?"

"No, but I'm game to try it if it's something that would turn you on. I have a few vibrators, so I like toys."

"You're serious?"

"I mean, yeah. Sex for me has always been boring and vanilla, and I've always wanted to spice things up with previous partners, but I didn't trust them enough. I trust you, though, so if you wanted to try it, I would. I know you won't hurt me."

It's official. I'm the luckiest man alive.

"I don't want you to feel like you have to do anything."

"I know I don't, but it does intrigue me a little, and I think it might be exciting to try new things with you. Have you ever used one with a partner?"

"No, that would've required the girl to stick around for longer than one night, and they never did."

"Got it. Well I don't plan on going anywhere, so I say order one, and we can figure it out together."

"You're serious?"

"Yes," she says. "I promise."

"Good," I lean forward, and my mouth finds hers. Her hand finds my cock and takes me by surprise.

"Wren."

"What? All that sex talk made me horny, and now all I can think about is hanging my head over the side of the bed."

"You're serious?" I ask again. She nods, stroking my shaft.

"Please fuck my mouth," she begs.

Fuck.

She begins to tug on the band of my underwear. My cock springs free. She wraps her hand around my length again, stroking me a few times before running her thumb over the tip, collecting the bead of salty liquid gathered there. Her finger meets her tongue, and I watch in awe as my girl sucks it clean.

"I want to take care of you first," I say, rolling to my back. "Sit on my face, and then I promise to make your fantasy come true."

I watch as she removes her thong and climbs toward me. Positioning herself above me, she straddles my head.

"Sit," I command, and she does.

I take her pussy into my mouth and watch as she grips the headboard above me. I work her center with my tongue, and she writhes against my face. Fuck, there is nothing better than her using me like this. My dick strains under the sheets, and I could easily come like this, but I know it's not what she wants.

No, my wild girl wants me to fuck her mouth, and who am I to tell her no.

My hands find her ass, and I push her up gently so I can speak.

"Tanner," she pleads, desperate for more. "Don't stop."

"Can I touch you here?" I ask, rolling my hands around her hips and over her ass until I reach her puckered hole.

"Yes," she nods.

"I'll be gentle," I promise. "Sit for me, baby," I urge her, and when she does, I suck her clit back into my mouth. My finger gently circles her asshole.

She moans and pushes into the finger. The tip gently stretches her, and another moan escapes her lips. "Fuck… Tanner…yesssss…fuckkkk," she says, grinding against my face.

I continue to play with her ass, lapping up everything her pussy gives me.

"I'm close," she says, her hips now moving quicker. My tongue finds her clit, and I inch the finger a little deeper. I feel her body relax above me as she meets her climax, and she rides out every last wave.

She moves down my body and takes my mouth with hers.

"It's my turn," she says, moving to sit up on her knees, turning away from me. I move out of the bed, and she pulls the T-shirt she's wearing over her head, giving me the perfect few of her back and ass.

"Fuck, you're sexy," I say. Leaning forward, I kiss her shoulder, and she turns her head, exposing more of her neck, so I place a line of kisses all the way up to her ear.

"You sure you want me to do this?" I ask. "I don't want to hurt you."

"I'm not some porcelain doll that'll break. This was my idea, so I'm very sure that I want to try it," she says, looking over my shoulder.

"I want to make sure I take care of you too," I say, taking a step back. I study the bed, and my mind tries to think through the logistics of what we're about to try and where I'll put my hands.

"You just did. Let me take care of you." She lays down on her back, tipping her head over the edge of the mattress. Her red hair cascades down, and I take a step closer to her.

A sly smile spreads across her face, and my cock leaks at the idea that I can turn her on like this and that she wants to try new things with me.

"Now tell me what to do," she says.

"Open," I say, and her whole body shivers. Her lips part, and I push my dick into her mouth. Her hands find the back of my thighs. She pulls me closer, opening her throat as she takes me deeper.

A moan escapes and vibrates around my cock, and I know

I'm not going to last long. I begin to pump my hips forward, and she takes me deep into her throat over and over again. Reaching down, I pinch and play with her nipples, and a long moan escapes from her mouth.

She whimpers around me, and I try to pull back, worried it might be too much for her, but her fingers dig into the back of my thighs and she holds me against her, taking everything I have to give. There's no way I'm going to last long, and despite my best efforts, I can feel myself nearing the edge.

"Look at you," I say, mesmerized by the sight before me. Her whole body is splayed across my bed, and her pink lips are around my shaft. "You're taking me so well, pretty girl. I'm almost there."

She hallows out her cheeks, and after two more pumps, the tension at the base of my spine releases. I coat the back of her throat with my cum. She hangs on, swallowing every bit of it. When I finish, I take a step back and carefully sit her up. Tears streak her face, and my heart drops a little.

"Did I hurt you?" I ask.

"Are you kidding?" she asks. Her blue-green eyes are still a little glossy, and her cheeks are flushed. "That was so fucking hot. We're definitely doing that again." Her mouth forms into a sexy grin, and fuck I don't know what I did to deserve her, but I know now that I have her, I can never lose her.

"You did so good," I say, sitting next to her and running the pad of my thumb over her cheeks. She leans forward and kisses me.

"Did you like it?" she asks.

"Did I like that?" I laugh. "Babe, that was the hottest thing I've ever done. Sorry it didn't last longer, but I just couldn't help it."

"That's okay. I have some ideas for how we can spice it up next time." She giggles.

"My wild girl. What am I going to do with you?" I ask, kissing her again.

CHAPTER 41: YOU CAME
WREN

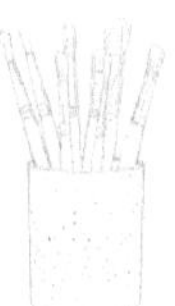

It's been one week since Tanner decided to officially buy The Local and told his father he was leaving Austere. From what he told me, I don't think his dad was very accepting of his decision, but he agreed that Tanner needed to show his face at the party tonight honoring the company's new CEO.

Despite the nerves I know he's feeling, he still managed to surprise me with a whole new outfit for tonight. When I got home from work, a beautiful emerald satin gown was hanging in my room. It's the green version of the iconic *How To Lose A Guy In 10 Days* dress that Kate Hudson wore. It's absolutely stunning, and it fits me like a glove.

I walk out of my room, and he's standing in the living room wearing a black suit, with a white shirt and a tie that matches my dress. His hair is pulled into a bun on the top of his head.

"Wow," he says, drinking me in. He spins his finger in the air, and I twirl. "You're a knockout, Wren Dawson."

He walks toward me and wraps me in his arm. "You feeling good about tonight?" I ask.

"I don't know. Part of me is so ready to move on, but it's

also a little embarrassing. The entire company knows Stuart was picked over me, and while I know I need to be there, I don't want to be."

"I think what you're doing is very honorable. I'm so proud to be your girlfriend and to get to walk into that party on your arm."

He releases me and tugs on his tie, loosening it a little.

"I wish I didn't have to be in a fucking suit," he says. "Maybe I should go change."

"Absolutely not. You might hate wearing it, but I will be the one taking it off of you tonight," I tease. "You look like a snack."

He laughs, and his shoulders relax.

"Also, we can still dress up nice and have a little fun." I pick up the hem of my dress and show off the sneakers that adorn my feet instead of heels. "Go change your shoes so you're a little more comfortable."

"Seriously?" he asks.

"Yes, we're in this together," I say, fixing his tie. "We make a good team, remember."

Tanner leans forward and kisses me.

"You're right." He heads into his room, and when he returns, sneakers adorn both of his feet.

"Better?" I ask.

"Much better. Let's get it over with." Hand in hand, we walk down to his car. During the drive over, we discuss plans for the bar, the progress I've made for my art classes, and the upcoming therapy session he has scheduled. His hand remains on my thigh the entire drive.

He pulls into the hotel that's hosting his company. The valet attendant opens his door, and Tanner makes his way around the car, opens my door, and helps me out.

"You ready?" I ask.

"As I'll ever be," he says.

We walk into the banquet room together. It's obvious a lot

of money was dropped on the event, and everywhere you look there are tables of food or bars. Four large crystal chandeliers adorn the ceiling. Waiters walk around with trays of hors d'oeuvres, and at the front of the space is an empty dance floor and a DJ playing music.

Tanner scans the room.

"Do you see your parents?"

"No."

"Should we get a drink then?"

"Yes, a drink sounds perfect." We begin walking across the room, and Tanner gets stopped by someone I've never seen before. "Hi, John," he says. "This is my girlfriend, Wren. Wren, this is John, my assistant."

"Oh, it's so nice to meet you," I say, shaking his hand. "Tanner has nothing but nice things to say about you."

John smiles. "I sure am going to miss him being my boss," he says, rocking back on his heels.

"You might be the only person I miss from Austere," Tanner says, tapping him across the shoulders.

"I'm going let you two talk, and I'm going to get those drinks," I say, squeezing Tanner's hand. "I'll be right back." He nods, and I walk away looking for a bar.

"What can I get you?" the bartender asks when I walk up to the first one I see.

"Can you make a cosmo?"

"Not here," she says. "If you go across the room to the bigger bar, they can make you whatever you want. This one only has beer and wine."

"Thanks," I say, smiling and heading toward the larger bar. It's mostly empty except for two men. I move by them, stepping up to the bar and grabbing the bartender's attention.

"How can I help you?" he asks.

"Can I get a cosmo, and then just a bottle of beer."

"Sure thing," he says, turning around to prepare my drink.

"It's embarrassing," the younger man standing to my right says. "If I were him, I wouldn't have even shown my face."

I scoot a little further away from them, trying my best not to eavesdrop.

"Always has to make a show," the older gentleman says.

"Yeah, but a bar." I follow the man's gaze and see that he's staring at Tanner.

Fire boils under my skin. I know they aren't talking about him like that.

"Excuse me," I say, catching both of their attention.

"Can we help you?" the older gentleman asks.

"It's just always been interesting to me how no matter where you are, you can always tell who the smallest men in the room are."

"I'm not following," he says.

"The smallest men in a room are always the ones who feel the need to cut down others. I didn't catch your entire conversation, but I heard enough."

"Excuse me," the younger man says, aghast.

"You heard me," I snap, turning to grab our drinks. I walk back toward Tanner, and I try to calm my rage, but it's no use.No wonder he wanted to skip tonight.

Fucking assholes.

Anger thrums through my body, and I sip my drink, trying to calm myself.

"I was thinking that maybe we just duck out early," he says as I hand him his beer.

"No, I'm not going to let these dicks make you feel unwelcome," I breathe out.

"You good?

"Oh, yeah," I say, trying to reign myself in.

"You sure you seem a little flustered."

"No, I'm good. Actually, you want to go dance?"

"There's no one dancing," he laughs. "I think the dance floor is more for show at these types of things."

"That's never stopped us before." I grab his beer and set both of our drinks on a nearby table.

We walk toward the dance floor, and the upbeat song shifts to "It Had To Be You" by Frank Sinatra. Tanner takes my hand, pulling me into him. His hands find my lower back, and mine wrap around his neck. He holds me close. As the lyrics continue singing about love, the entire room melts away.

"I'm so proud of you," I tell him.

"What made you tell me that?"

"I just know how hard this is for you." He pulls me in and kisses me on the forehead. We continue to sway in each other's arms, and when I look around the room, I spot the two assholes from the bar watching us with unamused looks on their faces.

The music fades, and "Shut up and Dance," by Walk the Moon begins to play. Tanner spins me out and then immediately back into him. We're still the only people on the dance floor, and I'm sure everyone in this stuffy room thinks we're nuts, but I don't care. All I care about is that when Tanner looks back on tonight it's a good memory, not a bad one.

The music continues to play, and song after song he twirls me, and we dance like no one is watching and we're the only two goofballs in the entire world.

"I need to run to the bathroom," I giggle, as he twirls me into him. "Can we pause the dancing for a minute?"

"That's fine. I'm thirsty anyway. I'll go grab us something, and then we probably do need to find my parents. I'm sure they've seen us by now."

He kisses the top of my head, and I head one way while he heads in the other direction. I quickly use the restroom and wash my hands. I'm fixing my hair, when I hear my phone ping. Pulling it out, I'm met with a flurry of missed phone calls and text messages all from my mom and dad.

My heart sinks, and my mind begins to race as I click on the text messages.

MOM:

Hey, sweetheart. Please call us when you see this.

DAD:

Wren, it's Cody. He had a grand mal seizure, and we're at the hospital. He's doing okay, but please call as soon as you can.

DAD:

They have us in room 4567.

I'm so sorry. I'm on my way.

Panic over takes me, and I need to get out of here—quickly. I need to get to my family. Cody needs me. *Fuck.* Without hesitating, I take off running to the front of the hotel, calling for an Uber as I move.

Three minutes away.

Through tears, I swipe up and click on Tanner's name. I stare at the blank text box for a minute, not entirely sure what to say.

I'm sorry to do this, but Cody had a seizure. I'm on my way to the hospital, and I'm not entirely sure when I'll be back to the apartment. I'll text you when I know more. 🤍

My Uber arrives, and I slide in the back seat. "If you could hurry—it's my little brother," I say, choking back tears and putting my phone back in my purse.

"I'll do my best," she says.

My leg shakes up and down, and I play nervously with

the bracelet on my wrist. Tears continue to fall, as she weaves in and out of traffic on the way to the hospital.

She gets me there in fifteen minutes, and I have the door open and my feet are on the pavement before she comes to a complete stop.

"I hope everything is alright," she says right before the door shuts behind me.

I barge through the doors and am met by the nurse working the intake desk in the emergency room.

"Hi," I say, shaking. "I'm here to see my brother, Cody Dawson. I think he's in room 3567 or maybe it was 4567. I'm sorry I don't remember." I reach for my purse and realize that, in my rush, I left it in the back of the Uber.

Shit.

"Wren?" My dad's voice comes from behind me, and I completely crumble at the sound of it. "Oh, honey, I'm so glad you're here."

I move quickly toward him, and he wraps me in a big hug. "Where is he? Is he okay? What happened? Dad, I'm so sorry I wasn't answering. I was at a party, and I didn't hear it or feel it."

"Calm down, sweetie," he says, pulling away from me and grabbing me by the shoulders. "Cody's alright. It was scary there for a minute, but the ambulance got there fast. He's a little tired, but he's going to be okay."

"Thank goodness," I breathe out, wiping my eyes. "Can I see him?"

"Sure, come on. I'm surprised you didn't call when you got here."

"In my panic, I left my purse in the backseat of my Uber. I want to lay eyes on him, and then I'll try to figure out what I need to do to get it back."

He leads me through the emergency room to room 4567. He knocks gently then pushes it open.

"Wren," my mom says, tears falling from her eyes. "Thank goodness you're here sweetheart."

She wraps me in a hug, and I breathe her in, trying to calm myself. "Hey, bud," I say, looking towards Cody and letting go of her.

Tears prick the back of my eyes as I walk over and wrap my arms around him. "I love you," he signs when he sees me, and I exhale for the first time since seeing my phone.

"I love you too. I'm so sorry I wasn't here sooner." I kiss his forehead and tousle his hair a little. "Where's his iPad?" I ask, taking his hand in mine.

"In all the chaos, we forgot to grab it," my mom explains. "The nurses got us a simple choice board. It's over there on the table."

Cody begins to nod off, and I know his body and his brain have to be exhausted.

"What triggered it?" I ask.

"The aid forgot to give him his meds," my dad says.

"You're joking," I say. Guilt strikes me, and for a split second I consider moving back in with my parents and handling it all myself, but I push it away. "Did you report her?"

"We did, but I truly think it was an honest mistake. She's new, and she was overwhelmed. Her supervisor is supposed to call us tomorrow."

"Regardless of how her day was going, he needed his medicine." I shake my head. "This could've been so much worse."

"Your mom already called his neurologist, and he has an appointment Monday pending that he discharges tonight."

"Good. Are they talking about keeping him overnight?"

"We're actually not sure," my dad says. "It was longer than they used to be, so that's why we called 911. We're waiting for the doctor to come back with his labs."

"Okay." I massage my temples and look down at my brother.

"Why are you so dressed up tonight?" my mom asks. "I like that dress. It looks really pretty on you."

"I was at a party with Tanner."

"Your roommate?" my dad asks.

"Actually…he's my boyfriend." I blush. "And before you freak out, it's new."

"What makes you think I'd freak out?" he laughs.

"I'm not surprised," my mom says.

"What does that mean?" I ask.

"I could just tell you two mean a lot to each other. It's not every day men do grand gestures like buying a lift for your brother."

"I'm really happy."

"That's all we want for you, honey." She smiles. "So where is he?"

"I saw your text messages and calls while I was in the bathroom, and I ran out of there so fast that I only had time to text him, and then I left my phone in the Uber like an idiot."

The room phone begins to ring, and my dad walks over and answers it.

"Oh, no, do you think there is any chance the Uber driver will bring it back?" my mom asks.

"Maybe. She was really nice."

My dad hangs up the phone and looks over at me. "Someone is down at the front desk asking for you. It must be the driver with the bag."

"Really, but I wanted to talk to the doctor."

"Wren, we are perfectly capable of talking to the doctor, and there is no telling when he will come back. Run down and see who it is. You need your phone and purse."

I squeeze Cody's hand before leaving to make my way back to the lobby.

I freeze when the door swings open, revealing Tanner at

the front desk. His jacket is draped across his arm, and his tie is undone and hanging around his neck.

"Ma'am, I understand that your policy states that patient family members are the only ones admitted to visit in the ER, but the girl I love's brother is back there, and she's not answering her phone, so could you please tell me where I can find Cody Dawson."

He sounds panicked, and I can tell he's doing his best to keep his emotions in check, but he's starting to waver.

"Sir—"

"You came," I say, breathless.

Tanner's head whips in my direction, and in three long strides he meets me at the door. His arms wrap around me. "Of course I did."

Tears start streaming down my face, and he holds me tight against his chest. "What happened?" he asks, soothing my back.

"Cody's aid forgot his meds and it triggered a pretty bad seizure, which isn't unexpected, but still really scary."

"Is he okay?"

"Yeah, he'll be okay. They're just waiting for the doctor to come in."

"That's good. How are you?"

"I'm okay. It scared me, but I'm glad he's going to be alright. I'm really sorry that I tore out of there so fast. I know I promised you I would be there for the big announcement."

"Never apologize for putting Cody before me. He means a lot to you, which means he means a lot to me too. I know we're still early on, but I'm all in. And I know that means that one day, if you'll have me, I'll get the honor of helping you care for Cody, so you never have to apologize for putting him first. I don't care what we're doing. If he needs us, we're there, no questions asked."

His words wash over me, and my stomach flips.

"I love you," I say without hesitation.

"Really?" he asks like he doesn't believe me.

"Yes, I love you," I say, smiling. "I love you so much, Tanner Mitchell."

"I love you," he says, pulling me into him. I'm overcome with emotions, and tears begin to fall again.

"Thank you for coming," I say, wiping them away.

"There is nowhere else in this world I'd rather be."

The automatic sliding doors open, and my Uber driver from earlier walks in holding my purse. "Oh, good," she says, a little out of breath. "You left this in the back of my car."

"Thank you," I say, taking the bag. I pull out my phone and am met with a flurry of missed calls and text messages. Every single one is from Tanner.

He shrugs. "I might've freaked myself out when you weren't answering me and panicked a little."

"Come on. Let's go see Cody. My parents were asking where you were."

"Ma'am," the nurse behind the counter calls. "He is not permitted in the ER if he's not family or a spouse."

"Then as far as you're concerned, we're married." I flash a smile towards the nurse, grab Tanner's hand, and pull him through the door.

CHAPTER 42: HOME
TANNER

The doctor came in thirty minutes ago to tell the Dawsons that Cody could go home. Fatigue covers everyone's faces, and I know they're ready to get him home and back in his bed.

"Thank you for coming," Charlotte says, giving both me and Wren hugs.

"I'll come by tomorrow to check on him," Wren says.

"We both will," I say, squeezing her hand.

"That would mean a lot," Paul says. "To him and to us."

Wren walks over to Cody's bed and messes up his hair. "I love you. Don't scare me like that again, you hear."

He nods and signs "I love you."

"We will see you tomorrow," I say, squeezing his shoulder. "Get some rest."

He signs "I love you" to me as well. And I swallow down the tears that threaten to break free. "I love you too, man." My eyes find Wren and her eyes are a little glossy.

We walk out of the hospital room and back to my car.

"I'm spent," she says. "Can we go home and cuddle?"

Home.

"Home?"

"Yeah, I'm so ready to go home." We open the doors of the car and slide in.

"I think that's the first time you've called it home."

"Is it?" she asks.

"It definitely is. Does that mean you'll go get all of your stuff and move in for real?"

She smiles and grabs my hand.

"If you want me too. I know this is all happening really fast, and it's all new to you, but I'd really like that."

"Do I want you too?" I shake my head, turning to face her. "Wren Abigail Dawson, I don't just want you for a little while."

Her eyes begin to water.

"I want to make you feel cherished every single day because I love you. I love that you're caring, compassionate, and driven. I love that you will go to the depths of the world for your family, and I want to be there by your side every step of the goddamn way. I want the apartment to be ours and I want your things next to mine. I hope your mattress never shows up because the only place I want you to be is in my bed. You just tell me when, and I'll rent the truck to make it happen."

"Rent the truck," she says, smiling. I lean forward and pull her into a kiss.

Although it's not long, Wren doses off on the way home. My hand stays interlocked with hers, resting on her upper thigh. I pull into my parking spot and quietly get out of the car. I walk around to the passenger side and open her door. Carefully I unbuckle her seat belt, pick her up, and carry her to our apartment.

"I could have walked," she says, stirring in my arms.

"You're tired, and I'll never complain about holding you." She nestles her head into my chest, and I kiss the top of her head.

Once inside, I walk her over to my bed and set her down. I

remove her shoes, and then she sits up so that I can help her out of her dress.

"You looked beautiful tonight," I say.

"Hard not to be in a dress like this."

"The dress had nothing to do with it." I walk the dress over to my closet and hang it up, and then grab a T-shirt out of my dresser. "Here, pretty girl, put this on." She pulls it over her head and climbs under the comforter.

"Heir with the Good Hair." She laughs while reading the front of the light blue shirt.

I shrug. "Are you hungry?" I ask.

"No." She swipes up on her phone. "Cody's home and resting."

"Good."

"Was your dad mad you left?"

"No, I told him I had to go to you, and he understood, and then I left. He texted an hour ago to check on your brother."

"That was nice of him."

"Yeah, he might be an ass to me, but he's not a total monster." I quickly change down to my underwear then turn off the light. Crawling into bed, I curl my body behind her, placing a kiss on her cheek.

"I'm sorry," she says, sleepily.

"Why are you sorry?"

"I'm too tired for sex tonight, and you said all that nice stuff to me at the hospital and in the car, and I feel bad."

"Never apologize for not feeling up for sex," I say. "You had a stressful night, and I know you're thinking about your brother and worried about him. I will never expect you to have sex with me, but especially not when we just left the hospital. I love you wholeheartedly, Wren."

"I love you too," she says. She moves closer to me, and her breathing begins to even out as she drifts off to sleep.

CHAPTER 43: I'M PROUD OF YOU
TANNER

Wren and I spent the weekend at her parents' house hanging out with Cody. Charlotte and Paul are so warm compared to my parents, and I feel really fortunate they've accepted me so easily.

I'm officially no longer an employee at Austere, but my dad asked that I stop by today to meet with him, and since I still needed to clean out my desk, I agreed.

At ten, I make my way to his office. I'm not really sure what there is left to say, but Wren encouraged me to tell him how I've been feeling, so I'm going to try.

"You can go in," his assistant says when I greet her. "He's waiting on you."

Knocking on the door, I push it open and find him behind his desk.

"Tanner, thanks for coming by," he says.

"Yeah, I had to grab the rest of my things, so it was no problem." I take a seat in one of the chairs across from him, and he looks me up and down, but to my surprise, he doesn't comment on my casual outfit.

"How's your friend's brother?" he asks.

"Girlfriend. Wren is my girlfriend."

"Right, how is her brother doing?"

"Good. He's home, back to his normal self. Sorry again about the party."

He shakes his head. "I understand. I would've done the same for your mother."

An awkward silence hangs between us, and I rub my hands against my thighs.

"I'm sorry Wren and I didn't officially meet," he says.

"Officially?"

"Funny enough, she spoke to your brother and I at the bar that night during the party, but we didn't know who the other person was at the time. I don't think we made the best impression, but she seems like a great girl."

"How do you know that was Wren?"

"I guess I don't, but she seemed pretty quick to defend you, and then I saw you dancing with her before y'all left. Red hair and a green dress, right?"

My mind runs wild with the possibilities of what she could've heard them say about me and I do my best to silence my insecurities.

"Is there anything else you need from me before I go?" I ask, ready to leave.

"No, I think we're all set from the business side of things, but your mother and I talked and I wanted to say that I know I've been hard on you, but—"

I scoff. "You think you've been hard on me? Dad, that doesn't even begin to describe the way you treat me. I know I'm not Mitch or Bella, but I am your son, and all I've ever wanted to do is make you proud, but nothing I do is ever good enough."

"Tanner, if you would listen. I'm trying to apologize."

"Apologize?"

"Yes, I might not agree with all of the decisions you make. Or understand why you want to waste your time with this bar project, but I do love you, and I want you to be happy."

I shake my head.

"Well you have a funny way of showing it."

He opens his mouth to speak but stops himself.

"Look, the thing is, I'm trying really hard not to care if you're proud of me or not and just focus on making myself proud instead. I know you don't think very highly of me owning the bar, but it's something that will make me happy. I've got a lot going on right now, so if I'm distant, it's because I just need some space from this place and from you. I really appreciate everything Austere has done for me, but I ask that you save your apologies or whatever you were just trying to do until you understand what you're apologizing for."

He stares across the desk but doesn't speak.

"If that's what you want," he says.

"It is," I say confidently, standing. "I've got to head out though. I have my first therapy session today, and I don't want to be late."

"Therapy?" he questions.

"Yeah, like I said. I'm gonna try to work on me for a while."

He nods, and I walk out of his office feeling a little lighter than I did before. I smile to myself, pulling out my phone as the elevator doors close behind me.

I did it

I told him I needed some space and he agreed to give me it

WREN 🐺:

I'm proud of you! I know that was tough.

It was actually a little easier than I thought it would be

Did you know you talked to my dad and my brother at the party

WREN 🐺:

Huh? No I didn't.

Apparently, you saw them at a bar and then they saw us dancing and figured you were you

WREN 🐺:

OMG! That was them?

What did you say

WREN 🐺:

I heard them talking about you, and I snapped. Essentially, I called them the smallest men in the entire room, but I would've never done it if I had known who they were.

LMAO

Thank you for protecting me

WREN 🐺:

Always! I'm really proud of you for standing up for yourself!

Me too

I'll see you at home

WREN 🐺:

I can't wait. Good luck in therapy 🤍 I love you!

I love you too

CHAPTER 44: FULL

WREN

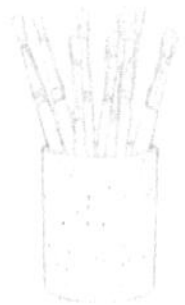

Wednesday 1:18 pm

TANNER 🦙:

Look what just delivered

TANNER 🦙:

<<Screenshot attached>>

> Is that what I think it is?

TANNER 🦙:

It is 🌰⚡

> Stop making me blush at work

TANNER 🦙:

Why you blushing

> Just thinking about later.

TANNER 🦙:

What's happening later

> Are you really going to make me say it?

TANNER:

Yes

> You're going to fuck me while I wear my new toy

TANNER:

Fuck

TANNER:

Come home NOW

TANNER:

I can't wait until tonight

> But it seems like such a good way to spend roomie night 😉

TANNER:

You're killing me

> You'll survive!

TANNER:

I love you

> I love you too! Be home soon!

———

Tonight is our first roomie night since we've said those three little words, and my body has been thrumming with need ever since Tanner texted me earlier.

I've never considered myself to be a person with any kinks, but knowing that the plug came in the mail today and that I get to try something new with Tanner has me excited.

I pull into the parking lot, get out of the car, and run up to the apartment.

"Tanner," I yell, swinging the door open. He walks out of his room—shirtless, black sweatpants hang low on his hips. My gaze drops to his crotch, and I swear I can see his cock harden below his pants.

"Come here, pretty girl," he says.

I drop my things onto the floor, kicking the door closed. He begins to close the space between us, and so do I. When our bodies collide, he picks me up, and I let out a little squeal. Wrapping my legs around his waist, I rock my hips against his length, warmth pooling between my legs.

Our mouths clash in a heated kiss that's nothing but tongues and teeth. His hands find my ass, pulling me tighter against him, and mine tangle in his hair. "Fuck," he says against me, laying me gently on his bed. He takes his time, removing my shoes and then my pants, leaving me in nothing but my thong. His eyes find the wet spot between my legs, and his pupils blow.

"Fuck, you're already so wet for me," he growls.

"I couldn't get here fast enough," I say, breathless. I sit up and pull my shirt off, tossing it to the floor, and then I reach forward and begin tugging on the band of his pants and underwear. Moving them down, he kicks them off, and his dick springs free.

"Do you have the plug?" I ask.

"You sure you want to try it?"

"Yes," I say, confidently. "I trust you, and it's all I've been able to think about since you texted me."

He grabs a box off the nightstand then disappears into the bathroom. When he returns, he's holding a bottle of lube and a small silver plug adorned with an orange gemstone where the base flares.

He kneels on the carpet, and in one swift motion, he pulls me towards him so that my ass is on the edge of my bed. My legs wrap around him, and his mouth finds my clit in an instant. He sucks hard on my bundle of nerves, and I yell out his name.

He continues to work me with his tongue. My hand finds his hair, and I grind against his rough beard as his tongue strokes my center.

My heels dig into his back, and he moans into me. Our eyes lock, and a sexy smile spreads across his face when he realizes I'm watching him.

"You like watching me taste your sweet pussy?" he asks.

"Yes," I whimper. He goes back to work, and one of his fingers finds my asshole. Without warning, he spits on my ass, and my whole body erupts with feral need. I let out a loud moan as he pushes his finger deeper, and I rock into the feeling.

"That's it," he says. His tongue finds my clit again, and I let out a scream when he sucks it into his mouth. My hand tightens in his hair, and I pull him towards me. "Fuck… Tanner…fuck…more…I want more."

"I want you to come like this for me, pretty girl. And then I want to feel your tight pussy clamp around my cock when I fuck you with that plug. You think you can do that for me?"

"Yes," I nod. He pushes two fingers into my center, so both holes are completely filled by him. Pressure begins to build low in my belly, and my head begins to spin as his mouth and hand work together to send me so far over the edge, I don't know if I'll ever return. I ride his hand and face frantically, chasing my release. The whole room goes dark as I soak his face, yelling his name out like a fucking prayer.

"I don't think I'll ever get enough of you," he says, laying kisses along the insides of my thighs. "Are you sure you want to try the plug?"

"Yes," I say.

"Okay, if at any point you don't like it, then you tell me and I'll stop," he promises me.

"I want it, Tanner," I assure him again. I scoot back onto

the bed, and he climbs to meet me. With his hands, he spreads my legs apart and runs the cold metal down my center. Goosebumps erupt across my body as he continues to tease me with the icy silver.

"That…fuck…" I say, breathlessly. His mouth erupts into a wicked grin. He grabs the lube, taking his time, carefully applying it to my ass and the tear-drop end of the plug. He gently primes me with his finger. "You okay?" he asks, his eyes finding mine.

"Yes," I say. I watch as he begins pushing the plug inside me, cautiously. The metal stretches me, and I do my best to relax into the sweet pain it causes. A moan escapes as it enters me completely, and my head lolls back at the full feeling.

"How does that feel?" he asks.

"Good, but I want you. I need your cock," I say.

His eyes rake over me, and his hands trail down my legs. "You're so fucking beautiful like this," he says, his eyes dipping to the little orange jewel.

"Babe, I need more," I beg. "Please."

He scrambles to find a condom, but I stop him. "I think I might want you to fuck my mouth later," I say. "Can you go bare?"

"Bare?" he asks.

"Yeah, I want all of you," I say, reaching out and taking his shaft in my hand. "You're my first partner since my last exam, and I'm on the pill. I know you haven't been with anyone since April."

"You're sure?" he asks, moving his body over mine.

"Fuck me bare, Tanner. I need you to fill me."

He lets out a low moan, lining his cock up between my legs. He inches forward, and I breathe out, trying to adjust to the size of him with the plug.

"Fuck, you're so tight," he says, continuing to push forward. "Do you like it?"

"Yes," I breathe out, as he stretches me wider.

"That's it, pretty girl. You're doing so well taking my cock."

Inch by inch, he sinks into me until the hilt, and then he begins to thrust his hips over and over, and I match his pace. His mouth crashes into mine in a feral kiss, our tongues twisting around each other.

"I don't know how long I'm going to be able to last like this," he breathes out. "You." *Thrust.* "Feel." *Thrust.* "So." *Thrust.* "Fucking." *Thrust.* "Amazing."

My legs wrap around his ass, and I pull him deeper into me.

"Wren, I'm going to come if you do that," he warns.

"Then fuck my mouth," I say.

"Just a little bit longer," he begs, pumping into me again. "It feels too good."

"Tanner, I want you to fuck my mouth," I say again.

"I want you to come again though."

"Then go grab my vibrator." His eyes darken, and he pulls out of me and jumps out of bed. "Bottom drawer of my nightstand. I want the purple one," I yell after him, as he runs across the apartment towards my room.

After a few moments, he returns holding it.

"Is this the one you wanted?" he asks, crawling back into bed and handing me my purple rabbit. I nod. Kneeling near my head, he turns me to face him, and he caresses my cheek. "Do you want me to wreck you, pretty girl?"

"Desperately."

"Then open." My lips part, and he pushes his cock into my mouth. I gag as he hits the back of my mouth, but I open my throat, taking him deeper.

"You taste yourself all over me?" he asks. "Do you taste how sweet you are?"

All I can do is whimper in response.

With one hand, I grab the back of his thigh, and with the other I turn on the toy and push it inside me, causing the plug to thrum with vibrations, and I almost come right then. I do my best to hold on. I don't want this to end—it's too fucking hot.

"Would you look at you? So fucking full for me," he says, rocking his hips forward. His hands gather in my hair, and he holds me in place.

He fucks my mouth over and over as I fuck my pussy with the vibrator.

It's rough, and filthy, and so fucking good.

My core tightens, and my whole body is overwhelmed with so much pleasure that it feels illegal. We're both a mix of nothing but moans and heavy breaths.

Every whimper that spills out of me is silenced by his shaft sliding deeper into the back of my throat, and when I glance upward, his eyes are locked on my hand. I move my other hand that's splayed across the back of his thigh to cup his balls, massaging gently.

"Fuckkkkkkkkk," he calls out. Upping the vibrations, I let out a long scream as I finally give into it all, and I fall harder than I ever have before. Cum coats the back of my throat at the same time, and I swallow it down, letting him ride out his orgasm against me as I continue to ride out mine.

When we're done, he collapses next to me, kissing my forehead gently.

"That was…um…" he begins. "That was hot."

"Yeah," I agree, trying to catch my breath.

He turns to face me and smoothes my hair.

"Has sex ever been like this for you before?" I ask.

"No," he says, kissing me tenderly. "This feels like so much more than sex to me. That was incredible. You are so incredible, my wild girl. I love you."

"I love you too," I say, moving off the bed.

"Where you going?" he asks.

"I'm just going to go to the bathroom, take the plug out, and then I'll be back. I promise."

Once I'm done getting cleaned up, I rejoin him in his bed, and he wraps me in his arms.

"You ready for the big move on Saturday?"

"So ready," I say, wiggling back into him. "Everyone is good to go, so after we pick up the truck, we can head over to my parents' and the guys are going to meet us there."

"Good. Have I told you how happy you make me?" he asks.

"You may have mentioned it."

He squeezes me again, and I let him even further into my heart, knowing that every bit he takes will be his forever.

CHAPTER 45: COUPLES WHO MATCH
WREN

I walk out into the living room dressed in jeans, my Vans, and my favorite Team Cody sweatshirt. It's dark green and has a big ribbon on the front.

"I like that sweatshirt," Tanner says. He's wearing a white T-shirt, gray sweatpants, and tennis shoes.

"Dink Responsibly." I laugh. "Nice shirt."

He looks down and chuckles. "I like yours better. The weather is supposed to be chilly today. You think I could get one of those?"

"Maybe. I'm not sure if there are any left, but I can look when we get to my parents' house. What time is the moving truck going to be ready?"

Dolly runs into the room chasing a little ball. She pounces on it, and it shoots across the floor, hitting my foot. "Morning, baby girl," I say, reaching down to pet her head.

"We can pick it up at nine."

I walk over to the fridge, pausing when I see what's waiting for me. There hangs a Post-it, and on it are the same dog and cheetah doodle that he's given me countless times, but they're sitting in front of a moving truck with little boxes all around.

"I love my doodle," I say, taking it off the fridge.

"What do you do with them?"

"They all live in the top drawer of my nightstand."

"You save them?"

"Yes, silly. Come with me." I walk back past him, grabbing his hand and tugging him into the room where my furniture is. Opening the top drawer of my nightstand, I reveal every doodle and note he's ever left me.

"I can't believe you saved them all," he says.

"Of course I did. They're one of my favorite things—the story of you and me."

He spins me around and kisses me. "Tanner!" I giggle. "We have to go, and I still need coffee."

"You're killing me," he says, checking his watch. "We may have time for a quickie if we hurry."

"I promise I'll make the wait worth your while, but we have to go. My parents are waiting for us to arrive."

"Fine," he pouts, kissing my nose.

We head back into the kitchen, and I prepare my coffee in a to-go cup. At eight thirty, we make our way down to his car and get across town to pick up the moving truck Tanner rented.

"I figured you could drive my car, and I'll drive the truck," he says.

"That's fine with me. Oh, I forgot to tell you Gwen called yesterday, and the adjustable tables shipped, so pending they don't go swimming in the middle of the ocean like my mattress, they should be here soon."

"That's awesome, babe."

I squeeze his hand, smiling that I'm one step closer to my dream becoming a reality. "Do you know when you close on the bar?"

"The lawyer emailed me this morning. A month from tomorrow. If all goes according to plan, the bar will re-open at the end of January, and then we will break ground on the pickleball courts at the end of February."

"You don't want to do it all at the same time?"

"I'm hiring all of the current staff, so I'm trying to minimize the time I'm having to cover salaries when they aren't working."

"I'm sure they appreciate it."

"It's a win-win. I get to keep Jerry's team, and they get paid and the holidays off."

He turns into the rent-a-truck parking lot, and I switch into the driver's seat of his car. "Do you want me to wait?" I ask, kissing him through the window

"No, you go ahead," he says, opening the back door, pulling out a little bag.

"What's that?"

"You'll see," he smirks. "Go, and I'll be there as soon as I can." He kisses me again and then begins to walk toward the office door, and I finish the short drive to my mom and dad's.

———

"Hey, everybody," I yell, walking through my parents' front door.

"Hey, sweetheart," my mom says. "Where's Tanner?"

"Just a little bit behind me. I dropped him at the rent-a-truck place. He shouldn't be long. Cody doing okay?"

"Your brother is fine," she says. "He's watching some movie with your dad."

We walk further into the house, and I greet my dad and brother.

"Where's your boyfriend?" Cody asks, using his speech device.

"On his way," I say. "Hey, Mom, do we have any more of these sweatshirts from last year's walk? Tanner was asking."

"I'm not sure. I can check." She walks out of the room.

"So, you're really living with your boyfriend," my dad says, making Cody laugh.

"Yes, Dad. I'm really living with my boyfriend."

"I'm fine with it. I just want to make sure you're protecting your heart. You were devastated when Chad broke it off with you."

"Tanner's not Chad, Dad."

"I believe you. He seems like a very fine young man. You're just my little girl, and I want you to find someone who will love you wholeheartedly."

I giggle thinking about the conversation Tanner and I had the night after the hospital. "I can assure you he does."

"Oh, will you leave her alone," my mom says, walking back in. "I couldn't find a sweatshirt, but I found a T-shirt." She lays it across the back of the leather chair.

A knock comes from the front door, and both my parents yell, "Come in!"

"Good morning, Dawsons," Tanner shouts as he walks into their house, holding the small gift bag.

"Morning," my parents say in unison.

He walks over to me, kisses me on the top of the head, and then walks over to Cody. "I got you a little something, man." He sets the bag on Cody's tray table, holding it steady while my brother removes the tissue paper. Tanner helps him pull out a small box, and Cody's face lights up.

"What is it?" I ask.

He begins to type, and I wait for his response. "Thor thank you," he says.

"You're very welcome." Tanner spins the box around, and it's a special edition Funko: Pop! Thor figurine. "I figured he needed the best superhero on his shelf," he says, laughing.

"How thoughtful," I reply with a giggle. "Everyone will be here soon. Should we start moving the boxes upstairs?"

"Let's do it."

Tanner and I make our way downstairs to the basement to begin moving the boxes. As we pass by the leather recliner, I grab the shirt. "I had my mom look for a sweatshirt and she couldn't find one, but we had some T-shirts," I say, tossing it in his direction. Catching it, he smiles.

"A T-shirt is perfect."

He pulls the shirt he's wearing off in one motion. His back muscles flex as we descend the stairs. "What are you doing?"

He stops at the bottom and pulls Cody's shirt over his head. "I figured I'd wear my new shirt."

"No, you're not. We are not one of those couples that matches our clothes."

"We could be."

"No!" I laugh. "That's so lame."

"Too late. You gave me the shirt, and I'm wearing it. I think we look cute."

"You think we look cute?"

I reach the bottom of the stairs. "Well, I think you look cute, and I like the shirt. Plus, think about how stoked Cody's gonna be when we go back upstairs matching."

"You're—"

"Insufferable?"

"I was actually going to say amazing, but you are a little insufferable."

The doorbell rings, and then heavy footsteps echo above us. "That'll be the guys," I say.

A minute later, Logan, Jacks, Donovan, and Enzo appear at the top of the stairs.

"Y'all are really trying to be one of those couples that matches," Jacks says.

"See, I told you," I say, giggling.

"Honestly, I would expect nothing less from Tanner," Logan says. "I'm surprised he didn't make you wear gray sweats too."

"Well, I considered it, but then I remembered all of you big, strong men volunteered to help me, so I went with jeans because I don't think I'll be doing much heavy lifting."

"Volunteered?" Donovan asks. "I think we all got volun-told by Lacey to be here."

"Regardless, I appreciate you all. These boxes, those paintings, and the couch all need to be on the truck."

"Couch?" Enzo questions. "Y'all already have a couch."

"No, we have a torture device that costs as much as a car."

"She's not wrong," Tanner laughs. "If my girl wants her couch, we're bringing her couch."

"Got it," Jacks says. "Any other furniture?"

"No, we'll leave it all here until we have more room for it."

"You're the boss," Tanner says, looking around the space. "Let's do this boys."

TANNER

Seven hours and forty-two minutes later, Wren is unpacked and officially moved into our apartment—and as fate would have it, her mattress is officially here.

When we got home from her parents' house, it was propped up against the door frame, and after some minor complaints from our friends, it's on her old bed frame.

There are two couches in our living room, and every one is sitting around eating pizza. I wrap Wren up from behind, and she leans back into me. Dolly circles our feet, and I've officially never been happier.

My phone rings, and my dad's name flashes across the screen.

"You should answer it," Wren encourages. I quietly excuse myself toward our bedroom and swipe up, shutting the door behind me.

"Hello," I say.

"Tanner," his voice booms through the phone. "Is now a bad time?"

"Wren moved the rest of her stuff over today, so all of our friends are here, but I stepped away. Is everything okay?"

"Yeah, everything is good. I was calling because your mother and I would like for you and Wren to come to Thanksgiving. Your brother and Farah will be moving the following week, so we thought it would be nice for everyone to get together. Fleur has an entire menu planned."

"Wren's parents invited us to their house for Thanksgiving," I say, thinking back to my conversation with Wren's dad earlier today. "And we said we'd be there."

"Oh, okay. Well maybe if you have time, you all can stop by."

A soft knock comes from the door, and Wren walks in. "You okay?" she mouths, and I nod. Placing the phone on speaker, I grab her and pull her in between my legs, her back against me.

"I'll talk to Wren and see what we can do," I say.

"Talk to you soon," he replies and then hangs up.

"They want us to come to Thanksgiving dinner, but I told him we had already committed to your family."

"Do you want to go to Thanksgiving with your parents?"

I shrug. "I feel like I shouldn't want to go, but they're my family. Mitch and Farah are moving the next week, and I don't know the next time I'll see them, and Bella is there."

"Then we should go. My parents usually do an early

lunch, and then we can pop over to your parents' house for dinner. Cody will probably be tired early anyway, so it's no big deal. Plus, I'd really like to meet Bella."

"You sure?"

"As long as you're sure, I am," she says. "How are you feeling about everything with him?"

"At the end of the day, I have you, and all of the people sitting in our living room. Soon I'll have the bar, and one day you'll have your camps, and I think I'm starting to realize I don't need his validation to know that I'm the happiest I've ever been."

She leans forward and kisses my nose. "I'm happy, too, T. I had this plan, this idea I was comfortable with, and you completely blindsided me and wrecked the whole damn thing, in the best way."

"I love you," I say, tugging her closer.

"And I love you."

Banging erupts on my door. "Stop doing it, you two, and come eat!" Enzo yells.

A giggle bubbles out of Wren, and we stand to walk back out to join our friends.

"Who's to say I wasn't eating?" I joke.

"Don't be so gross, Tanner," Lacey says, throwing a wadded up napkin at my head.

Poppy passes out champagne, and Wren clears her throat.

"Thanks for helping me move twice; we promise to hire movers the next time." She giggles. "If it hadn't been for everyone here, Tanner and I would've never met, so thank you, and cheers to wrecked plans!"

"Cheers!" They all toast, raising their glasses.

As I look around the room at the people in front of me, pure happiness settles deep in my bones, and I know that as long as I can do life with Wren and our friends by my side I'll always be happy.

CHAPTER 46: TANNER'S
WREN - ONE MONTH LATER - DECEMBER

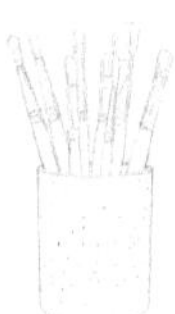

It's three days before Christmas, and Tanner officially owns The Local—or should I say, he officially owns Tanner's.

He pushes the key in and unlocks the front doors, pulling me inside the empty bar where so many of my favorite memories have taken place.

"It's so empty," I say, walking with him towards the bar top and setting down the gift I brought with me.

"Weird, right?"

"Very weird. When does the new furniture arrive?"

"In a couple of weeks. Looking at it this empty, I'm wondering if I should've taken Jerry up on his offer to give me the furniture, but I think I made the right call."

"I think you did too. And you kept the ping-pong table, which is the most important piece of furniture. Did you know that the girls think it's magic?"

"Magic?"

"Yep, apparently all of us who are now together started by playing a game on that table."

"Interesting." He shrugs, running his hand along the bar top. "When do I get to open my present?"

"Be patient."

"Do you want a drink?"

"Sure."

He moves around the bar and searches the shelves underneath it. "There isn't much back here, but there is a bottle of amaretto."

"That seems right."

He pours some of the amber liquid into two glasses and then walks over to the freezer and grabs out some ice.

"What's on your mind?" I ask as he slides one of the glasses in my direction. I take a sip, and the almond-flavored liquor tickles my taste buds.

"Isn't that the question I should be asking you?" He laughs. "I am the one on this side of the bar."

I push myself up onto the bar, moving to sit on the edge so that my legs are dangling. He moves in between them and sips from his glass.

"Now that I'm on the right side of the bar, may I ask the question, bartender?"

"You may."

"What's on your mind?"

He breathes out a long breath and stretches his neck. "I'm really wondering what's in the present."

"Be serious. You seem really preoccupied."

"Honestly, I think I'm in shock that it's all mine," he says. "And while I'm really happy and excited to have a place with my name on it, I'm scared that I'll fuck it up somehow and lose it all."

"You aren't going to fuck it up."

"How do you know that?"

"Because you're smart, and strong, and creative, and you aren't a quitter." I punctuate each adjective with a peck on his lips. "You are going to kill it here. Come on, tell me all of your plans."

"You know my plans."

"Humor me. What's going on that wall over there?" I ask, pointing to the blank wall behind the DJ booth.

"I actually don't have plans for that wall yet, but I was wondering if you'd paint something on it."

I stare at him a little stunned. "You want me to paint the wall?"

"If you want to…" He smiles. "I'd absolutely love for you to paint the wall."

"Do I have full creative reign?"

"Of course." He laughs, shaking his head. "What are you thinking?"

"Off the top of my head? Let's see." I pause, tapping my chin with my finger. "Maybe a big mural of our friend group, but animals instead of people. We could all be gathered under the name of the bar."

"Animals?"

"Yes, so like you'd be a dog, and I'd be a cheetah. And we could all be holding our typical drinks."

He chuckles. "I like that. And what kind of animal would everyone else be?"

"Hmm," I say. "Maybe we let them pick?"

"I think it sounds perfect."

"Good," I say, kissing him quickly. "Then I'll do it."

He begins to unzip one of my knee-high boots.

"What are you doing?" I ask, need coursing through me in an instant.

"You just look so pretty sitting here, and I thought we might need to christen the place." He unzips my other boot and tugs it off my foot before dropping it onto the floor.

"What if someone comes in?" I ask.

"The bar's closed. No one is coming in here." He sips from his glass, his eyes darkening over the rim, then works his hands up my legs and over my hips. "I love this little skirt," he says. "But you know what would make it better?"

"What?" I ask, my breaths already turning rapid in anticipation of his next move.

"Nothing underneath it. How attached are you to these?"

"Not attached at all. Wh—"

Before I can finish, he gathers the top of my stockings and rips them open in one motion, exposing my bare pussy to him completely.

"Fuck," I let out. "You really should rip my clothes off of me more often."

"Noted." He pulls the torn fabric off, and a sexy grin spreads across his face. "My wild girl. You're wearing the plug?" he asks, running his fingers along my inner thigh until he reaches the orange jewel that adorns it.

I nod my head and smirk.

His throat bobs as he swallows, and his pupils blow.

Taking both of his hands, he spreads my legs apart, causing my skirt to bunch around my hips. I lean back ever so slightly on my hands so that I'm on full display for him. "Fuck, I wish you could see yourself," he says.

I whimper under his praise.

Trailing his finger up my center, he dips one finger inside of me and then another, causing my head to fall back. "You're soaked, baby." A moan escapes my lips as he pumps his fingers in and out at a tantalizing speed.

Our eyes lock on one another, and he removes his hand. My lips part on instinct, expecting him to want me to suck them clean, but he doesn't. Instead, he brings both to his own mouth. "Fuckkkk," he says with a moan. "You taste amazing."

Another whimper crosses my lips as his eyes rake over me.

"Do you trust me?" he asks.

"Always," I say.

He finds his glass of amaretto and pulls out a large piece of ice. Bringing one of my ankles to his shoulder, he runs the cube down my leg, causing goosebumps to flare everywhere it touches. He continues to trail up my inner thigh, and when he reaches my pussy, he runs the ice up my center, and I let out a moan. "Does that feel good, pretty girl?"

"So good," I breathe out, swallowing hard.

The contrast between the slight burn of alcohol and the coldness of the ice on my clit causes my whole body to shudder. I watch as he circles my sensitive bud with the ice, winding me tighter. A wicked grin spreads across his face, and he pops the ice cube into his mouth.

HOLY. FUCKING. SHIT.

He lets out a moan when the ice hits his tongue, and then he pulls me forward so that my ass hits the edge of the bar.

His mouth crashes into mine, and he pushes the still not melted ice cube into my mouth, his hands working up my body. He only breaks away long enough to remove my shirt and his, and my hands trace the lines of his abs.

Covering both of my tits with his hands, he plays with nipples. I buck my hips forward, desperate for more.

"Fuck me," I beg, as heat gathers between my thighs. "I need you inside of me now."

"Soon," he says, bending down until his head is buried between my thighs. His tongue works me over and over again in long, filthy licks and flicks. My hands pull on his hair, and I writhe against his face.

"Tanner, please. I need more," I plead, desperate to feel him inside me. "And I don't want your hand." He stands, pulling me in for another kiss.

"Pants," he breathes out.

My hands find the button and zipper of his jeans. I undo them and then tug them down over his hips, freeing his shaft.

I line him up with my center, and he pushes forward in one motion. I take his cock until he's flush against me. I breathe through the sweet pain from the tightness of the plug. We rock into each other over and over. Our hands explore each other's bodies and weave into each other's hair. Our tongues tangle and our teeth clash. Feral need pulses through me; with every thrust of his hips, tension builds at the base of my spine.

He sits up slightly, and his thumb finds my clit. He begins to rub purposeful circles, and we both watch the place we connect.

"Let go, Wren. I know you're close, so let go. I want to feel *my* wild girl come all over *my* cock on top of *my* bar."

All it takes is one more thrust, and he catapults me over the edge. We both fall together as I moan out his name.

When we both finish, he helps me sit up a little straighter, kissing me gently.

I pop off the bar, grabbing my shirt. His eyes follow me as I walk to the bathroom. I've never felt more sexy or more desired in my life.

"Fuck," he calls behind me, and when I look back over my shoulder, his eyes rake down me, no doubt eyeing the little jewel and his cum that's dripping down my thighs. "I can't believe you're mine," he says.

"Yours," I echo, turning, so I'm now walking backwards. I swipe one of my fingers through his release and bring my hand to my mouth. Popping my lips, I suck the salty liquid from the tip and throw him a wink.

"You trying to kill me?" he asks.

I giggle, pleased with myself, and then continue towards the bathroom to get cleaned up.

When I return, he's still standing behind the bar, shirtless with his pants pulled up.

"Can I open my present now?" he asks, pouting his lip.

"So impatient." I giggle, climbing back onto the bar and pulling my shirt over my head. "But I guess you've earned it."

A wide grin spreads across his face, and he grabs the box.

Pulling on the paper, he tears it away, and inside is a comic book titled: *The Adventures of the Cheetah and the Dog.*

"You made me this?" he asks.

"No, someone else you're dating did," I deadpan.

"That's not what I meant. I just meant that I can't believe you made me a comic book."

"You like it?"

"Like it? I love it. Also, your dog and cheetah blow my doodles out of the water."

He leans forward, placing a chaste kiss on my lips, and then goes back to looking at the book.

"Well, I figured you needed your own doodles from me. I used all the Post-its you left me and tried to recreate our story. I'm no author, but I did my best, and all the drawings are mine."

"It's perfect," he says. "You're perfect. Will you dance with me?"

He takes my hand and leads me to the dance floor. Tapping his phone, "Wild Thing" by The Troggs begins to play through the sound system, and he spins me around and around.

"I love you," I say as he pulls me into him.

"I love you too, Wren," he says, spinning me again.

EPILOGUE
WREN - FOUR AND A
HALF YEARS LATER - MAY

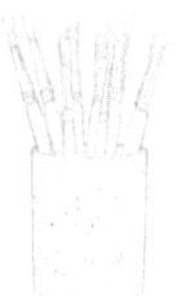

The Tortured Therapists Department

What time is everyone getting to Jacks and Lacey's tonight?

POPPY:

I told Lace hopefully no later than 6. There was a mixup with the car salesman (longggg story 😅), so we're waiting on the new one to come see us and then hopefully it'll be quick.

CHLOE:

You're going to LOVE your minivan. It's a total game changer!

LACEY:

We're ready for everyone whenever! Jace said Donovan, Enzo, and their girls will be here around five.

GRAY:

We should be there around 5:30. Hoping Max takes a nap so he's not totally cranky.

CHLOE:

My crew will be there around 5:30 too. Ava has a soccer game, so we'll be coming from that.

Sounds good!

POPPY:

Wren, Logan showed me the picture T posted today of you two and Cody at the campground a couple weeks ago. I think the pregnancy hormones are getting to me because it made me tear up. Y'all look so happy! I'm so sad I can't volunteer this year. I miss it. 😂

It's okay! You're six months pregnant. I wouldn't let you come if you tried!

LACEY:

Jace and I are so excited for this weekend!

He's seriously saving my life by agreeing to take pictures! I owe y'all big!

GRAY:

Stop! You're making me jealous. I wish I could come help. Maybe later this year when my little guy is older.

CHLOE:

Same!

LACEY:

Perks of being a DINKWAD and the forever cool aunt and uncle! And don't mention it. J was beyond thrilled you asked him to bring his camera 😊

> Y'all are too sweet. At this point I have a waitlist for volunteers. It's insane. Y'all help enough with the day camps and stroll and roll every year. I'm forever grateful!

GRAY:

Respectfully, waitlist or no waitlist, if I can come help I get first dibs as one of your best friends.

> Yes, LMAO! You all get first dibs at volunteering.

My phone rings, interrupting our conversation, and I swipe up on the screen.

"Hey, mom," I say, walking out onto the back porch of the home Tanner and I share. Dolly runs by me, jumping up into a chair sitting in the sun.

"Hi, sweetheart," my mom says. "How are you?"

"I'm good. Y'all okay?"

"Oh, yeah. Dad and Cody are watching baseball, and I'm crocheting a new blanket."

My eyes find Tanner as she talks. He's sitting on our porch swing, shirtless, with gym shorts slung low on his hips. A backwards hat sits on top of his long blond hair, and a short beard covers his jaw.

Need pools low in my belly at the sight of him.

God dammit, my husband is hot as hell.

He gestures to his lap, and I walk over, sitting down and curling against his bare chest. His hand finds my back and he trails his fingers down my spine, causing my skin to erupt with goosebumps. Kissing the top of my head, he gently rocks us with his feet.

"You there?" Mom asks.

"Oh, yeah, sorry. I got distracted." I set the phone down on the seat of the swing, tapping the speaker button. "You're on speaker and Tanner's here. What were you saying?"

"Hey, Charlotte," he says.

"Hi, honey. I was just calling to go over the plan for next weekend. What day are y'all heading up, and do you need anything?"

"I think we're good. We're leaving for the campground on Monday," I explain. "The volunteers are set to show up on Wednesday night, and then the campers will arrive Friday. We figured Cody could just stay in our cabin again this year, so we'll be close by if he was to need us. Did you see the email with the packing list?"

"I did, and you know you don't have to do that. He could stay with the other campers," she says.

"We're looking forward to spending some extra time with him," Tanner explains. "Plus, as the owners of the camp, we get to stay in the main cabin, so I know he'd be bummed if we didn't share it."

"If you insist."

"We do," I say. "You know our slumber parties are camp tradition."

"So you've said. Your dad and I will be dropping him off and then heading up to Charleston for a couple nights, so we won't be too far away."

"We got him," Tanner assures her.

My heart expands in my chest at his words. Every night I fall asleep thinking there is no way I could love Tanner Mitchell more than I already do. Then, every morning I wake up and he proves me wrong, making me fall deeper in love with him every day. I'll never know how I got so lucky in life.

"As you can imagine, Cody's thrilled! He can't stop talking about the talent show and dance party," my mom continues, laughing a little as she speaks.

"Well that's because those are the two best things. I really hope he and Wren have been working on their jokes and magic tricks." Tanner chuckles and tickles my sides teasingly.

"Because I've been practicing my yodeling, and I think I might win this time."

I giggle. "Absolutely not. You know my stand up routine with Cody is always the crowd favorite."

"We'll see about that," he jests, tickling me again and causing my giggles to erupt into full blown laughter.

"Please make sure someone films it," my mom deadpans. "Okay, well I'll let you two run. We'll see you Friday."

"Bye. We love you," I say. "Give Cody and Dad a hug from me."

"I will. Love you both."

I hang up the phone and nuzzle deeper into Tanner's arms. My mind wanders to how far my camps have come. What started out as a simple art class morphed into day camps, and then last year I officially quit working at Dogwood Manor and *Camp Butterfly* officially opened. Now, from May to September each year, we host one overnight camp a month. Every camp is full of light, life, and the promise of new beginnings.

Cody has attended every one and made so many friends. My parents have gotten to take vacations, and have even connected with some of the other caregivers. Tanner has been by my side every step of the way, and together we've built a community of volunteers and families that make life feel so full.

"I love you," I say.

"I love you too," he says, continuing to rub slow circles over my back. His phone vibrates, and he swipes up on the screen, letting out a laugh.

"What's so funny?"

"Bella is begging for us to come to my parents' for Memorial Day at the end of the month. Something about wanting me to make drinks for her and a couple of her friends since she's now twenty-one."

"Do you want to go? I don't think we have anything planned yet."

"Yeah, not sure how I feel about my little sister drinking, but we can plan on it."

"Good. It's pretty crazy how much everything has changed in the last few years."

He kisses the side of my head. "I'm really proud of us."

"Me too. I can't believe we're about to start year two of *Camp Butterfly*. I'm so nervous."

"I know, but you knock it out of the park every time. It's going to be a blast."

"I hope so. Is everything set at the bar?"

"Oh, yeah. Tony's got it covered. I've got my best staff working, so it should hopefully be a pretty uneventful week."

"Good. Speaking of Tony, I meant to tell you to tell him that the girls and I opened a bottle of that wine he made the other night and really enjoyed it. Chloe was asking if she could buy some."

He chuckles. "I'll be sure to let him know and see what I can do." He checks his watch. "What time did you want to head to Jacks and Lacey's tonight?"

"Everyone is heading over around five thirty. Poppy and Logan might be running a little late. They're currently buying a minivan."

He chuckles. "Logan mentioned that."

"I can't believe they're pregnant with twins," I say. "It's crazy to think there are going to be more kids running around soon."

"Right? We're going to need a bigger place to host group dinners." He laughs and starts counting our friends' kids on his fingers. "What will that be? Seven kids?"

"I think so," I muse. "You know, I've been thinking lately. What if there were eight?"

"Eight?"

"Yeah, like what if you and I started to try?" I shrug, sitting up so I can see him better.

"For real?" he questions through a wide grin. His eyes find mine, and I'm not sure I've ever seen him look so damn excited.

I nod my head. "I've been thinking about it a lot lately, and I'm ready. Are you?"

"Yes," he says, flipping me towards him so my legs straddle his lap. One of his hands finds the back of my head, and the other wraps around my waist. Pulling me towards him, our mouths crash, and he grinds his hips upward, causing the swing to rock.

"Tanner!" I shriek, pulling away and swatting at his chest. "Are you seriously trying to fuck me on this swing right now? The neighbors can totally see us. I was trying to have a sweet moment, and you're so fucking hard." I laugh.

"You just told me you want to try to have a baby, so I figured we should probably get to trying. Might've just unlocked a breeding kink I didn't know I had."

"You're insane!" I laugh. "I'm still on the pill, so we can't try until I quit taking it."

"Doesn't mean we can't practice," he says, standing and lifting me over his shoulder.

Laughter bubbles out of both of us as he jogs back into the house and to our bedroom.

Setting me down gently, his eyes rake down my body, and warmth pools low in my belly. He moves forward, crashing his mouth against mine and backing me up until we both fall into our bed.

"Did we just decide to have a baby?" I ask, pulling away and staring into his blue eyes.

"We did," he says, smiling. His mouth finds mine again, and our bodies tangle among the sheets. Reminding me once more, that him wrecking my plans all those years ago made all my dreams come true.

ACKNOWLEDGMENTS

To my readers: thank you for picking up When You Rec'd My Plans! Tanner has been one of my favorite characters to write since book one, so getting to give him his happily ever after was so special and genuinely a blast! I hope this story was a light in the midst of the craziness of life. I could not do this without each of you, and I'm forever grateful you took a chance on me and my stories.

To my husband, I love you. Thank you for continuing to support me on this journey and helping me silence my self-doubt. Thank you for bringing the cheetah and the dog to life!

To my children, never give up on your dreams. I love you very much!

Kalie, I can't believe we've been doing this for three books. I've said it before, but I'll say it again, I could not do this without you! I am forever grateful for your guidance and friendship. Here's to the next one! There is no one else I'd want in my corner!

Paige, three books later and there is still no one else I'd trust to bring my characters to life! Thank you for always putting up with me (even when I'm difficult)!

Tina, it was truly a pleasure to work with you. Thank you for your feedback and helping me make this story the best it could be!

To my wonderful beta team: THANK YOU! This book would not exist without your encouragement and feedback. Thank you for loving Wren and Tanner's story! You all mean so much to me!

To my sensitivity readers: When I started Romance Rehab, I wanted to include a story that featured a character with a brain injury because I've spent most of my career as a speech therapist working with individuals like Cody. Thank you for reading this story and giving me your honest feedback. Thank you for sharing your stories with me. I am so thankful for your help in bringing awareness to something so close to my heart.

Sam, Ginsa, and Grayce, thank you for your constant support! I love you all so much!

Samm, thank you for every brainstorm session and plotting call. Thank you for always building me up! Your friendship means the world to me! Tits up and out, baby!

Tony, what started as an accident turned into one of my favorite details. I think putting you in my book means you owe me a drink!

ABOUT THE AUTHOR

Jess Christine is a speech therapist turned contemporary romance author who writes cotton candy smut: sweet, fluffy, and utterly irresistible. With low angst and high swoon, Jess crafts stories that feel like the perfect indulgence. Readers will quickly be lost in the warmth of unforgettable characters, light-hearted humor, delicious spice, and feel-good romance.

Jess resides in Georgia with her husband and two children. When she's not writing, she enjoys binge-watching her favorite TV shows, spending time with her friends and family, and getting lost in love stories.

If you would like to stay in the know about Jess' upcoming books, join her reader group: The Cotton Candy Collective, or subscribe to her newsletter at https://jesschristine.substack.com/subscribe

ALSO BY JESS CHRISTINE

Romance Rehab Series

When You Left Me Speechless - Poppy and Logan's Story

When You Had Me Adapting - Lacey and Jace's Story

When You Rec'd My Plans - Wren and Tanner's Story

Book 4 - Coming 2026

Fairytale Season Series

A Dance of Sugarplums and Power Plays- A Nutcracker Retelling

ROMANCE REHAB BONUS CONTENT

Sign up for my newsletter and snag your free copy of When She Said Yes - Poppy and Logan's Proposal Story!

<u>When She Said Yes</u> should be read after <u>When You Rec'd My Plans</u> to avoid series spoilers.

ALSO BY JESS CHRISTINE

Romance Rehab Series

When You Left Me Speechless - Poppy and Logan's Story

When You Had Me Adapting - Lacey and Jace's Story

When You Rec'd My Plans - Wren and Tanner's Story

Book 4 - Coming Soon

Fairytale Season Series

A Dance of Sugarplums and Power Plays- A Nutcracker Retelling